Dedication

I wish to dedicate this story to the brave and dedicated men and women who serve and have served in
our armed forces as they protect our rights established by our forefathers in this great nation.

There are those, even now, who would take many
of those rights from us, reducing this nation to a
socialist governed one. Shame on them.

I would also dedicate this to the remaining congressmen and senators who fight to retain those
rights, few though they seem to be. Two of those
who still serve with common sense and a high value
of morals are my senator, Rob Portman, and my
congressman, Bob Latta. Thank you, sirs, for your
unswerving dedication to duty and freedom. This is
also dedicated to any others so valiantly serving in
spite of the opposition. Take heart, we will win!

A tribute to Donna Hinton, 9/8/1937 to 7/12/2015
Beloved wife and partner for 51 wonderful years.

Dearest Donna,

How do I find the words worthy of describing you and my love for you? As long as I shall write about, explain, or think of you I will always come short of being able to adequately reach into our language and find the proper accolades due you.

God bless you for your love!

In Him,
Will

VALLEY OF THE SHADOW

WILL RILEY HINTON

Published by White Feather Press. (www.whitefeatherpress.com)

ISBN 978-1-61808-135-3

Printed in the United States of America

White Feather Press

Reaffirming Faith in God, Family and Country

Prologue

April Seventh, 2023. The rural America that slid by under the wing of the Piper Cheyenne was a sleepy looking one. The farm houses dotting the patchwork quilt of spring crops showed no movement about them, and the lazy, winding creeks that watered the greening trees along their banks showed themselves to be a muddy brown with the spring run-off. The peaceful appearance was totally deceptive.

What had been a tranquil scene several months previous was now a subdued one with a pall of doom hanging over it. Morgan Montgomery worked absent-mindedly at his charts to check his position as he tried unsuccessfully to push that feeling into the far corners of his mind. The events of the last few weeks refused such efforts and screamed to be lived again and again.

His passengers, up since their midnight departure, were now asleep and he was entirely alone with his thoughts. Well, not entirely. The other Cheyenne just ahead and off to his right was banking to the left to begin the approach to the small county airport just ahead. The airport in question had been carefully selected because it was small and quite obscure, but that didn't mean it would be entirely safe, either. Never the less, they were committed, and would land at any cost. Morgan decided to allow his passengers to sleep on.

His youngest son, Cal, slept in the seat beside him, while Morgan's wife, Kay, and their oldest son Brian and his, wife, Sue were behind him. He felt terribly responsible for their well being and prayed fervently that he had made the right choice when he decided to flee the juggernaut of troop take over with his family. The instant replay continued to haunt his thoughts as he throttled back for the approach. As he advanced the mixture controls to full rich, the props to full pitch and began to trim for slower speed he tried to shut the horrors from his mind, but with little success. It was nearly impossible to accept the events of the last year, and even more impossible to keep the reality of the situation in perspective.

Chapter 1

Vice President of the United States Jeryl Roberts had a difficult time maintaining his composure as he approached the desk of President Marcus Deloyac. He knew what to expect from this power hungry man and also realized the problem would become his to solve.

"Mark, we've got a heck of a problem on our hands in the mid west. That paramilitary group in northern Ohio and southern Michigan has struck again.

"This time it's worse than before. They've bombed the city buildings in Detroit and Toledo and successfully attacked a Navy reserve base on Lake Erie where we've been training special forces. Who would ever have guessed something like that was going on in Ohio, for crying out loud?"

"They what? You better not be telling me what I think you are, Jer'. Are those buildings destroyed? Are there casualties?"

Roberts knew the last was asked only to satisfy protocol. The president of the United States couldn't care less who or how many were killed. His concern was regaining total control of the country, and the ethnic, racial, and supremacist groups were making it hard to do.

"No, Mark, there are no casualties. This is the group that brags about its ability to cause unrest without injuring. And the bombings were of minimal impact, apparently designed just to show us they could do it."

"They'll show what can be done someday, all right. They'll learn the hard way that we can locate and do away with them!" This was said harshly and with much bitterness.

The entire country was in turmoil. Ethnic groups were fighting among themselves and between groups. The various militia forces had actually begun to mount insurrectional offenses on different government bodies, and finally, congress had started to attempt a sort of martial law status. The church became the first target of this action. Somehow, congress decided that the country's preachers were at fault for much of the antigovernment sentimentality. This view was no doubt spurred on by the ever increasing attacks by the ACLU. As a result, many freedoms of the churches had been removed.

Chaos was building, but mostly in the big cities. Anyone with any sense of reasoning could tell, however, that it was only a matter of time until the juggernaut rolled on to the rural areas. The land of the free was in deep trouble, and everyone knew it, especially President Deloyac. It wasn't his concern for the country, however, that drove him; it was his desire to control the nation to suit his own interests in power. It was also this approach to total rule by his administration that had started the revolts in the first place.

As Jeryl stood waiting for orders he steeled himself for the racial tirade he knew would soon follow. It wasn't that he was a non-racist, he just didn't have the stomach for the ethnic cleansing that his commander in chief advocated. Nor did he include the Jews and Christians in his prejudice, it was only the blacks and Hispanics that needed to be removed from the country. Somehow, in his narrow, self-centered and greedy mind he felt those two groups were responsible for his lack of ascent to more power. After all, hadn't several such people been promoted past him in the military? All because of their race.

His mind was one that was typically closed to the fact that those he was thinking about were, one and all, more talented and intelligent than he. Narrow-minded people are like that; they tend to blame others for their own lack of progress. President Deloyac was even worse in that department. Even though he had attained the highest office in his country and was arguably the most powerful man in the world he carried a trained hatred for anyone not like him.

Raised by a KKK activist and grand knight he had been taught to hate and had learned very well. He had also learned to consider violence to be the best and most effective means of dealing with others. That outlook had contributed greatly to the country's plight.

Deloyac looked up at his associate over his glasses and issued the expected edict. "Go ahead and activate the martial law decree for the whole nation, Jer'. I'm tired of this garbage. See to it that the right people are in charge, too. Got it?"

Oh, he had it, okay. That meant the most unscrupulous and backhanded generals and congressmen he could muster. Not that he hadn't already chosen his favorite blackguards for just this moment. He knew all too well what his president would require of him and was usually this step and some times two ahead of the man. He thought within himself how it should have been *him* as top dog and Mark as the vee-pee.

He made his first call to a friend in Ohio, one who had been prepared long in advance for this moment. John Harvey Stokes was an unscrupulous man dedicated only to gain for himself and perfectly suited for the job of cleaning up the Ohio and Michigan area. Jer' knew the troops held in readiness there would carry out the orders of Stokes to the letter. The letters would not be pleasant to read by any who opposed him.

In only a few words the fate of many was changed forever. With but a few more in the right places martial law was declared for the entire nation and the juggernaut released.

Chapter 2

Father Simson heard the vehicle pull up in a rush and felt a surge of apprehension well up within. He didn't know why, but a darkness seemed to descend on the parish house with the sound of slamming car doors.

He went to the window to peer out just as the door was thrown violently open and two darkly clad men entered nearly as one. Without so much as a grunt for a warning they grabbed the hapless priest and threw him to the floor.

"Provost wants you to be a lesson for those so-called Christian niggers you claim to love so much, preacher boy! You're gonna wish you'd listened better before we're finished!"

The speaker was wearing sergeant's stripes, and Father Simson recognized him as one of two men who had delivered a message of warning just the week before. As the parish priest of a black congregation he had been warned that the area provost in charge of martial law was not fond of other races or Christianity and therefore wanted him to shut down the church. He had, of course, refused.

"You think your so-called Christ suffered like your big book there says, Parson, you ain't seen nothin'," the speaker continued.

As he did so, the others were in the process of binding his hands and feet while the speaker efficiently gagged him. They dragged him to the car where they quickly tossed him into the trunk and slammed the lid. His heart was beating furiously, and he was sick to his stomach, but could experience no relief because of the gag. Fear pierced his entire being like so many hot and cold knives and his head pounded from the elevated blood pressure.

He felt the car leave the highway no more than five minutes after the start of the journey. The trunk opened shortly, and he was dragged from it and tossed to the ground, where the men proceeded to kick him. They soon tired of that, and hauled him to his feet. He expected to be struck, and steeled himself as best he could against the onslaught that never came. Just as he felt a sense of relief that they may be finished with him, a wire was wrapped around his neck.

"They're going to choke me!" he thought, and began to struggle against the tape that secured his hands. He experienced only derisive laughter from the men for his efforts as they lighted a torch.

Total fear and panic consumed him then, for he thought they would set him afire and he renewed his efforts to free himself. The torch was touched to the wire wrapped around his neck and as the fierce pain from the red-hot wire assailed him he realized through the blanket of agony that they were soldering the wire together. Then he passed out from the intense pain around his neck.

Consciousness returned slowly, as though from a fog bank of torment, and he became slowly aware of the gentle rocking of a boat. As his mind cleared to allow the return of the full sense of pain around his neck he realized he was in a rubber boat.

Try as he might, he couldn't lay still and fake a continuing unconscious state, so he tried to stir ever so slightly. The movement was seen.

"Well, well. Preacher boy's back with us. Let's get on with this, I'm ready for a night out on the town and drinks are on me," the voice of the sergeant came pushing through the fog in his mind.

The gag was removed and just as the distraught man was about to cry out for mercy he was rolled over the side into the river. A terrible weight quickly pulled him below the surface by the wire around his neck. Panic set in instantly as he tried to breathe and found only water in the place of air! Then, just as he choked violently on the muddy water, air rushed into his lungs!

But the respite was short lived, for water soon replaced the air, and he realized in a new rush of panic that the wire holding him under was demonically calibrated to just the right length to allow him to breath a tiny gasp of air when the waves washed over him. Father Simson, friend of all, was being tortured as terribly in his emotions as he was in the physical realm.

He struggled for control of his mind, and willed his now unbound hands to stop trying to swim and instead reached down to grab the wire. He feverishly bent it back and forth to break it, not knowing it was aircraft safety wire and the toughest available. Then, as more water than air repeatedly entered his choking, tortured lungs, the physiological control was totally lost and full red alert took over. His arms and legs furiously splashed in an attempt to swim and escape the terrible cloud of senselessness that fought to consume him until the water for several feet around him became a white froth. To the observers in the raft, it seemed forever until the beating of the water slowed to nearly nothing, then ceased completely.

As the current alternately lifted and pushed his body back and forth at the end of the wire, the killers made sure that it would stay afloat to be seen the next day by attaching a life jacket. This was to be a warning to any and all who might desire to disobey the provost marshal of the area. Father Simson had paid the supreme price for his love and faith.

The rubber boat slowly pulled away towards the far shore of the river as the two discussed where they would spend the extra money the provost marshal had paid them for the grisly task. To men this evil, it was merely another good night's work.

Chapter 3

April 29, 2023. Morgan was more than a little edgy today. He'd just completed the biggest sale of sporting arms in several years, but something ominous seemed to hang over the deal. Hagan Marshall had seemed to be an honest man, but what would anyone want to purchase twenty hunting rifles for? When Morgan had questioned him, he'd been evasive, but the money seemed good, so Morg went ahead. Now he was second guessing himself, but he wasn't about to let the ATF agent across the counter know it.

"Look, Montgomery, I can close you down and lock you up if you don't give me more than that to go on," the man was nearly shouting, "When I say I want all the information, that's just what I want!"

Morgan replied in an even and very controlled tone, "And I'm telling you that you have all the information I have, mister. Now, you may think you're God, but I'm getting just a little tired of being called a liar, and I suggest you tone it down a little bit while *one* of us is still rational.

"You came through that door mouth first, you haven't said a cordial word since that moment, and while I'm a God-fearing, peace-loving man, your arrogance is wearing me thin.

"Now, I've cooperated fully with you, I've shown you the man's two permits, I even went to the library and ran copies off for you at my own expense, I've explained that he was buying for a new hunting ranch he intended to start in Tennessee, and I've identified his picture for you.

"I also showed you the bid sheet I submitted to him for

the high volume discount. Now, mister, that's it. You make one more threat or insinuation that I'm less than honest and I'm going to come over this counter and rearrange that arrogant look on your face, government agent or no government agent. Got it?"

Morgan knew he was allowing himself to become too worked up by this guy, but he had gone beyond the point of caring. It was then that his youngest son, Cal entered.

The agent, a Mr. Peters, turned to Cal and spoke gruffly to him. "I'm sorry, this store is closed for now, maybe permanently, so please leave."

Cal was a strapping youth of eighteen, tall, with the natural grace of an athlete and the disposition of a Labrador Retriever.

"I'm sorry, sir, but I work here, and I'm late getting my books balanced. You see, I do most of the bookkeeping now, and we simply won't let our paperwork get behind. Government regulations you see. We stay strictly within the guidelines here. My dad insists on it."

Morgan could have hugged the boy then, for it was obvious he knew nothing of who this arrogant stranger was. Cal followed this with the question, "Who is this guy, Dad, that he thinks he can close a store that isn't his? You're not selling, are you?"

Peters whirled to Morgan and spat out to him. "Don't think you've heard the last of this, Montgomery. You even breathe wrong and you're through. And if you're through, you'll also be making little rocks out of big ones, got it?"

"Mister, just get out. Now. You've worn my patience as thin as it can go and I want you gone. And if you do come back, you'd better bring help 'cause you're gonna need it!"

With flushed face and heavy steps the irate bully stomped to the door, pausing there for a second and looking back before charging out into the street. He nearly flattened old Mrs. Beaty as he hit the sidewalk. He growled an insult and continued on to his car. Squealing tires as he left the curb, he was soon out of sight.

"What in the world was that all about, Dad?" asked Cal.

"He's a government agent from the Alcohol, Tobacco, and Firearms division. Remember that big sale I made to that so-called game preserve owner? Well, he's supposed to be a terrorist, according to this character, and that guy's trying to say I'm in cahoots with them! Wouldn't listen to a thing I told him, just kept threatening me!"

"Do you think he'll make trouble? I mean, they've been jailing a lot of gun dealers and confiscating their businesses lately. Maybe we should get out of the guns and just sell hardware."

"Yeah, I know. I've had the same thoughts myself, with all the trouble that's been going on. But I hate to, the sporting goods section is our biggest source of income, son."

Gordon Montgomery had seen his share of hardships in his fifty five years, but had been enjoying the success of his business for the past ten years. He hated the thought of giving any of it up. He had been a flight instructor at the local county airport for nearly twenty years, owning and operating his own flight school for fifteen of those. Then, at forty-two years of age, he developed a heart condition that took him from flying. He had been grounded, with no chance of redeeming his FAA medical certificate.

There were three other instructors working for him at the time, two of them part timers and John Rosenthal, his full time associate. He had hired John, more frequently known as "Rosey," when he showed up from the east coast on a charter flight and inquired about employment in "these quiet, hick surroundings." They had become inseparable friends, and Rosey and his wife, Paige, spent many of their waking hours with the Montgomery's. When John Rosenthal made a friend, it was for life, as he didn't accept that many people into his close relationships, and it was an instant decision on his part to buy Morgan out as soon as he heard the bad news. He not only did that, he insisted that Morgan retain a part ownership and thus keep some income from the business until the Montgomery's decided what to do for a living.

If you asked any of the Montgomery family, God intervened quickly, for the local hardware suddenly became available for just the amount they had received for the flight school. Rosey sneered at the thought, but there was no steering Morgan from that belief. Both Morgan and Kay had been raised with a Christian background, though Morg hadn't actually become a Christian until his mid twenties. Kay had accepted Christ at an early age, had fallen in love with Morgan in high school, but refused to marry him because of his less than acceptable lifestyle. He had joined the "in crowd" with their drinking and such, and saw nothing wrong with "having a little fun." His flight school had been prospering, but he wasn't happy. He had searched every avenue he could to become satisfied only to fail at every attempt. Then an evangelist from a missionary flying service visited his church.

Morgan went with Kay at her invitation, and after the missionary pilot's message you couldn't have kept Morgan Montgomery from going forward to accept Christ if you'd have shot him! His life had changed drastically in an instant.He still had to prove himself to Kay, but their relationship had grown rapidly, and as he hungrily absorbed as much of the Bible as he could, she drew closer to him until one day she announced to him that she was ready. His baffled look had thrown her into a fit of laughter that further confused him. Then she threw her arms around his neck and proposed marriage. The rest, as they say, was history.

When Morgan had purchased the hardware he told Rosey of his beliefs, to be met by sheer skepticism. It didn't change his mind a bit that God had provided this for him, and a year later he had remodeled and added the sporting goods section. Business shot through the roof, and Morgan had come to slowly accept his non-flying status in the years that followed.

Chapter 4

Morgan, Kay, and Cal had just finished the evening meal when a car door slammed in the drive outside. Cal peered out the window and promptly announced that Brian and Sue had arrived. Brian was the oldest son at twenty-two, and he and Sue had been married a year and a half. To show up during the dinner hour was very unusual for them, and Morgan sensed an immediate chill. Sue entered with a somber look and slid to the side to allow Brian entrance. His dark, unruly hair was more disheveled than usual and his eyes glinted a steely gray that only showed when he was angry or stressed out. Both were the case now.

He stopped just inside the door and Sue slid her slender figure under his arm, slipping her own around his waste. They stood silent for what seemed eternity before Brian finally spoke.

"Mom, Dad. We just heard some terrible news." At that point he choked up and took several seconds to compose himself, then he spoke again. "Remember Father Simson, that priest we were telling you about?"

Kay was first to answer, "Yes, he's the one who was speaking out for his black congregation over in Oplatt, right? The government was trying to make them disband for some silly reason."

"Yeah. The silly reason was that they were black, and the area provost marshal said they had no right to be acting like white people, with their own church, and such."

"So what's happened, Brian? I know you were involved heavily in their building program as a carpenter last year. You re

13

pretty close to him, right?" Morgan asked.

"Not any more, Dad. They..." He choked up again, this time to fail completely in his efforts to regain composure.

"Oh Dad, they've just found him in the river," Sue choked out, "Tied to a piece of cement by a wire around his neck!"

"No! You can't be serious! Who would dare harm a priest? And for what reason?" Morgan's horror spilled out in a rush. There was a deafening silence for a very long time, then Brian collected his emotions and began to share his thoughts.

"Tom shared with me the last time I worked over there that the provost had made insinuations of violence, Dad. I think he had something to do with it. I really do!"

"No! I can't think that. Why, he's a government official sworn to keep the peace!"

The office of provost marshal was a relatively new one, established in an effort to squelch the militia's actions throughout the country. In the state of Ohio, the government had first broken it down to four counties per provost, making a total of twenty-two, then further established "precincts" in the larger cities of Cleveland, Columbus, Cincinnati, Toledo, and the Akron-Canton areas. Each provost had two-hundred troops at his command who patrolled the roads in all the precincts continuously. These troops had grown progressively more aggressive with the general public during the year of their existence and were sometimes referred to as the new SS. Some provosts had even developed hand picked "goon squads" to care for their own personal interests and elimination of trouble makers. Father Tom had become earmarked as one of those. Brian mentioned the fact at that time.

Kay's reply was to express doubt that any government official would sink to that depth. "I just don't see how you can believe that, Brian. This is America! Those things happen in third world countries, not here."

"Mom, they do happen here, and they are happening here," Brian replied.

"Dad," Cal spoke up, "Maybe you should share what happened today at the store with that creep from the ATF."

He received a stare from Morgan that suggested the topic hadn't been one he planned to bring up. It was too late now, however, so he went ahead and told them of the incident, with Cal filling in little details that Morgan had chosen to conveniently leave out in an attempt to spare Kay from worry.

"Morgan, I think Cal's right. I think we should stop selling guns and ammunition until this silly business has blown over and things are back to normal," Kay said.

He looked at her with the eyes of a teenage lover, drinking in the wonderful qualities this woman held that so drew him to her. She was, without doubt, the warmest and most loving of all women. But she kept within her a trait that was both inspiring and frustrating. She trusted all people and carried the ideals in her heart that mankind was basically good and should always be given the benefit of the doubt.

His voice was soft and gentle when he answered her. "Honey, I'm not sure you and I will ever see that time. I really believe we're seeing the end times the Bible talks about, and this is just the way for America to be taken from power in order to make us ready for the one world government."

She laid a gentle hand on his and replied, "Dear, even the apostle Paul thought he was living in the end times. Men of every generation have thought so. I just don't know, but I do believe we'll see the U.S. back where it once was."

"I sure hope so, honey, but don't hold your breath."

"Well, I just can't bring myself to believe this horrible thing wasn't the act of some perverted sect or...or something like that. It's just too terrible to even comprehend."

"Mom. You need to realize that I overheard some of the threats that came from the provost's office," Brian said. "They were even left on his answering machine with no regard or fear of the wrong person hearing them. I still find it hard to believe that someone could be so boldly brutal."

The sound of car doors slamming came from the driveway, and a very pale and drawn John Rosenthal burst into the house with anger bristling forth like a porcupine's quills.

"I tell you, Morgan Montgomery, I'm about ready to call it quits where this country's concerned," he started. "I just saw a sheriff all but ignore a problem that's totally horrible.

"I'm leaning more and more towards agreeing with you, John, but there's more serious things than that going on here.

15

Did you hear about the murder of the priest?"

"Hear about it? Morg', I was there. I helped pull him out! A student and I were on our way in when we over-flew the river and the student, Jimmy Clark, saw the body floating in the water. We called the sheriff as soon as we landed, then drove out there in a hurry. In fact, we got there before the law did. That's what I'm talking about!"

"Then you've had a horrible day! That's got to be awful, John!" Kay blurted out. "Does Paige know any of this yet?"

"No. I thought she'd be here when there was no answer at home. That's why I rushed over here. I'm about as shook as I ever want to be. First the phone call just as Jimmy and I were ready to go out for his lesson, then the awful sight of that poor guy when we pulled him out of the river and saw the weight wired around his neck!" Rosey gave a violent shudder, turned pale, and sat down on the nearest open chair with a thud.

"I mean, you want to talk about something brutal and ugly! Jimmy and I both lost our meals from the last week! I'm still queasy, I tell you.

"When the sheriff got there, he had a rubber boat with him, and after about fifteen minutes, he got impatient for a deputy to show, and asked us to go with him to help. I mean, we had no idea we were looking at a murder!

"All we could see was this poor soul floating out there on the current with a life jacket on. I said to the sheriff how strange that looked, then we pulled him out."

At that point, Rosey paused, drew a deep breath and shuddered. His face drew into a convulsive state as he fought to hold the tears back, and failing, he fell into a soft sobbing. Minutes later he finally composed himself and began to speak again.

"There was a plastic soft drink bottle tied to his back with a note in it. The sheriff wouldn't let me see it, but I looked over his shoulder as he read it and it was a threat of some kind towards the guy's church. I mean, I don't think church is all that important myself, but what harm can it do for people to go?"

"Just how blatant will these people get?" Morgan exclaimed.

Brian strode to the window and spent the next several

minutes staring at nothing. The rest of them set as though in a trance, each trying to grasp the fact that such a thing could happen in their small community. Kay was the first to stir, and she moved as though every move hurt.

She stepped to the fridge and began to dip ice cream into cones for each of them, not bothering to ask if all wanted one. She had to busy herself some way and to serve others was always her reaction. They all received their cones mechanically and remained lost in their thoughts until the phone jarred them back to earth. It was Paige.

"Hi Kay! Listen, is Rosey there? He should be home by now, but I haven't heard from him," she asked.

"Uuh, yes, Paige, he's here. Maybe you should come over, something's happened and we need each other right now."

"Is he okay? He didn't have an accident Kay, tell me he didn't."

"No, no, nothing like that. John's fine, but you really need to be here. Please," Kay returned. Then she did a very uncharacteristic thing, she hung up. If she could have seen the face of her friend as she rushed to the car she would have felt terrible, but the resulting arrival of Paige in record time more than made up for it.

John brought her up to date on the events, including the ATF man, and they consoled her as she tried unsuccessfully to remain composed. Paige Rosenthal liked to think she was pretty tough and resilient, but in truth she was one who needed support of others in all situations. Both Kay and Morgan had seen through her facade early on in the friendship and responded accordingly. It was their feeling that she could be reached for the Lord easier than Rosey and they trusted he could then be reached through her.

The seven shocked and saddened people remained together 'til near ten o'clock, and then began to quietly slip towards their own homes and private thoughts. None would sleep well that night; Brian and Sue wept the night away clinging to one another, Kay clung to Morgan as though she would fall from the bed if she let go while Paige spent the night softly soothing a husband imprisoned by recurring nightmares. Several states away to the west an unknowing elderly couple prayed and thanked their God for their son's faithfulness and courage. Their smiles would fade to tears with the next morning's news.

****

Breakfast at the Montgomery's was subdued, to say the least. Cal suggested to his folks that they take a day off and "go do a lot of nothing together." Morgan glanced at Kay with a question in his eyes, she smiled and nodded, and it was set. Cal would run the store and they would simply take off for parts as yet unknown for the day.

"I'll bet we end up shopping, what do you think, Cal?" a teasing Morgan asked.

"Write it down, Dad, now that you brought it up. Mom would never have thought of it if you would have been still!"

"Yeah, sure. Pigs start flying tomorrow, too, Son."

"Hey you two! Let's show a little respect and consideration around here for the weaker sex," was Kay's reply. "I've got to put on my face and then I'll be right with you Morgan Montgomery, so you just sit tight for a bit."

"Face looks fine to me, love. Just use the one you have on for today and we'll still have to whip every guy we meet because they flirted with my wife."

She gave him an affectionate ear pull as she passed his chair on her way from the room, taking the time to kiss Cal on the cheek as well.

"Thanks, Cal. You are so wise beyond your years. This is just what we need."

He grinned as she left and looked at Morgan, speaking more seriously. "What if that nut from the ATF comes back today, Dad? Do I toss him or listen?"

"My word, don't toss him, Cal! Just try to give him whatever you can and let it take it's course from there! We don't want to aggravate these people any more than necessary for cryin' out loud!"

The mischievous grin that followed told Morgan he'd been had by his youngest once again. This enigmatic lad had always been a study for him. Cal was a very serious lad most of the time, but on occasion he would spring forth with the most subtle teasing, usually when you least expected it. This was just

18

such a time.

Morgan arose and followed his lovely wife, wallowing his son's unruly hair as he passed.

"One day I'll be ready for you, buster. And when I am, you watch out."

Cal merely grinned bigger and poked his passing dad in the ribs with a finger. Morgan walked into the bedroom to find Kay with several outfits lying on the bed.

"I can't make up my mind what to wear, Hon," she mused as he entered.

"So what's new? Does the destination have any bearing on the decision?"

She turned to him with a questioning look. "Do you have something in mind?"

"Well, what if we have Rosey fly us over to Port Clinton and we take a ferry out to the islands? We haven't been out there for a long time," he replied.

"Oh Morg', that's a great idea. But what if John's tied up?"

He put his arms around her and drew her close as he answered. "Then I'll fly the darned thing myself. I haven't forgotten how, you know."

"Yeah, you'd do that in a minute, wouldn't you, Morgan Montgomery?" she answered. "That's all we need now, for you to have something happen while you're flying without a valid ticket. You get that nonsense out of that handsome head of yours, fellow. If John's busy we'll find somewhere else to go."

He laughed as he released her with a smack on the bottom and reached for the phone. "I'll just call old Mister Rosenthal right now and schedule a charter for us my dear."

His attempt at an English accent was, as usual, a total flop, but she smiled tolerantly just the same as if he were a proper butler. A harried and tired voice answered the airport phone on the fourth ring and Morgan could hear the frustration a bad night can bring. After all, before Cal's brilliant suggestion he'd felt the same way. Maybe Rosey and Paige would like to go. But no, that thought quickly passed, for he wanted the time with Kay to himself.

"Hi Rosey. You sound like I feel, buddy."

"Didn't sleep much," the voice on the other end growled.

"I'm not sure I'll ever sleep again."

"Listen, John, I need a favor, but if you don't feel like it I want you to be honest and tell me. okay?"

"Hey, Morg, I can do whatever favor you need with my eyes closed. All you gotta do is ask. What gives?"

"Well, Cal is going to tend the store today and I thought it would be good for Kay if we went over to one of the Lake Erie islands for the day. I wondered if you could drop us off on the airstrip in one of your Cherokees and pick us up just before dark?"

"Get your hind ends over here as soon as you can, then. I've got some military students at ten. I'll preflight and be ready for you. 'Course...." The statement stopped there.

"Of course what, fella. What you got up your sneaky sleeve now?"

"Look, Morg, you can still fly as good as you ever could, at least in VFR. If you want, I'll just look the other way while you take the one-eighty Cherokee."

"Rosey, you'll never know the temptation I have to do just that, but the law's the law, and I just can't risk it even if I would."

"You and your goody-two-shoes approach to life will cause you no end of grief some day, Morg. I'll be waiting."

"Okay,, we're on our way."

They donned shorts and grabbed what they could find for a picnic from the fridge and were off for the county airstrip. On the way across the Maumee river bridge Morgan shuddered and felt a terrible chill deep in his soul. He actually groaned softly.

"What did you say, Hon?" Kay asked.

"Nothing, I just realized that back there was where they found Brian's friend in the river, that's all."

"That's all? That's certainly enough! I wish I hadn't asked," she declared.

That caused all conversation to cease until they arrived at the airport. The white and red Cherokee was sitting at the gas pump and Rosey leaned against the wing gazing off into the blue of the sky. He turned at the sound of their car and climbed onto the wing and into the left seat. Morgan gave Kay a boost onto the wing , adding a playful pinch as he did so and received a cuff on the head for his trouble. As she slid into the back seat she wrinkled her nose at him and stuck out her tongue. Rosey caught the by-play and shook his head solemnly.

"I don't know how you two can shake off that dread so easily" he commented, "I've still got the heebie-jeebies."

"Why do you think we're going off for the day, John?" Kay responded. "We had to try and wring this out of our systems."

Morgan added, "We prayed about it nearly half the night, but we just couldn't leave it with Him. I kept putting it in His hands, then I'd reach out and grab it again. I guess my faith isn't as strong as I thought."

"You can try that "faith" thing if you want, you two, but as far as I'm concerned, John Rosenthal is carrying a piece from now on!" With that declaration he switched the magnetos on and cranked the Lycoming over. It sprang to life quickly and Morgan succumbed to habit long established and scanned the engine instruments for proper readings. All looked right.

Kay responded from the back over the loud engine as Rosey throttled forward and started his taxi. "What do you mean, a piece? Piece of what?"

Morgan turned and explained that the military definition of a piece was a rifle or pistol. They were never to be called a gun by military personnel. Then he turned to Rosey with a cold, misgiving feeling.

"You aren't going to tell me you're carrying a sidearm are you? Please tell me you're not!"

Rosey simply pulled his left arm high to reveal a small .25 caliber pistol nestled in a diminutive shoulder holster. The cold went to the marrow of Morgan's being as he saw his friend was serious. Being speechless, he dropped the subject.

"I think we'd like to drop into Small Bass this trip, John," he related. The pilot gave him a concerned look at the use of his proper name in place of Rosey.

"Small Bass it is, Morg."

Morgan picked the mike off its cradle and dialed in the initial Toledo frequency on the radio. After receiving the information being broadcast he then switched to approach control and informed them of their altitude and destination. He always enjoyed getting back on the radio, it seemed a balm to his injured soul where flying was concerned.

21

After getting clearance they scanned the sky around them in silence for other traffic. The mood had quickly returned to one of tension. The day was a rare northwestern Ohio one in that the wind was silent, which allowed the surface of Lake Erie to lie in a pristine mirror fashion. The brilliant blue of the water flowed away from them until it met the blue of the sky in an indiscernible blending. It appeared as though the lake simply wrapped all the way from beneath them to the atmosphere above.

The Lake Erie islands lay only a few miles from the shore so it wasn't long before Rosey throttled back to start his approach. Within a couple of minutes the Cherokee was settling onto the grass runway and rolling to a stop.

"How about a four o'clock pickup, John? Can you make that?"

"No Morg, it'll be either after five before I can make it or at three. I have another military student at four."

"Okay, make it whenever you can after that student. We'll get along just fine with the extra time," Morgan answered. He helped Kay down the wing to the step as the prop wash lifted her scarf from her head and sent it on its merry way into the weeds behind them. She squealed as her long hair attempted to follow and Morgan sort of held her from getting out of the air as quickly as she wanted.

Rosey laughed at the sight of their struggles and let the Lycoming have full throttle a little early to add to her dismay. The runway soon fell away beneath the plane, leaving the two wrestlers alone. Morgan held his wife close for a few seconds 'til she ceased to struggle and soundly kissed her when she did.

"Are you going to be difficult to live with today, Morgan Montgomery?" she asked with fire in her eye.

"Not at all, Missus Montgomery, ma'am. Not at all. You just be at my beck and call and all will be fine."

"So! You've only brought me to this island paradise to strand me here so you could ply your wiles upon me, have you?"

"Ply my wiles upon you?" he asked as he broke up with laughter at her questioning.

She chuckled and said with a rather contrite look, "That wasn't the best of use of the Queen's language, was it?"

Morgan just shook his head and smiled, continuing to hug her close. She stayed submissive for a few moments, then pushed him away.

"We can't be hugging and kissing in the middle of the runway for the rest of the day now, can we? What if another plane wants to land? Let's go rent a bicycle built for two if they still have one and tour the island again.

"Morgan! Wake up! Helloooo, earth to Morgan. Where are you?"

The last brought him out of the deep thoughts he'd been drawn into, and he chuckled as he went to retrieve her wayward scarf..

"What? What is it, buddy?" she insisted in her best scolding tone.

"Oh, nothing really. I was just remembering the first time we were here. Do you?"

She took his hand gently as they began to stroll towards the village to find a bike. "Yes I do. You had just accepted Christ and we came here for our own little mini-retreat. You were so eager to learn the whole Bible that I thought you'd never let me go home 'til you had all your questions answered!"

"Yeah," he chuckled, "I thought I could nail this Christianity thing down with just one session with you. Boy was I dreaming! Sometimes I wonder if I'll ever get it."

"None of us ever 'get it' until He takes us out of this world and changes us forever, Hon, you know that."

"Yeah, I do, but you know what I mean. I just think I'm making progress and then someone like that ATF agent comes along and I'm ready to pop him. I wish I could have your natural love and understanding for everyone, even the creeps."

"My outlook isn't natural, you know that. It comes from constant study of the Word and a lot of prayer. And I slip, too. I could hate the people who do things like this last terrible act! And I feel bad about it, but it's still possible.

"Let's forget those things and get going. I need to wear you down on a bike so you'll behave yourself."

"Hah! As if you could, lady," he replied, and they stepped up the pace towards the bike rentals.

****

The sun was reaching its peak as the two pulled their rented bicycle up to the north shore of the island and spread their picnic lunch on the ground. A small boat lay just off shore with a lone fisherman in the bow intent on his casting. As they slowly devoured the lunch, a larger boat appeared on the horizon and approached the smaller craft. The fisherman slowly boated his line and seemed to almost lazily drift towards the now anchored larger one. Morgan and Kay could hear the calls from one of the crew to the fisherman.

"Any luck with your catch there, sailor?"

"Yeah, some," replied the fisherman. "I can see a little bit of success developing if I use the right bait!"

Morgan looked at Kay with a very puzzled look at the statement as the conversation continued.

"I know a guy who likes to use a half-ounce sinker just ahead of a one ounce lure. He says that'll get what you want every time." This came from the larger boat.

"I don't think so," came the answer, "You tell him I'd use no more than a half ounce lure on that rig."

"He ain't gonna like it, but I'll tell him."

"You can also tell him I need to catch my dinner by this weekend, got it? He'll have to make up his mind by then or we're going with another charter captain."

"Okay, but it's your funeral, buddy." With that final strange reply the larger craft weighed anchor and chugged off towards the north, retracing its original path.

The starter rope was pulled on the smaller boat and it, too, left, charting a course towards the rental docks to the east. Morgan had an uneasy feeling about the whole thing and said as much.

"Why is that, Hon?" Kay asked.

"That guy in the small fishing boat looked strangely familiar. I just can't place him, but even at this distance there's a look that I know I've seen."

They finished their lunch and Morgan stretched out with his head in her lap. As she twisted her fingers in his hair he exercised the one gift he was blessed with that exasperated his beloved, he promptly went to sleep. Several minutes later he opened his eyes slowly to peer up into hers. She playfully placed her hands over his eyes and commanded him to sleep some more.

"Can't. That was enough to re-energize me, Hon. You know that."

"Yes, I do. And I'm jealous, you know. It just isn't fair that you can just drop off to sleep at the drop of a hat, sleep ten or fifteen minutes, and be refreshed. It isn't, I tell you, sir!"

He got to his feet, pulled her up, and squeezed her tightly for a moment. Then they gathered their scraps and such and trod off to the bike.

"Let's take this thing back and walk for the rest of the day, okay? I've seen enough of the long range stuff for today," he said.

"That sounds great to me. I've been trying to get you to exercise, maybe this is the breakthrough." She dodged the swat at her bottom and leaped on the back seat of the conveyance motioning for him to be seated. "Your throne, my lord."

He sighed, mounted, and with the admonition for her to be sure and help pedal shoved off. They made the two mile ride in a leisurely fashion, and when they pulled up to the rental place a familiar figure was just leaving. The tall, lanky form of the man jarred Morgan to a halt, and he muttered almost too low for Kay to hear, "Marshall!"

"What, Hon, is that man a marshal?"

Before he could answer the fellow was upon them. He held out his hand for Morgan's and greeted him warmly.

"Hello, Mister Montgomery. I didn't expect to see you here. How are things?"

"Not good at all since you came into my life, fellow. You've really messed things up at the store for me. You better be able to prove you didn't lie to me, Marshall, or...." Morgan had started to work himself up to a frenzy when he realized it and reined in his reactions.

"Look, Montgomery, keep it down, you hear? I didn't lie to you. I do have a lodge and hunting service and I am a licensed guide. It's just that it doesn't stop there and for that I'll apologize to no man. I gave you all the information you needed. Now, what's the problem at the shop?"

25

Morgan drew a deep breath before he started again. "I had an ATF agent in there yesterday trying to grill me about you and accusing me of being a part of whatever it is you're a part of. And I don't even want to come close to knowing what that is! I just want to run my store and be left alone. By everyone! Including you from now on."

"Okay, I see your dilemma, sir, and I understand your being upset. I didn't think they'd be on it that quickly. All the other buys took more time before they caught on. I'd be lying if I told you I was sorry, for I'll do whatever it takes to arm our people, and you'd be better off if you joined up with us now. They'll hound you, not just until you're out of business, but until you either break or they lock you up under some false pretense. This seems to be a purging of the classes for some reason or another, and mark my words, they are very good and getting better at it!

"I'll not bother you folks further, its best if you're not seen talking to me. But...If you ever decide to start fighting to keep your freedom, I'll send a messenger from time to time and ask my informants to keep track of you. After all, I guess I may have brought trouble your way without intending to and I owe you that much. Good day sir; ma'am."

With that he nodded briefly, turned on his heel, and was gone into the restaurant beside them. They both stood dumbfounded for a full minute and then strode down the road towards the airstrip as though in a trance. They had walked fully half a mile before either spoke.

"I know that man is doing things that neither you or I approve of, Hon, but he really does seem like a nice sort," Kay remarked.

"Well, that's what I thought, too. And he did seem genuinely concerned. Its a little late for that, though. I'm afraid the damage has been done. Plus...He ruined our day away!"

His distress moved her to wrap her arms around his right one as they walked and lay her head on his shoulder. "No, I think not. I'm here with the man I love in a beautiful setting knowing he loves me and knowing also that God is here with the two of us, always and everywhere," she answered.

Her warmth in troubled times never failed to bring tears of gratitude to his eyes, and his voice failed him for a few moments. She knew him so well! He knew as well that she knew he couldn't speak nor did she expect him to. God had been so good to him to provide this lovely women to support him in life!

Their time remaining on the island was spent sitting at the edge of the runway with Morgan leaning against a small tree and Kay laying back against him just making small talk and reminiscing.

Chapter 5

The Cherokee seemed as though the engine noise would crush his chest as John Rosenthal began his descent to the island airstrip. His heart was still beating faster than the Piper was flying and the cold, clammy feeling went deeper than he'd ever known. He was frightened, angry, and near tears once again.

It had seemed like the day was improving as it went along. The first military student had done well, and seemed to be more jovial than normal. Then the two civilian students that followed had done equally well and were two really sweet people besides.

He'd spent the rest of his day working on one of the charter ships to complete a periodic check until the last two military students arrived. They did okay, but he was getting very tired of both of them by the time the second one was down. They were both loud and arrogant men who liked to push people around. Rosey was a very pleasant guy, but he didn't push. As soon as he had the last man's logbook filled out he went to the rest room to disappear for a bit.

Placing himself on the stool furthest from the door he closed the door of the stall and leaned back. That lasted about two seconds when he heard the outer door of the restore open and someone entered. Being stressed out once again he raised his feet up so they couldn't be seen and tried to get comfortable. He refused to talk further to these crud balls from the local unit and would wait them out. Whoever this was surely couldn't take long.

It was then that the door opened again and another entered. Drat! His legs were starting to cramp. Hurry up, crud balls!

Just as that thought passed through his mind he recognized the voice of the sergeant.

"How'd you do today, Crawford? Learnin' anything from this slime ball civilian?"

"Yeah, Sarge, I think he's pretty good at this. I still feel tired from last night, though. I didn't sleep so good after that episode. It sorta haunted me every time I dozed off. I could still see that poor fool trying for all his life to swim with that cement wired to his neck I wish we'd just shot the fool, it'd been a lot easier."

"Listen you! You start to get choir boy on me and I'll shoot **you**! You know I will! This setup is too good to have someone jeopardize it because he ain't got the guts to perform a little tough stuff for us! Stokes paid us and paid us good, so you got no gripe comin'. That preacher boy had his chance and was too stupid to take it, so that makes him worthless anyway. That little play was nothing more than ridding the country of a meddlin' goody two-shoes and God knows we got too many of them as it is!"

By the time his speech was over the sergeant was worked up to a near frenzy and the other man seemed properly cowed. He muttered something unintelligible and left the room. Utter fear mixed with total fury engulfed Rosenthal as he waited for the sergeant to leave. The cramps in his legs forgotten, he stood and trembled under the mixture of emotions. He nearly collapsed when he discovered the little pistol was in his hand. He'd forgotten he was even carrying it during the day's activities and here he stood with it fully loaded and cocked in his hand! It was a wonder the men hadn't heard the action when he cocked it, but the anger of the higher ranking man had apparently held both their attentions for the time.

Rosey had waited a small eternity before leaving the rest room and then made straight for the Cherokee. He wanted out of there and **now**! He went straight to the Cherokee. The Lycoming had caught quickly and he was rolling immediately.

John's mind snapped back to the present and he realized that South Bass Island was right beneath him and also that he was still at three thousand feet! He pulled the carb heat, chopped the throttle, and spiraled down. "If Morgan's watching

I'll take a beatin' for this," he said aloud to himself. "Darned fool's not flown for ten years and can probably *still* out fly me."

As he slid in over the end of the runway he dropped the ship in from too high and bounced a couple of feet back into the air. Then it slammed back onto the grass and stuck fast this time. He slowed quickly and wheeled around only halfway down the runway to taxi back . He could see Morgan and Kay just now getting up from their seat against a small tree. That meant he'd been observed. Drat!

Morgan twirled his hand in the air signaling for him to keep the engine running and then slipped behind the wing to escort Kay to the step. Rosey reached over to unlatch the door and the two were soon seated and buckled in. Morgan never offered to critique the approach or the landing and Rosey realized the day had accomplished just what it was supposed to for them. He wouldn't have said a thing about his recent discovery if someone had held a gun to his head! These two were the second and third most important people in his life, coming right on the heels of his petite little wife and he'd be darned if he was going to ruin their day.

"You guys been waiting long? I didn't see you there on the approach, you must have been napping," he accused.

Kay laughed as she replied, "No, not napping. Morgan was reading to me from his little New Testament he always carries. I think we could have just set there like that for the whole day and been satisfied. That way, old 'I'm in great shape so I'll do all the pedaling' Montgomery here wouldn't have been so worn out!"

Morgan wheeled to look fondly at her and replied, "Et too, Brute? I'm *not* worn out, just catching my second wind."

The 180 horses in front of them began their cacophony of 2600 rpm and plummeted them down the grass of the runway, the nose rotated, and they were on their way back home. If one could have looked inside the three, they would have found a mixture of emotions that ran the entire gamut. In the two island exploring people, contentment, deep love, excitement, and peace once again. In the pilot, every negative thought one soul could harbor at one time from bitter hate all the way to fear, with murder and revenge sitting somewhere in between. John

Rosenthal was not the same man who had flown them to South Bass that morning, and the change was not for the better.

Once they were on the ground at the Henry County Airport he was able to present himself in a normal manner. He had successfully calmed the storm within and even joked with Kay a bit. With the Piper tied down and the terminal locked, the three went to their separate cars and departed. Morgan insisted on stopping at the store to check things out while Rosey went straight home. Morgan found the store already closed and Rosey found his house empty. It was twenty minutes past normal closing time at the hardware and at the Rosenthal's, Paige had left a note saying she needed groceries or they would soon starve. Rosey smiled when he saw it, something the diminutive little brunette could always make him do, even in the toughest of times.

He poured a glass of wine, grabbed the paper, and practically fell into the recliner. With the wine beside him and the paper on his lap he lay his head back and closed his eyes for a bit. Mental exhaustion took over and Paige found him just like that an hour later when she came in. She knew he was really tired for she had carried in the groceries and stored them before entering the living room and he hadn't even stirred. That just didn't happen with *her* hubby! He always heard her come in the driveway and would be at the door of the car to open it for her before the engine quit. "The true gentleman, you are sir," she mused to herself as she tiptoed back to the kitchen.

She soon busied herself with preparing supper and was merrily humming quietly when he finally awoke and came out for a snack. Then he looked at the clock.

"Seven o'clock!" he exclaimed. "Wow, how long did I sleep, anyhow? No wonder I'm hungry!"

"You sure were somewhere far off," she answered with a wink. "You must have had a bear of a day, I haven't seen my 'Mister Energy Man' that tired for years."

He dropped his head and sighed deeply. "Yeah, it was. I'm pretty stressed out over that deal last evening, and today didn't ease it any." He stopped there, not wanting her to know more lest she be more alarmed than she already was.

She smiled at him and handed him a plate. "Here, get what

you want and I'll bring you something to drink. I'll set the TV tray up for you, its too late to catch the news, but a little TV nonsense may relax you."

"No! I....uh, I...Well, I just want to eat at the table with you. Just you and me alone. No noise, no news, just you. I want us to spend more quality time, like Morg' is always preaching to me, okay?"

The look she gave him was one of mixed emotions. She was thrilled, yet realized that this man she loved so dearly was at a strange place for him. She would have to really pamper him for a while, she supposed, and knew she could help him through this crisis. She set the table and rubbed his back for a bit as soon as he sat down. Then they had a delightful meal together though she could sense the strain remaining in him.

Afterwards he helped her with the dishes and they then retired to the living room to relax. That, however, was too much for the normally hyper John Rosenthal. He was not the TV type, but had to be accomplishing something with his time. Tonight he attempted to read a new publication on the present aviation navigational systems being developed. Concentration was impossible and Paige could tell he was restless.

"Hon, why don't you take your shower now and I'll give you a hot oil rubdown when you're ready?"

"Lady, you've got a deal. I think my muscles are trying to become fiddle strings they feel so tight."

With that he strode off towards the basement shower while she headed to the bathroom for a bath. Knowing he would stay under the hot shower for a long time she quickly bathed, put on her best perfume, and began to rifle through her dresser for a long lost negligee. It had been years since she had enticed her husband this way and decided the time was long overdue. She returned to the bathroom to finish preparations and heard his footfall go past the door.

Once she felt properly arranged she viewed her petite, well rounded little body with its filmy attire in the full length mirror. "Lady, you still ain't bad, ya know that?" she murmured to herself with a girlish giggle. She warmed a bottle of body lotion under the hot water faucet then with rapidly beating heart slipped to the bedroom. She was now feeling very exhilarated at the prospect of their time together. The feeling didn't last long, for there on the bed lay an exhausted and totally comatose husband! His snoring was from deep within and she could tell he was gone for the night.

A tolerant and loving smile crossed her face as she covered him gently with the top sheet and turned out the light. She retrieved a housecoat from the closet and went to the living room to read for a while. She would awaken Rosey in the morning with her feminine charm, she thought to herself.

Ten miles away in the Montgomery house a contented couple lay asleep in each others arms, the crud and corruption of the world washed away by their day together and their faith in a loving God. Nothing would easily replace that in these two lives.

*****

It was two days later and the church council was together for their monthly meeting. Morgan had been on the council for several years now and could just about tell you how each member would react to any given situation. The business of the church had all been cared for and Phil Cooper was about to adjourn when Morgan spoke up.

"Just a minute, Phil. I think we need to discuss this deplorable situation at hand as a church council and take it to the congregation to make a stand against these things."

"What in the world are you talking about, Morgan Montgomery?" asked Julie Donspell. "I think we've cared for all we need to tonight. I was hoping to get home a little early."

Morgan was exasperated enough as it was and allowed his true feelings to leap out unabridged and with total candor.

"Julie, you *always* want to get home a little early! So do the rest of us, but we're here to do the Lord's business for this congregation and there's a dire need for action in this county!"

Pastor McVey quickly attempted to disarm the fireworks brewing with a calming influence. "Morgan, I think I know what you're getting at, but I'm not sure all of us here are ready to approach that. It *is* quite frightening for most of us, and I'm sure that sooner or later we'll need to take a stand, but now may be a bit premature, don't you think?"

That infuriated Morgan and he was off and running. "A *bit* frightening? A *BIT* frightening? My word, man, this scares the living begeepers out of me! How in the name of Jesus Christ can you say its a *little frightening?!* I wonder how our Lord feels about His servants turning their backs on the torture and martyrdom of one of His clergy? Mister," he said as he pointed his finger at the pastor, "That could have been *you!* Or maybe that's what bothers you. Is that it, Clarence? Are you afraid to take a stand because of that? They've accomplished just exactly what they set out for, haven't they? They've frightened, no, scared is a better word 'cause frightened is to nicey-nicey. They've scared the so-called church into silence, haven't they? If we stay silent on this, we're liars and hypocrites of the lowest kind, and further more...."

His tirade was silenced by the interruption of Phil as he slapped his hands together loudly several times. "You just get down off you pious high-horse, Morg'. You're out of line and I won't tolerate that here, this meeting is adjourned!"

"**WHAT!?** You can't do that without a motion! Listen to me, people, we...." The rest of his thoughts remained unsaid, for the others were in the act of walking out, some shaking their heads as though Morgan Montgomery had lost it and there was no hope for him.

Pastor McVey was soon the only one left in the room. He sat with a forlorn and hurt look as he stared at the floor. For a minute Morgan was filled with doubt and remorse at his comments, then the indignation returned and he stalked from the room. A soft murmur followed at his heels that sounded something like, "You're wrong, Morgan, you're wrong."

Kay sensed the tenseness in him as soon as he walked in the door. She waited for him to begin the conversation for she knew from years of experience that she would learn more after he calmed enough to talk rationally to her. He had come a long way with his old temper, but hadn't "arrived" yet and she was well aware of that.

"Hon, you won't believe what our church council is doing," he started, "They are choosing to stick their heads in the sand and ignore this whole murder thing!"

She walked over to stand behind him and rub his neck and back as he continued telling her in detail of the meeting and the controversy that resulted. When he had finished she gently spoke as she continued the massage.

"You need to think this through, Dear. Not everyone has your passion for fighting injustice and not everyone has your courage.

"Pastor McVey is a dear, dear man, but he's the timid type. You know how he hates to confront people on anything, even salvation. His alter calls are so few and far between that one could begin to think he'd abandoned the theme of salvation during a worship service. And when he does have one, it's so meek you wonder why he bothers.

"But Hon, you also know how he loves God and reveres teaching others about Him. You mustn't be too harsh with him, he's God's man at God's call and we shouldn't question that."

"I know, I know, but why would God call a pansy to the pulpit? And the rest of the council, what's with them? Is everyone but me afraid of this thing that's trying to ruin our world?"

"You have to reason this through for yourself, Morg, I can't do it for you. On second thought, that's wrong. You have to determine God's will for us in this, not our own and not based on feelings, but on facts from Him."

He reached over his shoulder and drew her down to kiss her cheek, then released a huge sigh as he sunk further into the chair. It seemed as though the day away had all been negated at the meeting and he was suddenly very tired again. Kay pulled him to his feet and marched him off to bed, knowing that sleep would help him to look more calmly at this come the morning. It always worked with this man she adored so completely, faults and all.

Chapter 6

Two weeks later the phone fairly rang off the wall before Sue could get to it. "Hello, Montgomery's, this is Sue," she answered.

"Honey, I've got the greatest news!" came from Brian on the other end. "Wait'll you hear what they just told me here."

"Well, mister, are you going to just sit there and wait for me to beg you, or are you going to tell me?" she asked after a waiting for him to continue.

"Maybe I should make you beg, or better yet, guess."

"If that's your approach to this so-called good news, it can't be so very good or you couldn't hold it in, buster," she replied in her best grumpy voice.

"They're sending me to Minnesota for two days to help fix a problem in some network stuff up there," he told her. "Its a great chance to show what I'm capable of and get closer to that raise we keep talking about."

"Oh Honey, that's wonderful. But..."

"But what, you? Go ahead and spit it out."

"I don't suppose they want your little wifey to go along to keep you company, do they? I'm not sure I can go two days without seeing you."

"Ha! That's the best part. They want a really tight time schedule on this, so they've chartered Rosey to take me there! You can go along 'cause he won't care and won't charge them extra for you, I'm sure! You know how that old rascal is."

"Brian Montgomery, I don't think of Rosey as an 'old rascal.'He's younger than your dad by a year. But that's great, do I pack big or small?"

"Take the least you can do with for two or three days. I'll call Rosey and make sure its all right. Gotta go now, bye!"

With the click of the phone at the other end she smiled at her young husband's enthusiasm and wondered aloud to herself if"He's considered that this is the Lord's way of helping us get away for a bit and still make a living?"

Brian had accepted Christ as a fairly young lad, but had slipped into a spiritual apathy lately that alarmed her to some extent. He easily overlooked the small miracles that occurred daily in their lives. She had started several weeks before the terrible murder to pray for a new awareness of God's presence for him, and was sure his friendship with Father Simson was an answer to those prayers. The young priest had spurred Brian to reading his Bible again as the two shared in their faith together. She gave an involuntary shudder at the memory of the tragedy. Could it be that the attack was from Satan and was designed to dim Brian's spiritual fervor? Another shudder racked her body and then she shrugged it off and proceeded to select from her closet the clothes she felt she needed. After all, Christ had already defeated the devil at the cross and she need not accept fear of him because of that! Christ would care for them.

When their car slid into the driveway with a beep and the tires threw gravel from the violent stop she knew her going was all right with Rosey. Brian only drove like that when he had good news to tell. Otherwise, he poked into the drive and slouched into the house as a dog with its tail between its legs. She chuckled at the thought of how well she already knew her husband of a year. Mother-in-law Kay had told her it would be like that.

"Dear girl, you'll get to know him better than he knows himself in a couple of years," she had said. It was proving to be true.

He zipped through the door to quickly kiss her and before he could erupt with the news she stalemated him with, "I'm going aren't I?

Holding her at arms' length by the shoulders and staring into her eyes he studied her a moment before answering.

"I just don't know how well I like this wife-knows- husband

stuff, girl. How could you tell? Aren't you getting to be pretty sure of yourself, huh? Huh?" The last was said with a little shake for added emphasis.

She giggled and replied, "Well, fella, if ever someone else were to drive into our driveway like an IRL racer I'd lock the doors and call the sheriff, but when its you, I know its good news and you're happy.If you don't like being read like a book, change some of the pages, buster."

With that saucy comment she freed herself and skipped to the kitchen to finish supper while he changed to his customary jeans and tee-shirt for the afternoon. He had never adapted to the white shirt world of computer programming, nor did he intend to! Most companies cared not what their people wore as long as it was clean and decent, but his boss liked to impress, so shirt and ties were the order of the day. "Bah! Humbug!" he thought to himself.

The evening was spent pouring over maps and travel booklets to find what was in the area to see evenings during their short stay. It was decided to rent two cars so Sue could be free to do as she pleased during Brian's working hours.

"You know, Hon, I may have some long hours if this is worse than we think. You could be alone more than we plan."

"I look at it this way, if I stay home, I'm alone, period. If I go, I get to spend all your extra money and still see you at night. How's that grab ya?"

"Boy! You're awfully sassy today, I may just have to take you down a notch or two girl!"

"Ha! Just you try it and I'll use my caruddy, or klig-fooey, or whatever those things are called, Buster. Then you'd be in a *real* mess of hurt!"

The wrestling match that ensued was short lived, and the two lovers were as happy and carefree as they had been for many weeks. The trip was already paying dividends.

****

The aging Cheyenne taxied slowly to the fence at the Ely, Minnesota airport and turned its tail to the fence before stopping. The props were still spinning when the door opened and Brian and Sue descended into the fresh spring air. A tall man in overalls walked towards them with extended hand.

"Hi folks. If you're Mister Montgomery I'm your greeting party. If you aren't, then I'll greet you anyhow, but you may have to find a different ride into town. My name's Greenly, Al Greenly."

Brian laughed and replied, "I'm *Brian* Montgomery, sir. Mister just doesn't fit too well yet. May never, for that matter. This is my wife, Sue. I hope you don't mind her coming along; we plan to do some sight seeing after hours and get some relaxing time in. We plan to rent two cars so she can enjoy her days, too."

"Wouldn't hear of it! We have two cars and she can use one of those while you're here. Won't take no for an answer!"

"But Sir, what will your wife do for transportation?'

"No, no. I mean *company* cars. She'll use one and you'll ride with me. You folks are staying with us, the motels around here are always full-up, what with all the tourists and such."

This revelation wasn't welcomed with open arms by the two, as they had planned on some time alone. Besides, if this gregarious fellow's wife was anything like him, well....It **could** be a long two or three days. Big Al Greenly was pleasant enough; just a bit overbearing.

They reluctantly loaded their meager belongings into the waiting van and settled in, Brian in front, for the ride. As they rode through the wooded countryside they were enthralled with the beauty of it. Evergreen trees lined the road for as far as they could see and every now and then the reflection of the sun's rays flashed through the trees from a lake's surface. During the last half hour of the plane ride the lakes were so plentiful they had noted the country seemed almost to be more water than land.

Twenty minutes later they pulled into a driveway nearly hidden by trees, passed down a lane for nearly a quarter of a mile, and pulled into the graveled parking area of what appeared to be a hunting or fishing lodge. The lot lay on the hillside overlooking a pristine lake with cabins lining the shore. The main lodge building perched in the middle of these and was slightly higher on the sloping bank. A rustic but sound looking structure, it was of peeled logs standing two stories high with a porch on both floors that ran all the way around the building.

Lounge chairs occupied the entire perimeter of both porches, many of them in use. On the lake, fishermen in canoes could be seen dotting the surface at various places. It was a beautiful setting.

Greenly allowed them a few minutes of gazing over the scene before interrupting their thoughts.

"This is our retirement package."

"Wow," returned Brian, "That's a whale of a package. I could go for this as a retirement home."

"Well, it ain't just a retirement home, you see, but an income. We'll move several hundred people through here every summer at a good return of cash for each one. Add to that the mail order business and we shouldn't have to worry ever 'bout income."

"Move them through how, Mister Greenly?" asked Sue.

"Wilderness camping and fishin', ma'am. We outfit parties with everthin' they need for trips into the area, includin' the canoes. Then we help them pick a route that suits them and get 'em started off. You'd love a trip into the Boundary Waters, I know you would.

"Why, you'll see moose, beaver, bald eagles, otter, bear, and all sorts of wild creatures. Usually, once a person has been out there, they keep comin' back year after year. That's what keeps us goin', the repeat business."

Brian was gazing wistfully at the lake, picturing a bass on the end of his line and fighting furiously.Sue gave a sideways glance at her husband and chuckled.

"You've just lost Brian, Sir. He's out there somewhere even now, and probably won't be worth a hoot until he catches at least one poor, helpless fish!"

The big fellow chuckled at the hurt look that passed from Brian to Sue, grabbed their luggage and trod off towards the nearest cabin. Depositing it on the little porch overlooking the lake he handed Sue a key.

"This here's yours 'til you leave, we'd like you to have supper with us since you haven't had time to get settled. Nearest restaurant's back in Ely, that's 'bout ten miles. Don't worry none about the computer stuff for tonight, Brian, we'll go into the warehouse in the morning and you can get us bailed out.

"I'll call you to breakfast around six in the morning, that okay with you?"

Brian chuckled as he nodded. "I like an early start. I'm not sure we'll get sleepyhead here out of bed for **anything** at that time, though."

The elbow that intruded upon his rib section was a familiar one, and he gave the appropriate grunt of simulated pain to go with it. He then grabbed her and carried her through the door, much to her dismay. The cry from Greely that it wasn't the honeymoon cabin didn't help and they tussled for several minutes before he properly subdued her on the floor.

Helpless with her arms pinned she glared up at him in mock anger and demanded to be set free.

"You give me back me!" she commanded.

At that he lost all composure for the game and fell laughing to the floor beside her.

"Give me back me?" he chortled. "Give me back me? Where'd you come up with that, girl?"

"Dunno. Just seemed right."

They proceeded to arrange the few things they had with them and settled in for the afternoon and evening, leaving the porch only for the evening meal. The rest of the time they spent just rocking and gazing out over the lake.

****

Morning dawned to a foggy lakeside and the ride to Ely was a crawl. Greely was one of those morning talkers, as though he had to get an early start in order to use up all the day's allotment of words. Brian sat silently taking in the other's rambling, thinking to himself how nice it would be to drive alone tomorrow. Upon arrival at the man's business he unlocked the door in silence and allowed Brian to enter first. The business proved to be housed in a metal building with the offices separated from the front by a cheap partition of dry wall. After showing him to the computer system Greely then proceeded to make a pot of strong coffee.

The morning passed quickly for Brian, as was usually the case on a job like this, and by late afternoon he had a handle on the problems with the software. It looked as though one more day would be plenty of time to care for it and he said as much to Al. It was an early quitting time for them as a result and Sue heard her husband's footsteps on the porch before four o'clock.

Running to grab him she covered his face with sloppy smooches and nearly choked him with the hug.

"Hey, woman, what gives here? You trying to drown me or what?"

"No, but this place is so lovely I just wanted you here all day to share it with me!" she replied. "I missed you."

"Well, I'm here now, so let's get a canoe after supper and do some touring, what do you think?"

"Wonderful. Missus Greely said to be at the lodge at five for supper, so you've got plenty of time for a shower. Or whatever," she added coyly.

He looked at her with yearning and said something to the effect that whatever and a shower both sounded right to him and then attacked her.

****

Water lapped quietly at the canoe as they drifted silently with the gentle breeze blowing across the lake. Sue was sure she had seen a large animal move in the brush along shore so they had pulled in their paddles and became silent. After a short time the bushes parted and a young moose not yet adorned with antlers pushed through to the shore, paused a moment to glance at the strange craft, then waded calmly into the water and proceeded to eat from the bottom plants in the vicinity.

They sat hushed by the intriguing sight of one of nature's largest animals on their continent methodically submerging for bottom plants and seemingly ignoring them as they perched less than thirty yards away. After a while, whether full or not, the animal turned and waded towards shore with the couple watching in rapt silence.

When the beast had disappeared into the forest Sue at last spoke. "Wow, I didn't think that thing was ever going to stop getting taller as it climbed out, Hon."

"Yeah, they sure are long legged things. Bet there's some great eating there."

"Great, all you males think about is either killing something

42

or eating. Or killing something to eat. Take me back home, Captain, before this ship ain't big 'nuff fer both o' us, ye blaggard."

Brian simply shook his head and started paddling.

****

Mid-morning the next day found him weeding out the root of the software problems and checking files with Big Al peering over his shoulder. The man was just overbearing enough to aggravate Brian by just being there, let alone peering over his shoulder and he was about to ask him to back off when Al broke into his thoughts.

"Now, there's a few of those files I'd rather you don't bother goin' into, young feller. I do a little extra business on the side and the less anyone else knows 'bout it, the better. Okay?"

Brian stopped immediately and whirled around in the swivel chair, nearly toppling it over in the process.

"I really have a bad feeling about that, sir. Are you telling me there's an illegal operation here that I now know about? You realize that would be traceable to me with this work I've just done, don't you? With our records and yours together I could be implicated in anything discovered by authorities and I'm really...."

He was working up to a very untypical and impassioned response as he went when the big man stopped him.

"Whoa, there. Just whoa it . I'm not doin' anything illegal, just some supplying of stuff that the fewer people outside of my clients know, the better I like it. Look, go into the file "survivor" and have a quick look. It ain't gonna put you, or anyone else for that matter, in jail to see it. I just don't want a wide knowledge of the activity broadcast."

Brian did as asked, clicking on the file and opening it. He saw a very innocent looking inventory of dried foods and other back-country needs. There were no weapons or suspicious things at all. He tilted the insubordinate chair back, twisted part way around and looked up into the swarthy face of his client.

"So what makes this file so special? It's just the same stuff you list in your catalog."

"That's right, but look at the quantities, Brian. You'll see there's enough supplies there to care for over a hundred people for three months! The government knows that, they'll want to know why. It ain't something I want them to be askin' about.

"As far as you bein' at risk for knowin' there's nothin there for you to be tellin' anyone about, so they'd not come to you if they saw that you were here workin' on the thing for me.

" I just don't want that many folks knowin' about this 'cause it'd open me up to thieves if'n this thing with martial law goes down. That happens, folks is gonna be headin' for the hills. I plan to take care of my own in that case, my own bein' family and friends around here."

Brian mentally scratched his head as he digested, or rather, tried to digest what the man had just told him. He didn't like the implication of mistrust he felt had been made and said so.

"So what you're saying is this, my knowing about this file may mean that I go around telling every Tom, Dick, and Harry that Big Al has all the food you radicals need to survive and you should go steal it. You know, that *really* ticks me off! Who in the world do you think I am that I'd even think of disclosing information I briefly went through while in the process of doing my job? And what in the world makes you think I'd even notice this? I don't pay attention to what files contain, only that they haven't been compromised by the problem I've come to work on. That takes me all of five minutes in a file and then it's on to the next one.

"So I'll tell you what, I'll just consider the job done so I don't put any more of your important' information at risk. You can take me back to the cabin, we'll pack and get the blazes out of your hair. How's that grab you?"

He had really worked himself into a frenzy by the time he was done and was fuming at the big man. His father's temper may have hidden deep within him all these years, but it wasn't so deep it couldn't surface with a little encouraging. And when that happened, he was willing to take on anything, large or small, and this fellow was on the verge of finding that out!

"Now you just calm down, Brian," the suddenly softspoken words came. "I wasn't sayin' this information was at risk 'cause you know about it. I'm sayin *you* could be at risk. I don't want that.

"You see, and I'm telling you this 'cause I really have gotten to like you and your missus, I'm sorta tied into a group that the government doesn't care much for. Now that's all you need to know. Any more knowledge and they could lock you up if the wrong things came out of your mouth at the wrong time.

"I have been collecting this stuff for over a year now, and other things listed in other files that you will *not* be privy to. Some of them can go bang-bang if used certain ways. Do you get my drift?

"You and your wife are really good people. I sensed that right away and I don't want you at risk in any way. You may not agree with what we do around here as a militia group...There, I said the word. Militia. Now you know, but try to forget you do. Unless you're looking for a group to join, that is."

"No way. No way at all. My folks raised me to be a God fearing, law abiding guy and I plan to stick to that, my friend. What you do is your business, but I want no part of it. Let's just leave it all at that."

"That's fine with me, Brian. But, if you *ever* need help in any way, and that includes supplies or goods of any kind, you be sure and let me know. I mean that. I'd hate to learn that you and that sweet, lovely little lady of yours were in trouble and I didn't help some way. Can I count on that? You'll let me know?"

The man's eagerness towards friendship and seemingly uncharacteristic softness melted Brian's reserve and he offered his hand. "Count on it, Al. And the same goes in reverse. You know, I have a friend I haven't told you about that could help you more than any stores of food or things that go bang ever could in times like these. His name is Jesus, and I'd sure like to tell you about Him. You interested?"

A tear formed in the corner of the big man's eyes and he lowered his head ever so slightly. " I know Him, Brian," he murmured, "I just don't know how brave I'll be to depend on Him if this goes haywire on us. I..."

Brian saw the choking up come and watched as Al turned away and walked from the room. He drew a deep breath and immediately prayed for his new friend to find strength and new faith. He then turned to finish the task before him. It took less than half an hour and he was done. Shutting down the system he rose, walked from the building and found Big Al leaning on the hood of the truck with his hands folded before him gazing off across the lakes. He turned from the hood, smiled, climbed in and started the engine.

"Don't you want to lock up before we leave, Al?"

A sonorous chuckle issued forth from somewhere deep in his chest as the big fellow shifted into neutral and climbed back down to accomplish that task. He returned with a sheepish grin that reminded Brian of his brother Cal whenever they caught him at one of his tricks. The comparison did nothing to dispel his liking for this bear of a man. The trip to the cottage was silent, both men deep in their thoughts and far away.

Chapter 7

She was kneeling at the rear of the lot, planting something in the small garden she enjoyed so much. The sight of her diminutive yet full and rounded figure caused him to pause in his progress in that direction. Though turned from him, he could picture the sweet beauty of her face, splendid in its pixy like features with the deep, dark eyes that could melt him with a simple glance. It was at times like these John Rosenthal's chest seemed hardly large enough to hold the heart that pounded within in harmony with the intense gratitude always sensed for the love he had been granted from Paige. How a true and beautiful lady such as her could love *him* he could neither fathom nor explain. He only knew it was so and he was totally committed to her. Almost to the point of worship at times, it seemed.

He carefully tiptoed up behind her and was about to leap to grab her when the soft, husky voice calmly spoke. "Don't even think about it, fellow, I know you're there."

"Wha...I mean, you, uh, holy cow, Paige, whaddaya mean, don't think about it?"

"I *saw* your shadow and those grabby arms of yours getting ready to haul me in like some lobster from a trap. You can't sneak up on *me* mister Rosenthal. No sir, not at all."

"Why, I never intended to, little lady. No sir, not *me!*"

"Bull. You were, you *would*, and you *know* it! And why aren't you at the airport? I thought you had some work to do on one of the Cheyennes?"

"That got sidetracked, **Missus** Rosenthal. Brian called for me to come get him and Sue, and I discovered I'd left my Jepp charts here. I tried to call and invite you to go along for the ride, but were you home? Ohhh, no, that just can't happen when I need you, can it? I figured you were either out with another man or out spending my money, or *both*! Come on, 'fess up lady, which was it?"

"Well, actually, mister nosey, it was *both*. I went down to buy some seeds from Morgan and we got to talking. All teasing aside, John, I'm really worried about him and that store. I wish he'd just close down the gun sales part, and I think Kay feels the same, though she would never say so."

"Well, I know what you're saying, but I don't think anything is going to come of this idiot from the ATF harassing him. Besides, if any more murders like the priest's happen around here, Morg' will probably be sold out of weapons in no time.

"But listen, what I wanted to ask you was this, if you're not too enamored with that other guy to go out with me I'd love to have your company for a few hours. How 'bout it?"

"Uh, I dunno, where to?"

"I have to pick up Brian and Sue in Minnesota and I figured it would be good to get you away from all those other men in your life."

While the required punch in the stomach wore off, she smiled and asked, "How much time do I have to get ready?"

"Not much," he gasped, showing a severe pain that was only half fake. She could punch!

Rosey looked forward to some time alone with just Paige, even if it was in the air. He needed her company desperately, though he would be the last to realize it.

Chapter 8

The Henry County airport was not the favorite place for Rosey any more. He had been struggling with depression for days now, and was about to just scrap the whole operation when he made a fateful decision; justice would be his to serve out. The big Sarge and his buddy were going to die and Rosey was going to be the executioner! He knew just how it could happen and no one would be the wiser.

Wednesday was their day to sky dive each week. The government was paying for their entertainment because "it is part of their training and they need to stay current."

Rosey had the door off the Skyhawk and was ready for his two clients before they arrived at the scene. His heart was racing with the terror of what he was about to do.

"Hey, flyboy! You're starting to catch on to who's important around here and who ain't!" the mouthy solder spouted before he even got all the way through the door. "You usually ain't got that door off before we get here!"

Rosey swallowed his nasty reply that the two couldn't be depended on to be on time or even to keep their appointments so he refused to remove the door 'til he knew they were there. He simply went to the ship and climbed aboard.

The two hired killers grabbed their 'chutes and hurried out to the waiting, and now running, Cessna. Rosey swallowed hard again, all was going according to the plan! The two usually double checked their chutes before donning them but his readiness to depart rushed them right past the safety check.

"How high you guys wanta jump from this time?" he

shouted over the wind and engine noise. "Were you serious about the low level jump for the first one today or is that too scary for you heroes?"

The jibe hit the mark as the big man screamed at him that they feared nothing and "Take us out where the jeep sets so we don't walk back to the hanger! We'll jump from eight hundred this time and then you better be ready for a good chewin' when we get down mister smart mouth. You'll learn a thing or two 'for I get done with ya!"

Rosey taxied the 'Hawk out and poured the throttle to it, shaking like a leaf and enduring the big man's scorn as he laughed at Rosey, thinking the pilot was scared of the chewing he had promised. That helped cement Rosey's resolve toward the completion of the plot to properly punish these two terrorists, at least as he saw it in his own mind. The Cessna seemed to lag torturously in performance as he climbed to the prescribed altitude and circled to the east end of the runway where the low altitude jumps were typically made.

As he made his run for the jump, neither man seemed to notice the lack of altitude, for Rosey was at a mere 500 feet. The two moved to set in the doorway side by side as he approached the place where the jeep was parked and just as the big man challenged their height Rosey hit each man quickly with a stun gun and flipped the Cessna onto its side. The two plummeted to the ground below with perfectly good chutes that never opened.

The Skyhawk trembled as he chopped the throttle, ran in full flaps and side slipped to land on the second half of the runway without a go-round. He taxied back as quickly as possible, shut down the plane and ran to the two badly crumpled bodies. Even though Rosey had seen battle and killing at one time the sight still sickened him; this was his own doing! The bodies were only a few feet apart, just as he had hoped for, and he quickly pulled their rip chords to release the chutes and then wound them together at the cords. The job was done and he prayed no one would be the wiser. As he called frantically on his cell phone for 911 he was trembling at the thought of what he had just done. Would he get away with it? Now the thought of possible failure to do so caused an all-encompassing sickness to envelope him. He was still bent double beside the bodies when the rescue squad arrived.

"Look Mister Rosenthal, I realize you don't feel like answering questions right now, maybe never, but I have to know all the little details of this incident for a proper report."

"Captain, you're right, I don't feel like it, but you just called this an incident and I call it a tragedy!" Rosey nearly yelled back at the military man across the desk. He didn't have to play-act much at being upset for he was now in the "why did I ever think I could get away with this" stage and his tense nerves were very real.

"And besides that," he continued, "I have a client to pick up out on the islands in another hour." This last was a lie, but part of his plan to avoid being discovered.

"I promise you I'll be through here in time for you to leave with plenty of time to make your appointment, sir. Now, please, go through the events one more time so I can record it accurately, then I'll have all I need."

"Well, like I said before, the men wanted to make three jumps today, a low level and two much higher ones. The Sergeant decided to make the lower one first even though I felt it should always be the last one. It's the more dangerous of the jumps and I just feel better that way, for whatever reason. No logical explanation, just my opinion.

"The Sergeant held fast so we went up for it. When I came around they both sat in the doorway side by side and went at the same time. That's not supposed to be done with the Cessna because of the strut being in the way for two guys going together. They can hit together and throw off the whole thing. That seems to be what happened, they just went on down even after the chutes opened. It looked like the chutes were tangled together but still somewhat filled with air, but I rolled up on the side and it looked like they hit so hard I couldn't imagine them surviving. I landed without going around. You know, I just came down hard and ran back there as fast as I could. A neighbor to the airport called and asked if a plane had just crashed I came downstairs so quickly. It didn't matter, I was just helpless to do anything."

The Captain finished writing, put the papers in his case and stood, offering Rosey his hand.

"Thank you for your help in this, sir, I am sorry you had to go through it, I'll contact you if I need anything more from you."

With that, he stiffly turned and stalked out the door of Rosey's office. By the time the officer was out of the airport drive Rosey was in the Cessna and taxiing out. He climbed to a low altitude, turned towards the lake and flew out until no boats or land could be seen from his two hundred feet and tossed the stun gun out the door into Lake Erie. He had wiped the gun down to try and eliminate any evidence, but still watched it disappear into the water with fear it could be found sometime. A life of crime wouldn't fit easily into his life any time soon!

Morgan, Kay and Paige were sitting around the kitchen table at the Montgomery's house discussing Rosey. It had been two weeks since the tragic accident at the airport.

"He's just not himself," Paige was saying, "he seems distant, almost like he's in a fog mentally and I just can't reach him. I'm worried he'll have some sort of breakdown."

"I know, I went through a similar time after I was grounded," Morgan answered. "Kay finally made me take her on a vacation trip to try and find a release. I know being grounded and losing my business didn't come even close to what Rosey is going through, but it was still quite a life-changing thing and very stressful."

"Maybe you two should try that, Paige. We could find a way to care for the airport business. You have two part-time instructors who could take care of the major part of that business, and I think maybe this renegade ex-pilot here could run the rest so you could be gone for a week or two." Kay looked fondly at her husband as she spoke and found him nodding to the affirmative.

"I can't possibly go anywhere right now. I promised my boss I would stand in for two of our other agents for a month while they get more training on the new real estate laws. Maybe I could talk Rosey into a hunting trip, he always seems to be willing to do that. Are there any hunting seasons in right now?"

Morgan shook his head, "Not that I know of, but maybe he

could do some exploring out in the Rockies, you know how he loves it there. He has that friend who guides him during the hunting trips, we could hire the guy for a couple of weeks as a present to John. Kay, what's your thoughts on that?"

"Hon, I think that's a great idea. Do you have the fellow's number?"

Paige spoke up, "I have it at home. I'll call right away. If we make the appointment, John can't refuse! I knew I could count on you two to come up with help!"

Kay spoke up, "And don't let him tell you he can't be gone, Paige. Morg can run the place for him, his two instructors can take up the slack, and Cal and I can run the store. Go make your call, sweetheart."

Paige left and went home to find the number. After finding it she called, rejoicing at the voice responding to the first ring.

"Hello. This is Paige Rosenthal, John's wife. He's hunted with you before and I want to surprise him with a trip. He's had a tremendous amount of stress lately and needs a getaway."

The voice on the other end of the line was soft and gentle with a slight drawl. "Well, Missus Rosey, there ain't any huntin' season in right now. Maybe we could do a ride back into the mountains for couple of weeks. I've been scoutin' for new territory for my hunts, and there's some really amazing country I could explore further that Rosey would love. We need two weeks of riding, though.

"Pick your dates and tell me when he'll fly in. I'll be at the strip waitin' for him. Tell him to bring his 44 Magnum for a sidearm just in case and I'll furnish the rifles."

"I want this as soon as possible, Mister... I'm sorry, I don't know your name; this business card only has your outfitting company on it. Plus, tell me how much to make the check for, please."

'I'm Roy Turnbull, ma'am. Ya know, this one's on me. Rosey has hunted with me for so many years, I can mark this down to a vacation with a friend. The wife just left to help her mother out for a couple of months, so the timing is perfect. Just let me know when!"

"Roy, that's really wonderful of you. I'll have Rosey call you before he leaves, but I plan to throw him out of here as soon as

I can."

"Great. And don't feel like he has to wait for a weekend, it can happen whenever he gets here."

"Thanks so much, Roy. He'll be calling, goodbye now."

"Bye, ma'am."

Paige hung up and called Kay right away. The two chattered for several minutes and then Kay turned to Morgan after they hung up and gave him a thumbs-up. The plot against Rosey was finalized.

When John Rosenthal pulled into the driveway after his last student that evening, there were streamers and balloons all over the porch and around the front door. He immediately figured he had forgotten an important date and was in trouble. The state of his nerves was such that he reacted with thoughts of rebellion.

The door opened and there was a demure Paige surrounded by the Montgomery's holding suitcases that he recognized as his own. Now he was really stressed. What was happening? Wait a minute, there were some rifle cases there as well! What in the world?

"Hi honey," greeted Paige. "We've got a surprise ready for you. I called Roy Turnbull and he's expecting you in a couple of days for a two week stay. He says there's nothing in season for hunting right now but he has fantastic trip back into the mountains planned for you for several days.

"I already PayPaled him the money, so you have to go. No excuses, no backing out, no arguments."

"What the blazes are you people thinking about? I can't leave now. I have an airport to run, students to accommodate, and a wife to try and keep straight when she gets hair-brained ideas like this!"

Morgan stepped between them and said, "Cal is running my store for two weeks and I'm running the airport. Your two part-time instructors are going to cover your students and Chet Silvan can do any charters that come along. You can't fly both Cheyennes so one is available for that.

"So…my friend, you have no excuses left, your sweet wife

has already spent the money, and, quite frankly, you're going if I have to hog-tie you and fly you out there myself!"

Rosey looked from one to another, shook his head, and seemed to deflate like a balloon punched with a pin.

"Okay, what's brought you people to this point?" he asked. "Have I been hard to live with?"

"We see your stress, sweetie. We see the lovable guy we know being totally different, not just once in a while, but all the time. This thing with finding that poor priest started it, and you seem to have drawn farther away from being our Rosey every day.

"You need to just get away, honey, and I know how you love the Rockies. Roy says he has the answer, so please don't fight us on this."

He visibly sagged, dropped his head and seemed to relax. "So…do I need to leave right now, or can I get a night's rest first? I have to make sure the new panel on the number two Cheyenne is finished and ready," He looked at Morgan and said by way of explanation, "I had a new flat panel put in and haven't flown it yet. The shop says its a go, but I prefer to test it myself. You taught me that."

The last was said in a defensive manner and Morgan chuckled. He put an arm around Rosey's shoulders started him toward the car. "In that case, I want to go with you and see this new stuff. I can't imagine the things it'll do compared to the stuff I had to use when they grounded me."

That spurred a typical pilot reaction as Rosey started enthusiastically explaining the benefits of the new instrument panel to Morgan. The two Cheyennes were quite old but mechanically sound but the instrument panels were alarmingly outdated. The cost of upgrading was as much as the airplane had originally cost, but a fraction of the cost of a new one. The two friends ended up being gone until after dark as Rosey instructed Morgan in the use of the new equipment, much to Moran's delight and amazement.

Dawn found John Rosenthal pre-flighting the Cheyenne with the new panel in preparation for his trip. He had decided to further "test" the new equipment by using this aircraft and leaving the unmodified one for the airport use. He felt innocent of playing "the boss" in doing so since Paige had insisted he deserved it. He would call Roy Turnbull later from the air to let him know his arrival time. The time difference was such that Roy was probably still asleep since the sun was just now peeking over the horizon to the east as if to check out the safety of showing its face.

John decided to just fly VFR (Visual Flight Rules) and ignore Air Traffic Control for this flight. Since he was the only occupant he had full fuel tanks and would fly non-stop to Cheyenne, Wyoming. He would refuel there and then make the remaining hop to Roy's strip on his hunting ranch, a five thousand foot runway. Even though it was grass, Roy's crew kept it in great shape and both of Rosey's aircraft had been in and out of there before when he took hunting parties on charter to Roy. That was how they had met, he and Roy. John had been hired to fly a party of three to Turnbull's for a hunting vacation and had decided to stay and hunt when Roy offered him use of all the necessary equipment. They had become great friends on that first trip and Rosenthal had gone out nearly every year since.

The Cheyenne had chased the sun across the sky in a losing race and it was near sunset when Rosey dropped into the strip in Idaho that rested peacefully on the R-T hunting ranch. The strip was a mile from the ranch buildings and Roy was waiting with a pickup that showed more use than Rosey's 1980's airplane. The tall, slender rancher stood leaning against the front fender watching as Rosey taxied back to the tie-down spot. He was dressed in worn and faded jeans with run-down riding boots and a Mackinaw. The handle-bar mustache moved rhythmically with the chewing action as he brutalized the gum in his mouth. Roy was never without his mouthful of gum and the sharp jutting chin never ceased its motion during his waking hours. Roy's wife had insisted that he continued chewing even in his sleep!

After the two turbo-props had ceased their turning and Rosey had finished his checkout he lowered the door and descended to find his hand engulfed in the huge mitt Roy claimed was a real hand. The fingers were long and slender, like the body of the man, with a grip of steel that matched the piercing steel-blue eyes of this taciturn rider. Roy was a definite throw-back to the riders of the west from decades before. Quiet spoken and always thinking, he was a rock to rely upon. The throw-back was also apparent in the ever present revolver strapped to his side from "get-up to lay-down" as he put it. "Too many rattlers to go without," was his answer to any who asked about it. The well-worn 44 magnum showed his constant practice with the weapon.

"Hi John. Welcome once again to Turnbull Hunting Ranch. You got your ridin' boots and your hikin' boots with you? I'm gonna run you through some of the roughest, meanest, rockiest territory you ever did see. Your wife said you really needed to get away from reality for a while, and I have some new ground to cover that may well be the richest hunting area either of us have ever seen!"

This was a typical greeting from one of Roy's stripe, and meant that he intended to get right down to business. Rosey chuckled and replied, "Does that mean we're leaving tonight before I get some sleep, Roy, or are you going to cut me some slack and let me at least catch a few winks?"

The slow smile lit the craggy face and he pushed playfully on Rosey's shoulder. "I might even let you sleep the night away, but I do have everything but the food already to strap on the pack horses at first light. Figured we might as well get at it right away.

"We're gonna be around three days just getting to the area I want to search out. We're ridin' mules 'stead o' horses 'cause there is some really bad spots and I want all the sure-footedness we can get. Means this ain't a relaxin' trip, just a get away one. We're gonna work at this, but I know you'll handle it fine. Real fine, and you'll be a big help as well. That's why I ain't chargin' you for it."

"What?! Paige said she'd already spent the money for the trip so I had to come! You mean she…"

The slow smile widened a bit and Roy just shrugged. "Reckon that's something you'll have to take up when you get home, John boy. I ain't goin' there, an' it sounds like I already spoke to soon and too much." An audible chuckle slid back over his shoulder as he turned to the plane and started unloading Rosey's gear.

As Roy cared for the unloading, Rosey tied the ship down, checked it out thoroughly in a post-flight inspection, locked the hatches and climbed in the truck. Roy ground the tranny into gear on the old warrior and turned toward the buildings a mile away. When he had decided to install a landing strip there was only one area with enough almost level ground for it, but he had well over a mile of clear runway, so the drive was nothing compared to the business it had generated.

Evening coffee and a robust meal laced with much catching up ended the day and the two found their beds as the night sounds of the Rockies awakened and began their serenade. The last thing Rosey heard was the howl of a lobo a long way out from the ranch. As it faded away, so did his consciousness and he was soon snoring.

"We're taking all mules on this trip, John. We need their sure-footedness where we're going. We give up the comfort for the safety."

"Comfort? How we givin' up comfort?"

"All my mules are stiff legged when it comes to travel. They feel like you're walking on posts with no give. But I tell you, when they put those feet down, they stay where they're put and they don't slip. You'll see why I want them when we get to the valley I've found.

"I had a party here that wanted different hunting grounds than they had seen before, so I went out alone after they left to see what I could locate. Took me three days, but I stumbled on an area I had never been to before.

"We know there are no unexplored regions left in the mountains, but I guarantee you this one is left alone. Takes three days of the most rugged travel you ever did have and another two days to get down in! That's five days of being whipped at day's end. The last two days also include sheer terror for most of the time spent climbing down into the valley.

"If a guide isn't collecting phenomenal pay, he ain't gonna bother with it. You'll help me find a better way down, John, and we'll bask in the beauty of the place for a couple of days. I have fishing gear along and we'll eat some of the biggest trout you never did see!"

This speech was the longest Rosey had ever heard from Roy at one time and he was quite impressed. This trip would be fantastic if Roy's predictions held true!

With three mules under loaded pack saddles and two ready for their riders, they mounted and Roy led off to the southwest toward the towering and alluring mountain range in that direction. Roy's evaluation of his mules' ride proved accurate and Rosey soon spent a lot of his time turning first one way and then the other to ease the pressure on his legs and body. Two hours of this and he called for a stop.

"Roy, I gotta get off and walk for a while, this mule is walking on cobblestones and I'm aching something terrible already."

"Ha! I told you about that, but you'll thank me later on for old Baldy, there, when you're riding with your eyes closed along the cliffs."

Rosey dismounted and began to walk beside Baldy while Roy remained in the saddle but slowed their progress to suit Rosey's pace. The rest of the first day passed with Rosey alternating between walking and riding. He had begun to think they would go until past dark when Roy finally called a halt. They had only made twenty miles due to the rugged terrain, but it was a well-earned twenty miles.

They camped by a gurgling mountain stream some twenty yards wide but shallow and swift. The small copse of trees gave some protection from any wind and Roy promised trout for supper. Rosey couldn't decide which he wanted most; food or sleep. Not being in good condition had told on him as every bone and muscle ached with loud protestations at every movement. He started gathering wood for the fire while Roy broke out the fishing gear.

Rosey was used to traveling the wilderness with Roy and knew he was expected to unsaddle the mules and hobble them while the quiet guide started supper. That start usually included catching fish before hand. Rosey also was expected to start the fire and prepare the utensils. After a few confusing minutes he slowly acclimated himself once again to camp chores and soon had everything in place, ready for the cook. Roy had rules for his campers, and the first and foremost was that he alone did the cooking. While he chuckled over some of the meals he had endured that had been prepared by some of his clients before he established that rule, he adhered strictly to it now. "I like eatin' real food cooked just right," he would say when asked about the rule.

Chapter 9

The canyon just ahead was quite imposing. It consisted of sharply rising stone spurs, each reaching at least two hundred feet at their tops, many going much higher than that, and some leaned at perilous angles, threatening to crush any invaders of their space with but a moment's notice.

As the two riders entered Rosey saw the floor of the canyon, which was more of a crevasse, actually, sloped upward in a rather sharp ascent. The way up required a twisting of directions by the invaders and in many places barely allowed passage without a scraping of the burdens on the pack mules. Rosey found his knees the frequent receptors of sharp stone invasions as well.

The colors of the walls of this canyon were spectacular; dark reds at the top, muted yellow in the next layer down, rust below that, and shading to a gray at the bottom. The sandstone composition had allowed much erosion through the centuries which only added to the complexity of the formations Rosey was seeing. It seemed a foreboding place to him and he said so to Roy.

"Hey Roy, I thought you said we were going to one of the prettiest places in the mountains. I sure hope this isn't it!"

"You gotta remember, John, sometimes life throws stuff at you that makes you go through ugly in order to get to beauty! You may not see the beauty of this canyon, but I do. Its remained here for a long time with little or no change other than a few little rock slides, and when the sun hits this wall to the west in the morning? Man alive, what a sight! And in the sunset hour? This east side becomes another realm in its own right. To bad we won't still be here come sunset, we're gonna miss the show."

"Not sure that grieves me at all, Roy. I don't particularly like this place!"

Roy only chuckled and drove his mule higher. After a steady four and a half hours of the climb they came to an impassable spot where the stones pinched together so closely the pack animals were too wide for passage.Roy dismounted and began removing the packs from the lead pack animal. Rosey followed suit and, to his astonishment, suddenly lost sight of Roy! He swallowed hard and called out to the guide who seemed to appear from nowhere by a short stone spire.

Roy procured the next pack and disappeared as quickly as he had appeared. He noticed the startled look of consternation on Rosey's face and broke into a wide grin.

"S'matter, John? You look like you just saw a ghost."

"Well, first you were gone, like up in smoke, then you weren't, then you were again! Sorta shook me up."

This is one of two places where we have to unload the mules to get them through narrow spots. I told you this would be rough going, didn't I?"

"What I don't understand is why you would ever venture through a place like this. What ever in the world possessed you to continue through here?"

"Well, John, I make my living like this. Sooner or later I've found there will be people coming who want to hunt where no one else has. Now, you and I know such a place doesn't exist, but if I put them through this sort of trial to get to a place, they are convinced they're the first.

"Not only that, but the hunting is unbelievable because of the remoteness. The game isn't as wary of man's presence, except for the predators, and its plentiful as all-get-out. I figure I can charge triple for a trip like this and have clients hooked for good."

"How long did it take you to search this out?"

"Ha. I was three years just getting to this spot, and another two finding the valley where we're going. My purpose for this trip is to try and find a better, or at least easier way in or out. If we get down in the valley day after tomorrow we'll have time to explore a bit, and just maybe find a way out to the south as well as from here. We're going in from the northeast right now."

They lapsed into silence as they led the mules around the twisting and narrow spot, then proceeded to re-saddle them and load the supplies. Some fifty minutes later they topped out on a promontory where there was a level spot with a couple of trees clinging to life on the stone terrace of the peak. Roy called a halt for their midday meal.

While Rosey searched for fuel for a fire Roy began laying out the food. He then unsaddled all the animals and hobbled them so they could forage on the sparse bunch grass poking through in places. He also began filling feed-bags with a couple of handfuls of oats for each mule.

The view was nothing short of spectacular as Rosey relaxed after their meal. To the south rose peak after peak of unique and varied rock formations while the western view showed itself to be greener with trees covering the slopes. He ended up sound asleep after several minutes of gazing.

When Rosey awoke he found Roy in the act of saddling the mules in preparation for loading the packs. Rosey jumped to help while scolding Roy for not waking him up to assist in the heavy chore with the supplies.

"You suggesting I'm not able to perform my guidely duties, John?"

"Well, maybe I am. But are YOU suggesting your client isn't able to be any help?"

"Huh! You're not my client on this trip, Johnny lad, you're my helper and I'm saving you for the really heavy work. You'll find that out when you start carrying these mules down into the valley!"

Rosey threw a small stone at Roy and proceeded to saddle the two riding mules. Within a few minutes they were on their way, winding down a narrow path similar to their ascent course. They continued the downward trend for several hours before the way tipped up again. All in all, Rosey had absolutely no idea of the directions they had traveled by the time dusk began to settle around them like a soft touch of quietness in the middle of a hectic city street as day surrendered supremacy to night.

Camp for the night was under a huge outcropping that would provide shelter from any weather finding its way to the area. The mantle of stars glowing down on them indicated the usefulness of the roof would be unnecessary. Rosey felt his body stiffen as he stretched out on his sleeping bag and groaned audibly. He heard a chuckle from Roy and threw another small stone at the dark mound that indicated the guide's spot.

"Ain't funny, Roy. You tortured me with that last ten miles, fella."

"Could be, John, could be. You probably had it coming for some reason or another."

"Ha! Little you know just how close to the truth THAT is!"

"Go to sleep, John, you're going to need all the rest you can get for the next two days. They might be brutal."

By noon the next day they had made their way west and were entering the area of forested slopes. Rosey was really starting to enjoy this scenery when Roy turned south again and within a few hours ride they were once again into the rugged, barren peaks. Their camp that night was a dry camp, and the water supply was used up for the mules and cooking. The only water left was the partially filled canteens.

"Roy, do we get water tomorrow? This could be a struggle without."

"Yeah, John, by mid-morning we'll hit a river. It's the one that flows through the valley we're aiming for. We'll follow it for several miles before it goes underground. When we get to that point, we're less than two hours from the valley. That's when we start a nasty climb."

"Oh joy, just what I wanted to hear, another climb! Tell me, Roy, why didn't we just bring a helicopter in?"

"That's how I first found the valley. But, these hunters who want hunting like this don't want an easy trip into the mountains, they want to experience the pioneer way of travel. When I give them that, I know they'll be back. And by knowing they'll be back, I know I can pretty much charge whatever I want. Believe me, they provide me with a quarter of my income for the year when I take a party of six or seven guys in for two weeks."

Rosey fell silent then, and the next few hours were

accompanied only by the sound of iron-shod hooves on stone. When they hit the river, they heard it a half hour before rounding a point of rock and finding themselves at the very edge of the rushing water. The clear, burbling stream promised wonderfully cold and fresh relief from their thirst and, indeed, delivered on that promise. After they filled their water bags for the mules and their personal canteens they sprawled out on a rock for a quick lunch. Roy indicated the need for expediency in their coming climb, wanting to be "on top" before darkness fell. They soon mounted and were on their way.

Rosey found himself short of breath as he looked out over Roy's valley. That shortness was not just from the nine thousand feet above seas level, but as much from the view as it was from that height. The verdant green floor was a good two thousand feet below their position. The walls dropped sheer at their feet, and it seemed to Rosey the valley was more of a canyon. He expressed his thoughts to Roy.

"Well, John, I suppose you could be right, but notice that it spreads out just to our left to around a mile wide and stays that way for nearly five miles. Notice the river, and I really do think its the same one, runs along that other side. There's trout in there nearly as long as your arm!"

"So we have trout for super, huh?"

Roy laughed and shook his head. "We won't have trout before tomorrow's supper, John. Our job for the next few days is to find a better way down into this place. The first two times I came here, it took us a whole day to get down in. If I can't do better than that, I'll need to abandon this as a viable hunting trip. Those guys bellyached the whole time because they knew the trip back out was gonna be even tougher."

"Wow. Well, I hope we can do it for you, Roy. Where do we start?"

"I think we need to get down in and then survey this entire side from valley level."

"Let's get to it, then."

"Well, what we're going to get at is setting up camp right over there. No need to start down this afternoon, we wouldn't get far enough to even touch base with the descent. I'll have to let you actually rest a bit today. I hate that, but it has to be!"

"Okay, slave driver. Give me those binoculars of yours and let me look this place over from here."

Rosey spent the better part of two hours perusing the valley side from his vantage point, but saw no decent place from which to descend.In fact, he failed to see how the point where they camped at the present that would serve as a good place to go down. Roy spent the time rearranging packs and baking in the Dutch oven so they would have plenty of sourdough biscuits for the next day's meals. He explained to Rosey that meals would be on the move while descending. With the smells of the baking and meat frying in the frying pan, they succumbed to hunger earlier than usual, then devoured an extra meal later in the day.High mountain air was not conducive to any diet restrictions. They also spent a lot of time prowling along the rim in exploration.

That night by the firelight Roy explained the next day's task. "We'll start down about fifty yards over there, and we can get a couple hundred feet down before we have to unload the mules the first time."

"Wait! Unload the mules the FIRST time? First of all, why unload them? Second, what do you mean the FIRST time!?"

"Well, John, if you'll let me continue, you'll understand. When we get down that little path for half an hour or so, we come to a spot several hundred feet in length where the ledge is too narrow for the mules to pass with the packs. There's barely enough ledge for their hooves, let alone trying to squeeze a pack through. We have three places like that, and we're going to let the packs down to the next level with ropes each time.

"During all that, we'll have traveled close to a mile to our left and another half mile back this way. Its going to be most of the day for us to get down, its much worse coming back up, but it can't be helped unless we find another way. You can see why this might well be a lost cause for bringing hunting parties here although the game down there is truly abundant."

"What has Paige gotten me into? We'll have a little talk when I get back, you can bet on that!"

Roy chuckled and walked back to the sleeping bags where he proceeded to crawl in and roll with his back to the fire.

"Better get all the sleep you can, John, tomorrow's a tough day no matter how we slice it."

The smoke from the fire woke Rosey the next morning as it was held to the ground by a wind blowing right across his sleeping bag. He awoke choking with burning eyes watering.

"What you trying to do to me, Roy? You taking to smoking everything like you do your hams? I'm not a ham, you know."

"That could probably be debated, John. I sure hate that we have this wind already; bodes no good for our descent. It can really get difficult with wind blowing along the walls. That valley is a two-thousand feet drop from here at this point and it acts just like a venturi to accelerate the speed from where it enters off to our right when it's a west wind.

"Today is a dangerous one, and I sure don't relish it. Eat, my friend, and let's get to it."

Rosey availed himself of the lavish breakfast laid out by the fire, mumbling all the while that Roy could start the fire and cook so much while he slept. As he ate, Roy brought the mules in from their oat bags and began to saddle them.

"We'll get about five-hundred feet down in before we have to drop-line supplies over the edge. By then we'll be nearly directly below this spot. We'll have gone half a mile east as we go down and then make a turn and come back in two shorter legs as we descend. This requires we have our total concentration on the task, John, it's easy to get distracted, and if you do, its just as easy to go over the edge! Don't do that. I don't want to have to haul your sorry carcass back up."

"Thanks, Roy, I love you too."

When breakfast was finished, dishes cared for, and pack saddles loaded, they mounted and Roy led off the edge. That first drop over the edge took Rosey's breath away as he realized he was now hanging onto a mere thread of rock ledge. His leg on the inside was less than an inch from the cliff wall! Roy called back to leave the mule alone and he would take care of everything better than if Rosey tried to make decisions for the animal. He drew in a deep breath, settled into the saddle, and tried to remain calm. Height in an airplane while surrounded by the cabin walls, windows, and plush seats was an entirely different animal than this. He was in control in the plane, not even close to that here.

The five-hundred foot descent took over two hours as they wound their way down, resting the mules every half hour. When Roy pulled to a stop Rosey could see just ahead where the narrow ledge necked down to what looked like nothing any animal could traverse, not even a mouse! They were not only on the narrow ledge clinging to the wall, but it sloped downward yet at a frightening angle.

"You aren't going to tell me we have to work from right here, are you, Roy?"

"Not if you don't want me to, John, but not telling you won't make any difference. We still have it to do. You can slide over your mule's rump to dismount if you like. I think you'll do fine unsaddling him there once you're off. "We'll tie our riding saddles together to lower them, then the pack saddles.

"Now, when its time to lower the pack saddles, tie the saddle and all to the end. Use a bowline knot so I can get it loose down there and then just drop it over the side and ease it down until I yell. Okay?"

"You mean I'll be up here alone, right?"

"Heavens no, John, the mules will still be here."

"Roy! This is no time to mess with my mind! I'm afraid of heights, and this is giving me the bejeebers!"

Roy simply smiled in his typical laconic way and replied, "How do you think we can untie the goods if we both stay up here, John? Once everything is down, we'll lead the mules down and rest on the ledge down there. It's a bit wider where we end up and we'll take a break. Relax, you have insurance."

The tall rider turned with that and proceeded to unsaddle his mount. Within minutes they were tying the saddles together on a rope and then Roy tied that rope to yet another.

"How long are these, Roy?"

"We're dropping the stuff around seventy feet, these are fifty foot ropes. You ready? If you are, let'er go, I'll be down by the time these are if you don't let go."

"Very funny, Roy. I'm beginning to think you've turned evil on me."

His answer was a wave from another twenty feet down the

trail as he walked at a normal pace in that direction. Rosey started lowering the saddles. He noticed the lead mule, Roy's mount, followed its master down the path with no urging from the guide. Maybe the rest would do the same.

It took very little time to lower the load to Roy, even less to pull the rope back up and tie on the next pack saddle. That lowering took him longer because the load was much heavier. Rosey heaved a sigh of relief when Roy called out and the rope went slack. Wow, three more packs to go!

For all the relative ease with which the task was accomplished, it was fully an hour before the last load was lowered, the mules below, and the saddles returned to their backs. Rosey had trembled with fear as he watched the mules rub against the sheer walls during the descent, hooves a mere two inches from the edge. If the saddles had been on, they wouldn't have had room to walk the ledge. Rosey watched his feet and kept his eyes on the point where the ledge met the wall; no looking ahead or down for him! Sweat poured from his total being and his heart pounded so fast and hard he feared he might have an attack. The farther he went the tighter his chest became and by the time he followed the mule ahead of him onto the wider section of ledge he was a wreck.

"Roy, that has GOT to be the worst thing I have ever done! I am SO glad that's over and done with. No more of that stuff for me!"

"Uuh, John, I don't know how to tell you this, but there's two more places that narrow we have to traverse. The next one is farther down, too, from the spot where we have to unsaddle. I have another section of rope to tie on. You think you can buck up and do it, or should we climb back up right now? It isn't too late to turn back."

Rosey just groaned and sat down on the ledge. After a few minutes he looked up at the sympathetic guide and said, "Let's saddle up, Roy. We've come this far, we might as well do it."

"That's my friend John talking now. We can get through this, but before you make your final decision, remember we also have to come back OUT of here, and that is, my fine feathered friend, UP."

A groan escaped once more from Rosey, then he stood up

69

and started saddling his mule. Roy smiled and duplicated the action.

Somewhere close to six hours later they had traversed the last of the bad spots without incident and had but a quarter of a mile of ledge left to descend. They had spent a lot of time walking and leading the mules where the ledge was too narrow for their legs to clear while in the saddle and had to shift the loads on the pack saddles as well for those beasts of burden to clear. Two of the mules were less than content to follow meekly and had to be pulled along in places.

"When you found this ledge from the chopper, what ever made you think it could be traveled?"

"Wasn't sure, John. Looked like the only place to come down, thought I had to try it, and here we are. Main mistake I made was in bringing a hunting party with me the first time before I tried it myself.Once I saw the beauty from down here and saw the amount of game I knew it was a gold mine for hunting. Wait 'til tomorrow morning, my friend, and you'll be wishing season was in!

"For now, let's make our way over to the river and set up camp. We'll set up in that grove of trees downstream a bit and do all our exploring from there. You are in for a real treat! Meanwhile, I'm gonna cook you a meal fit for a king tonight, 'cause I'm really proud of you and the way you stuck with me… that was no trip for the weak of heart or any kind of a greenhorn. You aren't either one."

That was a long speech for the quiet man from the mountains, and Rosey fairly glowed from the praise. He suddenly didn't feel as tired as he had moments ago.

As the shadows began their invasion of the area and the playful river gurgled happily beside the camp, Rosey sipped from his coffee cup and listened as Roy played softly on his harmonica. He could hear the night sounds of the wilds slowly come to life as the two friends languished by the fire. When the coffee was gone, Rosey stood and went in search of more wood for the fire. They would take turns stoking the fire during the night to keep some semblance of warmth available.

After the canyon walls had chased the daylight away and replaced it with a cobalt blue darkness Rosey lay on his back staring up at the stars in a sky that nearly took his breath away. These mountains had a way of casting a spell over a man that threatened to mesmerize and tranquilize him. He fell asleep without intending to, surrendering to a combination of fatigue and tranquility. The feeling failed to last, however, and dreams of fear and violence assailed his sleep until the cold, damp hours of the morning when he awoke with a start. His sleeping bag was a mess of rumpled cloth and he was half out of it, shivering from the cold that permeated his body.

Roy was still just a dark mound across the fire from him, attesting to the fact the time of day had not yet reached early morning. Roy was always up by 5:00, saying he didnt want the daylight to sneak up on him. Rosey climbed from what remained of his covers and put kindling on the fire, stirring the remaining coals and blowing softly on them to get a blaze going, shivering all the while.

Once the fire was roaring he lay back down wrapped in his sleeping bag. Another night like that and he might just forget sleeping altogether! He was sound asleep when Roy shook him awake two hours later. The sun was well up and he realized Roy had let him sleep in. His watch showed the hour to be seven o'clock; that was sleeping in to Roy.

"John, are you okay?"

"Uuh, yeah, Roy, I'm fine, why?"

"Well, you had a really bad night, tossed and turned, shouted out a lot, groaned a lot, and I began to think maybe I'd done you in yesterday."

"Just tired, that's all. I probably missed my bed. After all, you did strike terror into my heart with that confound descent yesterday. We don't have to do that again, do we?"

"No, but if we don't find a better way up, we gotta go back up that way."

Rosey answered that with a groan and accepted the coffee Roy was offering. Once they had eaten and cleaned the dishes, they took stock of their surroundings and Roy pointed to the east end of the valley.

"Best chance of a way in and out is down that way, I had the time when I had that hunting party in to look this end over, found nothing. Absolutely nothing."

71

"Man, Roy, I can't get over how level and smooth this valley floor looks! I think I could land a Cheyenne here."

"Could you take it back out again?"

"Maybe. You say this is five miles long?"

"At least that long. Winds are very unpredictable, though. I had a couple of that party set up what was downwind from some elk, suddenly they spooked and took off. I checked it out, the wind had shifted. Then, while I was explaining to the hunters, it switched again, that time to a ninety degree angle from either way. There's quite a swirl at times."

"That wouldn't keep me from going if I was light enough. With twenty-five thousand feet to play with, I could be at cruise speed before I had to pull up. If I kept to the center I would avoid any radical turbulence or downdrafts. I think I could fly parties in for you, Roy. Or…you could hire a chopper to bring you in."

"Not interested in that. John. I take pride in showing my hunters just what mountain life and hunting is like. If we flew them in here, the living is way too easy once they're here. Might as well go to one of those hunting preserves." The last was said in disgust.

Rosey knew his guide looked at those establishments with intense disdain because he felt they might as well tie the animals to a tree and shoot them. His quote was, "Only difference between them and slaughter houses is the animals they're killing."

As they talked, they saddled the mules. Rosey mounted first and headed down river, looking at the ground condition as he did. The smooth, level plain was really intriguing. He really could land the planes here! He pulled out his pocket GPS and entered the coordinates, saving them after he was done. The plush, green grass of the valley grew belly high to the mules and waved hypnotically in the light breezes as the two rode by the river. Small game flushed ahead of them as they rode, the mules occasionally laying long ears back at the interruptions, but never seeming startled.

The valley walls remained as vertical as their descent spot for the entire length of the valley, and was the same on both sides. High promontories dotted the southern rim like sentries guarding the way, not allowing men to ruin their peaceful kingdom without paying the price of real labor. There seemed no way whatsoever to ascend or descend on that side of the valley. Roy stated that even the wily mountain sheep would be hard-pressed to travel those areas.

As they neared the halfway point of the valley they saw it had expanded to its maximum width, with small groves of trees dotting the mile wide floor. Game was seen often as the groves provided cover from the strange looking invaders. Roy commented that the game had most likely only seen men once, and that was earlier in the season last fall when he had his only hunting party in. While wary, the animals also showed curiosity; coming to the edge of the covering foliage to peer through keen eyes at the wondering pair of riders.

Rosey noticed a deeper grove clear to the northern edge of the valley; it actually looked to be more of a full-fledged forest. Upon riding to it to investigate, he found huge boulders dotting the tree stand where they had fallen from the wall centuries before. The house sized stones had plowed a path through the trees before coming to rest. He was glad he hadn't been around when they fell!

"Hey John, look over here!"

Rosey rode to the spot where Roy had called from to find the rider to find him with a nonplussed look as he gazed at a ramshackle log cabin nestled in among the boulders and trees. It was all but invisible unless one was right on it.

"How in Casey's boots did I miss this before? We were in here for three whole days and I never found this!"

They dismounted and explored the structure. "Looks like the folks who built this wanted lots of room, Roy. This is a big cabin! Not much of a roof left, but the walls still look pretty amazing!"

"Right you are. The back wall there is leaning back pretty bad, but other than that, they're still good. I can't see as they're even rotting, John."

"Not much of a floor, though, Roy. Unless you want to call these weeds a carpet."

The two shared a laugh at that as they searched through the weeds that grew over the entire floor of the structure. The fireplace had collapsed for whatever reason, with the chimney laying inside the room. Roy was examining the stones when he jumped back with a shout, pulling his revolver.

"Rattler, John! Look around carefully, this place is a natural den area for them. Why in the world did I forget that possibility? Watch careful, we need to get out of here, but go slow and step on eggs."

They eased their way out of the cabin remains and returned to the mules. Both were breathing a little hard, Rosey claimed it was the altitude, Roy simply said he was scared out of his wits.

"John, I must be getting old to have neglected warning you about that possibility, and not even watching close myself! I've never been that negligent before. What is so bad is that some of these vipers don't bother warning a guy before striking. Most folks would deny that could ever happen, but I've seen it."

"Thanks for that little bit of information, Roy, I really wanted to know that. I'll be sure to dwell on it the rest of this trip!" His comment was made in the driest of humor.

They made their way out of the wooded area and turned again to the east. The cabin was about a mile from the eastern end of the valley and when they had covered that mile, they sat saddles looking up at the end of the valley. The wall across the end was not as high as the sides, reaching around a thousand feet. It was ragged and rugged and looked like the teeth in an alligator's mouth.

Rosey was no different than any other dedicated pilot, he automatically began to weigh the route over the end and evaluating the best spot to make his entry should he try it. Most pilots are a little strange that way, always searching out risks and ways to minimize them while adding the thought of new adventure to their flying. Rosey rode along the wall from north to south and stopped about three-quarters of the way down. There was a gap some fifty yards wide that was a couple of hundred feet lower than the rest of the rim. Roy sat watching his friend with an amused look on his face.

"What has you so captivated, John Rosenthal?"

Rosey jumped, having been jarred out of his contemplative state. "Aw, I was just thinking how a guy could come in a little hot, come up on one wing while holding opposite rudder and clip through that wedge-like place with plenty of room to spare. That would give him a couple hundred feet of advantage on an approach."

"You always have to imagine landing in tough spots, John? I hear the same thing from you every time you're out here. What is it with that?"

"What if a guy had problems and had to make an emergency landing, Roy? It's thinking things like that through that keep the mind sharp and ready for quick decisions in times of trouble. It's an exercise of the mind; keeps ya sharp."

Roy simply chuckled and turned his mule to the west. "Let's ride along the river and see how the trout holes look, I'm in the mood for a big rainbow all to myself for lunch!"

The rest of the day was spent searching the north wall for ascent routes, all to no avail. The rugged, perpendicular sides gave no hope of such activity as climbing with mules and supplies. By the time late afternoon arrived and they were contemplating another meal of trout they knew the valley was out of the consideration for Roy to bring hunting parties into it. He commented they would turn their attention to the south wall in the morning. For now, they went to the river with their fishing gear to catch supper. At least that part of the trip was successful!

Chapter 10

Two days later the men had surveyed the entire valley with no encouragement for Roy. Rosey had become very quiet during the last day and was shocked when Roy had questions after supper was done with.

"John, you know I treasure your friendship, don't you?"

"Well, yes, Roy. I guess I do, and I treasure yours."

"Okay John, then tell me what kind of trouble you're in."

"What?"

"Tell me what kind of trouble you're in."

"I'm not in any kind of trouble, Roy, why do you ask a question like that?"

"John, we've been sleeping out here for five nights now, and you have all but destroyed your sleeping bag with your tossing around like a rattler with someone standing on its head. Plus, you've been shouting in your sleep about killing something or someone, and about a gun to your head on one occasion. Now, if you don't want to tell me, that's your business, but maybe I can help in some way."

Rosey poked around in the fire with a stick for several minutes before he replied. When he had gathered himself emotionally he took a deep breath and proceeded to talk, "I killed two men, Roy. Did it in cold blood. They had it coming, but if anyone ever finds out, I'm cooked; finished; toast." He then told the taciturn guide the whole story, starting with the discovery of Father Simpson's body and sparing no detail right up to his flight west.

"Well, John, can't say as I blame you, but that doesn't make you any safer from the law. This kind of thing has a way of being revealed sooner or later. So what do you intend to do for now?"

"I have absolutely no idea, Roy. None whatsoever. It'll about kill Paige if I'm found out. I worry over that more than anything. Of course, I had no idea how killing another human being would effect me! It's really horrible, Roy! I don't think I'll ever shake the nightmares of seeing those two fall out. They are always looking back at me in the dream! Always, Roy!"

With that comment he broke into tears with silent sobs shaking his body. Roy sat quiet until Rosey had expended his grief. Then he stirred the fire until it was roaring once again after adding more wood. It seemed as though more light penetrating the darkness of the night shadows from the south wall would somehow alleviate his friend's grief. The river still sang its light-hearted melody as it rippled through the camp. Neither spoke for nearly half an hour, then the guide spoke first.

"John, do you really think you could land your plane here in the valley?"

"Well...yeah, no doubt in my mind about that. Why?"

"Well, if you thought it was getting bad back east, you could come in to my place, stock up with food, and come in here. It looks to me as if you could camouflage a plane back in the main grove over there, build a cabin, and hole up 'til things blow over. I could pack supplies in every once in a while, visit, and bring you any news of the outside world.

"We know folks back there could keep up with anything to do with your case. This situation has gotta get to a blowup sooner or later, and if Washington doesn't square around, I'm afraid we're gonna see another revolution. I've already been contacted by a couple of militia groups asking me to join."

"Wow, Roy, you're asking a lot. That would mean leaving everything Paige and I have worked for! And to ask her to come into a place with no modern conveniences...wow, man, that would be brutal!"

"As brutal as a firing squad for her husband?"

Rosey swallowed hard at that, felt light-headed for a couple of seconds and then shook his head. Silence engulfed them once again. As the night sounds once again invaded the camp, Roy arose and walked by the river, embracing the moonlight reflecting from the water while Rosey sat with head hung low, contemplating the hunter's words.

Morning found Rosey up before Roy, a first! He walked along the river as he surveyed the ground closest to it. He went from camp all the way to the western end, then moved to the north almost to the wall and retraced his steps. By the time he arrived back at camp the sun was high in the sky; he had walked nearly ten miles. Roy was preparing lunch by then.

"Wondered where you went off to, John. Was starting to think maybe I needed to come looking."

"I'm sorry, Roy. Needed time to think. I looked this place over good from the perspective of a landing site, I'd have to stay close to the river because the grass off to the north side is so tall. Which brings another question to mind; why isn't the grass even taller closer to the river?"

"There's little runs of water coming through from the rim that waters the grass as they come this way. They are absorbed by the sandy soil over that way so don't reach the river as little streams, but leach into the ground and come that way. You'd need to stay close to the river so's not to dig into that sandy soil or drop a gear into one of those little runs. You notice the ground seems to firm up here by the river."

"Wow, I was so deep in thought I didn't even notice the sandy soil or those little runs! Good thing you're here to keep me straight."

"So, you thinkin' on my suggestion, John?"

"I have to keep it in mind, Roy, but I don't see it as a possibility. I'll just have to hope nothing more happens back home. When do we start back, by the way? I'm missing that little wife of mine!"

"Me too, John. Well, I'm not missing YOUR little wife, but my own. The longer I do this, the more I dislike being gone for more than a couple of nights at a time. I gotta talk Florence into coming with me if I do this much longer. I can see THAT happening!"

They laughed, and started clearing the camp in preparation for packing the gear. As Rosey realized they were heading out soon, the north wall seemed to loom even higher and steeper than ever before. He was dreading the climb.

Chapter 11

Morgan chuckled at the customer's last comment and gave him a push on the shoulder. He started to go behind the counter to complete the purchase for the fellow when he saw a car whip into the angled parking place directly in front of the south set of doors of the hardware. Morgan was suddenly void of all reason and charged out the door to stand at the curb.

The ATF agent stepped out of the car and started to push past Morgan as though he wasn't there, only to find a pair of hands firmly grasping the front of his shirt as Morgan jerked the man back and spun him around. Morgan then wheeled the unfortunate fellow in a circle, slamming him into the driver's door of the vehicle. Morgan released his right hand to open the door, then hurled the man into the seat, making sure he banged the agent's head soundly on the top of the opening. The bump dazed the guy and he slumped into the seat.

"I told you to stay the blazes out of my store and out of my sight!" Morgan yelled as he shook the man.

"I'm here to confiscate all your records, Montgomery. All of them!"

"Like hob you are! You got a warrant?"

"I don't need a warrant for the likes of you, traitor. You're as good as locked up after this."

"Not by you, scum, not by you. I still have rights, and you don't have a warrant, you don't have any right to hassle me! Now, you start this piece of junk, back it out of here, and leave while I'm willing to leave you in one piece!" This last was said as Morgan shook the man by his long hair and then slammed the door before any more could be said.

The agent, looking dazed still, just set there for a few seconds before starting the car. He looked at Morgan with venom fairly pouring from his eyes, started to shut the car off and then thought better of it when he saw the small handgun at Morgan's waist. Morg' had pulled it around to where the fellow could see it. The car started backwards then, and with a look to kill, one less agent took up space in the street. The black tire marks testified as to his former presence.

The customer, John Dull, had slipped out through the north set of doors to the store and left the purchase on the counter. Morgan stood shaking at the curb for a long time before going back into the store. The whole reaction was so opposite to Morgan Montgomery that any who saw it would wonder at his forceful performance.

There are times in each life when internalized feelings can no longer be contained. When such times as these arrive, the individual often returns to their base instincts and reacts in that particular manner. Morgan Montgomery dropped into his former lifestyle at the sight of this extremely abrasive individual and dropped all guards against over reaction. He simply went code red with all his being and now, as the action ceased and the situation was over, his body, mind, and soul went into the next step which is usually a post traumatic shut down of all reasoning.

Trembling, he sidled back into the store, sweating and nauseous. What would the government man do, and how soon would he do it? What was Kay going to say? She had so much trust in him, and he had really blown it. There had been no such blow-ups for several years, and only one such happening since accepting Christ. Morgan grabbed a partly empty pop from below the counter and tipped it up to drink, relishing the warm liquid sliding down his throat as the fizzing sensation awakened his taste buds and served to distract him temporarily.

It was still an hour to closing time, just ten minutes until Cal was due to come to finish the day for him. Morgan realized he could not leave Cal to close the store alone in case the ATF agent returned. The cold chills engulfed him as he thought of the agent, and the gun at his side seemed to project heat that burned into his side. His hand sought the grip and he shuddered at the realization he might shoot another human being if he failed to control himself. Morgan slipped into the back room and dropped to his knees.

"Lord, I am so sorry! I wanted to kill a man just now. If I had another minute just a few minutes ago with him, I would have done it! I *know* I would have! Lord, please forgive my hate, and please strengthen me against the feelings that man brings out in me!"

He knelt there for several minutes in prayer, rising only when the door chime sounded its melodic introduction in the antiquated tradition of past times that a person had invaded the store. Cal soon poked his head around the door opening and greeted his dad.

"Hi Pops, how's the day been?"

"Not good, Son, not good," Morgan replied with a still trembling voice.

Cal sensed immediately that something was wrong, drastically wrong. His dad did NOT react that way to negative days!

"What is it, Dad? Tell me."

Morgan related the incident to his younger son, at least all he could remember clearly. Part of the physical action was clouded in his mind, but he told all he could recall.

"Wow, Dad, I've never seen you that angry, even at Brian or me."

"I'm really scared, Cal, what will I do if that idiot comes back? I'm afraid of myself, Son!" Morgan sobbed and collapsed into his son's embrace, crying for several minutes before collecting his wits about him. He stepped back, dried his eyes, and studied Cal. The youngster was calm, collected, and seemed to stand taller than ever before.

"You go home, Dad. That agent comes back, I'll handle it. We can close early if he does. I'll see him first and lock up right away. I can leave by the storage door in the alley."

Morgan slapped the lad on the shoulder, grabbed his keys and went out the back where his car was parked. He was home in five minutes. Kay had not yet come home from work so he climbed in the shower and let the water cascade over him for way too long before stepping out, drying off, and lying on the bed in his skivvies. Sleep claimed him in less than two minutes. The exhaustion of the stress had taken all Morgan Montgomery had to offer.

When Kay came home, she found him there, breathing deeply and having never moved from his original position. She let him sleep, knowing something must be really wrong for her husband to be sleeping in the late afternoon like that. Cal soon joined her and explained the day's occurrences to his mother as best he could.

The evening on East Maple Street was quite subdued that day, and beds were sought early as no one seemed disposed to stay conscious for long. Brian and Sue had been called, Rosey and Paige had not answered their phone because they were out celebrating Rosey's safe return from out west. They could be brought up to date tomorrow, no sense in all of them tossing and turning all night! Tomorrow would bring its own problems to add to the current ones.

Morgan opened the store as usual at 10 AM the next morning, and had barely energized the cash register when Rosey walked in. The shorter man strolled to the counter, leaned on his forearms and looked Morgan in the eye.

"What's this I hear from Kay that you've gone cave man?"

Morgan rolled his eyes and tilted his head back to gaze at the ceiling for a moment. "Whatever you mean by caveman, you Neanderthal, is inaccurate and I deny it. I guess you have a right to know the facts, but they ain't pretty." He then proceeded to relate to his friend the events as he could remember them. Morgan was shocked at how vague the facts seemed to him as he told Rosey about his actions.

When he was done his friend stood looking at the floor for a long time, drew a deep, deep breath and looked back at Morgan with difficulty. "Morg, I got something to tell you that you ain't gonna like. If anyone comes in while I'm talking I'll have to stop, and I'll soon be in such bad shape that I'll need to slip into the back. So…bear with me, old friend, and you'll see your little escapade is nothing.

"You see, I overheard two soldiers talking in the men's room out at the airport, and they were the ones who murdered that poor priest. They didn't know I was in there, and after they left, I was sick with grief and anger."

"I can understand that; that's horrible!"

"Morg, don't interrupt, this is hard enough as it is. I told Roy about this, but you'll be the only other person to know. Morg, I killed those two men!"

Morgan drew air into his lungs in a rush that threatened to explode his chest.

"It came to me that night while I was trying to sleep. I could tell they had been hired to do it, and by the guy over military and police operations in our region! I knew they would never be punished, even convicted, and, for that matter, probably not even arrested if I told my story to the law.

"So...I came up with this plan, foolproof, I told myself, and handed out my own justice. Now I'm not so sure the plan was as foolproof as I first thought it would be. There's this Army guy keeps coming back, asking the same questions, and always new ones, over and over. Morg, I'm scared as can be."

Morgan shook his head and replied, "All that, not to mention the horrible knowledge you killed another human being must be impossible to bear!"

"Oh, don't get me wrong, Morgan Montgomery, I'm not sorry I killed those snakes! I'm just scared as can be of getting found out. They needed killing!"

Morgan stood for countless minutes just staring at Rosey, trying unsuccessfully to comprehend what he had just heard. He saw in Rosey's eyes something never before seen through the many years of their friendship, he saw a hardness not easy to fathom; a quality he had not thought possible. Morgan shuddered, then looked away. His day might as well have been over for all the good he accomplished after that. He pictured Paige in his mind watching Rosey being hauled away, then he pictured Kay watching as HE was hauled away! Life was now a jumbled mess, thanks to two harsh men, him and Rosey not controlling their feelings.

Morgan closed early that day, taking his fishing gear with him as he left and heading for the river. He never caught anything in the river, but fish were not his goal; loneliness was.

He needed time to think. Cal found his note when he slipped in the back door with his personal key and smiled. His dad was a lousy fisherman and knew it, so Cal knew this was a thinking trip. He locked the back door as he left right away and walked the half-mile home, whistling as he did.

Had young Calvin Montgomery known the turns life was about to take, his whistle would have been more of the heavy breathing of a nervous person.

Morgan opened the next morning at eight AM, same as every other day. As he unlocked the south set of front doors from within he saw the ATF agent's car across the street! He steeled himself to be as courteous as the man would allow and then heard the back door through which he had entered, as always, open and bang shut. He looked around to see sheriff's deputy Ted Sawyer enter from the back room and walk past the end of the counter.

"Just take it easy, Morgan, please don't make this any harder than it already is."

"What's up, Ted? You look like your dog just died."

"Don't you know, Morg? The ATF guy out there has pressed charges against you for assaulting him yesterday. Why don't you let him in?"

Morgan had relocked the door when he saw the agent, and looked at the deputy with consternation showing on his face. "No way, Ted, he will NOT enter this establishment under any circumstances as long as I'm here. He has harassed me for six months, badgered me about every possible thing he could, and I have cooperated fully, supplied him with every record he has asked for, withstood his threats over groundless issues, and he enters only over my dead body. I'm sorry, Ted, but I gotta stand pat on this one. He's pushed me over the limit!"

Morgan was getting louder with each word until he was now nearly shouting. Sawyer waited patiently for him to finish, then quietly explained. "He has a warrant out for you, Morg, and I suggest you try your best to be calm. I have to take you in, there's no choice.

"If you don't want him in here, then we'll go out the back the way I came in. I know, though, that he's waiting for a judge to issue a search warrant and seizure order for all your records. He claims you not only assaulted him, but you're supporting terrorist groups. Now, I know better, the sheriff knows better, and the whole county knows better, Morg, but with these feds thinking they can run the whole shebang any way they want to, our hands are pretty much tied.

"Please, Morg, let's just go out the back, get in cruiser, and I'll get you over to the jail without your needing to have any contact with him. Okay?"

Morgan stared unbelievingly at the deputy, sagged in resignation and nodded. He looked through the locked door at the agent, spit on the door in front of his face, and wheeled around to follow Sawyer. As he exited the back door he carefully locked it and stepped to the cruiser. Just as he opened the car door the ATF man rounded the corner shouting at them. Sawyer started the car, put it in gear, and since the man had positioned himself directly in front of it, backed to the alley and turned there. They were on the road before the agent reached his own vehicle.

Morgan rode with his head down, trying to reason through the situation and failing miserably. He knew the local sheriff and deputies were friends and sympathetic to the old order when it came to both politics and military control. Their hands were tied, however.

Morgan took out his cell phone and punched Kay's speed dial number. Ted commented, "Its okay if you do that, Morg."

"I didn't ask," Morgan growled. When Kay's voice answered he softened his own and told her the situation.

"Oh Honey, you can't be serious! What are we going to do?"

"I have absolutely no idea, girl. None whatsoever."

"I'll call the pastor and get the prayer chain going!"

"Hmmf, don't bother. That coward probably won't pass it on for fear he'll upset someone."

"Honey, you're too bitter, that's not you! Just because you don't agree with his outlook doesn't make him an ineffective Christian!"

"Far as I'm concerned, he doesn't even exist after the chicken way he handled the last board meeting. I'm done with that church, sweetheart, they are a bunch of chickens; afraid to stand up for the gospel in the face of these trials."

"Morgan…darling…don't let this happen to you. The enemy is trying to destroy your peace and rob you of your victory and joy. You be the man I married in and through this; you hear me mister?"

"I hear you. Doesn't mean I gotta change how I feel, though. Hey, we're pulling into the county jail now, I have to go. They'll probably take my phone, so check in with the sheriff later to see what happens next. And Kay…"

"Yes, hon?"

"If that agent comes to the house, you shoot his tail off!"

He snapped the phone shut before she could answer and grabbed the door handle. This was promising to be a very long day.

When Ted had shut the cruiser off, Morgan turned to him, reached behind his right hip and unclipped his holster with the semi-automatic in it and handed it to Ted.

"Here, Ted, you probably oughtta have control of this."

The deputy turned a sickly shade of greenish white and swallowed hard. "Thanks, Morg, you just saved my job! I can't imagine what could have happened to me in there."

Morgan stalked through the door and leaned on the counter, looking the deputy sitting behind it straight in the eyes with a venomous glare. "Don't say a word, Jenny Hyde. Not one word! And if you call that pretend pastor of ours I'll throw up on you next chance I get."

"Morgan, I won't call anyone you don't want me to, but you need to calm down where Pastor is concerned. He feels really bad about your condemnation, and so do many of the rest of us at church."

"Then find him a new backbone," Morgan growled and emptied his pockets onto the counter top. His countenance was that of a true criminal at that time; his attitude one that would carry no patience.

The door to the right opened and Sheriff John Hall emerged, and stopped dead in his tracks. "Morgan, I am so sorry to have to do this. They left me no choice. Man, next time you decide to not be Morgan, do it to someone without power to swing things.

"Ted, get him booked and then make sure he's not with any undesirables. Morgan's our friend and we need to make this as friendly for him as possible."

"Sure, sheriff, I'll do just that."

"Morgan, I need the number off your concealed carry permit, would you take it out of your wallet, please?" Jenny said.

Hall stopped at that, turned and came back to the desk. "Morg, you're still carrying, even outside of the store?"

"Of course I am," growled Morgan. "These days, a man needs the protection with him all the time."

"You didn't have it on when you popped that agent, did you?"

"First of all, I didn't pop that knucklehead, and second of all, of course I did. You got a problem with that, John?"

"Wait a minute; you say you didn't pop him? He claimed you did. Said you hit him in the back of the head as he was getting out of the car and shoved him back in. Said you must have used something hard because he was dizzy from the blow."

"If I would have hit the...well... the liar, he wouldn't have felt dizzy, he wouldn't have felt ANYTHING!"

"Easy, Morg. So, now we have a different story, which is to be expected. But Morg, how am I supposed to prove you're telling us the truth instead of him?"

"You call yourself a sheriff? Check the back of the stupid jerk's head! For cryin' out loud, John, to think I voted for you several times!"

"Easy Morgan, easy. I can understand you being worked up, but keep it civil in case the wrong ears should show up. This guy has serious connections to big brother and I'm really worried about you. You're in a really bad spot here. I don't want to see you taken out of my custody, but unless I miss my guess, the jerk, as you call him, will push for just that.

"If he gets you away from here, no telling what they can do to keep you locked up far longer than the old laws allowed. This is a whole 'nuther ballgame now. I've never seen such stretching of the law, and there's been so darn little I've been able to do about it."

It was then the ATF agent entered. He looked at Morgan

and then accosted the sheriff.

"Why isn't this man in a cell?"

"Because he hasn't been completely booked yet, you suppose? Or maybe we need to prepare the greetings banquet room first? Get one thing straight, Peters, I run this jail, and if you climb all over one of my people like you did yesterday for no reason, I slap your sorry hide in a cell with that man there so fast it'll make you dizzier than you claim to be right now!

"Now, turn around and stand still." John Hall was working himself up to Morgan's level of excitement. The feds had pushed him farther than he ever wanted to be pushed and, as a man of integrity, he was about to the end of his patience.

"What do you mean, turn around? And you better lower your voice to me, mister, I don't tolerate insolence."

That was the absolute wrong approach by the fed. Sheriff Hall grabbed him, spun him around, threw a hammerlock on him, and started to handcuff him. Ted stepped in and grabbed Hall's arm, keeping him from locking the first cuff.

"Wait sheriff, let's look him over and then let him go. We don't need his kind of trouble right now. Or ever, for that matter."

Peters was sputtering and making threats as John grabbed the seat of his pants and lifted him onto the counter. John Hall was six foot and four inches with a weight of two hundred plus forty pounds, only twenty of which were extra. Peters weighed a rompin' stompin' 130 pounds and was now becoming aware of the fact that Sheriff John Hall and his staff had no fear of him or his position.

Jenny stood up from the other side of the desk and began ruffling through Peters' hair. Morgan almost chuckled at the sight because it reminded him of the monkeys at the zoo as they searched each other for fleas.

"Say, mister Peters, that's a nasty cut where he hit you yesterday. Where did you get the stitches done?"

Peters looked at Jenny and snarled, "You have a smart mouth, deputy. You know there's no stitches there."

"That's right. And if Morgan Montgomery had hit you as hard as you say he did, there would be some kind of bruise, cut, goose egg, or whatever there. There's nothing, sir, absolutely nothing. Now, hold still while I get a picture of that smooth head of yours; you know, the one with no mark of any kind."

Peters swore and struggled to climb from the counter but Hall held him there.

"This is illegal restraint! I'll have all your badges for this! I know…"

The sheriff interrupted him, "Yeah, we know; you know the big cheese personally. Remember this, MISTER Peters, we know mister Colt and mister Smith and mister Wesson personally, and we just might introduce you to them some dark and stormy night.

"We're getting pretty darned tired of you feds thinking you own everybody around here, and I won't be surprised if some sort of rebellion doesn't jump up and bite you on the behind. Now, I have papers here for you to sign that gave us permission to photograph the back of your head. Then you can sign the complaint against Mister Montgomery, here, and we'll lock the nasty man up and throw away the cell. Err, the key; we need the cell. You might need a bed tonight. Coppice?"

"You…you're threatening me? An officer of the federal government? I'll burn you for this."

"Ted, put Morg in a cell and then you and I need to show this federal agent where that poor priest was drowned. I think the wire is still there with the weight tied to it. If not, we'll use a rock."

Peters turned white, swallowed hard, and took on the countenance of a beaten man. He had seen the resolve of these rural Americans and had long ago realized the government put no fear into their hearts. These were the type of people who started the little fracas in 1776, for sure!

Ted looked him in the eyes and asked, "You sure you want to lock this innocent man behind bars, SIR?"

Peters glowered at each of them in turn, then wheeled around and stormed out of the office. Ted, Jenny, and John looked at each other and Ted shrugged his shoulders and said, "Guess not."

"Give Morgan back his stuff, including the gun, and throw him out of here," Hall commented.

"Listen, you guys," Morgan said, "You just stuck your

necks out a mile for me and don't think for one minute I don't appreciate it, but that was dumb! That creep will find a way to come after you!"

Sheriff Hall looked at Jenny, said to her, "Jenny, you need to check out the cells back there and make sure everything is secure. It should take you at least fifteen minutes to do that. Okay?"

She nodded, gave Morgan and Ted a strange look then disappeared through the door to the back.

"Morgan, I know you've met a man named Hagan Marshall. That's the reason you're here, but you're not the only one here who knows him. Ted, you want to tell him, or should I?"

"Go ahead, Sheriff. I'll watch the door." With that, Ted moved to the door to the outside and positioned himself directly in the way should anyone come through.

"Morgan, you need to absorb this information, then forget it unless you get in further trouble with the feds. Marshall has successfully formed a militia in this area. He's arming people for any possible assault to seize our guns, is developing a storehouse of food and emergency supplies, and training leaders for command.

"He has roughly three thousand people right now, mostly men, and more are being recruited. We're preparing for war, Morg, and we're serious about it." "You keep saying things like 'we', 'we're' and that kind of stuff. What's your meaning, John?"

"Ted, myself, and three other deputies, plus every single town cop are members. We see more oppression coming, Morg, and we are NOT going to take it. This is a free country, and we fully intend to see it remains so."

The news hit Morgan like a bomb and his body chilled from head to toe, causing him to shiver noticeably. He began to realize this situation was much worse than he had thought. Rural America was readying for battle and he and his family were right in the middle of it. All this, plus what had happened to the priest, the deaths at the airport at Rosey's hand, and the prospects of his family suffering because of him cascaded down over him in the hot and cold of tangled nerves. He was on the verge of panic.

Ted opened the door for him to exit, and stood patiently while Morgan gathered himself back together. "John, I appreciate your trust in me that you're willing for me to know this information. I'll never disclose it, no matter what."

"I know that, Morgan Montgomery. You're a man of integrity and a man of the faith, as are Ted and I. I told you with the hope you would consider joining us."

"John, I just can't. I mean, I stopped hunting years ago because I just can't stand to kill anything any more. Christ really softened my heart that day I gave myself to Him. The thought of deliberately harming another human just scares the bejeebers out of me. That's why this agent riles me so; he brings out that old Morgan I have learned to despise!"

"Maybe so, Morg, but don't discount that fact that God ordered wars and killing in the taking of Canaan by His people. That was ordained by Him, and was pretty bloody. We all hope and pray this doesn't get to that, but it doesn't look good."

"What do I do, John? About the store, I mean. I hate the thought of letting this crudball put me out of business, but it's starting to look like it just isn't worth the hassle."

"Don't you do it, Morg. Don't you do it. We gotta stand up for our rights. The second amendment gives us the right to keep and bear arms, and that means we have a right to purchase and sell arms. You paid for your permits, you exercise the rights those permits give you.

"Remember, you have our backing, and we're ready to protect you at all cost."

"John, that's what worries me! The cost! Man alive, I don't want to see anyone hurt defending me and a store that could survive without selling arms! You're talking about the possibility of not only losing your careers, but your lives! There's families to think of, John, yours, mine, Ted's, many others! Is it worth it?"

"Darned right it's worth it, Morgan. Men and women gave their lives to establish this great country, men and women have given their lives in numerous situations to retain this great country, and if that's what it takes again, so be it. This far, we've not been called on for outright war on our own soil since 1865, but that doesn't mean it can't, or shouldn't, happen.

"I shudder at the thought of killing other Americans, but if they send them against us to take away freedoms we already have, so be it. If those soldiers are willing to fight to remove America from its history, they have chosen wrong. And I tell you this, Morgan; I know of things going on in our military that would shake your foundations if you knew of them. If this comes to a war of rebellion, the rebels will have far more American soldiers fighting on its side than the government! That's the stupidity of our White House right now. They assume the Army is all theirs, but I tell you, they're wrong; dead wrong."

Morgan stood head down as he contemplated the things going through his tangled mind. This seemed a nightmare. Then he looked at his sheriff, smiled weakly with a nod, and slunk through the door still being held by Ted, walking head down to the waiting cruiser. He was numb and only wanted to hide under his bed at home.

Chapter 12

"Captain, I just don't know what else I can tell you that I haven't told at least a dozen other people, most of them Army. Don't you people compare notes? Is there some sort of non-trust among you that you don't share information?" John Rosenthal was getting frustrated with the new line of questions being asked, and, beyond that, he was starting to feel as though the military was suspicious of him in the deaths of the two soldiers. It wasn't a good feeling.

"Surely, Mister Rosenthal, you understand how we have to get every detail right and proper for the families of those two men. Those under whom the men served need to have more information so as to properly train against such an event happening again, also." The captain's voice sounded like oil sliding over a snakes belly to Rosey. He had zero trust in this man.

"The way you train against such an event happening again is to surgically remove all the ego and arrogance from your soldiers, Captain. Both of those men thought they knew more about my airplanes than I do, and neither one had the decency to ever thank me for a flight. It was all 'order the civilian around without so much as a how-do-you-do.' Neither one was very polite. Never! Their arrogance toward their craft is what killed them. I always objected to their low-level jumps."

"And what was their response to your objections, sir?"

"Always made fun of me for being a momma's boy. Treated me like I was a second class citizen."

"So you held a dislike for them?"

"Sure I did, but I had a job to do for my country, and I had a signed contract my government was paying for. Personal feelings can't be allowed to enter into a job like that. They had their orders, I had mine. Doesn't mean I endorse the low-level jumps, though. I think that's stupidity at its finest. With the controllable chutes we have now, a man can easily hit a target without taking such a risk."

"You fail to understand battle conditions, Rosenthal. There are times that demand the low-level jumps. What is your schedule for tomorrow here? I need to spend a little more time with you on this."

"Can't tomorrow, got students all day long, thanks to your troops. I don't understand that, either. Why is the Army paying for its men to learn to fly here when you have all the facilities to train them in military aircraft? What's that all about?"

"Don't you like the money? Maybe we should look into another flight school for them?"

The last was said with a snide smile on his face, as though Rosey was suppose to cave in and beg for his forgiveness in order to keep his contract. The Captain failed to take into account the type of man he was dealing with.

Rosey swore at him and then said, "Take your stupid contracts and go, for all I care! You're more bother than you're worth! You get in the way of my charter's; your stupid soldiers do stupid things that get them killed on MY airport, and then the likes of you hassle me to pieces because of that stupidity. Ya know what, I'm tired of stupid, and I'm tired of you. Get your sorry carcass out of my sight, this airport just closed!"

With that, Rosey pushed out of his chair, opened the office door, and motioned for the captain to leave. Thinking better of that, he simply stalked out and started putting airplanes in the hanger for the night. He was already late for supper.

The captain stalked up to him just as he was about to hook a tow bar onto a Cherokee and grabbed his arm. "Listen, mister, this isn't over by far. Our interview is over when I say it's over, and that is not happening yet! Now, get back in that office, set down, and listen close!"

It happened in an instant, and Rosey could no more have avoided it if he had hours to think it over; he smashed his fist

95

into the officer's nose and flattened him to the ground. As soon as the soldier hit he rolled to move out of Rosey's reach to get up, only to find the now thoroughly incensed civilian leaping onto his chest.

Rosey's hands grasped the man's neck and he choked him as he beat the head against the pavement, causing near unconsciousness to sweep over the captain. Rosey quit as he finally gained some control over his anger.

Still sitting on the man's chest he held onto the ears and lifted his head up until their noses were almost touching. The captain was coughing and trying to draw deep breaths as he struggled to free himself.

"Understand one thing, you fool; no man has the right to boss me around like you just tried, and no man ever lays a hand on me to force me to do something against my will! You ever do that again and I'll do worse than this to you, army or not! You got that?"

The man with the blurred vision and the beginning of a fierce headache nodded and held a beseeching hand up to the furious pilot. Rosey got off of him and let him get up, while offering no helping hand. He watched as the shaking hands dusted off the uniform while trying to stand without weaving. Then the captain started toward his car, shuffling his feet and making a crooked path as he did so.

Rosey called after him, "You want to talk to me any more about this, you call and make an appointment, otherwise, no tickee no laundry! Coppice?"

As the olive drab car slowly drove away he realized just how much he was trembling. John Rosenthal had been an athlete all his life and as such, had been involved in his share of confrontations. On both the football field and the basketball court he had exhibited a willingness to scrap that often drew penalties as well as his coach's reprimands. This was different; he felt his life was actually on the line with this, and what he had just done would more than likely backfire on him. The captain seemed already suspicious of his story, and this wouldn't help to make the man any more ready to just drop the questioning and go away. Just the opposite was likely to happen. The realization didn't help his attitude at all.

John locked the terminal doors, strode to his car, and squealed the tires away from the parking place. He went straight home and slunk into the house like a beaten animal. Going to the small cabinet in the basement where he kept a stash of liquor, he produced a bottle and tipped it up for a long drink, gasping as the strong liquid coursed down his throat and hit his stomach like coals of fire. As the drink slowly took hold he took another and then put it away. Paige found him morosely reading the paper when she arrived from work.

"Hi Hon! Got supper ready?"

He looked at her and growled a reply to the negative.

"Ooooo...Have I got a growley old bear in my den?"

He looked over the paper, suddenly realizing none of this was her fault, and that she would be his strength through all this.

"I'm sorry, Paige. I had an especially bad day. That army crudball was back digging at me for nearly two hours and I just got tired of him. I've had my fill of army people."

"Honey, why does he keep coming back? Haven't you told the facts enough times for them?"

"Apparently not. I think they're going to try and make a case against me for those two idiots' deaths. If I think it over enough, I'm worried they might try to stick me with the responsibility for the thing."

Paige looked at him with an incredulous look, mouth dropping wide open, eyes as large as possible, and her breathing strictly intake for several seconds. Finally, when she had to breath out, she put forth a loud moan such as Rosey had never heard from his bride.

"Ohhh, no! Honey, how could you think that? How could THEY think about such a thing? What's happening with us, honey, and with Morgan and Kay? It seems like the country is coming apart and we're the target of injustice! What are we going to do?"

The last came in a wail and Rosey, in spite of the anger it stirred in him, clutched her to him in a protective hug. She broke down at that and sobbed uncontrollably for a long time. In the years he had known Paige Rosenthal, he had never known her to lose her cool. She had always been a rock, and as he realized the scope of her panic he contemplated telling her the truth. Then he rejected that premise under the guise of "protecting" her. No need to stoke the fires of fear right now. He would tell her later if need be.

Paige eventually ran down and stood silently in his arms for a long time, then looked him directly in the eyes and shuddered. "If anything ever happened to you, it would be the end of me," she offered.

"Nothing is going to happen to me, or us for that matter. I'll see to that." The hidden valley suddenly popped into his mind as he made the statement. He would contact Roy tomorrow and see if he was serious about the valley becoming a refuge.

Kay Montgomery sat straddling Morgan with his ears clutched in her hands as she gently, for the most part, shook his head back and forth, her nose a scant inch from his. "You listen to me, mister monster man, you're going to dump those guns at the store and become strictly a hardware. Morgan's sporting goods is now out of business. Ya got it, buster?"

He chuckled and defied her order. "No, my dear wifey, I ain't 'got it'. Do you realize the paperwork involved in 'dumping' that inventory? Besides, that ATF agent would only consider that an admission of guilt."

"I'm sorry, mister, but I'm not buying that. Why would he feel that way about it? Seems to me anyone with a snippet of common sense would see you were cooperating with the government."

"There, my dear," he replied in his best Burt Reynolds imitation, "is where you err. The man involved has no common sense. He proved that when he claimed I had hit him in the head so hard. Did he really think no one would seek the proof of that? No, he isn't that bright. But he IS that vengeful, hon, and he WILL be out for anything he can get to put me away. Even if he has to fabricate something, I'm fair game for him right now."

"What do you intend to do, then? Do you have any ideas?"

"Yes and no. Sheriff Hall plans to keep track of all he can where this guy is concerned. He has a couple of people sympathetic with a group he knows, so he should be able to keep on top of anything Peters plans to pull."

"Peters is the ATF agent?"

"Yeah. He's a real piece of work. Seems to think he should be able to boss everyone around in any way he pleases. He's a real bully type. I think it stems from having the little man syndrome; he needs to prove himself worthy of any man's respect and goes about it the wrong way."

"Well, we'll just have to pray for him and let the Lord take care of the problem."

"Man, Kay Montgomery, you have to nail things down for me, don't you? I'm not too sure I can pray for that man and mean it! So…it seems to me the Lord will hear your prayers with more compassion than mine since mine would be insincere. How do I get around the insincerity? He knows my heart!"

Kay wrapped her arms around her man and simply hugged him for a long span of time, then kissed him and, with no answer, trouped to the kitchen to prepare supper, humming to herself all the while. Morgan stood transfixed as he watched her graceful figure disappear through the door. If he only had her love for others!

Chapter 13

Anson Peters took careful inventory of his appearance in the mirror as he readied himself for the next meeting with Stokes. If he could successfully put the man off guard with this situation, he stood a chance of causing Stokes to lose face with those higher up and therefore position himself for a new position. He was ambitious to a fault, and the ATF job was not to his liking. After all, shouldn't a man of his brilliance be more than just an agent?

Peters had planned for nearly two years for this chance and he did not intend to let it slip away. With all the posturing he had accomplished by harassing gun dealers and others into bending their knees to him, the final act for his play was ready to start. Added to this were the records he had of different non-profit groups, some of them even churches that had folded under his scrutiny. It mattered not that the ATF had no jurisdiction over them, the fear resulting from the pseudo pressure he had exerted had accomplished much. Anson Peters was about to close out the career of John Harvey Stokes with a final thrust of carefully constructed power!

Fifteen miles upstream on the Maumee river, Stokes was holding a meeting behind closed doors in the Defiance County court house. Outside the room stood two military aids with rifles at hand, allowing no one entrance.

"The little twerp seems to think he's set me up by doing all this, doesn't he realize how strong my hold is on the people of this area who swing the hammers?"

A cowering man in a Mister Rogers type sweater replied to Stokes with a wavering voice. "I don't know any more than what I've told you, sir. You asked me to report anything to you concerning arms movement and underground activity and that's all I'm doing."

"So Peters has paid you to undermine your militia group to make himself look good, is that it?"

The stooge nodded nervously while looking at his feet. His fear of Stokes was so overwhelming that he had never seen the man's eyes; his were always looking down. He had been persuaded to infiltrate the area militia under the pretense of selling ammunition and hunting arms as a sideline. Stokes had figured contact would be made because of the way they had set the business up. Contrary to the manner in which all the legitimate dealers were established, the permit had been faked and the local enforcement officials bought off. This was bait for the militia in the area, hoping they would enlist the man into their ranks. The ironic part of that was that those locals were smarter than Stokes and his cronies and made the contact knowing they could feed him false information through this weasel named Ronald Hill.

Stokes, the president, vice president and most other government officials all made the same mistake which was fired by their ignorant egos; they considered any man not in a position like their own to be stupid and easy to fool. Elected officials down through the centuries have made the same mistake time and time again. There were, of course, the honest and common sense possessing men and women who were honest officials, but, as history has proven, they were sadly outnumbered so were mainly ineffective in the overall scheme of things. This was the beginning of the downfall of the U.S.

As Hill shifted nervously on his chair another member of the group, Henry Stoddard, took careful note of Stokes' writing a memo to himself on a pad before him. Stokes looked up as he tore the sheet from the pad and dismissed Hill with just a nod of his head. The man nearly leaped to his feet and started for the door.

"Wait a minute, Mister Hill, you forgot something."

At the sound of Stokes' voice, the fellow nearly collapsed,

such was his innate fear of his position there. With trembling hand, he turned to see what his commander had in mind. John Stokes reached into his inner coat pocket, retrieved a bill of large denomination and handed it to an aid standing nearby. The aid walked to Hill and handed it to him with the look of a snake about to strike. Hill took the bill and, while thanking them profusely, backed all the way to door before turning and nearly running from the room.

Once the door closed behind the informant, all eyes turned to Stokes. He contemplated for several minutes before speaking. When he finally spoke, it was through clenched teeth.

"Peters has lived out his usefulness. We can eliminate him from our list of pests and use that for a good benefit at the same time. Miles, what's your take on that peon at the Henry County airport? You think he had anything to do with your two guys trying to make holes in the ground with their heads?"

The uniformed officer stepped forward and nodded. "If he didn't, he wanted to. He jumped me when I was just there and caught me with a sucker punch that put me out of commission for a few minutes. To me, that spells guilt. I think we should pull him down."

"Intel says he's close to the gun dealer in Liberty Center that Peters has been hassling, right?"

"That's correct, sir. Their families are together most of the time in the evenings."

"Good. I want Peters to investigate that gun store at the hardware at night. Break in, then see to it someone with him leaves him there for good. Understand? As soon as their little tin badge sheriff does his investigation, we'll be poised to raid both the airport and the hardware and seize the properties plus the families.

"I'm sure a man who sells guns will fight back when he sees his wife grabbed. At least that's the way it's gonna look when he gets shot. The airport guy probably carries as well and will try to help out. Too bad they both are too stupid to give up and have to die trying to avoid arrest, don't you think?"

"When do we take care of Peters?"

"Well, let's crank up the pressure on him to get some results with this Montgomery guy and see how he reacts. It should be soon, before he reveals anything we don't want people to know. Meanwhile, try to arrange a visit to that store to find out the best way to get in without triggering the alarm I'm sure they have. Hank, can you do that?"

Stoddard's heart leaped at the question and he simply nodded. This was perfect; he could visit Montgomery and warn him without raising suspicion. He could also get word to Sheriff Hall and his staff to slow down their investigation. He felt no guilt at not warning Peters; the man was a thorn in the militia's side and best gone. There was no Christian act of kindness in his heart; this was war and he was prepared to do whatever it took to win. Anyway, the faith thing was far over rated in his estimate; no one had proven to him that a god even existed. Hank took leave of the room and proceeded to his car, being careful to walk slowly and appear to be just leaving a normal meeting of whatever committee people might think he was involved in.

The sheriff's car cruising on U.S. 24 saw the old bright yellow Plymouth coupe flying in the other direction and flicked on his lights, making the turn east right through the median divider grass. It took the deputy two miles of pedal to the medal running to catch the old hot-rod, but he finally pulled it over. The Chevy V-8 rumbled low and with the loping beat of a high rise cam asking to be loosed to scream into the high RPM world. Ted Sawyer smiled at the throbbing sound of good design in a souped up engine.

"License and registration please. I'm sure you know the drill by now, Mister Stoddard."

"Yeah, yeah, I know the drill. Here, now write your blasted ticket."

As he handed the required documents to Deputy Sawyer, any observer would have failed to note the inclusion of a folded paper transferred with them. The deputy walked back to his cruiser and sat inside to write the information down. What an observer would have been unable to know was that this "ticket" was a blank piece of paper and important information had just been passed to the Henry County sheriff and his deputies.

Hank Stoddard's hopped up old Plymouth, painted a

bright yellow and capable of ridiculous speeds with the powerful custom drive train was easily recognized. Ted Sawyer cruised this route every night at the same time for just one reason; to watch for Hank speeding. If the coupe flew by he knew there was information to be passed and would give chase.

The ticket would be published in the paper, but never listed in the court records except to show that a payoff had occurred even though none had. This arrangement allowed Stoddard a nearly fool-proof means of communicating with Hall and his staff. Morgan Montgomery and John Rosenthal would soon know there was a killing order out on them.

Sawyer pulled his cruiser into the parking place in front of the Henry County jail and strolled purposefully through the door. As soon as it was shut he fairly bounded into John Hall's office and tossed the paper onto the desk. Hall read it and turned pale.

"Man, Ted, we need to get to these guys right now. I wonder if Hank knows of a time frame?"

"He never indicated, as you can see, but I had an idea on the way here. What if we snatch Peters somehow and keep him unavailable for a couple of days or so? Their main purpose in this is not only to get rid of Morgan and Rosey, but just as much to clear Peters from their midst. If they can't get to him, they have to delay the operation, right?"

"That's good thinking, Ted, but what excuse do we use? How do we implement it? And who do we use; hooded guys, official arrest, what?"

"All good questions, and I haven't gotten that far yet. We need more minds than ours on this, but we have to act soon."

"Agreed. Put out an APB on the guy who just left the Malinta gas station without paying."

The APB would go out, the owner of the Malinta station would file a complaint, and all members of the militia in the area would know to meet at the next assigned clandestine meeting place that night. The meeting place was on a complex rotating schedule to prevent discovery by the enemy. Sadly, the enemy was the government forces in charge of the area. Immediate action was necessary, so a meeting was a must.

Hagan Marshall held up his hand to signal for silence and the twenty men who were the leaders of the area militia quieted from the hushed conversations they had been having.

"We have a rather urgent problem before us, people. The enemy is planning the elimination of two of our local men, and possibly their families as well. Their plan hinges on murdering our dearly beloved Anson Peters in Montgomery's store and then having a fire fight as they try to arrest him for the murder."

A quiet murmur of chuckles ran through the group as a result of his referring to Peters as their friend. John Hall stood and related the information he had received, then outlined Ted Sawyer's idea. There were many who knew Peters who volunteered to accomplish the task! Marshall turned them all down for he knew the mischief they desired to inflict on this hated agent.

An outsider would have wondered about the total control Hagan Marshall seemed to have over the assembly, but when he had started the militia, the rules were made clear. This would be a military organization, run on the military example of both the esprit de corps and the chain of command principle. Any one signing on had to agree to those standards or be rejected. Officers were established based on performance and previous military experience. There were ditch diggers, farmers, office workers, and some unemployed who were high ranking as a result of this and no one questioned their authority.

The organization was far reaching, going from coast to coast, but centered in the heartland of the corn-belt. Hagan Marshall had dedicated over ten years of his life to the establishing of this movement and was among the top echelon.

Ted Sawyer stood and requested to be heard. Upon acknowledgement he spoke. "I've thought some more on this, and I think we need to call in someone from a different locality to do this. That way, should Peters ever get sight of a face, or anything like that, the people would be out of his area and less likely to ever be recognized."

"I like that, Ted. I like it so well that I've already requested three men from another place. None of you need to know where, but they're already on their way."

John Hall had told Marshall of Ted's idea and the man had acted on it without consulting the rest of the group. Should they have objected, the people on their way could have been sent back with no problem, but this way there would be no time lost.

Some low key discussion followed, but in the end, the plan was approved to capture the agent as soon as possible and secret him away for a few days. He would be allowed to escape, but would also be armed with the knowledge of Stokes' plan to eliminate him. Marshall desired to keep from any killing when he could, plus, the mistrust established would be useful to his group. He knew from his experience in counter-intelligence operations that any undermining of trust within a government, especially one of questionable goals, was invaluable. This was a case where government training was paying off in ways they had not intended. There were times when Hagan Marshall almost felt guilty over this. Almost.

The large red numbers on Anson Peters' digital clock showed 3:17 AM when he opened his eyes to answer the obnoxiously ringing phone. As he tried unsuccessfully to wipe the sleep from his eyes and replace it with alertness he knocked the receiver to the floor. Swearing and grumbling, he finally lay hold of it and growled a greeting of some sort. The voice coming through was hushed.

"You want a big bust, ya need to come to Sherwood. Slip in behind the station there and wait. Guns are being shipped yet this morning, but ya better hurry. And bring a few hundred cash with ya to pay me for my information, ya hear."

The line went dead and he blinked to clear his still foggy mind of debris. He had received prank calls before, but always checked them out just in case they might be legit. His thirst for power and position often overrode his judgment. He was out of bed and dressing before he even gave thought to where Sherwood was.

Peters left Defiance in a hurry, and when he turned onto state route 18 his tires were objecting to the speed with which he took the corner. Then he broke out in another fit of swearing as a large box truck blocked the road. It sat there across the highway in a manner that prevented his going around it and appeared to be abandoned. Peters threw the car into park and piled out. His intention was to either move the vehicle himself or find those responsible and straighten them out. His rage doubled when he jerked the driver's door open and found a loaded and cocked 44 magnum sticking in his face. He nearly grabbed for is own gun, but the arrival of a second weapon from beneath the truck convinced him it was useless.

He found his hands quickly bound behind him and a pair of men roughly dragged him to the rear of the truck. The vehicle started and backed into the driveway it had been exiting. The doors opened and a ramp was slid out. Peters found his feet being forced up the ramp as he heard his car start and had to hurry to get to the top before his car ran him down! As soon as both he and his car were inside, the ramp came next and he was forced to plunk down in a corner as he saw the doors shut, and felt the truck start to move. The abduction was smooth and precise, and Anson Peters was terrified.

Chapter 14

When the sheriff's car slid into a parking spot at the airport, Rosey had a bad feeling about it. Then when he saw Morgan exit the passenger side door, the feeling got worse. Morgan was not a man easily frightened, but his face was white and his hands trembled slightly as he took hold of the door handle to the terminal. Ted Sawyer was right behind Morgan with John Hall following. 'This isn't good,' he thought to himself.

"Hi John," was Ted's greeting while Morgan just nodded to him.

"Got anything going on in your office, John?" asked Hall.

"Nothing right now, but it looks like there's gonna be. Come on in."

"We have some information that really needs to be shared now, so we brought Morgan with us so we only need to go over it once." Ted was dead serious and both civilians shared a look of concern.

"What's it all about, guys? How does it apply to both of us? Morg', you look like death warmed over, so this must really be bad stuff." Rosey was starting to perspire as he took in the three men's countenances.

"Rosey, I know a little bit about what's happening; enough to scare the bejeebers out of me! Gotta say I don't like it one bit."

"Men, here's the story. The big-shot provost marshal has decided Peters is a liability he doesn't need or want. John R, he also has word of your little fiasco with Miles Trent, that army dude you roughed up. As a result, he's planning to have Peters break into your hardware, Morg, and be found there with a bullet in the head. That makes you a suspect because of your tiff with him.

"Good grief, you can't be serious! What the blazes am I supposed to do?"

"Only you can answer that, Morgan," replied Hall. "You and John, here, need to put your heads together and figure a place to disappear to for a while. And I'm afraid that's for a very long while!"

Rosey had turned pale during the conversation, but recovered his equilibrium enough to grab Morgan by the sleeve. "Morg, I may have it. Remember that valley I told you about? No one would ever wonder in there by accident." Great scott, Rosey, how in the world do we convince our wives to go native in a deserted valley, even for a while?"

"Hey bud, it's either that or visit our graves. Whadda you think they'll choose?"

"Listen, you maniac; we'd have to gather supplies enough to last for who knows how long, including, mister genius, utensils, stoves, tents, all the things we now use our houses for. I'm sorry, Rosey, but that's a ridiculous idea."

John Hall interrupted, "Morgan, you may not have a choice. Remember, we're talking about the possibility of you two being killed, here. Whatever you do, it needs to be quick, and it needs to get you far from here. Now, as far as temporary quarters and supplies, we have several avenues we can go to for those things through the organization. This is one of the situations we have discussed many times, and didn't just talk about, but prepared for."

The two friends stared at one another for several seconds, then Morgan breathed deeply and shook his head. "I'm sorry guys, but I'm not going to subject my family to this sort of disappearing act. Kay and I have worked hard for our home, and I'll fight to keep it. I won't even put our little dog through living in a tent somewhere in those God-forsaken mountains you're talking about."

Chapter 15

"John, I got word from Hank that he needs to see one of us," Ted whispered to the sheriff.

"Any idea what's up, Ted?"

"None whatsoever. He just left the coded note in my car. I figure if it's coded, he must need it soon."

"Yeah, you're right. It could be about Rosey and Morgan. What's the location for the meet?"

"The forest shack on road fourteen. Tonight, between seven and eleven. Couldn't pin it down any closer than that."

"Okay, you come in from the north edge of the woods and I'll keep watch while you do, then half an hour later, I'll slip in from the east. Let's be there early, as soon as dusk slips in. If he has to wait, too bad, but I don't think he'll try to get there in broad daylight."

"Ha, you know Hank, he might be there right now! The guy has the patience of an Indian."

"Ted, Hank IS part Indian. Algonquin, I think."

"Seriously? I didn't know that. Well, I need to go home and let Julie know I possibly have a long night ahead and grab a quick meal. See ya later."

That evening the shack buried deep in the woods along county road fourteen found an occupant in the tall maple tree to the west gazing down at it. Henry Stoddard was firmly planted in the branches just above the area where the trunk split into two large limbs. His ear buds that were attached to the scanner were silent, but he left them in just to be aware of any radio activity from the military. This was probably his most dangerous time since infiltrating the provost's organization, but two lives were to be directly affected and two or more families just as much the same.

A faint sound of cloth on brush made a slight whisper from his right and he quickly looked that way. A shadowy form slipped silently toward the shack, pausing after every other step. The little shack, scarcely ten by ten and not even six feet high appeared to hunker down at the stranger's approach. The darkness inside waited for any with the audacity to invade the space, and a sort of foreboding atmosphere prevailed.

When the dark form reached the opening that served as a door, Henry heard a low whisper, "Who's waiting here?"

"Up here, John. I see another coming from the east, slip inside 'til we know who it is, I'll cover you."

Sheriff John Hall drew his weapon and slipped in through the door, needing to bend nearly in half in order to do so. Within a few minutes more the second shadowy form slipped stealthily up to the door and whispered a like question. Hall replied from within and Henry Stoddard lowered his body from the tree after a final scrutiny of the area.

"What's happening, Hank?"

"Well, John, the provost is stepping up the hit for Rosey and Morgan. He's also ordered their families taken prisoner and shipped off to who knows where to avoid anyone questioning the disappearance of Rosey and Morg. He's decided to just have them all vanish instead of trumping up charges. Says it's easier that way. Next week is the designated time. You have to get them all out of here, and fast."

"Good land, Hank, Morgan is digging his heels in, says he'll stay and fight."

"Tell him it isn't just him, but his family. That includes his sons!"

Ted spoke up, "I'll get hold of big Al Green and have him start putting supplies together for them, but I still think we need to have another supply station like his in the Midwest, one just isn't enough, no matter what the risk is of being found out!"

"I couldn't agree more, Ted, but now isn't the time to be campaigning for that, now's the time for a move!"

"You're right of course, John, but as soon as these folks are safe. . ."

"Yeah, I know, and we'll jump on Marshall to get after it."

Hank slipped from the shack without another sound and was gone into the darkness. He was confident the two lawmen would care for the rescue; his job was done. Ted and John whispered plans for a few minutes, then each of them slipped away as well. Morgan Montgomery was going to have to succumb to reason.

Brian Montgomery was surprised that morning as he opened his email. There was a message from big Al Green in the code he had explained to Brian when they were together. Brian had insisted he would never use it, but Al had won out and they had covered it thoroughly before Brian had left the lodge in the Boundary Waters.

His eyes seemed to be fooling him as he deciphered the communiqué telling him all the supplies for a month would be ready and waiting at a small county airport three days from then. Further instructions on which building would hold them and the coordinates of the airport ended the cryptic message. What in the world was this all about?

He called his mother and questioned her, with no more information being offered from her. She was shocked and questioning. He then called the store,

"Dad, what's going on?"

"What do you mean?"

Brian explained in short, terse sentences that they needed to meet immediately. "I can't talk now, Dad, but you simply HAVE to meet me at home NOW. I'll be there in ten minutes." The line went dead as he hung up and Morgan knew he might as well close up and do as his number one son said.

"So you see, Dad, something is drastically wrong here, or Al wouldn't risk contacting me, and he wouldn't go to all the bother of getting things ready. Dad, he even gave me the total weight of everything he'll have ready!"

Morgan was about to reply, and not too nicely, when a car pulled into the drive. A man exited the passenger's side and came to the side door. He was about to knock when Morgan swung the door open.

"Can I help you, sir?"

"Are you Morgan Montgomery?"

"Yes, I am."

The dark suited individual wordlessly handed him a paper, turned and stalked back to the car. Once inside, the car backed out of the drive and disappeared. When Morgan opened the paper, he saw it was a subpoena. In anger he slammed the door and stomped to the kitchen table.

"What is it , Dad?"

"It's a . . . waaaaiit a minute. Brian, look at this!"

As Brian looked over his father's shoulder, he saw the paper was an official looking document on the outside, but a handwritten message from John Hall on the back. He had used this means of contacting Morgan to avoid suspicion. There was no doubting Hall's handwriting, for he had filled out many a paper in the store.

"Brian, are you reading this?"

"Yes, Dad. I'm also trembling as I do! Do you think we can trust it?"

"I'm afraid so, son. I know John Hall too well to doubt him. They've receive word somehow. They're giving me no choice, son, now I have to go along with Rosey's crazy scheme, at least for a while!"

"Dad, do you really think Sue, Cal and I need to disappear as well?"

"Son, if John says so, we better do it. Remember your Catholic friend while we're going through this. That was the most heinous thing I can imagine some human doing to another. These people are being led by Satan and his minions, and they have no scruples. I've gotten that message loud and clear now. We'll do the disappearing act for a while until we can find new ground from which to work our lives back into society. If ever we can!"

The last was added with a bitter note. "I need to go to the store and start a list of what we take from here. That means I need to weigh everything, too. Wanna help?"

"Of course."

Rosey climbed from the Cherokee and turned to help his lady student down. She handed him her flight case and then her hand as he bowed deeply from the waist in a mock act of knighthood.

"Why, thank you sir Bowsalot, you are so gallant!"

"Nothing at all, my lady, nothing at all. After all, that last ILS approach was your best yet, so you earned a little extra respect. Note, please, the key word there was LITTLE."

"Hey, that just blew it, coach! Here I thought we had reached a breakthrough between instructor and student."

"We have. The breakthrough means that now I can start getting you ready for your instrument check-ride and then be rid of you! Rid of you, do you hear?"

"Not so fast, oh stealer of my money, now I want to start on my commercial license! You're not getting rid of me that easy, fella, chivalry or no chivalry."

He let go with a sigh and opened the door into the small terminal for her. John Hall was filling out some papers at the counter and smiled at the local doctor's wife. "Afternoon, Dawn. You and Doc still submitting yourselves to this slave driver?"

"Yes, sheriff, and I don't understand why, but I guess it's a matter of charity for us, he looks like he needs the money, he's so thin! I need to talk to my husband about this unhealthy specimen still flying. He has to be dangerous to those on the ground!"

The debriefing of the flight took ten minutes and when they came out, Hall was still there. As Dawn drove away, Hall dragged Rosey into the restroom.

"I know this probably isn't bugged," he started in a very hushed voice. Rosey could barely hear him. John Hall spent the next few minutes explaining to Rosey what was to happen the next week, and had no trouble convincing him the escape, if it was to be called that, needed to be immediate. He also assured Rosey the Montgomery's were preparing as well.

As the sheriff drove down the lane leading from the airport Rosey pulled his one Cheyenne from the hanger to the fuel pump and topped off all tanks. Even if the load was going to be so heavy they needed to leave a tank down for weight, tough, the bird was just going to have to lift more! He had never ignored a weight and balance calculation in his flying career, but this was different.

Once the ship was topped of, he towed it to a remote "T" hanger far from the main buildings. He then repeated the action with the other Cheyenne, finding another "T" hanger near the first. They could load the planes there, out of sight of the public eye. He left both hangers' doors open. Then he returned to the office and charted the route to Turnbull's for Morgan. He decided they would attempt to fly together all the way there, but just in case...

When Morgan and Cal were in the store, Cal cared for the customers while Morgan collected equipment for their trip. He placed the collection in a sequestered corner in the back room. It consisted of at least one sidearm for each man, all but one of those being .44 magnums, the other a .45 since he lacked enough of the magnums for all four men. He had three .44 magnum rifles on hand, so they would have plenty of ammunition that would switch from handgun to rifle. He then took seven 410 gauge revolvers, all he had, and the ammo for them.

In addition to that collection he took all five thirty-ought six rifles and all the ammo for them as well as for the .44's and stacked that with the firearms.

Then he took every arrow in the store and three bows for the growing pile. After he was satisfied with the collection of fire-power and a knife for every person he started on the camping gear, choosing carefully with both room and weight in mind. Who could tell how long they were going to be called on to exist in the wilds?

While the two were busy in the store, Brian was in a chat mode with Big Al Green. After an intense hour he had a list of all the goods to be left at a small county airstrip on the way. He even had weights listed. As soon as he could close down he left for home. He picked up Sue and they headed for Morgan's house for final planning. Sue was a wreck emotionally, and he wasn't far behind. This was upsetting the tranquil life of the peaceful Midwest couple and their family as never before.

At the supper table in the Montgomery house, it was a

very quiet and hushed meal. Rosey and Paige were with them, and the planning had been covered before Sue and Kay put the food on the table. They would pack immediately, procure the equipment from the store, and leave during the night as soon as possible. The tension was such that a knocking on the door caused no end of jumping of nerves and gasping of breath by each and every person.

Rosey pulled his little "pop-gun" as Cal called it and stood ready to defend all of them single-handedly. Morgan pushed him into the dining room with whispered instructions to "Stay there!" He followed that command with, "That .25 caliber will get you killed yet, I'm gonna throw that useless piece of junk away as soon as I get this cared for, whatever it is. You've got to have a REAL gun."

When he opened the door, expecting the worst, it was Ted, dressed in civvies instead of his uniform. He looked troubled.

"I don't want to intrude, looks like you have company, but this is urgent. You need to get out of here tonight, I just got word they've stepped up their program for you guys. Peters escaped the guys holding him, didn't believe our guys about Stokes wanting him dead, and he is no more. They did him in and will haul the body to your store as soon as it gets dark. You want anything from there, better get it now, and I mean NOW!"

Not another word was spoken as the four men joined Ted and rushed to the store. Parking in the alley, Morgan tripped a hidden latch he had installed years before on the small equipment door and slipped through. Cal followed him and the two of them started handing things through to the others while Ted stood watch. As soon as the things were loaded in Morgan's van he and Cal headed for the airport while Rosey went to pick up Paige so they could pack the personal things they would take. Ted followed Rosey at a discreet distance since he felt the Rosenthal's would be the primary target until the dead ATF agent was dumped in the hardware store. Ted was ready for a gun battle if necessary, his jaw clamped firmly in a set that boded no good for any he had to fight. The illegal automatic weapon beside him would have no hesitation applied in its use should he have resistance from any source.

The Montgomery house was a disaster of activity with

Kay and Cal grabbing what they thought they needed, with Kay getting Morgan's stuff around. Cal did the carrying to his car while she packed. Kay picked some kitchen utensils she felt they would need, but Cal rejected them on the basis that Morgan had taken special lightweight camping gear for that purpose.

As the sun tipped the horizon, Kay and Cal turned into the airport drive. Cal pointed to their northeast at where the back road exited the woods and when Kay looked, she could see Brian's car appear just behind Rosey's. Now, if they could just fit everything into the airplanes!

All three cars drove into the tee-hanger since Morgan and Cal had the Cheyenne's pulled out already and had the number one ship Rosey would fly nearly loaded with all the equipment from the store. His family would all fly together in the other ship, so he gave Rosey the bulk of the equipment so as to distribute the weight properly between the two planes.

Clothing was quickly loaded and Morgan called them all together. "This isn't the way I like to fight; by running, but we have been given no choice. Brian has the instructions as to where we find the supplies to be left for us, as well as the frequency to monitor for emergency contact with his friends' organization should it be necessary.

"We'll fly low, very low, and have no communications between us on the radios, but I have two walky-talkies here we can safely use. They're such low power they'll never be monitored and can plug into the twelve volt outlets in the ships. Any questions? Rosey, you lead, you have the new stuff for navigation and a lot more recent experience than I have. Let's pray together now, then we're out of here."

The last was said through a choked up voice. They clasped hands, even John and Paige, and Brian began praying before any of the others could collect their thoughts.

"Lord, we don't want to do this, but we have to. We didn't choose this trial, but we have it. We're frightened, angry, and full of mixed feelings, but here we are, and we know You are with us, whether we're right in this that we do, or whether we're wrong. We haven't had time to consult You first, so please forgive us if we should try another approach.

"We ask for Your great protection, comfort, and the peace that passes all understanding as Your Word promises. We ask for You to show us how to fight these battles, and take us safely to Your destination. Thank You our Heavenly Father, we pray this in the precious name of our Lord and Savior, Jesus. Amen."

Not another word was said and the trembling group of refugees climbed numbly into the airplanes and stared straight ahead as Morg and Rosey started the engines. The turbines whirred into life and soon four propellers were dragging the heavily loaded ships toward the runway. Darkness was rapidly chasing the sun such that it tried escaping by ducking behind the horizon. As it succeeded, dusk laughed its way onto the little county strip and soon two vessels of mercy roared down the 5000 foot runway together. Rosey hadn't bothered with a preflight run-up, they had no choice but to go, so why bother? As flaps and landing gears came up to nestle in their appointed places, a sob from more than one throat was drowned out by the roar of the turbines. Stress and "code red" hormones filled the cabins of both airplanes to the extent of seeming liquid with their presence. Silence settled in except for the now-silent weeping of those not busy with flying chores. Morgan wondered if Rosey was having as much trouble seeing the instrument panel as he was.

Chapter 16

At the little county strip in the boonies of Nebraska the lead Cheyenne went to full pitch, one notch of flaps and gear down as soon as it was on final approach. Morgan had taught John Rosenthal to keep his speed up until on final because, "Hey fella, why do we fly? To get there quicker, right? Then why slow down before ya have to? Final approach is plenty soon for all this slow stuff."

All Morgan's family in the following ship watched nervously as Morgan set down in formation within seconds of Rosey, wasting no time in a separated approach. He stayed just off Rosey's right wing and landed military formation style as Rosey called it. They had listened on the assigned emergency frequency for the message to abort the landings because of danger from the local officials, and, hearing none, rolled on to the hanger as instructed by Big Al to Brian.

Two men exited the hanger and guided them to a ramp just to the side. As soon as the props quit turning, two others ran toward them pushing carts loaded with supplies. The loading was accomplished in little time without a word spoken. When they were done, the four men wordlessly shook hands with the pilots and ran to a truck, roaring out of the airport as fast as possible. The engines were soon whining and taxi under way. They were airborne in less than fifteen minutes from their landing time. Roy Turnbull would see them later today.

The low power walkie-talkie scratched at Morgan's ear as Rosey told him to go ahead and land on the long, grass airstrip below. Rosey would buzz Turnbull's ranch buildings to let him know someone was there. As Morgan taxied back down the strip he saw Rosey already approaching on final. The tired, hungry, nerved up passengers climbed gratefully from the Cheyenne and simply plopped their bodies down in the grass by the plane.

Tension was high, moral was low, and tears pushed to escape from every eye as Rosey and Paige departed their ship. Paige silently walked over to sit by Kay, snuggle up to her and begin sobbing silently. That broke the dam for Kay who then joined her in the shaking shoulder society. Sue was soon wrapped around the two of them and together, the three women cried out their pent-up emotions. Were it possible to read the minds of the four men, one would have seen envy over the freedom of their ladies to release the day's troubles in that manner.

As it was, if that same one would have examined the eyes of the men closely, moisture in copious amounts, just begging for freedom would have been detected. Roy's four wheeler interrupted the spell as he roared up.

"John! What in the world are you doing here? With TWO ships? Man, guy, I'm booked up in three days! Why didn't you . . . wait, I get it. You had to run? Man, John, this really stinks, I mean, it REALLY stinks!"

"These must be the family you told me about last time we talked. Folks, we have a little time to get you set for John's valley, then we'll start on getting you some civilization over there. For now, you're going to have to rough it. I'll start with the food prep first."

"Never mind that, Roy," spoke Rosey, "We're all set there. All we need to steal from you is three or four tents for now and a chain saw with fuel.

"By the way, Roy, meet Morgan Montgomery, my best friend ever, his wife, Kay, son's Brian and Cal, Brian's wife Sue, and my BEST best friend, also my wife, Paige. Folks, Roy Turnbull, one fine hombre."

Hands were shaken all around as the taciturn Roy just nodded to each as they clasped hands solemnly. "Folds, I truly am sorry you've been pried loose from your good lives so blamed suddenly, please know I'll help you get by in every way I possibly can, and I think we can get through this together. John's canyon will be safe for a long time if we hide the planes and tents well, and I think I know just how to do that. The satellites can't look at that location from the right angle to see what I've had in mind for John once we started talking about this possible need for stealth. For now, let's get you to the house, you must be hungry, tired, and just plain bent out of shape. Can't say as anyone can blame ya for that. Load the ladies first, I'll come back for the guys. If you want anything from the planes, grab it now and we'll be off."

Two hours later, Roy's wife Joan had served the weary travelers a hot meal, sent the ladies off for a relaxing bath, and prepared beds in three cabins for them. Tomorrow's trip into the canyon could wait.

"I've looked that canyon over for a long time, John and Morgan, and it's absolutely the ideal for your needs. There's an unbelievable shelf of rock overhanging the northeast corner of the thing, and I seriously doubt if the satellites can see under there.

Roy continued, "There is room enough for you to conceal both planes and, if you wanted to build a house or two, there's even room for that. I've known that place for long enough to feel confident no rock will be falling for decades."

"That's all well and good, Roy, and getting in is easy enough but there's those little streams in several places that would tear the planes up if we drop a gear down into them. We have to do some leveling before we can put a plane the size of these two in there safely!"

"Well, John, I remembered you pointing those out to me when we were in there, and with the things you told me on that trip, I knew that needed to be cared for.

"So here's what I did; I muled some culvert sections in, dumped them over the side, and destroyed most of them when I did so. When that had failed, I contacted some people I know who are sympathetic and they choppered sections in for me. We've placed those in and bridged all those little streams and bad places during the last month. You're all set. Now, be advised, those sympathetic people are gonna be lookin' at the place as a possible refuge for more folks like yourselves. Things are heatin' up all over, and we'd like to have a strategic hide-out for a center of operations for the militia.

"You've not known this, John, but I was contacted for such things two years ago. I joined in right then, been searchin' for the best place ever since. Couldn't get the canyon out of my mind all that time, and as soon as I showed it to them last week, it was a definite go. I hope you don't mind, but there's no help for it, we need a center of operations that's well hidden, and that's it."

Morgan looked at all those in his party. "I'm not the happiest about that, Roy; that could put my family in even more danger than we are now."

"Hey, we're all in more danger than we realize. This thing is close to rebellion and shooting, and it's getting' closer every day, Morgan. The canyon is your best bet. You'll be there alone for several weeks. I know that's likely to be hard on your ladies and youngsters, but you have to keep them looking up. Make it an adventure. There's enough game in that canyon to feed an army, so you can start hunting your winter meat. I'll show you how to smoke your meat for preservation, and there's time to plant a bit of a garden once I get the necessary tools and seed into you.

"When John told me what was going on, I started planning for your survival and for your needs for other things, like comfort. You'll be glad to know we're planning on some houses in there fairly soon."

"Houses! You can't be serious! Just how long do you think it will take to mule train supplies in and get down the canyon walls?" Rosey was thinking of the difficulty he and Rot had experienced just getting down into the canyon to hunt.

"John, have you pilots ever heard of helicopters?" The sage humor of their guide slipped right beyond their grasp as he chuckled.

"Hey, just where do you think you'll find a chopper you can trust, and how much can what you and your boy scouts find carry, Roy?"

Rosey was getting worked up and waved his arms excitedly.

"John Rosenthal, it's obvious to me that you still don't comprehend the magnitude of the militia we're involved with.

They have whole bases pretty much dedicated to the resistance. Naturally, they have to be careful to keep it as hushed as possible because of some troops being loyal to Washington, but these people are good at what they do best, and what they do best is clandestine operations. Trust me; your families won't be that alone all that long. Granted, some of the people coming in won't be model citizens, but they can be controlled."

"I'm liking this less and less the further we go," said Morgan.

"Like we have a choice, with the government after our scalps, c'mon Morg, we gotta do it!" Rosey was getting excited and starting to wave his arms as he talked.

"HEY! I know that, doesn't mean I have to like it, so get off my case Rosenthal!"

Brian stepped in between the three and tried to calm things down. "Listen, we'll do whatever it takes for however long it takes, but you guys are going to calm down for now and settle into the planning."

"You're right, Brian, you're right. Roy, how long is the strip you put culverts in?"

"I can't rightly say, Morgan, maybe three quarters of a mile at the most. Maybe a tad less."

"Boy, that's going to really cramp us, being loaded like we are. How's the wind usually doing there?"

"Most generally from the west end, the end opposite the strip. But there's several miles of clear ground from that way and you could be down really low and set up to touch down at the very end of the smooth part."

"Uuumm, I don't like that. Mountain flying is touchy, unpredictable at times, and I prefer to always be into the wind regardless. We'll have to look it over when we get there. Rosey, let's be off as soon as the light allows in the morning and go have a look. We'll plan on landing to the west, according to what you've explained to me, but keep our options open. Sound okay?"

'You bet, Morg, you're the ex-duster pilot, I'll follow your lead. By the way, out here, the expression is 'first light' for when we start. If you're gonna be a cowboy, ya gotta learn to talk like one."

That comment earned Rosey a smack on the back of his

head that really wasn't all that gentle. He cracked up at that, knowing he'd won the little exchange of barbs.

Two loaded Cheyenne's circled the valley, or canyon, whichever term one chose to use in reference to the long hole in the ground, and Morgan and Rosey were on the low powered hand-held radios as they did.

"Rosey, keep circling, I'm going to drop down into the valley from the west and see how the place feels. This is ridiculous; those walls must be a couple thousand feet high!"

"That's close, Morg, go for it."

Morgan slowed the ship to approach speed, dropped flaps as soon as the speed was down far enough, and slipped down into the west end of the valley. He then accelerated back to cruise, with raised flaps, and zipped along the valley floor at twenty feet. He didn't like what he saw.

Applying full power and pulling into a steep climb he soared up and out a half mile from the east end and looked for Rosey. The other Cheyenne soon joined him from the north.

The radio crackled with Rosey's voice. "How's it look?"

"Nasty. The sage growing on the floor of the valley is laying nearly straight down with the wind from the west end, just like he said was likely. We don't have a choice as to which end to go in from. I did see a break in the wall right at the east end, I'm going to take a look at that. Follow me."

"Roger that."

Morgan circled the east end of the valley and saw the split in the wall he had noticed. It was roughly a hundred feet wide and was a good seven hundred to a thousand feet deep. The distance through looked to be from five to six hundred feet. If the turbulence was not bad, it would serve them quite well.

"Cheyenne two."

"Yeah, go."

"Remember the maneuver I taught you for going between two trees with the Pawnee?"

"Uuuh, yeah . . . what about it?"

"We're going to slow to best angle speed, drop flaps and gear, and then hit that split in that manner. Just remember to give full power just before rolling onto one wing. Keep in mind how heavy these beasts are loaded and plant your opposite rudder to the floor! Right wing down is best because we need to slip over to the right a bit for the final line-up with the so-called smooth section. That means all the left rudder ya got."

"Roger, I'll see how you do from above and try to monkey you. For cryin' out loud, be careful"

"Always."

Morgan swung to the east and slowed the plane to approach speed while dropping to an altitude far below the imposing rim of the canyon. He eyed the notch in the rim as he lined up on it. The thousand feet looming above him was frightening, to say the least, but at over a hundred miles an hour he was now committed!

He purposely lined up at an angle to the notch and at the last minute he snapped full right aileron and left rudder combined with full throttle and back pressure on the yoke. The result was a curving knife-edge flight directly through the notch and they popped out into the canyon.

He immediately throttled to full idle, flaps down and gear extended and let the ship fall like a rock. A hundred feet from the bottom he eased throttles in to slow, even arrest, the descent and assumed a nearly level attitude to cause the plane to slow its plummeting path and simply let it thump to the earth under nearly full power. A true short field approach with a "couple" of variations!First, it was short field approach over a THOUSAND feet obstacle; not the FAA's typical fifty foot obstacle; and second, the Cheyenne literally blasted onto the runway. But he got it stopped in no time at all and found a spot where he could pull of to the right to allow Rosey access. To say there was sweat on his forehead was an understatement! He was afraid to look at his passengers to see how they were feeling.

"Piper two, carry plenty of power after you set the final decent up on this side and get way behind the power curve with your attitude and you'll be fine. I sort of splatted down, but could have done better if I would have slowed the fall sooner. I waited a bit too long to apply power and really left my marks, I'm afraid. We'll be praying for ya."

"Roger that. I don't mind tellin' ya, you're nuts. I mean just plain nuts. It looked to me from up here like you actually crashed into the ground. Hang on, here we come!"

Taking his cue from watching Morgan's maneuver, Rosey stood the plane on the right wing with full power but as soon as he was through the notch he chopped the power until he had flaps and gear fully down and had descended half of the thousand remaining feet. Then he pulled the nose up and applied partial power until the ship was near stall speed and shoved the throttles forward "to the firewall." His touch down wasn't as hard as Morgan's, but Rosey was much more current as a pilot than his friend and had the utmost respect for any man who could master the big Cheyenne after several years of not flying at all!

They shut down and climbed out, beginning a survey of the canyon to see where they could best camouflage the planes, if at all. Rosey pointed at the end they had approached from and they walked the half mile back to their touchdown spots.

After finding nothing in the way of cover there, they continued to the very end of the canyon and discovered a place around a bit of a curve in the north wall that hung out over the floor an almost frightening distance. They stood next to the wall and looked up to find they were a good two hundred feet under the outcropping! This was their hanger.

Leaving the family and Paige behind, the two trekked back to the planes to taxi them back. As they did, Cal and Brian began to move large stones to clear a path for the parking area. The very nature of the overhang above them would allow them to effectively camouflage the presence of the two large ships and also give a place for the tents to be rather hidden from high up seeking eyes.

Roy had promised help as soon as he could arrange it, and they counted heavily on his supplying them with information as to the conditions back in Ohio. Maybe they could be out of here fairly soon.

The two Cheyenne's whined their way to the chosen place and whistled relief at being shut down. Morgan and Rosey climbed out, retrieved the tow bars from the back and proceeded to push, grunt, grumble and manipulate the heavy monsters into a suitable parking place, tails to the canyon wall and tied down close together. Then they proceeded to unload all the supplies and equipment. Tents were pitched, fire pits dug and lined with rocks, and water bags filled.

Rosey's experiences as a hunter in the mountains proved invaluable when it came to establishing the camp as a livable community for the three families. It was decided that Cal would have his own tent before they left Ohio, so they had loaded a smaller one for his use. That made a little settlement of four canvas structures nestled together. Morgan had wanted to make the camp next to the old abandoned cabin ruins Rosey and Roy had found on the last trip in until Rosey informed him of the rattlesnakes who had claimed it. All of them shuddered to think of the prospects of those creatures and Rosey cautioned them to always be on the lookout for the snakes. Paige voted for them to sleep in the planes when she heard of them!

The campsite was well established by mid-afternoon and the troops then started looking for ways to improve on the comfort of the "home site." Small saplings close together found hammocks swinging between them while larger trees suddenly sprouted food supplies suspended between them at heights above the reach of wildlife.

Morgan set up a screened tent for their dining room while Rosey and the boys set a second one up as the artillery tent with all the guns and ammunition stored at the readiness for action they all prayed would never be needed. It was decided everyone would carry a sidearm at all times, and the three ladies were presented with the 410 gauge shotgun revolvers for their use. They would receive training tomorrow on the care and use of the weapons.

The men strapped on the heavy 44 magnum revolvers that would provide them with the most power available from a sidearm. The weight of the guns was a detriment, but the fire power at their command was worth the encumbrance. Rosey was sure there would be grizzlies in the valley. He reminded them of the fact that even the mighty 44's would be small in comparison the angry power of such a bear. Avoidance was the best policy when possible.

As the day began to drift into long shadows from the west they started their fires and tried to settle into an evening of rest. The unfamiliar surroundings, the terrible strain that sent them there and the uncertainty of the future weighed heavily on each and every one of them. Sleep would not come easy that night, nor would it be restful once it did slip into their bodies.

The following morning found the little troop shivering in the fresh, mountain air. Back in Ohio the eight hundred feet above sea level didn't supply the same temperatures as the seven thousand feet at the valley floor. No one had dressed for the night's chill and they were even more miserable than before. The fire was built to a roaring blaze so they could get warm enough to change into the day's outfits. If one would have listened closely they would have heard much grumbling about the temps.

"Roy should be starting out today with his mule train, so we should see him around three days from now."

"Great, Rosey, and what do you think he'll do with the frozen bodies he finds here?" Kay asked.

"Darned if I know, but whatever it is, I'll help him. Don't be such a pansy."

Chapter 17

If they had been able to observe Roy at that moment, they would have watched as the taciturn guide traced his finger along a map for the watching group of men in uniforms or rugged hunting outfits. The oldest, with the eagles of a general on his collar, was grilling Roy as to the air time involved for the trip and what the extra equipment and food provisions were for.

"I can help you, but the logistics aren't gonna be easy. Getting lumber in there will be the hardest, and there's no power within miles, so everything will have to be done with hand tools. You say you have the means to facilitate the lumber delivery, can I ask how that would happen?"

"Sure, Mister Turnbull. Remember, we're made up of thousands of different people from hundreds of different occupations and that includes military personnel. We can get a big chopper from a contractor in here that can lift and deliver enough lumber for a small building on every trip in. We can even get a few army engineers to help if we need to."

The secretive smile accompanying the statement sort of grated on Roy, but he said nothing. His guest continued with explanation of the proposed venture for another fifteen minutes and then went quiet, leaving the ball in Roy's court.

"I was glad to show you the valley I knew would surely fill your need, I even have the coordinates written down at the house. Sounds like I better erase that record, though, in case the wrong people come calling.

"Look, I'm in total agreement with what you people are doing, but never had any contact with you until recently. Mister

Marshall, how did you hear of my place? I'm a little nervous about that, 'cause I've only talked to one individual concerning this situation we find our nation in and he wouldn't have mentioned it to anyone because he figured on having need of the valley in question for himself."

"You guided a hunting party two years ago from upstate Minnesota and one of our charter members was in that party. He vividly remembers the valley and how you had such a hard time getting in and out. He thought at the time how like a retreat it seemed to be for fugitives. You see, we started the militia on a nation-wide basis five years ago, and big Al was in on the beginning of it."

"You mean..."

"That's right, Roy, he means me," Al Green spoke up. "I never forgot how much I hated the descent down into that hole, and hated even more the climb back out! I was never so glad to see our flat lakes area back home as after that!"

Roy looked the big man over a bit, then said, "I thought you looked familiar all this time, Just couldn't place you. You were my last group into the valley, and really, only the second group ever. I had too many complaints on the rugged trip, so gave it up. I did take a friend in just a few weeks ago, did some looking for a better way in so I could use the valley.

"I mean, the hunting is so fabulous in there it seems a waste to not use it. Had no success at all, though, so I wrote it off entirely. It's ideal for your ideas of a hidden escape settlement. I have no idea how many people you might have in mind for refuge, but if it's anything like my friend told me about, the need is going to increase. He's in deep trouble; and to be honest with you, is there right now."

"What part of the country is your friend from?"

"Northwest Ohio."

"Ahh yes, either Mister Rosenthal or Mister Montgomery, by any chance?"

"I'm not at liberty to say, but how would you know it's one of those two?"

"Okay, Roy, one thing you need to understand, we are an underground network involved in insurrection against the United States government. As such, it is our intent to take this country back for the conservative people living here and to stop the fascist take-over attempt by those people like the White House has right now. Congress is going to find the split down the middle is about to swing to the right, and in a drastic fashion. If that includes revolution, so be it, we have most of the military poised and ready. This all means we know what is going on over the whole country. We were instrumental in those two families escaping."

"You can't be serious, Hagan!"

"I'm dead serious. The main danger is having doubts about which upper echelon people can be trusted."

"This is getting scarier by the minute. I want to be included in anything that can bring this country back to the Christian nation it used to be, run by the people for the people and all that. But I hate like blazes any thoughts of Americans killing Americans to achieve it. We don't need another civil war like the 1860's!"

"I totally agree with you. Roy, but sometimes the only way to remove would-be dictators is the route of violence. Not good, not nice, but often necessary. I hate it as much as you do, but I have the experience, knowledge, and expertise to run the show, so I have to be ready to use what the former government taught me. And I am."

"Once again, General, I have people in the valley already. They need this stuff to help settle in."

"I don't like you putting people in there without checking with me first, Turnbull."

"Then get your sorry carcass back in your sorry helicopter and shashay on out of here, mister. It ain't your valley, I don't have to show you the place, and you're not in charge of this expedition OR who does and doesn't live there. I am. You either accept that and get off your high horse or get the blazes out of here and quit bothering me."

The two men stared at each other for a very long minute, neither giving ground until the military man realized Roy was right. The general had met his match in this civilian and would get nowhere without him. He finally gave out a low grunt and nodded, allowing a twitch in the corners of his mouth that threatened to become a smile.

"Okay, okay, cowboy, you win. I forget not all men are under my command. Heck, even some of my commanders tell me where to go if I get out of line. But tell me, just who are these people you have there and why are they there?"

Hagan Marshall stepped in and addressed the general, "General, they're some key folks from back east who ran afoul of the military and the provost because of their expression of freedom. They are, I assure you, as patriotic for the old USA as anyone you know, and very valuable to the cause, even though they aren't aware of it yet. They needed to get out or die; it's that serious for them."

"I have to trust your judgment, Marshall, because you're actually the man at the top on these operations. I look on you as my commanding officer, for you started this movement; you have orchestrated the formation of it, and know more than any other what makes us tick. I yield to you and to mister Turnbull, here."

"Good, then let's get aboard and let Roy take us to his valley."

Shortly after, the chopper rose from the Turnbull strip and banked south. The ride would be around and hour and the men settled into their places in silence. Roy Turnbull carefully observed each man during the flight, not liking everything he saw. He resolved to refrain from further judgment until he had the time for more observation of each individual. One thing was certain; none of these men realized the kind of man who was guiding them. Turnbull was old school western, and any who crossed him needed to understand the possible consequences.

Morgan, Rosey, Cal and Brian stepped carefully as they approached the site of the ramshackle cabin remains, looking before each step for the possible rattlesnake presence. It was their mission to reduce the snake population significantly during the afternoon. Morgan suddenly stopped and said, "Shhhhh. I hear a chopper, a big one."

They looked at one another for a few seconds and then took off on the run for the tents. If any invaders showed up, the women needed their presence! Sure enough, the sound grew louder and louder until a shadow flitted past the shadow of the overhanging rim and the large military ship began a descent into the canyon, aiming for a place just in front of the Cheyenne's.

Rosey had grabbed a 30-06 on his way past his tent while Morgan settled for a twelve gauge semi-automatic shotgun. They knelt by some of the larger boulders as the dust from the rotor whipped around them. Before the craft settled completely to the earth, figures leaped from it and as the canyon dweller's guns were leveled, Morgan saw Roy waving both arms frantically.

The rotors ground to a reluctant stop and silence settled into the area, the dwellers could hear Roy clearly then.

"Hold it guys, these men are peaceful and on your side. I brought them here to parley with you."

Morgan and the others rose to their feet and slowly started forward to meet the invaders. Rosey still carried the 30-06 somewhat at a ready position.

"What's the deal, Roy?" asked Morgan.

Roy explained the reasons for the presence of the men with him, stressing the need for a reclusive hide-away for others just like them. When he had finished, the pompous general stepped to the front and spoke to them.

"You men understand that I'm in command here, no matter . . ."

THUMP! The loud, sodden thud was followed immediately by a gasping for breath as the general doubled over the barrel of Rosey's 30-06. The rifle remained buried deep into his solar plexus. The look on Rosey's face was a combination of anger, fear, and pure meanness.

"You're an invader, mister; you ain't in charge of anything but puking your miserable guts out when I pull this trigger; WHICH I will do if anyone even twitches over there. Climb back into that blasted chopper and smoke on out of here or I'll blow your miserable innards out through your stinkin backbone. NOW MOVE!!"

Roy began laughing out loud, much to the consternation of a couple of the others. Big Al, had a smile on his face, as did Hagan Marshall. The general had forgotten himself again!

Both Roy and Hagan stepped forward to calm Rosey. "Easy, John," said Roy. "The general there keeps forgetting his place, but he really does have good intentions. He surely understands there's no place of command for him here since he's a late comer. Actually, he won't even be returning to the valley again, will you general?"

There came a nearly understandable grunt of agreement from the hurting soldier as he attempted to back off from Rosey and the offending rifle barrel. The barrel followed a couple of steps and then, as Rosey relented, it eased away. It did, however remain aimed in the direction of the portly midriff.

'I don't know what you mean, Roy, bringing these people here, but I don't appreciate it one bit,"

"I'm sure you don't, John, but please give me a chance to explain. You see, Hagan Marshall, here, is the head of all the nationwide resistance organization. Your problem wasn't the only such problem in the nation; there are many.

"Each one poses a unique situation where the martial law wielders feel threatened, so they react with violence and murder. People like your two families are crucial to the resistance effort, as well as in danger just for being patriots. We need a place of relative safety for those people to hide for a time. We also need a central base from which to operate for our clandestine operatives that is hard to detect.

"These men think this is the perfect location. I, however, have their agreement to forget this is here if you people don't approve. I mean, this group I'm with didn't discuss that agreement, but it's in place regardless of their approval. You see, those who disagree don't have to ever return from this trip."

As he spoke that last, the nasty, sharp metallic click of his 44 magnum revolver being cocked echoed through the area. Silence cascaded onto the group like a spring rainstorm. Hagan Marshall quickly diffused the situation by stepping forward.

"As commander of the resistance, I certainly agree to that, and since that makes me the head of all those with me, that makes it law. Am I right, gentlemen? General; any objections?"

That worthy simply glared at him, but gave a slight nod after a few seconds. Big Al Green stepped to Rosey and held out his hand, unafraid of the rifle.

"My hand and my trust goes out to any man that ready to defend his territory, mister. You've got a friend in me. Brian! It's good to see you again, son. I knew you were on your way, knew your pickup of the goods was successful, but brought you more just in case."

"Thanks, Al. Good to see you, too."

"People, can we have a parley here? Men, I think your women need to have a voice in this, too." Marshall looked in the direction of the tents as he spoke.

"Let's go on over to the living area for that, we can talk there," spoke Brian. He was starting to have a slowing of the heart rate caused by Rosey. He had been sure there was war to be had when the man he knew affectionately as "Uncle Rosey" had plunged his weapon into the general's midriff.

As the group slowly took positions around the large campfire in the center of the pitched tents, the ladies were introduced to each of the outsiders. The general seemed affable enough as this took place, so it seemed as though the tension had disappeared. The only person still rather on guard was the military pilot from the chopper.

"Here's the proposition we have for you folks here in the valley," Hagan Marshall started. "We have the means to place several modular homes and double wide homes in here and make this a bit more comfortable for all concerned.

"We would want to not only have a settlement of refugees here, but also a central intelligence camp. We would put in the necessary electronics for that, along with generators for power. We can set you up with many of the comforts you have been forced to give up.

"We also will sequester quick transportation vehicles for you in the form of small choppers in the case of discovery. You original settlers would be in charge of those. I understand two of you are pilots?"

"Yes, we are, but we've never flown choppers." answered Morgan.

The general spoke for the first time since the "incident", "We can provide the training for you. You got those other ships in here; you are definitely capable of learning quickly."

Rosey just looked at the man, but Morgan nodded agreeably at the comment. Maybe he was learning. As he contemplated the possibilities of what Marshall was proposing, Kay spoke up.

"Are you telling us we might have to stay here for several

135

months? And are you saying we might have others come in here who have the same plight as ourselves?"

"I can't say how long you misplaced folks might have to be here before it's safe to return to Ohio. I can't even promise you your property back there is safe from the corrupt government. As far as others like you coming here, we already know of several we are hiding out who could benefit from this open space. Right now they are cooped up inside except at night, and it's a heavy risk for them to even go out then." Hagan Marshall was sincere with his answer.

"And would those houses, real houses, be here before winter?"

"Absolutely. We have things already in place for some of the things we've mentioned."

"Then I see no recourse but to invite you here," Kay proclaimed in a ringing voice. "I don't want to spend winter in a tent!"

Morgan chuckled and looked at the others of his party. "Anyone else feel the same?"

All heads nodded, the decision was made, and permission was granted.

"Only one thing, we want the right to reject or have removed any person we feel detrimental to the community. We want the leadership of this community to be left to us until some better knowledge of those coming here is obtained. And ... our word is law. No conflict, no argument, we're in charge." As Morgan spoke, he looked at both the general and Hagan Marshall. They nodded in return.

"Then it looks like we have a town," Morgan said. Those in his group cheered and clapped their hands. The others soon joined in, even the general and his pilot.

Chapter 18

A week later in neighboring Idaho, a low power short wave radio sparkled to life and a coded message was delivered. If Mister Morris could have heard the way his code had changed he might well have spun in his grave. The message was relayed from low powered set to low powered set until the word had passed to every ear the leaders needed to have informed and activity began in seven states around the area. The low power was a sort of insurance against being overheard by government agencies as it was relayed between many operators and spread in that manner verses blasting the information out to men far away.

Building supplies were being gathered by many and were trucked to many varied locations for pickup by other truckers. An abandoned airstrip seventy miles to the northwest of Roy Turnbull's hunting ranch was the final destination before the supplies were to be transported into the hidden valley. Included in those supplies were even three modular homes ready for transporting.

Roy Turnbull had been informed the militia had access to any one of three Sikorsky Skycrane helicopters within a few hours notice and, should the need arise, even a huge Chinook double rotor chopper from a military base. How they could accomplish that was beyond Roy, but the less he knew, the better.

Within a space of a week, the crew returned once again to go with Roy into the valley. Only Al Greene was missing as he had returned to his operation in Minnesota.

Once they landed in the valley, the space was carefully surveyed for ideal placing of the village. It was finally, after much discussion and some bit of arguing to settle into the eastern end where there was the most tree coverage and the possibility of discovery was less. The cliffs overhung the base of the walls in many places by a good fifty feet or more and even though the possibility of some rock scaling off and falling was discussed, that area became the final place for their use.

"Men," Roy began, "I don't see how we're gonna get foundations in for those modular homes, or any other structures, for that matter. We need some equipment in here for that work, this is stone right up close to the surface, and the frost line is really deep in here."

Hagan Marshall smiled as he placed a hand on Roy's shoulder. "Do you think a backhoe would do the trick, Roy?"

"How you gonna get that in here?"

"Roy, if a Skycrane can haul half a modular house at a time, do you think it's going to even grunt over a backhoe?"

"He's right, mister Turnbull," spoke up James Caldwell, a general contractor. "We can have one in here tomorrow and start digging. As to the frost line, if we get to bedrock for the foundation, we'll be fine. Now, we need to determine what we'll do for water supply."

The planning and design work went on until very late afternoon and when they lifted off in the chopper, all were satisfied that a good portion of the planning was cared for and could be accomplished within a couple of weeks. Roy had also tried to convince them to smooth the floor of the valley for a few thousand feet for a better runway. That idea was rejected as the current valley floor was plenty good enough and would not look like a runway from a satellite.

Two weeks later as Morgan stood with his arm around Kay looking at the beginning of the settlement from a point high above the valley he reflected on the beehive of activity they had been immersed in for the period.

"Hon, what do you think of our situation here. I mean, REALLY think?"

"Well, husband and father of my children, it looks to me as though God has made lemonade for us. I find it unique that He led us here through unbelievers, don't you?"

"He has used many such people down through the centuries to bless His own, Love, and will no doubt continue to do so. I just wish I could get Rosey to listen to the Gospel for once. Have you tried to talk to Paige anytime since this nightmare started?"

"Yes, and she just smiles, pats my hand as if to reassure me I'll get over it and walks off. Sometimes I could just shake her and scream! Do you think that might work to convert folks?"

He chuckled and squeezed her tighter and replied, "It didn't during the inquisition, Love"

"Have you heard anything about new people coming in yet? We have our three homes in place, the generators are functional, and two more buildings will be done by the end of the week. Wow, I can't get over how fast these people get things done!"

"Yeah, I know. But the answer to the question is, no, I haven't. They'll be coming in soon enough, I guess. I think we should get back before it gets any darker, don't wanna step on any rattlers!"

"Ugh, you had to bring them up, didn't you? That's the worst thing about this place. I hate them."

"Me to. I think we've done for a huge percentage of them, though. Kay, can we ever get used to living here in this isolated place?"

"I guess we can, as long as we remember Jesus said even the foxes had a place to sleep but He didn't even have a place to lay His head. I don't like it, though. I hate what it might do to our sons and their families. I mean, will Cal even have a chance to HAVE a family?"

Morgan sensed her nearness to choking up as she contemplated that part of their fate. He hugged her tighter as they descended the narrow trail to the valley floor. He kept his hand on the 410 gauge pistol he wore for the dispensing of snakes. He couldn't believe he had brought them each one of the handy weapons for that purpose. The ladies failed to even complain about carrying the heavy pistols. Five 410 gauge shells in a revolver might not be so much for a guy, but the ladies, not used to any firearms at all, found them much in their way and another strike against this forsaken valley they were being forced to call home for a season.

139

The next morning found Cal chopping wood when the sound of a chopper interrupted his thoughts. It was not one of the huge jobs used to transport equipment or housing. He grabbed his now ever present rifle and ran for the house.

"Mom, Dad, chopper coming! Not one of the usual ones, we need to be ready!"

Rosey had heard and was running to his assigned "battle alert station," armed to the teeth. Brian could be seen farther down the valley at his post, he had been hunting when the sound came to him.

By the time the chopper descended to a landing on the normal area, there were guns aligned on it from three sides. The refugees had strategically planned their defense plans and stood at the ready for any development.

As the rotors wound down their whining song, the side door nearest the settlement slid open and the general stepped out. He held his hands out in front of him in a gesture of restraint.

"I'm afraid we have some good news and not so good news, my friends. The next house is going to be delayed a few days, but we have your next resident with us today. I dearly hope the tents are still here."

Morgan shook hands with Sikes and looked curiously at the rotor craft. A young man in his late twenties climbed to the ground.

"Morgan, all you others, this is Brent Shaffer."

Greetings were made by all the valley people, and then Sikes explained the situation as some large cases were being unloaded by two soldiers.

"Brent has been an engineer for Sascom, a large supplier of government surveillance equipment for several years. Someone in the defense department has found Brent to be much too conservative for their tastes so they began to build a false case of stealing secrets from Sascom. His family is now in danger as well as him.

"Since Brent has been accused of this heinous crime, he came to a certain cohort of ours and has provided us with, indeed, stolen secrets. Best part of that is, those stolen secrets are in the form of electronics equipment he designed himself! And . . . equipment that will be of great benefit to the valley."

"What are we looking at, General?"

Brent broke in and explained, "This unit will throw a protective electronic net over the settlement that will not allow satellite imaging to see anything we don't want it to see, sir. It will take me a couple of days to program it to hide us here, but when I'm done, any imaging they might glean from the eye in the sky will show a barren and empty valley. No dwellings, no airplanes on the ground, no nothing. We feel it's necessary to hide all we can as far as evidence of inhabitation or they'll find us sooner or later. Give me two days, and we no longer exist!"

"That's great news, Brent! I've been really concerned that sooner or later some clown would be searching the imaging and see the settlement in this forsaken hole. Then someone else would decide to investigate and we'd have to shoot some Americans. Not good." Morgan breathed a sigh of relief at the release of that particular tension. This young engineer had hit upon a prospective problem and the solution for it that had bothered Morgan for several days.

As the boxes of equipment were unloaded, strategies were discussed by the visitors as to the provision for electrical power on a continuing basis. Solar power, generators, how and how many of whatever. It was a problem they finally approached the young engineer about.

"Oh, that's an easy call, at least in my mind. If we go generators we have to continually bring in fuel, and there may come a day when that's not possible. You'll see I have solar panels providing power to each of my satellite disks to care for that aspect. We can do the same for each home by putting them on the roof of the individual houses as they go in place. We already have them set aside at a secret location." He finished his statement with a boyish grin straight from a Dennis the Menace cartoon.

Brian and Cal gravitated to the young man and soon involved themselves with helping unload the many boxes of equipment. In a matter of an hour the three youngsters had cemented friendships among them and were working hard at depositing the goods in the locations suggested by Brent.

When Rosey started toward them to help, Morgan caught him by the arm and gently shook his head.

"Rosey, let's you and I let those three work together for now. I think my boys need the contact with the outside world, such as Brent brings with him, and we can be more help by letting them alone."

Rosey looked at him, smiled and nodded. "Good idea, Morg, good idea."

The military people spent time planning their next step in bringing in the housing, and the next day was targeted for the arrival of the first unit. Brent overheard and vetoed the date.

"Listen, give me two days before you do that, otherwise there's the chance of discovery by some jerk on government equipment. Two days from now, not a chance!"

The general just nodded, and the plans were changed. In a matter of hours all matters had been decided, a calendar of movements was established, and the chopper lifted off, leaving the cargo and Brent behind.

Two days of long hours later, four satellite discs were in place and cables run in the ground to connect them. Brent had insisted on burying the cables, though just below the surface. Being below the frost line wasn't necessary for a wiring harness such as those and the job went fairly fast considering the length of the cables.

"Well, who's going climbing with me, guys? I have one last unit to mount, and it doesn't need any cable, it's wireless. I wish I could have had a couple more weeks before coming here so I could have set all these up wireless, but they wouldn't hold still for it, and now I've seen why."

"I'll go," said Cal. "Why do we have to climb?"

"This unit will scan the valley floor several times a second and transmit the appearance to the central brain which will apply that appearance to the picture seen by the satellite. After all, we can't have this area being green like right now if the rest of the valley floor is snow covered, can we? This unit will care for that."

"Wow, you've thought of everything, fella! I'm impressed. Let's get the beast mounted and this stuff working, I want my mom to have her house!"

"I understand that, fella, I'm not too excited about living in a tent myself. I don't know how Sally will take it, either."

"Who's Sally?"

"My wife. I didn't tell you? She's back at Turnbull's until I get us to disappear."

"No. How on earth did you come to think this stuff up?"

"No one told you? I was working for the military developing equipment to track American militants and other so-called enemies of the government when I came to realize how wrong their approach to the public is. I sabotaged the project in a manner that set them back a good two years. It was not discovered because of the way I did it until a couple of months ago. The longer it took the rest of the team to discover the sabotage, the farther I set them back!" He stopped to chuckle with satisfaction as he looked back on the project.

"Well, the chief engineer finally got suspicious and started checking on things. I had, in the meantime, found the militia and was in close contact with them. I told them he was starting to suspect something and they insisted Sally and I disappear when it was discovered someone was watching our house closely. So . . . here we are."

He ended with that Dennis-the-menace grin the refugees had already come to know.

"Wow, you're in the same boat as the rest of us. Let's get this done so your wife can join us and feel safe!" It was significant that Cal already accepted their location as safe. There had been many family and group discussions since arriving in the canyon and everyone had come to feel their decisions had been for the good. Morgan went so far as to say that "God orchestrated this whole escape thing, so we owe Him the glory and can rest assured He is in control." The comment brought a low snort of derision from Rosey who then received a little, pointed elbow from Paige.

"I'm ready to test the system, if you want to know. I came with the batteries charged so we don't need to wait on the solar panels to do that job. Let's get back to the main panel and see what happens when we make some stuff disappear!"

Two days later there was a hail from the north rim and the party could see mules starting down the precipice. Morgan called the group together with the prearranged signal and they took their defensive positions. Since Roy was coming the hard way instead of by chopper, there must be danger afoot and they needed to be at the ready just in case.

Several hours later the lanky guide rode into camp on his favorite mule with a bedraggled, weary, and thoroughly terrified but lovely in spite of it young lady. Brent let out a "Whoop!" and ran to rescue her from the mule's back. The two of them melted together in a hug that threatened to be endless until Roy stepped in.

"Here, youngster, let her go for now. This girl is probably tireder and scareder than she's ever been. That decent is pure terror for a tenderfoot. Right, John?"

"Man, truer words were never spoken, Roy! I'm still not over my first time down!"

The two separated and Sally was introduced all around. As soon as that was finished she grabbed Brent again and started sobbing on his shoulder and trying to tell him something that wasn't coming out very intelligible.They walked her to the campfire and plied her with coffee and kindness, finally getting her to calm down enough to speak slowly enough for understanding.

"Oh Brent, they have Jennifer and are holding her to try and find us when we go looking for her. She's in...!" She broke down again, sobbing uncontrollably. Roy took over the explanation.

"We got word three days ago, not twenty minutes after the choppers dropped us off, that spies for the militia in their hometown had discovered the government seized the younger sister and planned to hold her to draw Brent to her. One of the spies works with those who planned the grab. He tried to warn the family, but got nowhere with that. I started here the next morning, was afraid to wait for choppers to get the word. Then the general contacted us and said it was risky at this particular time to have choppers come for us, so I guess I did right."

"Okay, people, let's have a war council in an hour. Ladies, please prepare a meal for us, Cal, Brian, and Brent. No, not

Brent. You just sit with your wife and try to comfort the two of you for the next hour. Cal and Brian, get trail supplies ready for two men ready for a week. Make it as light as you can, but be sure there's enough.

"Rosey, you're in charge of weapons and ammo for the trip as well as anything else you can think of that you and I will need to free this girl. Roy, you show me the place where they have her and the best way there once we get to your place. We'll need a car, truck, whatever you can furnish to go from your place and back once we have her. Okay, you all have your assignments, get hopping, please."

Roy and Morgan poured over the maps Roy had brought along. The savvy guide had anticipated this sort of response from the group, and had already formed a plan for the operation. As he went over the plan carefully several times, Rosey joined them to learn the procedure for himself. Once most of the directions had been absorbed they took time to feed the mules their grain and cared for their comfort. They would be driven hard for the next couple of days. Roy figured he could cut a day off the three normally taken for the trip back to his place if they went first light to last. They then organized all the armament and loaded it onto packsaddles, splitting it up in equal numbers to allow for possible loss of a loaded mule on the ascent tomorrow.

Cal and Brian showed shortly after with the food and utensils for the trip. When the call to supper sounded the somber group gathered around the rough-hewn table they had constructed and once Morgan had prayed they all pitched in silently. Some, like Sally and Brent, had little appetite, but Morgan, Rosey and Roy knew the value of nourishment in time like this and piled in with a vengeance.

When all had ceased to eat, Morgan gave his instructions for the group for the next several days. "Ladies, I would like a large breakfast ready before dawn tomorrow. We'll be moving, as all the westerns say, 'at first light'. I don't care if the rest of you are up yet or not.

"Also, while we are gone, Brian is in charge. Be alert, be safe. I would like for you all to have prayer several times a day as a group. Pray for our safety, wisdom, discernment, and courage. This will be, well, for lack of a better word, dangerous for John and I.

"You may wonder why he and I are the ones to go, but experience and age are the main criteria here. I don't want to do this, but we simply have to. Roy already had a plan in place by the time he and Sally arrived here, and the three of us have gone over and over it until we know all the routes and such by heart.

"We know the layout of your home town, Sally, as well as you do! Roy went on the 'net and got a great overview of it. The spies there even gave him the address and schedule the people who have you sister are keeping. They don't expect two mossy-horned old men like Rosey and I, they expect Brent. The spies will help us all they can once we're there, but they have to be careful to not be discovered so they can continue to be effective. Any questions?"

Both Paige and Kay approached their men and Kay suggested they pray as a group right then. Brian noted the look of confusion on Brent and Sally's faces as well as the blank look on John Rosenthal's. He glanced at Paige and saw her face contorted in both fear and confusion. He determined to try and speak with her tomorrow.

After Kay was done with her prayer, Brian spoke out in prayer and then Morgan. Morgan's request was simple, "Lord, please direct us in our quest to rescue this young lady and keep us all safe. Please make it possible that we do not have to injure anyone, and may it be your will for us to return here unnoticed. These things we ask in the powerful and mighty name of Jesus Christ, our king, savior, and lord. Amen."

"Well guys, go and be safe, or as God told Joshua, 'Be strong and courageous!" With that admonition, Kay threw her arms around her husband and kissed him soundly. She had no tears, and no qualms. Morgan noticed those facts and smiled at his wife's faith.

The next morning after they had eaten and prayed together again, he went to a mule, mounted up, and waved goodbye. The little caravan started its way to the imposing north wall of the canyon. Those watching stood until the first corner was rounded and they lost sight of the mules. They knew they would be able to see them again in a while as the treacherous passage wound in and out of the canyon wall, but they went about their tasks instead of waiting.

Paige sniffled a bit, then placed her arm around Kay's waist and asked, "How can you send him off like that and not cry? I don't understand." She wiped a tear from her cheek as if to demonstrate her meaning.

"Don't be mistaken, Paige, I love that man more than life itself, but I trust God to bring him home safe. God has shown Himself to us way too many times through the years for us to doubt Him now. Morgan will be fine.

"Tell me, dear friend, how do you feel about God right now, do you believe in Him?"

"Well, I guess there could be a God, but I don't think, if there is one, that they would bother with insignificant beings like us. I mean, why would he bother, we're not important."

"That's where you're wrong, sweetie. He created us after His own image so we could fellowship with Him. Then, when He needed to, He was willing to send His Son to earth in the form of a human to be a sacrifice for our wrongs so we could be forgiven! That Son was Jesus, and He died for us, so if the Son of God would die for us, then we MUST be important! Do you see?"

"No, I don't. I'm not sure I even buy that there is a god, let alone one who would die for me. Why would he have to do that anyway?"

"Honey, let's go to my tent and let me show you what God's Bible says, then I think you'll understand."

Paige just shook her head and turned off toward her own tent, head hanging low and her steps mere shuffling of her feet. Kay prayed immediately for her friend, her heart deeply troubled for Paige. She was a little startled when an arm circled her shoulders from first one side, then the other. Two strong young men had her firmly in their grasp. She looked at them and smiled as her two sons walked her to her tent, smiling possessively at their mother.

"Nice job, Mom, not in her face, but still a gentle challenge," spoke Cal, the younger of the two. Then they kissed her on each cheek at the same precise time and wheeled away to begin the chore of building the noon fire.

Chapter 19

Fifty miles west of the tiny town of Nordvald, Iowa, a pickup truck left the highway and traveled three miles north on a gravel road. The two occupants were tired, bedraggled, and hungry. They had been on the road nonstop all day and half the night. They passed by a side road and saw the lights of another vehicle suddenly light up. The car pulled in behind them and flashed its brights twice, then three times, then twice again. They pulled over to the side and stopped.

Morgan turned the lights out on the pickup and both he and Rosey armed themselves with the .44 Magnum revolvers they carried. The car behind them also killed its lights and two men exited on the passenger side and walked into the field by the road. One of them lighted a cigarette, holding the flame an extra length of time to give the weary travelers a good look at the faces of the two.

When the flame was extinguished Morgan and Rosey got out and walked attentively toward them, separating themselves by a few paces.

"Looks like a nice night for fishing for big mudcats," one of the men said.

"Never heard of a mudcat," Morgan answered in the fashion in which they had been coached .

"They don't swim, they craw," was the answer and all breathed easier, for the codes had been satisfied. Nothing so ridiculous could have been faked.

They introduced themselves with false names and the two locals started their explanation.

"The local government guys decided they want Brent Shaffer really bad, so they must have figured holding his young sister-in-law would persuade him to give himself up. We been keeping good track of them ever since, but we don't dare do anything or we'll lose our cover. We're essential to the underground here; no one is even a little bit suspicious of the two of us. After all, we're just a farmer and a plumber, what can we know?" The last was said with a chuckle of derision.

"We understand completely. We were driven into hiding, and don't want anyone else to go through what we have. Or still probably will." Morgan was becoming angry as he said that.

"Brent is a local boy made good, and the smartest kid to ever graduate from the local school. He became something of a local hero when he graduated college suma cum whatever. We plan to keep him and his family safe. His folks and younger brother have been taken into hiding since Jennifer was stolen, and so have Sally's folks."

The other man spoke up then, "We have the guardians' schedule all mapped out for you. They aren't all that smart, they do everything according to the clock with no variation. Do you have any sort of knowledge of the town at all?"

"Let's go over where we can have headlights and I'll show you what we have. You can verify it for us."

Five minutes later, the taller of the two spoke up. "You have it really down, fellas. Now, here's their routine. Every morning at 7:30 the one just coming on duty takes Sally to the local diner for breakfast. Then they walk back to the car, which is always parked two blocks away for whatever reason. It's an older Buick Lucerne, dark blue. Has government plates on it, so that identifies it for you.

"After that, they return to the motel on the highway east of town and settle in for the morning. It's about a mile from the diner because it's way outside the town limits. There's a truck stop beside the motel, but they never eat there. Who knows why?

"Then for lunch, they walk her all the way into the diner for exercise. When they leave the diner the car meets them and they change guards. They return to the motel until supper time when they drive back in and park in the same place. When they go back to the motel a woman takes over for the night. Come morning, they change guards again and start the whole thing over.

"You can plan it however you want, of course, but if was me, I'd take her away from the woman."

"We'll study on that a bit, but I want to look things over in the morning and then decide what to do. Is the getaway car nearby?"

"Yep, just up the road a ways in a barn on the east side. We'll take you there now."

They went another mile or so and pulled into a driveway by a ramshackle building that had seen many better days. The two undercover men opened a creaky sliding door to reveal a four door sedan facing out. It was a non-descript four door with Nebraska plates.

"Plates are fakes. We'll take them off the day after you take her. Then we'll put the right ones on her and keep her for the next maneuver. Hope we never need her again." The tall fellow was sincere in his thoughtful statement.

"We hope the same. We'll back the truck in beside the car and get some sleep," Morgan said. Rosey had not spoken since they had arrived.

"Listen, we have beds and food ready for you on up this road a ways. Back your truck in here and ride with us. We'll have you back here before daylight. You'll get showers and rest and be on top of your game before you attack."

"You sure that would be safe for you?"

"Yep, safe as can be. Back that truck in there and let's get you refreshed."

The next morning found the two travelers clean, rested, and fed. As they finished the second cup of coffee they related the plan for rescue Roy Turnbull had formulated before they left. Harold, the taller spy and farm owner of the house where they had slept, nodded his approval of their plans.

"That all sounds good to me. You definitely want to wait until the evening meal, and, if possible, even until dark. We forgot to share one thing with you, in fact, maybe the most important part; the one guard always has to have a late coffee and pie break and he and the woman exchange Jennifer at the restaurant when he's on the late shift. That might be the best time to snatch her away. I think it very important for you to be making your run for it after dark."

"I definitely agree with that. How else can we make the switch to the truck? I say we just hit the hotel room and take her from there. If we have to shoot a woman, so be it," was Rosey's comment.

"HEY!" Morgan was angry. "We do this without bloodshed if possible, Rosenthal! I don't know what's gotten into you lately, but you just settle down, and right now!"

"Hey right back, MISTER Montgomery, who died and put YOU in charge? You seem to be getting a bit high and mighty lately. Tell me, who are YOU to give the orders here?"

"I'm the guy who is taking command of the camp and the force stationed there, friend Rosey. When Roy and I planned this out, you were right there agreeing with everything, including me being the leader of the group. That's the way it was agreed on, that's the way it's going to be. You have any objections, you have two choices. You can stay in this little town and we'll bring Paige to you here, or you can go see where Roy can take you to hide. Either way, you decide you're staying in the valley, you take orders from me. Capice?"

Rosey sat for a terrifically long time, staring at Morgan before he answered. "For now, SIR, I'll go along with you. But when we get back, IF we get back, we take a vote in the camp."

"Hey, we took a vote before, that's why I took the lead. What's happened to you, Rosey? You've never been this cantankerous before. I hate what this garbage has done to us just as much as you do, but we still need to live our lives according to the scripture."

"YOU may need to, but I don't. I don't buy into your Jesus thing, and you know it, so don't go putting your values on me, I go my own way."

"Wow, that's quite a blow to me. I thought we were best friends. Is that history? What's the deal? Help me out here, Rosey, I don't believe this is happening between us!"

"It happened when you got too big for your britches and wanted to take charge, BUDDY."

"John, John, I didn't WANT to take charge. But we agreed there needed to be one person at the head, and I was elected. You voted for me, too, fella. If you remember, I nominated YOU!"

"Sure you did. You had nothing to lose, you knew your family would vote for you, that made it a wash. Might as well have been fixed, far as I'm concerned."

"Man, this really bothers you, doesn't it? Okay, you can let it scratch your nerves raw if you want, but you're not going to do any unnecessary shooting on this trip. You do, and I'll crack your sorry head open for you. There, see? Now you've got ME threatening violence. Man, Rosey, we have to calm down here, or we're gonna blow the whole mission. Just take a walk and think things through, okay? That's what I'm gonna do right now. I'll be back in a few minutes."

With that, Morgan rose and left the room. He strolled out to the barn and went through the stalls, petting any animals tied there for the night. He failed to see Rosey leave the house and start up the road in the other direction. He was nearly running in his frustrated state.

As John Rosenthal cooled down, the guilt of his words and attitude started to take hold and he got even madder. He fussed and fumed for several minutes before getting a grasp on his feelings, then walked another half mile before turning back. When he arrived back at the house he found everyone seated at the kitchen table. They all carefully ignored him in an attempt to keep from agitating him again.

"Morg, I'm sorry. I don't know what got into me, but everything you said was right, I'll not cause any more problems, and I won't do anything crazy. This has just torn me apart with all that's happened."

Morgan leaped to his feet and threw his arms around his friend in a bear hug. There was a pregnant silence for several heartbeats, then sighs of relief could be heard. When all had quieted, Morgan still was bothered by his friend's blow up, and the incident held him captivity for long into the night.

The next day found the two eating breakfast at the diner in question. They watched carefully as each patron entered until a woman in a business suit opened the door and ushered an attractive young woman into the diner and guided her to a booth containing a tall, football player type of guy with a pock-marked face and bushy, unkempt hair that was a mark of rebellion in its styling; or a lack of same.

Rosey's elbow gently contacted Morgan's ribs as they tried to observe without seeming to gawk. The others' booth was almost directly behind where they sat at the counter. They finished their coffee, paid the waitress, and left the diner.

"Man, Morgan, did you see the size of that guy? We surely need to wait and get her from the broad, no doubt about it. He could crush our car!"

Morgan chuckled and nodded. They waited until nearly half an hour later before the couple came out of the diner and climbed into a car. The woman left walking and entered a store in the opposite direction. When the man and young lady left, the two followed at a safe distance to find where they were staying. The car pulled into the motel a couple of miles out of town and they watched as the guard escorted his charge with a hand on her arm. They entered a first floor room and the door closed behind them.

Morgan drove back to the farm to discuss what they knew of the pattern of behavior by the prey. When they arrived at the farm Harold met them and guided their car to a spot behind the barn. They then exchanged the information they had gleaned.

"That all jibes with what we've seen," Harold offered. "Now, something we need to cover for your escape. Where this gravel road turns off the main highway there's a hayfield. It will be mowed today so it will be short. Do not, I repeat, do not turn on the road. Instead, turn into the hayfield and run over the ridge in there before you turn back out to the gravel road. If you turn on the road, they'll be able to see the dust you make and know you turned there. If you go over the ridge first, the dust will be hidden when you hit the road again.

"Another thing, there's a switch just under the dash on the driver's side that disables every light in the car. Be SURE you turn that off before you leave town! Otherwise, if they're chasing you, they'll possibly see your brake lights go on when you turn. You can see where to turn by taking note of the big oak tree a couple hundred yards before the gravel road. Any questions?"

"How do the local cops enter into this? Are they sympathetic to our cause, or the government's?"

"Not ours. That's why they can hold this poor girl. It seems the area government guy got their people in the places they wanted them before this crackdown on liberty ever started. Why they targeted little Norvold, we'll never understand."

Morgan looked perplexed as he answered. "I think they tried everywhere, your locals were just susceptible to it more than some others."

Harold nodded, "Yeah, you're probably right. Both our sheriff and the town cops are out to be big shots."

"Well, let them be, they'll pay sooner or later. Now, Rosey, let's get in a nap this afternoon so we can run all night tonight. What say you?"

"I can go for that, Morg. You're always the best night guy for staying awake, you take first shift? Or would it be better if we save you for the deep night turn?"

"Let's make that call when we have the girl safe with us. We'll see who's the most ready guy."

"Okay, sounds good to me. Now, about that lunch before the snooze?"

Morgan looked appreciatively around the local hardware as he picked a roll of duct tape off the shelf. He went to the register, paid for the tape without a word, and left through a side door. Rosey pulled forward and paused just long enough for Morgan to climb in and drove away to the east down the main drag.

They drove to the inn and pulled around the back, backing the car into a spot near the back door of the office. Morgan opened the bag of food from the local fast food dive and the two settled in for a long wait. It was still a couple of hours until dark.

Nine PM finally slid into the day with a subtle smile of darkness and the pair of would-be rescuers slipped into the office back door. They did not bother with masking their faces, but when their perusal of the area failed to show any other persons present, Rosey drew his big 44 magnum and confronted the man at the desk. He was a man of medium height and dark skin wearing a turban.

Those bright, snapping dark eyes popped to twice their normal size at the sight of the wheeless cannon in Rosey's hand. His hands flew to the vertical position and he stepped back a step.

"Please sir, I do not have the combination for the safe, but I can give you everything in the register!"

"We don't want your money, mister. I want a key to the room where that young girl is being kept prisoner and I want it five minutes ago. Got it?"

The dark face was suddenly split by a beautiful white smile and the eyes fairly glinted with sparkles of pleasure. He drew a deep breath and lowered his voice.

"Do not speak too loudly, sir, the room is the one next door to the office. I pray you are rescuers? That poor Jennifer, she is such a sweet young thing to have people do this sort of thing to her. They won't even allow me to bring her extra snacks or anything. Please, tell me you are saving her!"

Morgan stepped close and nodded. "We're taking her to her brother-in-law and her sister. Can you tell us where her parents are?"

"No, I am afraid not. But I do know of people who could help you if you could contact them. But I warn you, they are hard to find, and even harder to talk to. I cannot help you to do either."

"So tell us, are we hearing you say you are sympathetic to Jennifer and others like her?"

"Sir, I came to this country nine years ago with a green card. I found some of my people, secured a job, and worked my way into buying a part ownership in this inn. I wanted to escape the big cities, and to just be a good American. I took my oath as soon as my time was fulfilled and," at this point his slender chest swelled out as he continued, "I have now voted twice in these local elections and one national election!"

They could see tears of pride form and glisten in those dark eyes as he looked from one to the other.

"Good for you. Now, the key?" Rosey still held the gun and waved it for affect.

"I will do that now. I would beg of you that you then bind me in some way so I cannot be accused of helping you, for they have treated me badly during the stay here just because I spoke out against them. Also, the local constable does not like me; he is sympathetic to their actions.

"When you leave here, go east to the first road, then north one mile and then turn west. I don't know that you are going west, you understand, but should that be your desire, that's what I would do so you don't go through town. That would-be big shot lawman follows every car he sees after dark. The east west road goes about seven miles and dead ends. Then you can go wherever you might think is the right way."

The last was said with a sly wink; this fellow knew more than they would ever get from him! Morgan went around the desk and duct taped him to his chair, making sure it wasn't too uncomfortable. As he started to leave, the fellow said, "Wait, a strip over my mouth, please, or they will still think I could have helped them and retaliate. They do not like me as it is because of my ethnicity."

Morgan smiled and complied with the request, then they went to the door, paused long enough to give the fellow a military salute with a smile, and after receiving a wink and a nod in return, quickly unlocked the door of the first room.

They barged in, guns drawn, and as the woman captor started to jump to her feet Rosey slapped her and knocked her back to the chair she had occupied. Unnoticed by him, one of the men was in the room! Morgan soon covered the man and cocked the monster pistol in his hand.

"You move, I make one heck of a mess of you right here, right now, girl snatcher. Siddown!"

The big man was the one Rosey had commented on, and for a moment he glanced around at possible moves to resist, but when the water main sized muzzle failed to waver, he set as commanded. The woman was starting to curse at Rosey until he slapped her again with the command to shut up. They placed the two back to back on the floor and used the entire roll of duct tape to secure them, including taping their mouths by simply wrapping the tape clear around their heads, making sure it covered their mouths and not their nose so they could breath. Their eyes? Covered them, too.

Jennifer sat immobilized in total fear as she watched the two men work rapidly. Tears flowed freely from her eyes.

She was led into the bathroom by Morgan and the door closed behind them. "Listen, Jennifer. We're taking you to Brent and Sally! We're friends. We haven't time to explain further, but grab what's yours in here and we have to go quickly."

The girl settled down and quickly collected her bathroom supplies, placing them in a shopping bag. "This is all they let me bring when they grabbed me."

"We'll take care of that, now let's get you out of here. I'm Morgan, by the way, and that guy out there is John."

"Where is Sami?" she asked.

"Who's Sami?"

"The clerk, he's a dear man and my good friend since they brought me here. He really took some chances trying to help make my captivity better. They didn't treat him very well."

"He's fine, insisted we tape him up so they couldn't hold him accountable, but I put the phone close to him so he can call for help by using a pencil grabbed in his teeth after he gets the tape off his mouth. He won't have to wait too long to do that so it doesn't get too uncomfortable. I left the tape with a bit of a free end so he can do that. You can say goodbye on our way out the back door."

They slipped out, turned out the lights, and locked the door behind them. On their way through the lobby Jennifer slipped behind the desk and gave Sami a quick kiss on the forehead and a tight hug then ran to the car. Morgan put her in the back seat with instructions to lie down out of sight and drove very calmly out of the inn. He followed Sami's advice and went east to the first road.

Some forty minutes later they turned into the freshly cut hay field and drove over the rise with lights out. Morgan stopped the car then to allow their eyes more time to adjust to the darkness. Thankfully, the moon was in a show-off mood and the clouds had honored that mood by staying away and allowing it to shine. After a bit, Morgan drove back to the northbound gravel road and slowly drove on. When they came to the barn and turned off, the large doors started to slide open before them. The undercover agents were there!

As they climbed out, Harry went to Jennifer and hugged her. "Listen, young lady, we have your folks safely hidden, along with Brent's parents. Don't you worry a bit about them. I suspect the group will see to it they follow you soon. Can't say for sure, but that's my bet."

The other fellow spoke up then, "You'll find some lunches in the back seat of the truck, and her bags in the bed, covered with a tarp."

"My bags?"

"Yes girl, your bags. We broke into your home and packed everything we thought was probably yours in a couple of suitcases we found and put the rest in grocery bags. Now, get you going, people, times a wasting!"

Harry spoke, "Go north out of here to the second paved road before you turn west. Follow that some fifty miles before you come back down to the US highway. Then I suggest you go a mile south of it and go west another thirty or so before getting back on the main route back to your guide's place. Good bye to you, take good care of our little one there, and God speed and God bless."

Chapter 20

"Pickup coming, Roy!" Brad Sommers hollered.

Roy Turnbull trotted to the pilot and took the binoculars from him. He studied the road for a bit, then smiled at the young flyer.

"That's mine, Brad, the guys are back! I just hope and pray they have the girl."

"Me too, Roy, we need a little better scenery around here. Your ugly mug is getting to me."

"I see. And what about my wife's mug, Bradley Sommers? Huh? Tell me about that!"

The pilot chuckled and replied, "No you don't, fella. You're not getting ME with that trick. I never insult a lady, especially if she's the cook!"

Roy laughed, placed the binoculars back to his eyes to observe the truck raising a dust cloud that was still several miles away. Roy's guide service was over twenty miles back from the main highway and the road was of gravel. No paving here, Roy felt the remote location aided in the appeal of the place.

"We might as well park on the porch, Brad. It'll be a few minutes yet. Jane! Company comin', and likely to be hungry! It's our truck!"

"I'll be ready for them, anyone following?" The cry came from some where deep in the house.

"Nope, they're alone!"

Some twenty minutes later the pickup slid to a stop in front of the porch. A bedraggled looking trio descended from the cab, with Morgan coming out of the back door while the other two staggered from the front. Morgan looked like a thundercloud as he held out a hand for Roy to shake.

"I see you got her safe and sound, Morg," Roy said.

"Yeah, she's pretty worn out, but considering what she's put up with for the last few weeks, she's doin' good. That's a pretty tough young lady there."

"Did you have any real problems with the captors?"

"No, more problems with the rescuer than the captors," Morgan grumbled.

With that comment, Rosey snapped to attention and glowered at Morgan. Roy looked from one to the other but received no clarification of any possible problem.

"Right now, we just need to sleep, eat, and sleep; in that order," Morgan continued.

"Jane is fixing a quick meal right now in case you would like to switch the first two around, Morg. Meanwhile, I want you two to meet Brad Sommers.He will be your instructor for the chopper training they promised you. A smaller one is already in the valley, but there's a larger bird out back under a camo net that will be yours when you're both qualified. You'll be surprised at what's happened to the settlement in the three short days you've been gone!"

"Such as?"

"Well, you now have water pumps in the river, and that means running water up by the houses. It's not in any of them yet, but soon will be. There's a hole dug, just waiting for the fuel tank to be taken in. There's a five-hundred gallon tank on its way, and you'll find that all of the choppers are turbine powered, so that means one fuel for all the ships, including the Cheyenne's."

"That's good, Roy, that's real good. Now, about that food?"

They trudged toward the house as both Morgan and Rosey shook hands with Brad. The young pilot studied his new students with an appraising eye as they entered the house and seated themselves at the table. Jane plied them with several dishes of warmed up leftovers and stood waiting to serve them in anyway she could.

Hunger satisfied at last, they trooped off to the bunkhouse kept for Roy's hunting parties. Except for Jennifer, that is;

she was escorted to the master bedroom for privacy and quiet. All three were gone to dreamland in a matter of seconds after hitting their pillows. Roy would leave them alone for several hours, but he also went to the new low-powered short wave set and contacted the valley, using a code they had established to let the valley dwellers know the party was back safe with their goal in tow. Tomorrow would see the arrival in the valley.

Brad went through his initial instructions with both Morgan and Rosey, then they did rock, paper, scissors to see who flew first. It was obvious to the others that the twelve hours sleep had changed the outlook of all three travelers. Brad motioned Rosey into the right seat of the chopper and shook hands with Roy and Jane before he entered. Roy had explained to the valley trio how Brad would be living with them until he was satisfied with the skill development of the two experienced pilots. Being single, he was free to do that, but also didn't expect to be there long considering the experiences of the two "students."

Guiding Rosey through the start up and checklist procedures, he waved to those on the ground and the craft lifted off. Jennifer was on her way to her new, if only temporary, home.

The trip to the valley was uneventful, and the three day trip by mules was reduced to three hours with the chopper. As they descended into the valley at the east end, they could see the group gathered to receive them waiting near the landing area. Rosey did a credible job as he followed Brad through on the landing, and the turbines were soon whining their acceptance of the contact with terra firma and the order to shut down.

Kay was the first to hit the departing passengers and nearly flattened Morgan as she tackled him with a hug, smothering his face with kisses. Paige wasn't far behind and it was a couple of minutes before Brent and Sally could get to Jennifer. When they did, the crying and hugging took over the moments and it was quite a while before anyone else could reach the new arrivals.

Once pandemonium settled down to a mild roar, Morgan gazed in wonder at the settlement. His estimation of the military efficiency exploded into a huge blossom of respect.

There were now three houses setting on foundations! In only three days! How could this be?

Kay chuckled as she observed her husband's astonishment. "You wouldn't have believed the number of uniforms swarming around here, hon. If I would have stood still for even a second, they would have either mounted me to a foundation or painted me! It was simply amazing."

Rosey heard the comment and asked her, "How could they have brought six halves in three days with one chopper, Kay?"

"They didn't. There were five choppers doing the lifts, and three personnel carriers bringing in the troops and other workers to do the foundations on the first day, and the dwellings the next two days. It was an organized madhouse."

Heads were shaking as they toured the houses and were given the fifty-cent introduction, as Cal put it. "I'm still tenting it, but Mom says you guys can move in today," he said with an eager look.

Sally, with her arm around her sister, pointed to the third house in the row. "This is our new home for a while, sis. You'll share this with Brent and I."

Jennifer swallowed hard and unsuccessfully tried to hold back the tears in her eyes as she nodded. Words wouldn't form right then, but the sense of not having her folks absolutely safe and visible overwhelmed her.

The remainder of the day was spent getting each family settled in a dwelling and trying to persuade Cal to live with his folks. He insisted on his tent and finally won out. By the time the sun had traversed the east to west pathway, a peace seemed to settle in where none had been before. Except for Morgan's thoughts, that is.

Morgan screamed at Rosey to stop, but the beating continued. The woman's face was cut in many places and her nose flattened and bleeding profusely since Rosey had doubled his fists. Morgan screamed again and felt his body shaking violently.

"Morgan! Morgan! You have to wake up! Morgan honey, it's me, Kay!"

He slid slowly from the torture of his nightmare and eased

162

his way through the fog surrounding him. He sat up and swiveled his feet over the edge of the bed as Kay continued to rub his back.

"Honey, you were screaming at Rosey to stop something. What were you dreaming?"

"Uumph, uh, nothing important, hon, just a bad dream I guess."

She roughly shook him and put her face close to his; close enough that he felt her breath as she spoke, "Morgan Montgomery, don't you start lying to me at this stage of our lives. You've been withdrawn all evening and now this. Talk, fella, and be quick about it."

The last was said with an even more violent shaking by the shoulders. He ran his hands through his shaggy crop of hair and then put his head in his hands with his elbows on his knees.

"Hon, I can't believe what Rosey did back there at the motel. We crashed in to the room where they were holding Jen and held the two, a man and a woman, at gunpoint. The woman started to stand up from the edge of the bed and Rosey slapped her. Slapped her as hard as he could. It was a horrible sound.

"Her head snapped back hard and she groaned kind of loud. Then, as we tied her and the guy up with duct tape, he jerked their heads together harder than needed and slapped her again! It went against everything I've ever known about Rosey. I can't get the picture out of my head!"

"Hon, all of us have been under a terrible strain for many weeks. We've all reacted in ways we don't normally react. Remember how you addressed the church counsel back home? That wasn't the Morgan they knew."

"But hon, you and I know I had a nasty temper before I accepted Christ. I just let the old Morgan slip back into me for a bit. Rosey's never been like that since we've known him, and he's not accepted the Lord so there's no change for him to come back from. He's always been so calm and cool until the murder back in Ohio. That seemed to change him, and not for the better."

"Dear, Paige and I have had conversations you guys don't have; we've talked at length about our men and their qualities, so I may know more of Rosey than you do because of that.

163

"I'm not saying he's like what you saw, but she shared once that he spent a bit of time with a gang before meeting her. He didn't like what they did to others so he left on his own.

"Now that shows his inherent good attitude, but the underlying carnality is there, just like it is with all of us. The experience you had at the church counsel meeting was the old, pre-Christian Morgan coming out. You know, and I know you know because I've heard you teach it from the scripture, that our carnal nature remains until God calls us home to be with Him and we receive our new and glorious bodies. Then we're changed forever. Keep that in mind as you witness to our great friend. He simply needs Christ, as we did; and for that matter, still do, but in a different way.

"Now, cuddle up here and try to go back to sleep. Rosey is going to be okay."

"I'll try, dear wife, but make no promise. If I start screaming again, just put a pillow over my head."

She laughed and cuffed him gently as she turned away and snuggled down into the covers.

Chapter 21

"I think I can turn you loose with this thing, Morgan. You've caught on to the differences between fixed wing and choppers pretty quickly once you got some time under your belt after your long hiatus from flying, period."

Brad had worked Morgan exceptionally hard on all the maneuvers with the chopper, holding him in a hover facing a cliff face for nearly half an hour. The old skills had long since returned and the new procedures, some of which seemed to go against his highly trained fixed-wing skills were now second nature to him. Rosey had been turned loose by Brad two weeks before and was away to the north in the larger chopper at the request of the general.

Plans were in the making to provide three more houses for the settlement. The militia was in the process of spiriting more key personnel out of the government's clutches and expanding the settlement's usefulness as a depot for insurrection activities. Washington had stepped up its attempts to ferret out key militia members and the reaction in the upper echelon of the militia was to increase the activities in undermining the slow removal of freedoms in the US.

Several provost marshals had found themselves in the clutches of underground groups who ferreted them out of the country to the long abandoned prison in Gitmo in Cuba. The regime that had started the deterioration of democracy early in the century had closed it down but hadn't signed it over to the Cuban government, so it was simply a desolate facility waiting for someone to sneak in and occupy it. The six former provosts housed there were treated humanely, but had zero contact with the outside world. They were under constant watch and given several chances on a steady basis to recant their government's stand on military rule. None had dared to do so.

In other areas of the country, spies were experiencing the need to go further underground. The typical human reaction of rejecting loyalty for money or false promises of safety forced many loyal militia members into hiding. The country's moral decay was rapidly gaining momentum.

In the wake of all that, the moral of the settlement had also taken a dive as the strife between Morgan and Rosey had somehow surfaced. No one knew just what had triggered the revealing of the tiff, but it was there nonetheless. The facts were not known, but the tension was definitely there. The third week after their return with Jennifer everything finally came to a head between Morgan and Rosey.

Rosey had just returned from a trip north with the smaller chopper as Morgan was pre-flighting the larger one. Rosey did his post-flight inspection and then walked over to the other craft as Morgan was completing his walk around. Rosey walked rather brusquely up to Morgan and said, "You got a few minutes before you have to go?"

"I'll take a few, Rosey. Let's sit in the door of the chopper here, out of the sun."

"Can we walk instead? I need total privacy for this."

"Sure, whatever you want. What's up?"

"Let's stroll down by the river, I got something to say to you that can't wait."

They came to the north bank of the rapidly flowing mountain stream and walked slowly along toward the place where it disappeared into the canyon wall at the east end. When they came to a long, flat shelf of rock Rosey stopped and turned to Morgan. Morg' tensed up because Rosey's mannerisms were those of confrontation.

"Morg, you and I have known each other for how long?"

"Whoa, wow, that's a good question. I suppose it's been… what, close to thirty years."

"Thirty one years and five months, Morg."

"Man, where'd they go, Rosey?"

166

"I don't know Morg, don't really care at this point in my life, 'cause they're all in the past and this is now. There's a crazy, stupid, greed driven and power hungry government with much of mankind out of control now! Where did our great United States go, Morg?"

The anguish had built during the speech and came out in almost a cry for help at the end. Morgan felt a lump building in his throat and his vision was getting blurry. He hesitated a minute to gain control before answering.

"Rosey, I wish I knew, and I wish I knew how to put it all back right. But I don't, and I'm not sure anybody does, unless it's God."

"There you go, back to God again. Blast it, Morg, can't you have a conversation without God jumping in?"

"I pray to Him I cannot, Rosey. I never intend to leave Him out no matter who it offends. Not you, not the general, not Marshall, not anybody; so you might as well just get used to it. Seems to me you'd have picked up on that somewhere over the last thirty one years and five months." Morgan's voice picked up a few decibels as he spoke.

"Easy, Morgan, easy. I'm not here to knock your religion, and I'm not here to start any trouble. Just the opposite, Morg. Please hear me out."

"I'm listening; go."

"Morg, when I showed up a wondering teen and got the line crew job at the airport, you had no idea where or how I showed up. You befriended me right away and showed me the ropes on fueling and hangering the ships; sorta kept me in line while I learned to fly and take care of the line duties. I owe you for that. But...you couldn't have known or cared where I had been or what I had done.

"Those first fourteen years of my life weren't very pretty, Morg. My dad was a drunk who liked to bang on people when he had too much, which was always. My mom was a run around, which I think is why Dad drank like he did, and I developed a real mistrust of adults in general. I especially mistrusted women because of Mom.

"When I met Paige, she changed my life where that's concerned. And when I met you, my attitude toward most people changed. Then you married Kay and I saw what a family was supposed to be, or at least in my mind. I came to realize that my Dad had his reasons for his outlook, and I still blamed Mom for it and figured she had ruined a good man. I always wanted to believe my dad was a good man once."

Rosey's eyes clouded up and he paused to collect himself. After a few moments, he continued. "I can't explain or evaluate our friendship, Morgan, except to thank you for being part of my life. There are times when I just wish you would forget about this Jesus thing where I'm concerned; it wears on me. But...no matter what else you do, you at least try to live what you say. That means everything to me.

"Morg, I did you wrong on that trip. So bloody wrong!" He choked up and turned away, standing with head down and trembling slightly. Morgan knew he was crying softly. After a few moments he turned back, tears streaming down his face.

The words came hard because of the huge lump in his throat. He struggles through in spite of it. "How I could accuse you the way I did after who you've been to us...I don't know what happened to me, Morg! I am so sorry, so bloody sorry!"

He lost all composure at that point and Morgan felt the freedom to put his arms around his desperate friend. It was an eternity before they broke the hug. Rosey walked around a bit, then came back to confront Morgan once more.

"Morg, when we broke into that room, I saw my mother. That woman, even though she was lots younger, looked just like my mother. I lost it when I thought of her destroying another life like she did my father's, Morg! That's why I hit her. I know how wrong it was, but I just couldn't hold back. Something snapped inside me and I just let her have all the aggression I've held in all these years.

"Then, when I was taping them together, she spit at me and I nailed her again. The thing I hate is how good it felt to hit that person and watch her pain, Morg! It scares me that I could do that. What makes a man be like that, Morgan, what?!"

Morgan swallowed hard, took a deep breath, and said exactly what he knew Rosey hated to hear. "I know you won't like this, dear friend, but you asked. Every human being has the ability in them to be like that, Rosey. You, me, Paige, Kay, my boys, everyone. It's the result of the sin nature of man. Now, just hold off that negative reaction for a bit, okay? Remember… you asked. I can only give you the answer of what I believe is the right one."

Morgan went on to explain the gospel in detail. This was the first time Rosey had ever allowed him to go all the way through the explanation of Adam's sin causing the fall of mankind and how God sent Jesus to pay the price on the cross for each person's sin. As he told Rosey how he could accept Christ and be guaranteed eternal life he saw the light in his friend's eyes go dim with rejection and broke off the testimony.

They walked slowly along the river on the way back toward the settlement. Rosey finally broke the loaded silence. "So, you won't forgive me unless I do this accept Christ thing, is that it?"

"Of course that isn't it. I'm not God! I have already forgiven you for those things. You didn't have to ask me to forgive you, I love you like a brother and nothing will break that bond we have. Nothing, you meat head, nothing!"

With that, Morgan gave a mighty push on Rosey's shoulder that nearly put him in the river.

"Hey! You trying to get me soaked? I'll…"

He cut his statement short as the sounds of a chopper came to them. They took off at a run toward the settlement, drawing sidearms as they did. The rule had been established that no aircraft could land at the settlement without those present taking their assigned defensive positions until the identification of the newcomer was established. They were to be ready to shoot should the order be given and Morgan was first in line to give that order. Rosey was next in line.

The chopper eased onto the grass and the whine of the turbines began its swan song as they started winding down. Not until the rotors had stopped and the engines totally silent did the side door slide open. A burly soldier in camos stepped down with his hands held high. He pulled an automatic 45 from a holster and laid it on the ground. Then he side-stepped ten feet to his left and stood at parade rest.

When he was still, another trooper departed the craft with an assault rifle in his hands, held high above his head. He laid the rifle with the former man's pistol and joined the first. This action was repeated four more times, and when the six were in formation, their leader saluted the armed defenders and reported.

"Messengers from General Sikes for the commander of this base. There are two men left on the ship; both civilians and unarmed. The pilot is also still aboard. Who do I address?"

Morgan strode forward and faced the leader. "Be at ease, soldier. I'm Morgan Montgomery, acting chief of the camp. What can we do for you?"

"Sir, we have these two with us who are supposed to take residence here with you. They are threatened and quite valuable to the cause. The General said you should be able to accommodate them in some manner. Tents, perhaps, until more can be done for the settlement?"

"They're welcome here, we turn no one away as long as they understand our rules. Bring them out."

The sergeant quickly walked to the sliding door and stuck his head inside for a moment. Two men then jumped down from the aircraft and stood looking around at their surroundings. One was of medium height and dressed in a suit & tie while the other was a wizened little man with beady eyes and a ferret face. His big ears protruded and the buzz haircut only added to the impression of a weasel. He glared at everyone for moments then stalked forward to Morgan.

"I'm Tyler Monsinger and you're no longer the big cheese here. I've been under fire and in the trenches for the last year and I'll be calling the shots from now on."

All 130 pounds of the fellow suddenly became airborne and he was carried high in the air by the strong arms of Cal who unceremoniously tossed him into the chopper. There was a crash, a yelp of pain, and then cursing. The little guy started to leap from the door when he was suddenly facing a shotgun and two pistols, the first shoved under his chin until his head was forced back.

"I will hate to mess this fine chopper up inside with what few brains you seem to have, but mess it up I will if you even blink."

Cal spoke in a calm voice but with a conviction the man fully understood. The pilot called back to them, "If you're going to spread his head all over something, please, please take him out side to do it! I've had all the guff I can take from him for a lifetime and don't want to try and clean all the crap outta this ship that must be inside that worthless head! Okay, fella?"

"Sounds to me like you're not a very popular person, mister, so what'll it be?"

Morgan stepped in at that point and pulled the shotgun away from a stubborn looking head and spoke softly, "You need to understand, sir, that the Army doesn't own this valley, the militia doesn't own this valley, and we were here first. That means, and the two I just spoke of have agreed to this, that we do NOT have to accept anybody we don't want as either visitors or occupants. If you insist on pursuing your intentions of running the place, you'll stay right on that ship and go back with it. And…if you decide to stay and give me any kind of problems once you're here, we'll ship you back. If you fight against it, I have some pretty big boys here who can strap you down and handle you. Those are my terms, I was elected as the head of the settlement, so the rest agree with me, and you have a decision to make.

"Another thing, you stay, you pay. That is…you work just like the rest of us. You will be assigned tasks to perform and if you fall behind, we'll have someone help you if it's warranted. You continue to fall behind, there's a free one way ticket out. Do you want to stay, or are you going back with the chopper?"

A furious stare from the little man locked on Morgan, then shifted from him to Cal, then Brian, and lastly onto Rosey, who held the second handgun on him. Something in Rosey's look froze the man, and he took a deep few breaths before answering.

"I don't have a lot of choice, they nearly got me the last time. I'll stay, but know this, any of you cross me and there'll be the devil to pay."

"Pilot, take this man back with you, he's not welcome here." Morgan turned to the solders and said, "You have him as your responsibility since you brought him here. If he gets off that ship, we'll shoot him. Am I clear on that?"

The burly sergeant laughed and replied, "You know, sir, you tempt me to toss the little piece of garbage off just to rid the militia of him. He's a non-royal pain. However, I've heard nothing but good about this place and the folks living here, so I'll hold back on that."

He held out a hand and smiled as he and Morgan shook. "You'll do fine here, sir, and should you ever need help, we're only two hours away with a small platoon that's armed to the teeth. Here's the frequency for us, I was told to be sure you get this, and to tell you to only call in an emergency. But...you're to call today just to make sure contact is possible.

"Good day, sir, we'll get this man out of your hair."

"Thank you, solder, my apologies for your return cargo. Please tell the general to be a bit more careful after this. Safe flight."

The turbines wound to a start, then spooled slowly to a whine and the rotors began to turn. A hateful face stared out of the window as the craft lifted off and Morgan had a cold feeling he would see Mosinger again. He motioned to Cal and Brian to follow him.

The three walked to the river and started upstream, walking until they were at least half a mile form the settlement. Morgan had given Rosey the frequency card and requested he contact the other end as requested.

Stopping by a large flat rock that jutted out over the fast flowing stream, Morgan plopped down and motioned his two sons to sit beside him.

Before he could speak, Cal opened up. "I'm in trouble, aren't I Dad?"

"Well, sort of. But not like when you scratched the fender on your mom's car. Listen, I want to know what in the world possessed you to respond the way you did back there?"

"Well Dad, I remembered how Rosey did with that arrogant general when he tried the same thing. He doubled that fellow over with a rifle barrel in the gut and backed him off once and for all. I just figured I could make the same sort of move work on that guy."

"Cal, I'm going to tell the two of you some things about my dear, dear friend John Rosenthal that you must never, and I mean NEVER, repeat. We raised you boys as Christians, and you both have accepted Jesus Christ as you Savior, and I want you to respond in like manner. That was NOT what happened back there. Two things are the possible result of your action.

"First, we now have a dangerous enemy we might not have had if I could have handled it differently, but second, and most important, there is no way any of us can ever witness to that man about his need for a savior. That is the main loss because of your actions, and it is a serious one."

"Aw Dad, I am so sorry; I just reacted and didn't think about consequences like that. Now I feel lousy."

"Never mind that, Son. Just keep this in mind from now on. We are going to face circumstances during these terrible times that will test our Christianity to the limit, and we'll ALL fail at times to react as He would have us react. However, we might also face things that require us to actually cause bodily harm to another, and we have to be prepared to do that. The tricky thing in all this is to know when to do that and how to make split second decisions.

"Here's an exercise for you. Dream up situations for each other with two possible results, then challenge each other as to how you might react. Judge the results as though it is a manner of life or death. That will prepare you a tiny bit better to react in the right manner."

"Okay, we can do that. But Dad, what do you think Rosey did wrong with the general? It worked."

"Unless a weapon is threatening you, you always talk first. Rosey didn't react that way. Keep in mind; I have known Rosey longer than you boys have been around, and I've loved the man that long. We are truly best friends. But his standards are not OUR standards. His standards are those of the world."

"But Dad, he's a really good guy. Nobody I know would say otherwise."

"I know, Cal, but being a good guy doesn't get you to heaven, and being a good guy doesn't give you the right to be cruel and violent.

"Listen to what I'm telling you about him carefully. I tell you men this because you need to more fully understand what a world view verses a Christian view can cause. Remember, never a word to anyone.

"Remember those two army jumpers who died at the Henry County Airport? Rosey heard them discussing the killing of your priest friend, Brian, and they were the ones who killed him! So Rosey did what he thought was right; he planned and executed their deaths. He stunned them with a stun gun and pushed them out of the plane. He murdered them, boys. In cold blood.

"He and I just returned from the rescue mission. On that mission he lost it and told me I was getting too big for my britches in so many words because I was giving orders. Then, when we burst into the room where they held Jennifer, he slapped the woman there so hard she nearly went unconscious. No more than five minutes later, after she was TIED UP, he hit her again!

"That's where we were when the last chopper came in; he was apologizing for all that. He explained the woman looked like his mother, who he still despises.

"Guys, I love that man like a brother, and will until I die, but I want; I NEED for you to understand that he is not the example I want you to emulate. Christ, and only Christ fills that role."

The two young sons sat in stunned silence for a long time. Brian spoke first, "I never would have thought he could ever do those things, Dad. I can see, though, how I could want to revenge Danny Simpson's evil murder with my own hands. I still have nightmares over my friend and the diabolical murder he suffered."

"I know, Son, I know, and I can't deny having such feelings myself; but we have to fight against them. Don't think I wouldn't have pulled the trigger on that big guard when we rescued Jen if he would have tried anything.

"My point in all of this is to caution you as to your faith verses your feelings, and in hopes that you think daily about what we are, who we are, and Who we serve. I love you boys, I am proud of you boys, and I wish with all my heart we didn't have to go through these trials. But…here we are, so we must make the best of it.

"Remember, God doesn't put us in any spots without giving us the strength to go through them. These trials are something we are to use for others' benefits, and for His glory.

"Now, Cal, one more question."

"Yeah Dad?"

"How in the world did you pick that crudball up and throw him six feet?"

Brian broke up laughing, Cal's mouth dropped open for a second before he replied.

"C'mon Dad, you know I was benching two-twenty during football last year. That 'crudball', as you called him, probably only hits half of that."

Both Brian and Morgan cracked up and pushed Cal into the fast flowing river. Brian yelled out to his unfortunate brother, "Bench press THAT, brother mine!"

The river flowing through the valley was mostly shallow and fast flowing, but very cold and Cal came out sputtering and threatening vial revenge on both his father and older brother. He tried to catch them, but they had a good head start and easily escaped to the settlement ahead of him.

Kay was watching her three men's rapid approach and noted her baby's soggy condition.

"Okay you two, what's going on here? You two have to gang up on my little boy?"

When Cal heard that he ran to her and grabbed her in a soggy and cold hug that brought out a scream worthy of a wildcat.

"Thanks Mom, I'm glad somebody loves me!"

"I may have once, but not any more, you Cretan! Go away from me; don't come back until you're ready to do all my chores for me for the next two years!!!"

In only a moment the rest of the camp was gathered around the hapless lady and her dripping son, who happened to still grasp her firmly in his arms. She squirmed and fought, all to no avail until everyone there was laughing uncontrollably. The moment eased the tension that had permeated the camp since the chopper had arrived.

Morgan noted that Rosey stood off to the side only smiling at the display and soon turned and stalked off into the house he and Paige occupied. He worried about his friend, and prayed silently for opportunity to help him. He knew John Rosenthal carried a big load at that time and yearned to lift it from his back.

175

Morgan was suddenly aware of the passenger who had departed the chopper with the arrogant Mosinger. He stood quietly smiling at the display by Cal and his mother; a look of both amusement and warmth on his cherubic face. Morgan approached him and offered his hand.

"Welcome to our settlement, sir, I'm Morgan Montgomery."

"Thank you sir, my name is Sean McTavish and if you accept me into the settlement, I'll be very temporary. Of course, I imagine the rest of you also consider yourselves in the same category. But I should be done in just a week or two if all goes well. Can we walk a bit?"

"Sure, Sean. But...I must advise you that we hold no secrets here in the settlement. I don't think it's healthy in our situation."

"Of course, but I only want to present you with my reasons for coming here so you can help the others with their decisions as to whether I'm allowed to stay or not. By the way, most people call me Mac."

"Okay, Mac, but what's the reason we might not want you here?"

"Well, to try to keep it brief; I'm an independent business man who happens to be an engineer and scientist working on a newly developing invention that just may prove valuable to the resistance movement. Which also means the military still faithful to the present government will also want it. That must be prevented."

"I see. And just what is this invention?"

"I really shouldn't refer to it as an invention, it's more of a continuing development of a rather old concept that no one considered pushing on to new horizons. You remember the airborne one man rocket conveyances from years ago? I have been developing those to present to the public for commuting at some future date. My units bear little resemblance to the originals.

"Thing is, they would be ideal for invasion forces to use in heavily populated areas, wooded areas, and places such as that. That's why those familiar with my efforts have suggested I come here to solicit help from you folks in the form of allowing me to work here.

"You see, if I run tests of actual flights in populated territory, they'll be seen. This canyon is so ideal for my testing; your brilliant young man's electronic camo net over this area, the high walls of the canyon, and the altitude above sea level all combine to allow me almost unlimited testing with little or no chance of discovery.

"If I have success here, I can succeed anywhere on earth."

"So, help me understand this better. You want to build and develop your units here and make them available to the militia?"

"Not exactly. Test and develop, yes, but I moved my manufacturing facility and my family to Australia two years ago as I saw the government sliding down the precipice of power grabbing desire to govern by dictatorship. That's not for me."

"But, Mac, we have little to no means of doing any of that here. How is this supposed to work?"

"Well, I talked it over with General Sikes, and he's prepared to bring in all I need to continue, providing you people approve this. He was adamant that yours is the final decision, that this is not a military owned establishment, but private."

Morgan chuckled aloud at the thought of the general's change of heart since his initial visit. His respect for the man went up a few notches.

"So, what happens next after we tell you yes?"

"We contact the General and he puts the wheels into motion. They already have what I need to continue There's a small building with all my chemicals and tools in place that needs no foundation,

"They bring the portable lab in for me. You see, I already have two basic units built, and the fuel cells are partially completed and need only testing for possible further development. The fuel has been the biggest obstacle.

"There's been several reasons this concept has not developed farther, but fuel efficiency and safety has been the biggest. I think I have that solved. I need to prove that and see exactly where I stand with progress so far."

"Let's go present this to the group, I'm confident the answer will be positive."

The two strolled back to the settlement and Morgan slipped into his dwelling to see if Kay was successfully dried out. He was chuckling to himself as he knocked on the bedroom door. From within came the voice of his bride.

"I hear you laughing out there, Morgan Montgomery! You started this when you cast your poor little boy into that cold, dangerous river, you cur. You, sir, are in my doghouse!"

"He slipped, young lady! I had nothing to do with it! Now let me in!"

"Not on your life, I'm not decent yet."

"And since when has that ever mattered, mother of my children? I have important things to tell you about our latest arriving member."

The door swung open and a fully clothed but disheveled lady stood just inside looking him in the eye. "This better be good, buster, 'cause this old wet hen ain't real happy with you and our eldest right now."

He cracked up at that and grabbed her, pulling her close. "Best lookin' old wet hen I've ever seen, lady. Let's go get the others, this is important."

They systematically rounded up the population of the settlement and gathered by the community fire pit where Mac presented his request to all of them.

Rosey spoke first, an air of excitement in his voice.

"I sure vote yes, fella! Providing I get to fly one of those rascals, that is!"

Mac chuckled and nodded. "I'll need test pilots, of course, but most importantly, I need greenhorns to try them, too. Not many, in fact, most of those using these will have any flying experience."

As each member was solicited, they all responded positively and the session was quite brief. As they broke up the meeting, Morgan called Brent to his side and sent him to contact their interim radio server. Brent had become very proficient with the modified Morse code being used. The message was simply to be, "Big yes on flitters." Flitters was the code name chosen by the general and his staff for the rocket sleds, as Mac called them.

Chapter 22

Life in the valley seemed to settle down to an almost normal atmosphere in the next two weeks, and Mac's lab was scheduled to arrive any time soon. The gardens they had planted were being weeded daily, though it was not needed that often. Most people in the settlement just wanted to feel useful.

Cal, Brian, Brent, and Brad were cutting, splitting and stacking wood in preparation for winter. Roy Turnbull had cautioned them about the need for that work. Rosey, Mac and Morgan were building a smoke house for meat they planned to prepare for the long winter months. Although food supplies would be flown in on a regular basis, they chose to not become totally reliant on the militia's provisions.

Jen, who had the communications watch during the mornings, came out to Brent and passed the message that the work shed for Mac was on its way. Brent had written a program to instantly decode the modified Morse code into text as it came to them. The remote antenna two-thousand feet above them on the rim was proving to be very efficient for the low powered transmissions being used by the team.

Brent went to Morgan to pass the word and the group picked up their ever present weapons and took a much needed break. They had close to another hour before the arrival, but were always ready in plenty of time when they were aware of a pending chopper landing.

Rosey squatted down in the grass by where Morgan was reclining. "You know, my friend, if you and I are going to compete with these youngsters for the hunting of elk, we better get some target shooting in."

"You really think we need it? I thought maybe we should give them a little handicap so they might have a ghost of a chance to out-hunt us."

"Seriously, Morg, we don't need to be downing too many of these animals considering how few folks we have staying here. This game will be here all winter, maybe not so plump as now, but still open for harvesting when we need them."

"You're right, of course. I wonder why Roy was so insistent on five of those big fellows?"

"I don't know, but we're talking a lot of work to dress them out and smoke that many."

As they talked about the preparations for the coming winter, though it was still four months away, the bond between these two underwent a lot of repair, and when the sound of choppers interrupted them it was with chagrin they broke off and went to their assigned watch stations.

The choppers were unloaded and the portable shed set in place on the beams that served as skids for it. They had watched, fascinated as the Sky Sleds, as Mac called them were unloaded from the second chopper. The contrivances stood seven feet tall, with the outer shell being a clear acrylic of some sort that was more or less a cocoon of sorts. The platform to stand on was the bottom except for small rollers under in a triangle pattern. Inside, the control panel was quite small with a screen display being the major portion of the panel.

A key, much like an ignition key graced the center of the bottom edge of the panel while two control sticks were mounted on each side of the panel, leaving just enough room for the pilot to slip by them. Directly below the control sticks were the thrusters. They were cylindrical and sported several nozzles sticking out to give directional thrust as well as the main thrust cone at the bottom of each cylinder.

At the top of each of these cylinders was a cap firmly locked in place where the fuel cells were installed when needed. Mac explained the cells could actually be changed in flight if done one at a time.

All the men stood fascinated and eager to try the machines.

180

The second sled was bigger than the first with room and power for two people. The unit had double thrusters on each side. Morgan was doubtful of the abilities of these units because of the small size of the thruster tubes and said so. Mac smiled and assured him the power was more than adequate.

"Previous experiments with jet packs utilized burning fuel, these use chemical reaction to create thrust. It's much more effective, more efficient, and much cheaper. The main thing it provides, however, is the tremendously longer duration of the cells. You drop the two cells into just one tube and you have two hours of flight on the one place unit, an hour and almost a half on the two place machine. My job at this point is to further develop the chemicals for longer duration and possibly more thrust per unit than they have right now."

"So when do I learn to fly the thing, Mac?' Rosey was fairly bouncing in place with eagerness. Morgan hadn't seen his friend this excited for months!

"What's wrong with right now?" Mac asked with a smile.

He guided Rosey into the jet pack and showed them all the controls to be used. He also emphasized how to release the chute should it fail to activate automatically.

"After thrust is achieved, if it goes to zero without the control being responsible, the chute deploys and is close to a zero-zero chute. Anything above ten feet and you'll drop like it was five feet. The landing impact is basically negated." Mac went on to explain the rest of the unit to all, then showed Rosey how to load the cartridges and fire it up.

With a smile that Brian claimed would have to be surgically removed, Rosey touched off the skimmer and slowly lifted off. He hovered a couple of feet up as Mac had instructed, wavering a bit back and forth but basically stable as he did so.

After a few successful turns and pivots Mac waved him off and it was instantaneous for Rosey as he shot up at full throttle! He was at the canyon rim in no time! They could hear the loud whoop of joy as he stopped the ascent and made some turns, then shot off down the canyon.

"You see how quickly one can master the skimmers with only a little training," Mac offered. "When he gets back I'll show all of you how to tip the unit forward a little and get top speed out of it. He's only at about sixty percent now at that attitude."

"How fast will it go?" Cal asked.

"Close to one-twenty"

"What! You can't mean it?"

"That's right, we've timed them both, and we're developing new acrylic shields that are more streamlined in hopes of even more. Making the thrusters angles more adjustable with the controls will also speed it up."

"You said you originally wanted to market these for people to go to work on, do you think people should be turned loose on a hundred mile an hour machine that has no designated roads?" asked Morgan.

Mac chuckled and just shook his head. "Thought of that, but never crossed the bridge on it. Too busy developing the beast."

Morgan smiled as he watched his older son enter the single passenger unit. Cal was looking over the two place unit and Mac raised his eyes at Morgan as though in question. Morgan nodded slightly, giving permission for Mac to put Cal in the skimmer.

For the next several hours the crew took turns in the skimmers, with even the younger ladies taking their turns. The units were so easily controlled there were no problems manifested at all. Mac was greatly pleased at the high praise his inventions received.

Once the shadows threatened to overcome the valley, they called a halt to the fun and most retired to their meager dwellings. Kay snuggled up to Morgan by the community fire pit and sat in silence. After long minutes he sensed she needed to talk and asked her about it.

"What you thinking, Honey?"

"I don't want to be here, Sweetheart. I want to go home to Ohio. I want to throw something at the neighbor's dog to chase it out of my flower bed. I want..." and she sobbed a silent sob in her homesickness. Morgan could only hold her close and pray for them for peace.

The sun slid behind the west rim where the canyon swerved slightly to the north as they held tightly to one another until the fire died down and the night chill slowly crept in to their circle of light from the embers. The two slowly rose and walked arm in arm to the house designated as theirs and disappeared inside for the night. An observer watched from in the same house as they slipped quietly to their bedroom with no meal. Mac sadly hung his head as he felt the couple's deep sorrow over their plight. Surely these terrible times would pass, and hopefully without blood in the streets as most were predicting.

The next morning was Sunday according to Morgan's calendar so they gathered around the fire pit for church. All but Rosey and Paige, that is. Brad played his guitar and they sang several worship songs before Morgan offered a devotional message he had used before at a different time and place. Many prayer requests were made and the prayer time was quite lengthy. Kay expressed her pleasure that the younger people all prayed aloud and with freedom.

Several weeks passed and during that time the little group was very busy with winter preparation. Although they had the military connection to bring them supplies and there were two choppers now stationed there for their exclusive use no one, including Roy Turnbull had any experience or even an idea as to what winter in the canyon would bring.

They downed three elk and butchered them, jerking one and smoking the other two. The little garden had actually been a success and they dried what they didn't eat to put up along with the elk. Wood was chopped, split and stacked and Rosey made a trip to Roy's for the four wood stoves he had informed them were there for them. It was during that trip he was told the government had found a leak in the militia's people and was watching General Sikes and others very closely. There wouldn't be any more military help for quite some time.

Mac had enlisted the help of any who were willing to assist in the manufacture of skimmer fuel plus some experimental parts. He had to turn many of them down, for all volunteered. During those weeks he felt, through testing, he had the final analysis on the fuel formula and was ready to make all they could in his little shack. The problem was, he needed more of the key ingredient to finish the necessary sample.

The room in Mac's shop was very limited and he ended up

with only two "employees" working side by side. Man chose the two youngest members of the settlers, Cal and Jennifer. Cal did the chemical measuring and mixing while Jen carefully read the necessary ingredients to him and served as his quality control supervisor. They constantly goaded each other with good natured jabs and threats for several hours each day while far exceeding Mac's production target for the week he had set aside for the project.

"Listen you," said Cal, "If you insist on all this nagging and harping you're gonna find yourself tossed in that cold, cold river down there! I know what that's like, and you ain't a gonna like it, see?"

With a chuckle Jen replied, "And just what makes you think you can accomplish that task, little fella? That river's a long ways away and I'm a heavy little package! Especially when I can whip you."

"Oh, so you think that, do you? We'll see about that when we quit today."

"Ooooh, I'm shaking." With that dig she bounced her hip against his and chuckled her challenge.

"You'll be shaking with the cold once I finally let you out of that river," he threatened.

Two hours later Mac entered and surveyed their day's accomplishments. He expressed his pleasure quite enthusiastically. "You two are a marvel! You have accomplished far more than I expected. We can fly one of the skimmers and see if this stuff works, and if it does, at the rate you work together I can send a sample off to my family within a week! Good work" Then he added, with a mischievous twinkle, "Now you won't have to put up with each other for a while. In fact, once I get the ingredient needed, if you want I can put a couple of others to work on the project."

The two of them just glared at him until he cracked up. "Okay, okay, if you're stuck on the JOB, I'll concede."

Jen pinched his cheek and shook it gently as she walked out the door, giving him a fake scowl and a wink. Cal just walked by him and gently pushed Jen in the back.

"Move outta my way, lady, we got a date with a river." With that, he grabbed her and swooped her up into his arms and took off toward the river at a run. Jen screamed and started kicking furiously as they drew closer to the rapidly flowing water.

Her scream drew the attention of Brian, Sue, and Cal's parents. They all stopped to watch the spectacle, wondering the cause of the attack.

By the time Cal reached the bank and paused, Jen was thoroughly convinced she was soon to become a splash and was begging Cal to relent. He stopped and looked her in the eye. Their close proximity was intoxicating to both of them and they nearly gave in to the temptation of that closeness. Jen caught herself just before their lips touched and pushed away, returning to her kicking and squirming. She whispered, "Not here, buster, now put me down. Pleeeeaase?"

Cal jerked with a start and then slowly lowered her to her feet. "I wasn't really planning to dunk you. Honest."

"I didn't really think so, but do you realize we have alerted the entire settlement to our little struggle?"

"So what? C'mon, let's get a snack." He took her hand and drew her along with him as he started to the house of his parents. She meekly went along, self consciously leaving her hand in his while blushing all the way. She saw Mac standing in his shop doorway smiling at them.

The following morning Mac approached the group at the morning fire ring.

"We've done all that can be done at this time except for flight testing. I want to put both skimmers in the air right away after breakfast. Who wants to fly today?"

Most of the hands went high and he looked at Cal first. "Calvin, you've worked hard on this, so you get first dibs. Jen, would you like to fly the other one?"

"I would love to, but I've never been checked out! I don't know how!"

"Mac, I've flown both skimmers, can I take Jen in the two place?" Cal tried to ask that in a casual manner, but failed to hide his eagerness.

"I don't know why not, Cal. Jen, you want to do that? What I mean is, can you two get along well enough together that long to not murder each other?"

Jen threw a stick at him and nodded. The group broke up

185

over that.

"Who's next in the single place? Brian?"

"I can do it for you, but I think our resident engineer is about to have a conniption fit wanting to go. Brent, am I right?"

"I would be so honored and excited! Is that okay with you, sir? I don't have much time in the unit, but I think I can be safe."

"I think the fact that you're not a pilot and are fairly new at it is a perfect fit for the testing. You three get some warmer clothes on for the altitude increase and meet me at the shop in twenty minutes."

Everyone gathered for the test flights as Mac gave final instructions to the flyers.

"Cal, since you will have the heavier load, I want you to really wring it out. Go up over the rim, fly back away from it and set down. Shut it off completely, let it set a few seconds and then fire back up. I want to know how it performs starting from the higher altitude with a full load. Well, almost full, anyway. Jen, you need to fill your pockets with rocks so you weigh more than a hop toad for this."

She squealed and shook her finger at him. "A hop toad? A HOP TOAD? Just what is that supposed to mean?"

"Well, you hardly weigh much more than the afore mentioned beast, that's all." He chuckled and waved them off, then gave Brent his instructions.

Cal and Jen climbed aboard the two place and Cal turned on the switch. There was no sound when he did, but the digital panel before him lighted up and requested they both fasten safety belts. As soon as they complied, Cal clutched the short joy stick and twisted it for thrust. They immediately felt the thrusters respond and with a slight pull back, they lifted off, tilting a bit to the right. Cal adjusted and then pulled further back as the two lifted higher and higher.

He took them up a few hundred feet and started forward down the valley, climbing steadily as he did. A quarter mile out he then gave it full command for climb straight up. Jen squeaked as they shot up like a rocket.

"This is better than Cedar Point back home!" she shouted

in Cal's ear.

"Ya know, little lady, you don't have to break my eardrum; there isn't any noise to shout over!"

She laughed and apologized. "It is just so exciting I got carried away."

"Just remember what happened the last time you got carried away, lady."

"And just what was that?" she asked petulantly.

He failed to respond as he was suddenly busy sliding over the rim and looking for a place to set down. Finding an open spot among some large boulders, he was able to ease his craft to a fairly soft set down. Shutting the panel down he turned to her.

"In answer to your question, you nearly got wet."

"And what else, Sir Galahad?" As she asked the question she put her face closer to his while staring straight into his eyes. Their lips met in a hesitant kiss at first, then into a full fledged gentle kiss lasting many seconds.

When they pulled away, Cal whispered, "I think we better get on with our test flight or we might not get back by dark."

"I think that is a very valid observation, mister. You're very wise as well as being very handsome and smart. Not a bad kisser, either," she chuckled into his ear.

"And just how many do you know to compare that too?"

She grabbed his cheek in a gentle kiss and put the end of her nose right against his as she replied, "I'll never tell, just know I liked it." Then she said seriously, "And I like YOU."

He kissed her gently with a little peck and turned the panel back on, listening for the tiny whisper beneath their feet the thrusters started making and easing from the ground as soon as they responded. The skimmer lifted as though it was at sea level and he gave it full thrust, shooting high above the rim and whipping out over the canyon wall at 120 miles per hour. The speed was achieved in seconds and performance was not affected much by the extra altitude.

Cal looked to his left and saw Brent doing some crazy patterns in the air; figure eights, climbs and dives, and he guided his skimmer over that way. They met and formed up together to return to the settlement, Cal descending first, with Brent right behind.

Cal gave Mac his findings and then Brent fairly bubbled over with his excitement at the performance of the unit. The fuel was a success and Mac was very pleased.

"We need to make all we can before winter sets in so I can get a substantial sample out to send to Australia for my people to manufacture in bulk. I've not told you this before, but you need to know now that the militia is counting on several thousand of the skimmers to be in their hands by spring. We plan to mount an offensive at that time and using the skimmers will all but assure a victory.

"I won't tell you where that is to happen; suffice it to say that if successful, we could be a huge step forward in reclaiming this great nation!"

"How soon can we get the other chemical in for you?"

"I need for one of you to get me to Roy's where a truck will pick me up and take me out to our contact for the stuff. Arrangements have been made already according to the last message coming in, so the sooner the better for the trip. I have to go in order to make sure the stuff is the right grade and composition."

"Hey, get ready to go. Rosey and I will take you as soon as you can be ready. We need to bring back another two barrels of jet fuel anyway just in case they're needed. We planned on taking the big chopper tomorrow, we can move up a day."

Rosey turned on his heel and walked toward his dwelling, shouting over his shoulder as he went, "Gotta get my charts, be back in a flash and ready to fly!"

Mac took off to his lab at a trot and Morgan followed suit toward his house. Kay trotted beside him. "Honey, I hate it when you leave the valley, I'm always afraid you won't come back. I know I have to trust the Lord, but it only helps a little when you're gone. Please be careful."

Morgan stopped in his tracks and grabbed his sweetheart, engulfing her in a huge hug as he assured her he would return. Then he continued on for his flight bag.

The three were in the air inside of twenty minutes with Brent on the transmitter key contacting the Turnbull ranch. At the last minute, Brad had tossed his suitcase into the chopper and announced he was finished with the pilots' training and would be leaving. He had signed both Brian and Cal off for solo flight and turned them over to Rosey and Morgan for further training. The valley was losing its guitar player!

In a matter of three hours Mac was in a beat up pickup truck on his way to "somewhere" southeast of the valley and would be gone several days. The extra fuel for the choppers was loaded in four barrels instead of the two planned. They would be a drop in the bucket as far as the large chopper, but still made the pilots feel more secure in their fuel supply in the valley. They would hand pump it into the buried tank there and keep that camouflaged just in case of invasion. It was only a matter of hours before the two were back in the valley and the chopper tied down and secured. The fire was burning brightly and the other residents were merrily celebrating their return by roasting elk steaks on a grill shelf supported by rocks. The aroma was enough to make a vegan want some!

As Morgan hugged his wife she whispered softly to be sure and locate where their youngest was sitting and then take special note of who set beside him. When they broke their hug and walked to the fire Morgan noted his son was lounging on the ground beside a seat occupied by Jennifer. Their places were not what caught his eye, it was their close proximity. Cal was leaning against Jennifer's hip and her hand was on his shoulder as they waited for the elk steaks to finish. It appeared there just might be a relationship developing there.

Later in the house Kay caught him up on the time after the two test flights were over and he had left with the chopper. The two young people had walked toward the river hand in hand and been gone for several minutes before showing up again. Their faces were flushed and they had sheepish looks as they separated and went different directions.

"I can recognize young love blooming when I see it, Mister Montgomery. You mark my words, we're going to need a minister in this valley some day. Or…maybe back in Ohio." The last was said reflectively, with the yearning of homesickness flowing from her face.

Three weeks had passed since they had delivered Mac to

the Turnbull ranch when there was a loud "Hallo!" from the rim accompanied by three booming shots. Cal grabbed the binoculars and searched the rim until he cried out, "It's Roy! He has at least one person with him!"

Three hours later, after the valley residents had watched the mule train of six animals make its way down the precipice with Roy in the lead the group arrived. Two other men were following at the end of the train.

Morgan had a bad feeling as he watched their friend arrive at the bottom and mount his lead mule. He kicked her into a trot while leaving the other five mules to the two men with him.

The lanky wrangler was off the mule before she came to a complete stop.

"There's heck to pay, people. It's the worst news in months for us. Get everyone to the fire pit 'cause we have to palaver big time."

Morgan waved his arm in a circle and dropped it to a horizontal position pointing toward the fire pit. It was a sign they had established when they first organized their settlement. In a matter of minutes they were circled around the pit on the crude benches established there for meetings.

"Good people, first things first, these two men will remain anonymous to you for your own protection. I don't even know them. They're Gus and Sonny if you need to address them for anything. They have been cleared by Hagan Marshall, as he personally delivered them to the ranch. They're listed as hunters on a hunt guided by me for the sake of security. They'll tell you the news that's so bad we had to come by mules rather than risk a chopper. Guys, it's all yours."

The rough looking "hunter" stepped forward and addressed them. "I'm Gus, at least for now, and I've been militia since the first group organized. I'm known to the government and not safe for you to know. We got word three days ago that Sean McTavish has been captured by the government people and will be transferred back to DC next week.

"He was exposed by a sneak turncoat double agent named Monsinger. This Monsinger was meeting with some other spies when he spotted McTavish and contacted an official near their location.

190

"They're holding McTavish in a little burg some hundred miles southeast of here named Struthersburg. It's over into Colorado and is apparently a switching point for intelligence operatives to meet so as to remain unknown. We know about it because we have our own double agents. They have furnished us with detailed information as to location, dates set to transfer McTavish to those who are to escort him east, and timing suggestions for rescue efforts.

"Sonny and I cannot help, we are known to those holding him. Roy has told us of your rescue of the girl recently, and we hope you'll agree to give it a try to get this brilliant man back. If he goes east, we guarantee he will be tortured for information and eventually terminated. Will you try?"

Kay turned white at the question and Paige let out a low moan of anguish. Rosey looked at Morgan and, while pale of face, gave a slight nod; he was willing. Morgan stood and called Kay, Paige, and Rosey to follow him to where they could talk alone.

Once in Morgan's house they sat down at the kitchen table and just looked at each other in silence for a long time. Kay was near tears and Paige looked as though she might pass out.

"Kay, Paige, this is your decision," Morgan began. "The two of you have all to lose if anything goes wrong and I, for one, refuse to put your peace of mind at risk unless it's with your blessing."

"I feel the same," Rosey said. "I rely on your wisdom and feelings, and on Morgan. What he says goes for me double."

Kay wiped a silent tear from her eye and took Paige's hand across the table. "Paige, honey, I never make a decision like this without praying about it. Will you go with me to a bedroom where we can have total quiet and hear His voice?"

"I…I'm not much for praying. But…I'll go with you, you'll have to help me."

"I will be honored to help and to guide you. Come."

They stood and left for the bedroom in the back while Rosey and Morgan stayed at the table.

"Rosey, I think what Kay is doing would be helpful for us as well. What do you think?"

"Aww, Morgan, you know I don't put much stock in your

God stuff. I love you like a brother, maybe more than that, but I just can't get my head around there being a god of any kind. I'll stay here with you though. Unless you prefer being alone for it since I feel this way."

"No, my dearest friend, I want you with me for the rest of my life."

Morgan opened the Bible lying on the table and flipped it open. He knew Kay was also searching the scriptures in the bedroom. He leafed casually through until he stopped at Deuteronomy. He scanned the words until he hit chapter 20. As he read it silently his eyes grew wide with excitement.

"I believe He is showing me His decision on this. Listen to this. 'When you go to war against your enemies and see horses and chariots and an army greater than yours, do not be afraid of them, because the Lord your God who brought you up out of Egypt will be with you. When you are about to go into battle, the priest shall come forward and address the army. He shall say : "Hear oh Israel, today you are going into battle against your enemies. Do not be faint hearted or afraid; do not be terrified or give way to panic before them. For the Lord your God is the one who goes with you to fight for you against your enemies to give you victory."'"

Morgan read the passage aloud and then looked up at a pale Rosey. "You believe that is there for you and I. Morg'? Can God really do that?"

"Rosey, this is not the first time God has directed me to a scripture when an important decision was necessary. This is only one way He guides his people. There are many others. What I want you to realize is, I seldom read the Old Testament. Very seldom, and never in this particular book if I do! Kay is the old testament scholar in the family, I pretty much stick to the new.

"Now, we need to pray about this scripture and about our decision."

Morgan started praying softly and continued for several minutes. Rosey listened carefully, absorbing every word Morgan spoke to God. He noted that several references to Jesus and faithful answers to prayer were made as well as to Jesus' unfailing love for all. There came over him a feeling of another presence that caused the goose bumps to rise on his arms.

Kay and Paige returned at that precise time and plopped down at the table. Paige was openly crying and Kay was white.

"Honey, God led me to Deuteronomy 20 and I prayed long about this. We had a good discussion about this and we have agreed that you need to go. We don't like this decision, but we believe it's God's choice. Right, Paige?"

"Yes," she sniffed, "He made it perfectly clear. Honey, I think I've changed my mind about this faith thing these two dear friends have been telling us about. There's been too much happening back there to be skeptical any longer. We can talk later about it."

Rosey just stared at her before a quick nod came forth. "So, are you telling me that God had you reading the very same part that Morgan just found? That is scary, but there's no way to discount it."

Kay sniffled through a handkerchief and spoke, "Morgan Montgomery, you have frustrated me so many times over these wonderful years we've been man and wife with your adventurous nature; your crop dusting, your sports cars, your lust for speed, so many crazy things I can't remember them all right now but here's been one feature about that crazy nature that I cannot deny; others mean more to you than your own desires.

"I know this is not from your sense of adventure, and I know it comes from your sense of duty. Not just to Mac, but to the cause of winning back this country. Now, that may sound like a dramatization to many, but I know your love for the U S, and I know your love for all of us. You must go God has told me you will be under His will and, therefore, under His protection. Go."

With the last word, she started to openly and silently weep.

Her face had a definite glow to it, and neither Rosey nor Paige could look away. Her tears were not those of sorrow or fear, but of joy at the touch of her beloved Creator and they could tell.

When the four returned to the fire pit, they found Brian and Cal putting together small packs in readiness for the trip. Those watching couldn't help but notice the weapons included in the mix. Brent was fueling the skimmers with fresh fuel cells while the two militia men had their maps spread before them.

"This is the little town, you can punch in the coordinates penciled in here, they take you just to the west of town by seven miles. When the government established their post for their underground activities, our people searched the area and found this honeycombed mountain at these coordinates. They sent some spelunkers in and found the place to be an ideal spot for a base.

"They spent weeks laying out several groundhog routes and marking them for possible use."

Cal and Brian raised their hands at the same time. When Gus nodded at them, Brian asked, "What is a groundhog route?"

Gus smiled and replied, "I thought you Buckeyes would grab on to that with no problem. When a groundhog digs a den, he always has at least two entrances. That way, if one is blocked by a predator, he can go out the other way. That's what we have there.

"Also, they strung rope along the main route so a person can follow the path without light if need be. I addition, they found a huge room they made into a weapons storage room. If you need it, it's probably there. That room is about two hundred yards from the opening just above the highway that leads into Struthersburg.

"The rope guided route leads through over two miles of cave and exits nearly due north of the highway. That location is at the coordinates listed here. There's a large shelf with an overhang giving room to land a small chopper and you'll have no problem putting your skimmers down there. You can then follow the cave rope and emerge about a hundred yards from the highway and a couple hundred feet above it.

"You can find your way down easily because our people spent some time clearing the way. They didn't expose it though, it's well hidden. Just across the highway is a huge mountain lake, a natural one. Once down to the highway, a car will pick you up and deliver you to town. There will be an old blue Buick setting across from the town's only restaurant with the keys in it for your escape vehicle.

"I won't lie to you, the whole town is subversive, including the town marshal. Once you make your move, you'll have no friends. Well, except for one. He's a young fellow who will drive the car and deliver you to the drop off spot. If it goes well, fine, if not, he might not be able to stop long enough to drop you off and the plan will then become to simply run as long as needed. Any questions?"

"Yes, is there a time frame already set in motion?"

"As soon as you leave here, Brent will contact those in the know and the mission is then underway. At that time, food will be delivered to the cave storage room for you for both going and coming."

Morgan looked at the other three with a question in his eyes, and the two women nodded while Rosey stood up and strapped his big 44 magnum around his waste. They were ready.

Gus nodded. "Okay, there's enough time yet today to make the cave and be dropped in town. You might end up affecting the grab after nightfall, and that isn't a bad thing. Goodbye, and good luck."

With only brief hugs all around, they headed for the skimmers and mounted up. Brent ran to the communications hut and sent his message. He returned just in time to watch the lift off. The rescue was underway less than an hour after the men had arrived in the valley. As soon as the skimmers disappeared over the south rim, Roy motioned the two others to the mules and they left for the climb out of the valley.

"If we make the top today, we can get back to the ranch in record time. If we wait, we lose a day, so let's go."

Gus moaned when he saw the saddle on his mule, "Oh man alive, I hope this sacrifice brings me a medal of some kind, maybe a distinguished riding cross?"

"Hey fella, how would you like to make your living on one of these critters? Just wait 'til you get back and try to get comfortable in a recliner!" The taciturn guide then chuckled all the way to the ledge up.

Brian gathered all the settlement together and started a prayer meeting for the task to succeed. He smiled to himself as he noted Cal and Jennifer sitting together, sides touching. He looked at Sue and found her eyes on his with a knowing smile when he tipped his head in the direction of the young couple.

The auto pilot guided by the GPS slid Morgan's skimmer onto the shelf beneath the tremendous overhang at the north entrance to the cave. Rosey was right behind him. They shut down the autopilots and executed a low hover that took them far into the large opening of the cave. Once they were far enough in to hide the evidence of any presence of the skimmers they shut them down and gathered their small packs. Both men carried revolvers on their side with a second pistol in a shoulder holster.

They drew a big breath and located the rope guide that would take them through the two miles of cave.

"I'm not in love with this cave idea, Rosey. I don't much care for tight places where I can't see everything around me. You wanna go first?"

Rosey laughed and commented, "You know, Morgan Montgomery, I've seen you do things I would never think of trying, and I've watched as you stuck your head in places not meant for man to go, but it's so hard for me to believe your claustrophobe AND your fear of heights! You, of all people! You, who flies airplanes; you, who faced down a bully at a ball game last year; you who lays in the belly of an airplane bucking rivets for hours on end, and yet you don't do this sort of thing eagerly. Man, my friend, you are a complex dude!"

"Just lead on, mister philosopher, and make it snappy."

Rosey cackled loudly and located the rope, leading off into the darkness with his headlamp piecing the gloom. The cavern rambled through the mountain in a series of ups and downs that worked their legs and bodies with the exertion. When they arrived at the huge storage room an hour later they were glad to flop to the soft pallets they found there with sleeping bags for padding.

As they searched the space with their probing lights, they discovered an armory that would do a drug cartel proud. "Look there, Morg', RPG's, and if I'm not completely nuts, there's some old world war two bazookas! I can't believe that! And some AK's with ammo, hand grenades; sheeesh, what do these guys think they can do with all this stuff?"

"Well, I guess they're willing to take whatever they can for weapons like beggars can't be choosers. I tell ya one thing, bro', these guys are as serious as a heart attack."

"You got that right. Well, time is creeping up on us; we better get down to the highway or we'll miss our contact and have to walk to town!"

They stood, stretched, and grabbed the rope guide and climbed the steep grade leading toward the last two hundred yards of tunnel. When they stepped out into the fading sun their eyes still objected to the sudden glare. They stood for a while to acclimate, then searched for the way to the highway. As the two men had instructed, they reached the highway and slipped down behind a large boulder to wait. Their tired bodies stiffened with the hard setting and lack of motion. It was over fifteen minutes later they heard the sound of an approaching vehicle.

A beat up pickup truck roared by, went around the sharp turn a hundred yards away, and then stopped. The truck backed up very fast, stopped by the boulder, and a young man in his very early twenties stuck his head out the driver's window.

"Anybody home? We need to go quick if you are "

They ran to the other side and climbed in. "Why did you go on by, we thought you weren't our ride."

"I needed to get around this curve right up here to make sure no other cars were coming. Didn't want nobody to see me pick you up.

"There's a change of plans, I can't drive the getaway Buick, 'cause they'll maybe see who I am. But, the keys are in it, and you can see the way back out here no problem. How you're gonna hide the Buick, I don't have a clue.

"Best bet is to drop two of you off here, go on up the road until you can find a place to dump it and have the others pick you up with one of those airborne things you have. There's a driveway some two miles back that way and you can take the car back in far enough to have it not seen, then climb out of the place until you disappear into the rocks.

"I'm really sorry about this twist, but I just found out I'm under suspicion and likely being watched."

"We'll manage someway, don't let it bother you."

"Good, I appreciate your understanding. Now, town is just another five miles up this way and I'm gonna stop just this side and have you get under the tarp in the back. I'll drop you off in a little park two blocks behind the jail. That's where they have your man. He's guarded by one man and there are no other prisoners. The guy who is the jailer right now is a n old dude and can be really nasty, but he's a base coward, so you should be able to shut him up okay.

"I moved the car from where your instructions said it was so it would be easier for you. It's directly across from the jail. As soon as I drop you off, I'll slip around and start it if you like, that will save a few seconds for you."

"Don't do that, it might draw attention we don't want. We might want to look things over a bit before we make a move, anyway. This whole thing has been one rush, rush cycle of craziness. We just started this, this morning!" Morgan was getting nervous about the whole thing and Rosey wasn't far behind him. They were not trained military men who knew a lot about this sort of mission!

About that time they entered a glade of trees within sight of lights ahead. They jumped out and climbed into the bed, slipping under the tarp spread out there. They were barely under when the truck jumped ahead. Potholes bounced them around with little to no mercy, but it was a mere eight minutes before the truck stopped again and the youngster banged on the rear window as a signal to exit. They jumped out to find themselves in another little grove of trees, these with picnic benches beneath them.

There was enough light from the street lights ahead for them to examine the map they had of the town. They located the jail by that, then looked over the pictures of the jail interior included with the paperwork Gus had given them. Once they felt familiar with their surroundings, Rosey stood and loosened his 44 in the holster.

"Wait a minute, cowboy, we can't go yet."

"Why not, why wait?"

"Because we haven't prayed again, that's why."

"Oh. Well, remember, that's not as natural for me as it is for you. Okay, get with it, then."

Morgan chuckled in spite of the seriousness of their plight, then lowered his head and prayed for safety and success, not forgetting to pray that they would not have to harm anyone in their effort. Then he grabbed Rosey, turned him to face himself, and, swallowing hard, told him how deeply he loved him.

"Hey, Mister Montgomery, you know that isn't necessary for you to say. But…I appreciate it, and you should also know all that love is coming back to you. Now, before either of us has a chance to chicken out, let's go free Mac."

They slipped up a narrow alley running beside the jail, which was a squat, small brick building. They pulled their coats together against the chill, which wasn't all air temperature, and stood in what they hoped was a nonchalant manner at the corner of the building. The street was deserted.

Morgan looked at Rosey and nodded. They moved quickly to the jail door and Rosey turned the handle; or rather attempted to do so. It was locked!

"Now what do we do?" Morgan asked.

Rosey quickly knocked hard on the door and cried out, "Open up, state police! Hurry up, unlock this door!"

A few seconds elapsed before a voice on the other side asked, "Whaddaya want? Door's locked at five and stays that way 'til mornin' so get lost."

"Didn't you hear what I said? We're the state police, and we need to talk to someone here. Open up or get dragged out in chains, buster!"

"Tell me what you need through the door. I open this and I get worse from the chief than you can give me."

"Then you better call him and get his sorry tail down here, and make it quick!"

Morgan looked at Rosey as if he was crazy, but Rosey just motioned for him to slip around the corner and wait. Morgan quickly obeyed.

"Chief ain't gonna like me calling his cell phone, he's in a big poker game tonight."

"If you don't call him down here, I'm not only going to tear this door down, I'm gonna haul your sorry rear end off in irons. NOW GET WITH IT!"

He heard mumbling from inside, then the fellow said, "He's on his way, and I wouldn't wanna be you when he gets here!"

Rosey drew his 44 and slipped it inside his coat, keeping

his hand on it, then hunched his shoulders and stood facing the door. It wasn't long before a pudgy officer came stomping down the sidewalk from the opposite direction he and Morgan had come from.He let the man walk all the way up to him before turning.

"What in blazes you want, you…"

The words stopped abruptly as a loud, double metallic click quieted him as the 44's hammer was pulled to a full cock and the muzzle ended up against his nose. The eyes crossed as he looked unbelievingly at the barrel and then he stiffened even more as another double click sounded against the back of his head when Morgan's 44 bumped solidly against him. He had slipped behind the fellow as soon as he had passed.

"Tell your man in there to open the door. You better sound normal when you do, we don't want to blow your head off before we blow the lock off that door. Move."

"M…Murray, it's okay, open up, we need to come in."

Much grumbling and shuffling was heard before the lock clicked and the door started to open. Rosey shoved the officer through before it was even half open, knocking poor Murray onto his bottom with the officer on top. Morgan quickly closed the door behind them.

"Murray, get the keys to the cells, this is an old fashioned wild-west jail break. Exciting, isn't it?"

Morgan nearly choked on hearing Rosey say that. He would have laughed out loud if not for the seriousness of the situation. Murray leaped to obey, nearly falling over the officer as he did so.

They were amazed that no threats or other exclamations came from the chief. They walked the two back to the cells, finding Mac sound asleep in the first one. The other cells were empty, just as Gus had told them.

"Mac, wake up, you're going on vacation!"

The little scientist looked up through owl-eyes, trying to realize where he was and what was happening. Then he jumped to his feet with a huge smile.

"Wow, rescue. This is great."

They freed him, then locked the other two men in the cell furthest back, taking the keys back to the office, then slipped out the door and across the street to the old blue Buick setting there. They climbed in and Morgan quickly started the car and eased it away from the curb. As he drove carefully out of town they saw two cars roar up to the front of the jail and men jumped out to run inside.

"How did THAT happen?" Rosey yelled. "How did they know so fast?"

"We didn't take his cell phone, we're a fine couple of outlaws, Rosey! How could we overlook that?"

The town disappeared from the mirror as Morgan tromped the gas pedal to the floor and abandoned all attempts at not being noticed. It wasn't long, just before the next curve took them out m of sight again, before he saw headlights coming behind them. They had only about a half-mile head start!

The old Buick, a 2004, was no dog and Morgan was driving it right on the edge as he careened around curves with squealing tires. He was eating up the miles to the escape spot very quickly.

"Morgan, how we gonna ditch this car and get away?"

"I have a solution! You guys buckle in really good. Mac, buckle in behind me, then lie down and buckle the other belt on Rosey's side around your chest. Can you swim?"

As Mac affirmed he could swim, Morgan was running all four windows down.

"What you doing, Morgan, you think we can go faster as we freeze, or what?"

"The car will sink faster with the windows down and maybe be out of sight by the time they get here! Now Rosey, when we go off the road, cross your arms in front of you and put your hands over your face so the air bag doesn't stun you."

They were now just a quarter of a mile from the sharp 90 degree curve that was directly in front of their desired climbing spot. As Morgan's intent dawned on Rosey, he yelled at Morgan to forget it, it wouldn't work. Morgan had the big car rocketing along at near top speed and as soon as he saw the curve, he yelled for them to hang on.

As the poor Buick rocketed into space Rosey screamed at him,

MOOOORRGAAAAAAAAAAA AAAAAAAAAN!!!!!!!!!

The faithful Buick leaped from the cliff, nosing down with the weight of the engine immediately as Morgan turned the key off to kill all lights as soon as possible and then crossed his arms in front of his chest.

The thirty foot drop took no time at all and the car slapped the water nose down with a frightening crash. Air bags deployed in the front, he heard Mac let out huge grunt in the back when they hit, and then all was quiet except for the rush of freezing cold lake water pouring in through all four windows. Morgan released his belt and felt to his right for Rosey. The man was struggling away from him so he assumed he was exiting the window and turned to check on Mac.

He felt the little man's body as it slipped through the back window so pulled himself out through his own window. By then they were several feet under the surface, as he had counted on, and he swam in the direction of the shore underwater as far as he could, hoping the others would do the same.

There was no need to be concerned, however, for when he broke the surface he saw the lights of the other two cars plummeting along the highway a full quarter-mile beyond their position.

"Over here, there's a shelf!" Mac had been the first to the rocks.

Morgan heard Rosey muttering as he swam that direction, then the splash as he exited the water. Morgan was the last to arrive.

"I outta shove you back in, Morgan Montgomery, I just outta! You tried to kill us! You crazy…"

Mac was laughing through chattering teeth as he searched for a way up the sheer cliff as the cold grabbed all three. Mountain lakes are never really warm, and this one was typical in its temperature. Couple that with the high elevation night air and you had three miserable guys trying to climb a sheer cliff.

"Over here!" Mac had found a place that seemed promising, and fifteen minutes later he and Rosey reached down from the roadbed and dragged Morgan the last couple of feet to safety.

"Guys, we need to run for it. They won't go very far that way if they're not seeing lights ahead of them. Come on!"

They ran the hundred yards in soggy shoes and clothes, practically leaping up the path to the top when they got there. Ten minutes later they were at the mouth of the cave. They were miserable and shaking such that Rosey had a hard time turning the light on when he finally found it.

Two hundred yards of twisting, turning, climbing and descending cavern later they burst into the large room and quickly went to the firewood already laid out for lighting. Mac grabbed the lighter and fired the tinder beneath the wood, watching eagerly as the flames licked upward. That wasn't fast enough for Rosey and he grabbed a bottle of lantern oil and tossed a splash onto the wood. There was a whoosh and the flames leaped up and out at them and then settled into the desired fire.

Morgan grabbed three blankets off the pile he had noticed before and tossed one to each of the others. He quickly stripped out of his soggy clothes and wrapped the blanket closely around him as he spread the clothes out by the fire.

Mac and Rosey needed no urging as they followed suit. They were soon huddled as close to the fire as they could get without catching their blankets on fire! It was many minutes, long minutes later before any of them began to settle into a normal breathing rhythm.

"I wanna know what in the world got into you to try such a crazy stunt, Morgan Montgomery."

"We had to ditch the car and get away without them catching us. How could we have done that if we went on to the driveway the kid told us about? This way the car disappeared and so did we. Right where we needed to, by the way, just in case you hadn't noticed." His sarcasm was wasted on Rosey, who just glared at him for a few seconds.

Then Rosey broke into a huge grin. "Just wait til we tell THAT story to the settlement! Kay might never ride with you again, brother mine."

They all started laughing, with the laughter becoming a stress release until it was raucous and loud. They continued for several minutes, then settled down. Mac retrieved three more blankets for them and suggested they get some sleep. He stoked the fire until it flamed high and hot and they rolled further into the blankets and attempted to do just that.

It was many minutes, however, before hearts slowed down enough for sleep, then when it came, it came hard and the three became as stones.

Many hours later it was Mac who first awakened. He roused the other two and tested his clothing for dampness. The fire had died way down without anyone stoking it during their sleep but there was just a hint of dampness in the heavier articles. They were donned anyway, though with quite a bit of grunting and groaning with the stiffness in their bodies. All three stood by the freshly stoked fire and shivered noticeably.

"What time you got, Morgan?" Rosey asked of his friend.

Morgan checked his watch and visibly reacted with shock. "Guys, it's after nine AM! We gotta get out of here! They'll be searching this area, maybe they are already, and we might not be able to take off if we can't sneak along the ridges."

They trekked back to the entrance, sneaking slowly to the opening as they heard the sounds of a chopper nearby.

"Drat! Men, we slept too long, that chopper will keep us here today!" Mac was clearly alarmed at the thought.

"What do ya think they're doing? Sounds to me like it's hovering right down there."

Morgan peered around the edge of the rock and quickly ducked back.

"They've spotted the car," he said in a hushed voice. "And they're climbing the rocks heading up this way. Guys, we have to get to the skimmers and try to sneak out of here."

Rosey's reply was to take off back toward the room muttering as he did about the "Blasted clear mountain lake water."

During times of conflict there are certain people who suddenly come to a point in their lives where they decide, much against their nature, that it is time to dig their heels in and make a stand. That decision is not necessarily always one of courage, though it could be, but sometimes simply occurs because it seems to be the only choice that is right. John Rosenthal had reached that point.

He ran the two hundred yards back to the cache of weapons, grabbed an outdated rocket grenade launcher and a sniper's rifle and charged back toward the entrance. When he passed Morgan and Mac he shouted something that sounded like they should run to the skimmers. Morgan tried to tackle him and failed.

"Mac, we have to catch the idiot, we can't make a stand here!"

It was too late, for they heard the rifle bark once, twice, and a third time. They had no way of knowing two of the searchers were even then falling from the rim with severe wounds from the rounds.

As Rosey watched in fascination, the military helicopter slowly raised up over the rim, seemingly in slow motion. It pivoted toward him and as it did, he grabbed up the old RPG launcher praying it wasn't too old to work.

He fired almost at the same instant the chopper launched a rocket from a battery of rockets on the left side of the ship. The two missiles passed within inches of each other and the larger modern one found the cavern entrance and went several yards into it before pounding into the wall of the cave. At the same time as that horrific explosion the RPG round struck the remaining rockets in the launch tube on the helicopter and they all exploded at once.

The twin explosions shook the very core of the mountain as the helicopter seemed nothing more than a monstrous ball of flame sending burning fragments the size of Volkswagons in every direction while the cavern entrance shuddered with a landslide of epic proportions.

Within seconds the cavern had disappeared under hundreds of tons of rock and shale. The entrance was totally clogged and now non-existent.

Inside, Morgan and Mac got up from where they had fallen with ears ringing from the terrible explosion. Neither one could hear the other as they both scrambled to find the light. Morgan found it first when he saw a tiny glimmer through the dust filling the air around them.

He grabbed it, and ignoring Mac he charged back toward the entrance. He didn't get very far before finding the pile of stone that now choked it for many yards. He started clawing at the stones as though he intended to move them all in an effort to find Rosey. Mac tackled him to the floor and just held him with his arms pinned to his side in a bear hug for several minutes.

Morgan was reduced to a sobbing, trembling wreck of his former self as he stared at the tomb of his best friend. They lay there for well over an hour as Mac was content to just hold Morgan in an attempt to comfort him. When Morgan finally turned his dirty, tear stained and miserable face to Mac he gently pushed free of the other's arms and stood to his feet. He stumbled away in the direction of the vaulted room not even asking Mac to follow.

They gathered some meager supplies once they were there and started the trek to the other end of the cavern, both seemingly in a stupor of unbelief. The price for the rescue had turned out to be very high. They weren't even sure they could still take the skimmers out without being detected, but were in such a state of shock it never occurred to them they might be seen.

Mac helped Morgan into his single place skimmer and buckled him in.

"Morgan, are you sure you can fly this thing? We could leave it here and take the twin place if you want."

Morgan growled something sounding like a positive answer so Mac ran to the other skimmer and climbed aboard. As soon as communications were established he told Morgan he would lead out, that Morgan should follow him. Getting no answer, he fired up and slowly slipped from the overhanging shelf and turned immediately to the east and followed a crevasse twisting and turning for several miles before forcing him to rise up over the rim.

Morgan was right behind him even though he was totally silent, not answering any of Mac's queries as to his status. It was mid afternoon when they slipped into the valley through the notch Morgan and Rosey had used to fly the Cheyenne's through on that first day that seemed a hundred years before.

Morgan recovered from the shock of losing his friend sufficiently to start worrying as to how he could break the news to Paige and the rest of the settlement. He was trembling as they set down by the fire ring. The first person he saw running toward them was Paige...

Chapter 23

Cal and Jen watched as the skimmers disappeared over the south rim and then strolled to the lab where Mac had them working on the fuel development. Cal was obviously concerned, and Jen could sense his tension.

"Cal, your mom obviously supported your dad doing this; how do you think she can do that?"

"You need to know my folks better, Hon. Their faith is incredible."

"Did you just call me Hon?"

"Errrr, I guess I did. Do you care?"

"Hmmm, do I care? Yes, I care, I care for you. You can call me what you want, but maybe it's a bit early in our relationship for that around the others. Ya think maybe?"

"I'm sure you're right, but I've admired you from the day you set foot in this place. You are so pretty, so sweet, and seemed to be nearly an orphan that you grabbed my heart right away. This crazy situation has turned so many lives upside down that there's no room for normal relationships, whatever normal is."

"Sooo…what does that mean as far as you and I, Cal? I guess I'm not too sure exactly what you're thinking as far as our relationship goes."

"Well, I guess I never did believe in love at first sight, even though that happens in books a lot; but something triggered inside me when I saw you and heard you speak to your sister. I just sort of folded over then and wanted to know you better right away."

"But you didn't even talk to me for several days, Cal. You even seemed to avoid me."

"I know, I was afraid I might really make a fool of myself until I knew you better. Then, when Mac put us together in the lab, I was sunk. Totally sunk.

"Then you treated me like you've known me all our lives. I'm a pretty shy guy around girls, so when you patted me on the back when I hit one of the formulas on the head, it nearly blew my mind and gave me a lot of confidence to try to know you a lot better. You'll never know what that did for me, Jen "

"Then I'm glad I did my normal thing there. I'm what my sis calls a toucher, so that pat was just me being me. Cal, I don't know where we are going to end up, but from what I already know about you and your family, I hope it's wherever you are. I think I'm in love with you, fellow, so there, I said it!"

He stepped close and pulled her into a soft, warm hug with tears running down his cheeks. They held on for many minutes, just enjoying the closeness together.

A pair of bright blue eyes looked on from a vantage point high above them as the pair stood together. Sue Montgomery loved climbing the rugged face of the north wall for her meditations sometime around mid-day. She could see the settlement, and beyond that; the rushing river and the wildlife feeding beyond the opposite bank. She gleaned an intense peace from the tranquil scene. She smiled when the couple parted and walked away hand in hand.

Sue closed her Bible and started her five minute climb down. She skirted the remains of the old rotted cabin known to them as "the rattlesnake ranch" while keeping a close eye on her steps to avoid any of the abominable creatures. When she reached the settlement she found Brian and collared him.

"Hey, husband, I think we might have a budding romance on our hands."

"Why do you say that? Did you see the mule flirting with another four-legged creature?"

That earned him a punch in the ribs that forced a grunt of major proportion. "Hey! Don't do that! I'm easily bruised, ya know."

"You haven't known bruises yet, husband mine. You just

wait 'til I really hand you one. Now, stand still and listen. I was up on my perch when I saw Cal and Jen come out of the lab. They were talking very seriously from the body language and then there was a really, really long hug. I mean a HUG, mister."

"So, you were spying on a private conversation, were you? I think that makes you a nosey little snitch who needs a trip to the river to baptize you for your sins."

He grabbed her up and ran toward the river with his arms full of a whirling dervish as she knew he would use any excuse whatsoever to administer to her a dunking in the cold water. When she managed to flip herself up and get her legs around his neck she knew she had him. If she went in, HE went in with her.

"All right, all right, I give, no baptism. I'll let you down if you let go."

"Not 'til you put me down first, mister. I don't trust you. You set down in the grass and then I'll let go with my death hold."

He did as required and then started laughing as she released him.

"How in the world did you do that?"

"Never you mind; it was just my superior speed and skill. Now, you listen to me. You need to have a little talk with that brother of yours. You know; the big brother advice column and all that."

"WHAT? You gotta be kidding; big brothers don't give love advice to little brothers, especially when the 'little' brother out weighs him by twenty pounds of pure muscle! Forget you, girl!"

"Brian, I'm serious. Cal and Jen are still very young, and to be dropped into this forsaken valley in such totally traumatic conditions opens them up to the same responses that we read about with love on the rebound. You promise me you'll talk to him."

"Well, I know I won't get any peace until I do, so, okay, I'll talk to him. But if I get a black eye or dumped in the river, you're gonna hear from me!"

"Oh, get real; you know Cal is a gentle guy at heart. And... he almost worships the ground his big brother walks on, in case

210

you haven't noticed."

"No, I hadn't noticed. Now, go 'way and leave me to walk my last mile."

She giggled, kissed him, and ran to the house area.

Brian had to search for quite a while until he found Cal on the bank of the river with a fishing pole in his hand. He had cut the pole and fashioned a hook from a pin in order to try for trout. Roy Turnbull had provided them with rod and reel outfits on his last trip, but Cal was really more about killing some time and thinking things through, so he chose the old fashioned way.

"Hey little brother, how many trout ya got for supper?"

"Dunno, I lost count right after two dozen. What you doing roaming around? Sue trying to put you to work so you need to disappear for a while?"

"Oh, she's putting me to work all right." He plopped down beside Cal and just watched the water run by for several minutes. Then he spoke.

"Listen, Cal, this really isn't any of my business, but Sue thinks I need to talk to you about you and Jen. You mind?"

Cal looked down at his shoes for a bit, then shook his head. "I know anything you, or Sue, for that matter, say will be out of caring for me, so go ahead,"

"Well, she happened to see the two of you in a very close hug, and she's concerned about maybe the two of you are in a similar situation as someone who just lost a lover and are on the rebound. I guess it's a natural thing to be concerned about, considering the way all of us have been dumped in here. She says I should caution you to go very slow. Aaaaand…I guess I would agree to that advice. What do you think?"

Cal laid the pole down and leaned back on his elbows for a bit before answering.

"Here's the way I see it. You probably expect me to tell you it's none of your business, but I don't feel that way at all. Mom and Dad have driven this family thing into our heads and hearts until we should expect all the other family members to care, and I do.

"But, you remember the talk we had with Dad several years ago about the western novels he reads? We were discussing

211

how the characters always fell in love in ten seconds or so. Remember Dad's explanation? He said it wasn't so far fetched because of the numbers, rather, the lack of numbers of people as the west was settled.

"People were thrown together and just naturally accepted the fact they didn't have a lot of choices for a mate. Well, I'm not sure that applies to Jen and I, but I fell quick when she came here. She's bright, witty, mischievous, and seems to have a big heart.

"Brian, that girl is the one. I hate this valley with a passion! We came here to keep Dad and Rosey out of jail! Yes, it's beautiful to see, and the hunting is phenomenal, but I hate it.

"I want to be back in Ohio! And I want all this big government to be gone, all the graft, all the meanness, all the power hungry fools running Washington. I want them GONE! But if I can't have that, then I want to see my parents and my brother and my friends have some semblance of a normal and happy life. Whatever that takes, count me in.

"But for now, Jen is the closest thing I have to a contact with normalcy."

"But Cal, you still have all of us here."

"Yeah, and it isn't NORMAL! I see Mom and Dad eating supper at a fire ring at night instead of at the family kitchen table. Yeah, I know that's gonna start happening soon once we get some furniture built, but it still won't be the same.

"Mom and Dad worked hard to get their house, and it was paid for! You worked hard to get your place, and even though it isn't paid for yet, all your work was tossed down the toilet by a corrupt government!

"I just want to be back on Ohio with all of Washington GONE! I'm tired of these cracker boxes we're living in, I'm tired of no pick up basketball games at the school. And I'm even tireder of not seeing more people than just our few here. Not that anyone here isn't great, but I want more. I want to go BACK! And I can't. And that makes me hate this crazy stuff even more.

"Do you get me, Brian?"

Brian nodded, then said, "I get you, Cal, and I mostly agree with everything you've said. But...we can't go back for a long time, if ever. Now, I don't plan to stay in this remote valley forever, but neither do the rest of us, so try to hang tough. As far as Jen is concerned, just keep your head straight and treat her like the lady she is and you'll be fine. Don't let this situation govern your morals or passions, look to Christ for that, okay?"

Cal looked at him with tears in his eyes and clutched his shoulder. "I know, brother, I know; and I understand your concern, but we'll be fine, and we'll somehow weather this hell we're going through. But...I don't have to like it."

"You sure don't, and neither do I. Let's go see what the others are doing to cope with Rosey's not being with us any more. Ya know, it's crazy, but it somehow seems if I don't say his death, or killed, or anything like that it will maybe let him come back someday."

The two brothers walked arm in arm back toward the settlement, heads hanging and eyes blurry at the thought of Rosey's death.

Indeed, the entire valley seemed under a shadow, the shadow of death.

Meanwhile, to the southwest a hundred or so miles, the setting sun found a figure with three saddled horses in tow slipping furtively toward the dinky little Colorado town of Struthersburg. He slipped in from the south and tied the horses in a small copse of trees just a couple hundred yards from the town hall and settled down to wait for dark.

When the sun had set and another hour had silently crept by, that shadowed figure left the shelter of the trees and slipped stealthily to the back of the building, settling in under a window that was slightly cracked open to let in the cooling night air. He listened with bated breath at the conversation going on inside. He recognized the voices except for one. Then, as he listened closer, he caught a name and realized who the third person was. It was the little man, Monsinger, who spoke so vehemently.

"Look, they told me I would get whatever I wanted here to try and find the nest of snakes up there in the mountains. Now, I want that man in there tomorrow and I WILL have him. You say you need to cast that shattered leg first thing in the morning, NO! I want that left free because I WILL use it tomorrow."

213

"What do you mean, you'll use it?" That was the town marshal's voice.

"You ever hear a man scream when you twist a broken leg like that one? I'll have him begging me to write down the coordinates of that nest tomorrow."

"Now you wait just a minute, buster. I don't hold with torture and that ain't happening in my town."

"In case you haven't noticed, big shot, this isn't your town. This is the government's town, and as of yesterday, I'm running it. Now, I'm getting some rest so I'm fresh tomorrow. I want you to lock this place tight, and I want you out of here. I'm sleeping in the next room for the night just in case some hero tries to break that bum out of here. Scoot!"

The other two men were muttering between themselves as they left, and the shadow settled down for a long wait. The lights went out fifteen minutes later; the intruder waited another thirty before easing the forgotten window open.

Quiet as a shadow he slipped over the sill and stalked to the room he knew held his prey, the wounded man they had spoken of. When he eased the door open he saw a figure on a bed, hands handcuffed to the tubular head of the bed. It was a cruel position in which to leave an injured person, and that would be like Monsinger to instigate such treatment to soften up his victim.

The shadow pulled a large hunting knife from his belt sheath, reversed it so the handle was sticking out by his little finger and gently bumped the door with it. He stepped behind the door and waited. Soft footsteps were coming slowly along the hall.

The door was thrown open and Monsinger leaped in, gun at the ready, only to be met with by a backhanded swing with the handle of that large knife soundly meeting his left temple. He dropped like a sack of potatoes.

A soft light came on after being retrieved from a backpack on the visitor's shoulder and showed the form on the bed to be looking at the body on the floor. His eyes were clouded with pain. Monsinger was quickly searched, then, from the wealth of the backpack came a roll of duct tape. It soon found its way around the little spy's wrists behind his back. The next few strips went around his mouth, then his left leg was pulled up to meet the wrists and taped fast.

Once the trussing up was done, the invader slipped down the hall to the office, light in hand, and searched the top drawer of the first desk he came to. No luck. Another top drawer, then at the third desk he found his prey; the handcuff keys!

Returning to the invalid, he quickly freed him from the cuffs. "My friend, you surely got yourself into a mess. That leg must hurt like blazes. I have a little something for it, even though I gonna have to carry you out of here."

He dug into that backpack again and came out with a vial of pills and a bottle of water.

"Doc says these will dull your pain really quickly, but you're gonna go out on me. With what you're gonna go through tonight, you need to be out, and not just a little."

The wounded man shook his head and pointed frantically to his ears with both hands. His voice cracked as he hoarsely whispered, "I can barely hear you, my ears are ringing really bad!"

"Okay, here, take these, and drink slowly while I work on you." He handed the bottle and two pills over, then reached for that seemingly bottomless backpack again.

Out came two long sections of some article in a kind of roll. He cut the leg of the pants off at the knee and whistled softly when he saw the shattered leg. It was a multiple compound fracture! The would-be rescuer had dropped out of nurses training when the government takeover had started, but had gotten far enough to have some basic knowledge of handling such injuries.

A soft pad with an ointment was wrapped gently around the leg and then one of the rolls was opened up, it was a section of tree bark from some form of birch or something similar. That piece went around the leg in the front and was taped at the top and bottom, away from the wounds. Then the other was placed at the back of the leg, overlapping the front, and was also taped in place. When he was finished, the leg was nearly immobilized from the knee down.

He then helped his charge from the bed into a chair and took hold of the unconscious Monsinger by the right leg. He dragged the body over to the bed, and leaving him on floor, lifted the leg high enough to handcuff the ankle to the head of the bed. Monsinger had only his head and shoulders on the floor with the arms and left leg behind his back.

The rescuer smiled at the nearly unconscious wounded man a said, "I'm full blooded Shoshone and my people have been accused of more torture than this creep ever dreamed of finding out. That's a false reputation, but I'll live up to it anyway for now. By morning when they find him, he's gonna wish he'd never been born!

"Now, let's get you safely out of here. I hate what you're about to go through, but Doc said those pills would work really fast, so try to hang in there and leave this all to me! Okay?"

He then pulled a tiny bottle from his diminishing pack and spilled some on a cloth. The strong smell of chloroform filled the room and he quickly put the wounded one to sleep.

"There, Doc said this would be a mercy, so I trust him. Now, let's you and me go camping!"

He wrestled the man onto his shoulders in a dead man's carry and slipped out the back door into the darkness. The couple of hundred yards to the waiting horses was a nightmare, and by the time he was ready to load his burden into the saddle, he was nearly exhausted.

A few seconds to catch his breath, then he hoisted his patient into the saddle and proceeded to tape his hands to the saddle horn. Then the uninjured right leg was taped to the stirrup skirt and the left, above the knee, likewise. A tightening of the cinches and he looped the lead rope of the pack horse to the man's saddle and the lead rope of the rider's horse to his. He left town by a trail that paralleled the highway for about a mile, checked to make sure the unconscious man was okay and not about to fall from the horse, and hit the deserted highway at a trot. That would be full speed for fully five miles.

Less than an hour later he found the place he wanted and veered off to the north into a narrow valley between two steep sided mountains. Within a half hour the Indian was deep enough into the mountains he could stop the horses to rest and check over his charge. He feared what this was going to do to the man, but it was better than what Monsinger had planned. He had the feeling that once the creep had the information he wanted, his patient would have simply disappeared.

After a half hour's rest, he continued on. His first destination was at least two hours away and dawn couldn't be far behind.It was daylight when he found his spot, a deep overhang that could be called a cave if one wished. It stretched a hundred yards under the lip of the eastern mountain and was no more than twenty yards from the mountain to the west. He had spent many nights there while avoiding the law in Struthersburg. His roll as a spy had been suspected for a few weeks now, and he had needed to disappear from time to time.

A makeshift manger of saplings cut and tied together inhabited the back of the cave and had been filled ahead of time with good timothy hay. In a plastic barrel was a couple days' supply of oats for three horses with some cut down plastic buckets beside it for the animals to eat from.

Shoshone college dropout Kenny Morningsong loosed his charge from the saddle and gingerly unloaded the floppy burden. While he was a strong six footer, it was all he could do to keep from dropping the man as he hauled him down from the horses back.

He wrestled his burden over to the crude bed with the sleeping bag on top and managed to get him in place. He quickly unbound the leg and inspected it. There was a lot of blood, and a seepage that looked very unhealthy. They were going to need a few days there if that leg was to be saved. He knew he certainly wasn't about to try an amputation!

Once he had cleaned and rewrapped the wound and put the crude splints back in place he then unsaddled the horses, the pack animal first, and tethered them to the manger with substantially long lead ropes. They then got a portion of the oats dished from the plastic drum. It wasn't that big a drum and was nearly empty, but would last them close to a week if necessary.

Once they were done with their oats he untied them and walked them to the stream to drink, returning them to the manger once they were done.

His next task was to start a fire and heat some broth and noodles. Pulling the wounded man to a near sitting position he shook him to wake him. It took a lot, and when the eyes opened, they were clouded with intense pain.

"Easy fella, I'm gonna get some broth down you, you simply have to have some replacement of energy. I know it hurts like crazy, but this has to happen. Can you handle it?"

There was a slight nod, so he began to spoon the broth into a very pained mouth. The session was successful because the patient even downed some of the noodles contained in the broth. Some ten minutes later Kenny could feel the slackness of exhaustion suddenly arrive and he allowed him to slump back onto the makeshift cot.

"Listen, that's it for now, you need to go back to sleep, you've been through more than any man should ever have to go through. I'll get you two more pf the pills, that will surely help, but do you also want me to use the chloroform?"

"Nooo" croaked the dry throated victim, "Makes me sick."

"Yeah, I remember you emptying about a weeks worth of… well, you gotta be weak from it. We're gonna be here a few days if we can to let you gain some strength, so just relax, I'm going to take good care of you. Plus, you should like to know that Doc is on his way to check you out. That old cantankerous sawbones is sure one of us. Sleep tight, pardner, real tight; and I'll see you next time you wake. When that happens, I've got plenty more of those red and white soup cans in the packs! You don't want any of MY cookin', that's for sure!"

With that, he sauntered off to prepare his own meal, and once he had eaten, collapsed in his own bedroll. An observer would have noticed the 30-30 Marlin lever action laying next to him as he faded away into sleepy land. His first goal had been accomplished, the militia man was free!

Chapter 24

The tiny, dilapidated wood shack in the forest in northwest Ohio was, at the present, empty. However, nearby were two pairs of eyes in separate observation posts scanning the surrounding forest for movement. Their vigilance paid off as, after some two hours' vigilance, a shadowy figure was stealthily approaching.

An owl hooted from one of the spots. The newly arrived figure returned the call, to then be echoed by the third figure from another source. They then converged on the shack.

Henry Stoddard was the last to enter and squat down along a wall. No light was brought forth and Sheriff John Hall spoke first.

"Ted, you find out anything from the preacher?"

"No John, he tried his best, but Stokes had nothing of value to say to his request."

"I could have told you that would be the result. Stokes hates preachers of any faith, but Christians most of all. I have information from our last meeting that will curl your hair, and if that preacher would have known about it, I doubt he would have consented to go meet with Stokes."

Silence hovered for a long pause until Ted Sawyer could stand it no longer; "Well, out with it, what's the deal, Henry?"

"Well, he same as admitted to having Anson Peters killed because he was getting dangerous to 'the cause', as he puts it, and is planning on another sweep of what he calls antagonists to the cause and eliminating them. This isn't to be another attempt like he did to get rid on Morgan Montgomery and John Rosenthal, this is to just have some of the suspects, as he calls them, disappear. We have very little time to try and find out who he has targeted before he goes into action on this!"

"How much time, Hank?"

"Two days at the most."

The deputy muttered a curse and Sheriff Hall spoke quickly, "I have a better solution than finding out who the targets are and getting them away. It's radical, but the time has come to declare all out war on this crudball. I'm gonna take him out. Let's get our heads together, we need to plan this well."

The other two held their collective breaths for a bit, then muttered their assent.

"Listen," spoke Henry, "I've about run the course of being undetected as a spy, why don't I just put a round in the back of his head and go west?"

"NO! You're still valuable there. Let me think a bit. Meet here tomorrow night the same time and I'll have something ready."

When Sheriff Hall drove out of the airport the next morning he had what he needed for a decision as to how to rid the area of John Harvey Stokes once and for all, and John Rosenthal had provided him with the information. Rosey's actions had been devilishly clever, as attested to by the fact the army had thus far failed to turn up the evidence of his guilt regardless of their being convinced by now of his actions.

Hall parked in front of the office next to the court house just as Ted Sawyer slid in next to him. "Mornin' John. Have a good night's rest?"

"Yeah Ted, I had a great night's rest. And I should rest even better tonight"

Anyone hearing the two would place no significance to their conversation other than a normal first morning greeting. Sawyer, however, knew he was about to hear his bosses plan for the freedom from the provost marshal. He was impatient, but held his curiosity at bay until tonight's meeting. They both began the day as though it was just one more in a dutiful job.

Once darkness had arrived late that night, the hoot of an owl again resounded in the woods southeast of town and the shadows once again moved to the tiny rundown shack.

"Okay, John, whadaya got?"

"I think I know exactly how Rosenthal took those two murdering thugs out, and we're gonna copy cat the process. It won't be as natural a setup as he had, but it'll work.

"Henry, you're a pilot, right?"

"Yes."

"Do you think we can come up with a need for Stokes to fly undetected to somewhere?, I mean, just any way to get him in an airplane without any fanfare?"

"That's no problem; I can fake a message from the guys who were holding Anson Peters that they want more money or they'll squeal, I guarantee I can get him on board if I offer to take him there to straighten them out. Only problem, he's gonna want a gunman along for the ride."

"Hey, you just get him and his henchman here to the airport and we'll do the rest. Now, are you two ready to commit murder in order to clear the air around here a bit? That's what I have planned, but I have to tell you, I see the time as ripe to start the blood in the streets phase of taking back the U.S."

"I was game six months ago as far as Stokes is concerned. I can personally list two killings and three frame-ups he has ordered. I'm pretty sure of a couple more, but couldn't prove them. Even if I could, the accusations would get nowhere. You know that."

"Yes I do, and that's why I'm ready to move this resistance movement up a couple of places to rash activities like this. Okay, here's the plan…"

Two days later a car drove into the Henry County airport under the cover of darkness. Three figures got out and approached the hanger next to the terminal. After attempting to open the door with no success, one of the figures motioned for the other two to follow.

"Come on, I know another craft we can use. It's used for jumpers, and I happen to have the keys for it since I know the club president."

They got to a Cessna 172 and Henry proceeded to untie the plane. Stokes grumbled about using a slower ship like that, but was reassured it would do the job of carrying them to their destination just fine. When they walked up to the door of the plane, a pistol was shoved in their faces from inside and they were ordered to lay face down in the grass.

Stokes was furious! He cursed and threatened but all to no avail. The provost and his hit man were handcuffed and then forced at gunpoint into the back seat of the plane. John Hall then looked Stokes in the eye as he shined a light so they could see.

"Stokes, I find you guilty of murder and sentence you to death by drowning. And you, whatever your name is, I find you guilty of executing those deaths and repeat the sentence for you. You two have about half and hour to make your peace with whatever God you might have before you land in Lake Erie. You, Stokes are the first casualty of the socialist government trying to ruin our great nation. I hope they find you in a few days when you wash up on shore or something, because you're going to send a message that cannot be ignored. Now, I suggest you get to praying."

Stokes began to threatened loudly until duct tape went in place over his mouth.. It matched the tape being wound around his feet. Cold fury emanated from him and then cold fear. The killer next to him had shriveled to a trembling wreck of a man. Tears ran down his cheeks as he shook his head from side to side silently. All of the killings he had done for money now seemed to rise up in his mind and choke off any sounds he might have wanted to make.

The door was removed from the Cessna and Hall climbed in, signaling Stoddard to get underway. John Hall produced a note encased in plastic and heat sealed that he taped to Stokes' shirt. It informed the authorities of the reason Stokes was murdered and explained that the militia was now in a state of war with the government of the United States.

John Hall knew he had no authority to makes such a declaration, but figured this would force Hagan Marshall's hand. There would be no turning back now, at least not in northwest Ohio.

Two large hangers at the airport in Perth, Australia, had been cleared of all previous occupants many years before and stood empty for that period of time. They were now under attack by enough people to make it look like ants at a picnic.

Manufacturing machines were being bolted to the floors in one while lab equipment was being installed in the other. In just three short weeks of long hours the two had been converted from empty to thriving production facilities.

Phyllis McTavish smiled with a thrill as she watched the production lines seemingly flying along as they produced skimmers piece by piece and assembled them into completed units. A somewhat strange but not unpleasant odor of chemicals drifted in the air from the other hanger. Fuel cells were dropping into cartons by the hundreds.

This had been one of the quickest establishments of a manufacturing facility of this size anyone there had ever seen. The thousand jobs that opened up immediately had spurred a wonderful reaction of hustle and efficiency and now the goal of a thousand skimmers by December was not only a possibility, but more than likely would be nearly doubled. Her husband would be so pleased to see his sacrifice bring results. He had gone into hiding while shipping her and their two children off to the land of Oz for their safety. These things could likely be instrumental in freeing them to reunite. It was her fervent prayer to have it happen.

As things were accelerating in America, many places throughout the states were in a near panic of covert communications within the militia. Hagan Marshall was frantically trying to keep it all together as one solid organization with only a small measure of success. The aid of General Sikes became the single most stabilizing force within the militia. He might have been pompous, but he knew how to command. Hagan was vastly relieved by the help coming from him.

Kenny Morningsong was carrying a bucket of cold stream water toward his patient with which to try and cool his temp when he heard the chopper. He quickly checked the horses to make sure they were far back under the roof of the cave and when he saw they were, he continued on to the bedside of the tossing and turning man.

Mopping the fevered brow with the nearly ice cold water

for hours had kept the fever from completely burning the fellow up, but he was really in a state of mind bordering on delirium. Kenny had continually been a praying nurse during the last two days and had forced the pills down the patient when he could.

The voice was faint, and hoarse because of the dehydration, but Morningsong heard him clearly, "Is…is that…hunting us?"

"Yes my friend, that chopper is hunting us. He's been around here for two days now, but the only bad part of that is that he's keeping Doc away. Once that thing gives up, Doc will skat for this place like a waterbug from a trout. I think your fever is about to break, friend, so I would like to feed you some more broth if you think you're up to it."

"Yes, I…can take…it. Who…who are you? I should know…you."

"Remember coming after a guy where you were to rescue him from the spy center of the west? He was a scientist or something?"

"OH…yes, vaguely. Can you…talk a little louder? My ears are …ringing something…awful."

"Yeah, I bet they are. Is that loud enough?" When he received a nod, he continued on. "Remember being picked up just below the cave you came through? That was me. I brought you to town. Say, what do I call you? I'm Kenny Morningsong, and thee and me are gonna spend a couple of weeks or so together, so I probably should have a name for you."

"It's Rosey. That's short… for…Rosen…thal."

"Okay, Rosey. Now, you lay back with that cold cloth on your head while I go fire up the grill for a couple of steaks. Or… maybe just some more broth." He chuckled and, after placing a newly saturated cloth on John Rosenthal's forehead, proceeded to the fire ring.

Starting a small fire with totally dry wood, he heated the broth and proceeded to feed Rosey, telling him what had happened as he did.

"When you guys escaped, I slipped out of town behind all the fuss and went on to that other drive I had told you about. Say, whose genius idea was it to drive over the cliff into the lake to get away? THAT was pure genius!

"Anyway, I stayed there overnight, and next morning I

heard the chopper and all the shouting from those hunters. I took my rifle and climbed to the top where I was only a few hundred yards from the cave. Don't know what I could have done from there, one against the whole bunch, but figured I had to try.

"Man, when I saw you step out of that cave entrance with the RPG launcher in your hands, I knew all heck was gonna break loose. You fired, they fired at the same time, and even as far as I was from the blast, it shook me.

"Their rocket went back into the cave quite a ways, and when it exploded it literally blew you a good hundred feet away. That, my friend Rosey, is why you ears are still ringing! It tore your leg up pretty bad when you hit in the jagged rocks.

"They let Doc look at you because they wanted to force information out of you as to the location of your base. They don't know he's part of the resistance, you know. He checked your ear drums, says you'll likely heal and get all your hearing back, but then they made him leave without patching up your leg.

"I'm sorry, Rosey, but that leg is really bad, and if Doc doesn't get here soon, it might not be salvageable. I don't know enough to help a lot, but Doc gave me the ointment to use and told me how to splint it for the ride. He said the ride would be as terrible for it as the initial blast was.

"Say, that chopper hasn't been around for a while maybe he's moved on to another area. If so, good ole Doc might get here tomorrow; he's a ridin' fool, Doc is.

"Well, that's enough information for now. Oh yes, your friends made it away. I slipped around to the other end of the cave the next day, took me almost all day, to check it out and your slick little air machines were gone. Worst part is, they most likely figure you dead under the tons of mountain plugging the south entrance of the cave. I'm truly sorry for that, but there's no changing it now. Listen, go to sleep if you can, I'll be right here."

Kenny spent the next twenty four hours constantly going from the creek to his patient's side with cold cloths to try and keep the fever down. Truth be told, he was getting very concerned when nothing seemed to change. Then, on the afternoon of the next day he looked at the horses to see they were all standing alert with ears forward and facing down stream.

He placed the cloth he had been bathing Rosey's face with on the forehead and grabbed his rifle. He ran to a place previously picked and climbed to a shelf some twenty feet above the creek level. It was but a short wait before a rider with two pack horses rounded a bend in the waterway, riding in the stream bed. A grin split his face as he recognized Doc Cole.

Scrambling down from his perch he ran to meet the old gentleman. Doc had been the one who delivered Kenny Morningsong as a baby and the two had become inseparable right from the get-go. It had been Doc's influence that inspired young Kenny to begin nurse's training. Doc's intentions were to influence the youngster to then continue toward a medical degree and become his replacement in the Struthersburg area. That was before all the government downtrend had occurred and definitely before the spy network had decided a tiny burg like theirs would be ideal for a liaison center for the underground government spies in a four state area.

Doc was a feisty old guy who was dearly loved by all locals who knew him. When Morningsong grabbed the lead ropes of the pack animals he gave a questioning look at Doc who responded with a glare.

"Before you ask, the devils wanted to blame ME for some young buck stealing their prize prisoner. How you managed to get the blame thrown at me, I'll never understand, but I owe ya one, and you aren't going to be happy when I pay it to you, young man."

Kenny just stood looking at him until Doc pushed by him to examine Rosey. "How's he been, Kenny? Looks really flushed, feels hot, and not so good over all."

"No Doc, he's had fever since before I got him here. The ride was tough on him, like you said it would be."

"Grab my black bag from the lead pack horse, son, I need to get on this man right now."

Kenny did as instructed and then started relieving the horses of their burdens. He stowed the pack saddles and packs at the back of the cave and then led all six horses from the cave to a cove where there was limited grass for them to graze on.

He both hobbled and tethered them and then returned to the cave shelter.

"Ran out of hay yesterday, Doc. The cove where I have them grazing right now might support them a couple of days, but no more. Are you saying you aren't going back to town? Or, rather, CAN'T go back?"

Doc just grunted with a head bob as he continued examining Rosey. When he saw the leg after unwrapping it he groaned.

"This looks really bad, Ken. I hope the next twenty-four hours show me a difference once I pump some of this stuff I brought with me into him. Otherwise, we might have to cut. That would be a real tragedy for him, and almost as bad for us. We might not get him out of here if that comes to be.'

"Wow, Doc. You talking gangrene or something?"

"Well, not necessarily that, although it's a possibility, but for now it's just a very bad infection."

He was already reaching into his large bag as he spoke, immerging with several vials and needles. He spent several minutes washing the area of the break with alcohol before plunging a needle directly into the wounds area. Rosey never flinched and Kenny realized the old doc had knocked him out with a sedative.

Doc spent some more time trying to adjust the break, realizing a certain amount of healing had actually taken place, preventing a perfect setting of the breaks. Once done, he nodded with a measured amount of satisfaction and re-bandaged the leg.

Once done there, he administered another series of shots to the shoulders before standing and stretching at length. He looked at Kenny and smiled as he then greeted his young friend with a hug. Doc wasn't a very demonstrative man, but this young man was like a son to him and he was pleased to be with him in this tough situation. It wasn't as though Kenny needed him to help survive, but that Rosey needed him and he needed Kenny for survival through this.

This young Shoshone knew the mountains for fifty miles around them as well as anyone and better than most, having lived out in the wilderness on his own most of his life. Whenever the local school let out for the summer, Doc knew he could count on seeing a rider towing one pack animal heading for the mountains, never to be seen again until a week or two before school was to begin again. It was just who and what Kenny Morningsong was.

Having lost his parents at the age of ten to an accident, he had moved in with Doc, and the old guy had raised him the best he could as a single parent. Kenny had once asked Doc why he never married to receive the answer that doctors didn't have time for marriage. They were too busy treating people to saddle a spouse with that kind of a part time relationship.

Kenny had known several doctors who were married and seemed happy with it, but Doc was Doc, and he never raised the question again.

Kenny collapsed onto his bedroll and fell asleep in seconds. He had been up continuously for two nights and it caught up with him. Doc fished around in the packs and prepared a meal for himself and the patient, and once he got Rosey awake was able to feed him a limited meal. Then he fed himself and walked around to unlimber his creaking body. Doc wasn't as young and resilient as he once was and nearly a day on a horse had taken its toll.

Kenny woke the following morning with a start. He laid perfectly still and listened to the sounds of his surroundings with a careful ear. There was no sound! He jumped to his feet, rifle in hand, and crept out of the cave with the firearm at the ready. He slipped in the direction of the horses, hoping against hope they were okay; he had not brought them into the cave for the night and feared for the kind of night they might have had.

All five animals were quietly cropping grass until they sensed him near then greeted him with soft wickers, expecting oats. Not ready to stop his exploration just yet he left them there and continued prowling the area. Nothing but intruders could cause the birds and animals to be this quiet!

When he came to his "perch" he soon located the source of alarm for the animals. Doc was sliding down the opposite hillside in an approach to the stream, sounding like a rolling boulder.

"Hey, what in the world you trying to do, raise the dead?"

"Nope, though it might have taken that to get your sorry hide up."

"Well, what are you doing over there? The patient is over here."

"Yep, he sure is. You ever hear of being regular, kid?"

"Oh."

When he thought of the reason for his alarm, it got to be funnier and funnier until he finally gave in and began to howl with mirth.

"You old reprobate, you scared me out of nine of my twelve lives! Why didn't you get me up first?'

"What; you think you needed to hold my hand? Listen, take John's temp for me while I wash up. And wash your own hands first, there's hot water on the fire."

Kenny chuckled as he obeyed and went to Rosey's side with some apprehension as to how he might find his condition. He could see there was a fairly fresh cold cloth on the forehead as he approached. He put the instrument in the ear, triggered it, and when it beeped he was ecstatic.

"Right at a hundred, Doc! That's a couple degrees down, right?"

"Right you are, my lad. Good, now for another series of shots and I bet we can get out of here by tomorrow. I looked at that leg earlier while you were playing lazy boy and the color is a lot better Now, get some food in that sorry carcass of yours before I have two patients."

Kenny ate a breakfast of trout Doc had caught and then took grain to the horses. Camp chores took up the rest of the morning as the two prepared for their departure the next day. Kenny spent a couple of hours manufacturing a stiff support on the saddle Rosey would ride so the injured leg would be fully supported, then started arraigning the supplies in packs that were in the order of their need. His life as a mountain raised man was paying off.

Rosey had a much more restful day, even commented on the decrease of the ringing in his ears. As Doc explained their next two weeks activities, he grew apprehensive, however. Kenny had been through these mountains by the intended route many times and it was a week's journey for him, but with an injured man to care for, the rugged terrain would take its toll.

"Doc, I know your horse, but are those other two from Clyde's stable?"

"Yes they are."

"Good, 'cause we need good, stable mountain rides right now, not some skittish hay burners that can't act like mules. We're gonna be going down one descent that will have you thinking about using some of those cusswords you hate on me because we don't have mules."

"If you can do it, Rosey and I can do it, redskin, and don't you forget that."

The fondness the older man had for his charge came through loud and clear in his remarks, and Rosey took note of them, gaining confidence in the two rescuers as he did so.

The next morning found Rosey tied to a saddle and somewhat comfortable in spite of the leg sticking straight out with the new hip to foot splint. Kenny struck out upstream with Rosey, then with Doc following. Kenny led one pack animal with Doc having the other two. They were now looking at two weeks in the saddle.

Chapter 25

The man standing in front of Phyllis McTavish's desk seemed alarmed as she showed him the month's figures.

"But...these are all single place skimmers, ma'am. We desperately need two place for the first operation to succeed! We're down to four to six months to complete and deliver the needed numbers."

"I assure you, sir, we can go to more people on each shift, switch to the two-place production, and get you what your superiors want.

"I can hardly believe the efficiency of these people here, they are simply put, the best ever. You want two-place skimmers, you'll have them! Now, do you have any word for me from my husband? Is there a chance he can make it out of the states and come visit his loving wife?"

Even though she said that with humor there was still the sound of hope in her voice.

"I can't really comment on that, ma'am, at the risk of being overheard. All I can tell you is that he has the total support of the resistance in whatever way he needs that support."

She nodded and turned to hide the tears forming. Had she known what was developing in the valley of the shadows she would have been of a different mind.

In the turmoil of grief over Rosey's death, the militia was still in and out of the valley on a constant basis. Mac had finished all the research needed for his fuel needs and was negotiating for a departure that would see him to Australia.

General Sikes himself had finally ordered a clandestine

operation to pull Mac out of the settlement and put him in a fighter jet for an unknown base in South America. From there he would be taken to Perth via a friendly nation's transport aircraft. Mac would be the only passenger, but would be riding with a load of raw materials destined to become skimmer parts. The farewell was poignant and exciting as the group bade him goodbye. All but Paige, that is; she was not anywhere to be found and as soon as the chopper left with Mac aboard, Kay went hunting her.

Paige had become more and more despondent with each passing day until the group was quite concerned about her well being. Kay had begun following her every time she left the settlement, keeping her distance so Paige would not suspect.

It was Sue who found her much later in the afternoon. Sue had climbed to her favorite perch far above the canyon floor and was gazing around at the beautiful panoramic view of the area when she spotted Paige.

There was a ledge similar to "hers" as an outcrop about two hundred yards down the canyon wall from there and somewhat higher. Paige was just standing at the edge looking off into space. Her stance frightened Sue into a frantic descent from her ledge and a hurried run right through rattlesnake alley without even looking for snakes.

Sue found the logical place for an ascent to where Paige stood and started climbing rapidly. When she was close enough she called to the petite lady in what she hoped was a normal voice.

"Hey Paige! Wow, you found a better ledge than mine, didn't you?"

When there was no response she continued her frantic climb, talking all the time. It took her fully fifteen minutes to reach the ledge, and when she did, she cautiously approached the distraught woman.

Sue, talking all the time, didn't know whether to reach out and touch Paige, take firm hold of her arm, or just talk and try to get a response. The normally prim lady's hair was a mess, there was no makeup, and her clothes needed pressing in the worst way; this was NOT the woman she knew as her mother's best friend. In addition, Paige had a wild, indescribable look in her eyes.

Sue finally made a desperate choice; she gently took a firm hold on the back of the vest Paige was wearing with her right hand and slipped her left arm in front of her in a very light contacting hug.

"Paige, I'm so glad to see you. Do you come here often? It's a great view isn't it? I love to sit and pray as I look at the wonderful view from up high."

When there was absolutely no response, Sue cautioned Paige that she was frightened of the height and wanted to call for help in getting herself down. "Or," she asked, "Could YOU help me down from here? This is soo much higher than MY shelf. Please, Paige, please help me down, I really do need you."

Paige finally turned her head a bit and studied Sue carefully. "You're Sue, right?"

Through the shock of that question, Sue was able to nod and choke out a "Yes."

She followed that with another plea for help. Paige finally turned to her and drew her toward the way down. Sue allowed her to guide and pull and push until they reached the bottom many minutes later.

"Thank you so much! Can you help me to the house; I'm still so frightened and shaky?"

THAT is not a lie, Sue thought to herself. She was convinced Paige had been contemplating jumping. They arrived at the settlement and Paige led Sue to Kay, who was just coming around the corner of her house. She had been searching in the opposite direction.

Because Kay had raised the alarm, the others began collecting by the fire pit. It was normal that all would head there, for that was the "family" meeting place. At least until winter set in.

Sue began telling them of the beautiful ledge Paige had found and how it was so high that she, Sue, had become frightened and needed Paige's help to get down. Cal looked over at Brian and gently shook his head for they both knew what a daredevil Sue was with heights.

The conversation went to other matters with everyone trying to include Paige until she finally stated she was very tired and left to go into her dwelling. Then the discussion quickly became quite animated. It was decided one of them would be assigned to watch Paige each day. They would concentrate on the ladies doing it because that would seem more natural to Paige. However, the guys would still keep a close watch whenever possible.

Kay told Morgan she intended to sleep with Paige that night just in case. He quickly agreed it was a good idea. The rest agreed and then assignments were made for the following days as to who would be the caretaker. All this brought an even darker shadow over their "valley of the shadow."

Hagan Marshall and General Sikes sat across from each other in the general's office, downing strong coffee as they discussed strategies.

"McTavish assured me he could get us four thousand two place skimmers in three months. That would give us eight thousand men for a coupe. I think we should plan it for November or early December. Give the nation an early Christmas present. Your thoughts?"

"I agree, but we need to make sure of those eight thousand troops. I want half of them involved in the D.C. invasion, and we can assign the rest to the Pentagon and other key state capitols." Hagan looked the general straight in the eye as he stated this last.

"I don't know, Hagan, how many of those would you think we need at the Pentagon? That's a huge place full of military men!"

"You're right, general, and most of those military men are ours! Those we have there have no idea when or how we plan to invade, but they know we DO! They understand their rolls when it happens. The green armbands are in their possession and ready to don, and their sidearms are within reach. I don't think it will take more than three or four hundred troops to take the place.

"I also have the key state capitals infiltrated with our military people. They are already in place, just waiting. I really am upset that some dimwit jumped the gun in Ohio by dumping that provost marshal in Lake Erie with a declaration of war pinned to his chest! If I ever find out who that was I'll nail his hide to the wall. He just made us move our plans ahead by at least a year!"

"Yes, I know, but I like it; because the government people were getting bolder and bolder there in Ohio and that was going to spread into the other districts if they kept getting away with that kind of stuff. You know, monkey see, monkey do."

"Yeah, but still…"

The planning continued well into the night as maps were consulted, numbers decided on, and strategies completed. The militia's plans to take back the states were rapidly coming to bear.

President Marcus Deloyac screamed at vice president Jeryl Roberts as he slammed his fist down on the desk in front of him. "I couldn't care less about some would-be provost marshal getting bumped off, we have others to take his place! But what I WON'T stand for is some upstart bunch of hoodlums trying to make it seem like they have some sort of power to start a revolution! I'm telling you NOW, Jeryl to get your sorry bunch of troops into Ohio and spread some fear into those worthless farmers' even if you have to have a couple of public executions by firing squad! GET WITH IT NOW!!!"

Roberts just sat and looked at him for a very long minute. Then he scooted back, deliberately placed his feet up onto the president's desk and lighted a cigar. He didn't reply until the stogie was well lighted and he could blow smoke at his boss.

"You want some 'worthless farmers' shot, you go shoot them yourself. You're not stupid enough to actually believe that would work at this point do you? Remember, you haven't gotten this nation's guns yet. So…just how do you propose we go about shooting some worthless farmers? And which worthless farmers do you want to choose, Mark?"

He knew Deloyac hated being called anything but Marcus and was deliberate in his mild taunt. The president stared at him, furious that Roberts would dare confront him like this, then slammed his top drawer shut and stalked out of the oval office. Roberts sat there with a satisfied smirk on his face as he contemplated the approaching melt down by the president. He was sure his own presidency would start as soon as he could cause Deloyac to either burst a blood vessel or get himself shot by some assassin.Roberts might even see what he could do about arranging that last. It would take very careful planning, but he considered himself a master planner and had no qualms about such a thought as knocking this disgusting power hungry man out of the picture.

Hmmmm…maybe if Deloyac were dumped into Lake Erie bound with duct tape and a similar note tacked to him those worthless farmers would get the blame and he would be free and clear. One way or another, he had the president marked for a killing. The man was just too arrogant to leave alive.

John Rosenthal was wracked with pain, but that had become the norm during the past week. Doc kept his pain level down as much as possible, but the jarring of the horse over rough terrain kept it prominent in his mind. Doc would approach him every so often to question him on the pain level, but Rosey hated the effects of the meds Doc used for the pain so he just denied the severity and rode on.

"We'll get to the descent tomorrow around noon if we keep making this kind of time, guys," shouted Kenny back at them. "You've really surprised me, Rosey; you're doing wonderfully for all that injury you have."

Rosey just waved a hand and gritted his teeth. They had been climbing continuously for the last two days, and that made the ride even rougher as the horses strained against the slopes strewn with boulders, etc.If Rosey had felt better he would have been completely enthralled with the scenery of the passages they had traversed. Morningsong definitely knew these mountains thoroughly. They had come to a branch of the creek the second day and the Indian guide had not hesitated to take the right fork. On the fourth day he left the stream to begin their climb, and it was gradual at first. Then it steepened considerably until Rosey wondered if the horses could keep up the pace Kenny was setting. The horses? The devil with the horses, could HE keep up the pace?

That night Rosey posed the question of distance to the Shoshone and received the shocking news they had covered only seventy miles in the three days.

"And how many miles are we going?"

"I figure it's around two hundred total. We'll be there in another few days."

"TWO HUNDRED! And there wasn't another way for us to get there? Why couldn't we have stolen a car? Or used Doc's?"

"Because there's a road block, subtle though they are, on every road out of Struthersburg. When they established that as the center for their liaison network they set up those government check points in the pretense that drug cartels were working out of the mountains. That gave them an excuse to control all the movement to and from the poor little town."

Rosey became very quiet for the rest of the time until he collapsed into his bedroll. Kenny was always kind enough to cut pine boughs to pad the ground for him, and he actually slept rather comfortably once Doc nailed him with his "blasted needles."

A day later Kenny halted them early in the afternoon and started to set up camp in a little copse of trees, explaining they were going to make the horrible descent during the next morning.

"The horses need to be at the top of their game for this, and you're both gonna hate my guts before we're down," he said with his mischievous grin. "Good thing is, though, we're cutting off three days by doing this. We'll be down by mid-morning and well on the final stretch. Tomorrow we'll be within range of our spot."

"Just what is this 'spot', son?"

"This will be the Henchlin ranch, Doc. They are a center for the resistance in these parts and you never know what all you'll find there. It might be a bunch of troops drilling, several fighter planes doing operations for practice, or nothing."

"You mean they have an airbase there? Fighter planes need RUNWAY!"

Morningsong chuckled and explained, "These fighters are stolen choppers or some bought from military boneyards and refurbished. Our side hasn't forgotten good old Yankee ingenuity! I've seen as many as 500 troops there at times."

"Okay, young man, just what's so terrible about this descent of yours?"

"Well, Doc, it's steep, narrow, and should be made with mules. We need to devise a different support for Rosey's leg for the trip down because otherwise he's gonna drag it on the side. I haven't really come up with a good solution yet, either."

Rosey spoke up, "Why can't I ride sorta side saddle? Just stick my leg out over the left side?"

"That was a thought I'd had, but I'm worried as to how stable your seat might be."

"How long in time are we talking about?"

"A bit over two hours."

"I can hold on with my teeth for that long, don't worry about it."

"Good for you, Rosey, I'll fix you up as best I can."

"I'm curious, youngster, you said you're full blooded Indian?"

"Right. Shoshone."

"So that's why you know these mountains so good? It's your native territory?"

"Actually, no, our people were really a state and change north of here. I'm a misplaced citizen." The last was accompanied by that twinkle of eye and little boy grin.

"Ha! You're misplaced? You ain't seen nothing where misplaced goes! I'm misplaced from Ohio!"

"Really, that isn't completely accurate. You're really misplaced from Europe, right?"

"Whaddaya mean?"

"Well, by your name you might have a Jewish background, and I guess that would actually be from the Middle East. Now, THAT'S displaced."

:Well, if you want to go there, my background folks were from Germany. That could be called twice displaced, couldn't it?"

"Yep, so I'm not as far displaced as you. Thing is, we both have grief in our backgrounds that caused that displacement, but we can both grasp onto an even greater displacement if we will just take advantage of it."

"What are you getting at?"

238

"Well, Rosey, Doc and I are really citizens of a place as far away as one can go, yet as close as the blink of an eye."

"What kind of game are you playing here, Kenny Indian boy?"

The youngster stood and walked around the fire to kneel in front of the patient. He looked steadily in Rosey's eyes and explained, "We are citizens of heaven, my friend. You see, a Jewish carpenter named Jesus Christ died for us, and if we accept Him as Savior, He promises us heaven. And that's where my heart is. So, you see, we're misplaced until we die and go home to Him."

Rosey sat there shaking his head from side to side, just chuckling to himself. Kenny looked at Doc and the good doctor shrugged his shoulders. They waited for the wounded man's comments.

Finally, when Doc could no longer stand the wait, he asked, "Well, what's so blamed funny, mister Rosenthal? What's got you by the horns now?"

Rosey leaned back and tossed the remains of his coffee to the side and then set the cup down. "All my life I've been my own guy. Then I run into this man named Montgomery. He was the first man to take me for who I was and to accept me into his life like one of his own family. He not only took me as a friend, but eventually as a business partner. His wife and my wife are the best of friends, really closer than some sisters.

"We'd been together for a few months when they all started telling us about Jesus. Paige, my wife, and I, we had no need or desire, at least as far as we knew, for any religion. Fought them off like crazy.

"But ya know what? They never changed their attitudes toward us. We did everything together. Well…everything but church, that is. Fast forward to recent. We were about to be imprisoned back in Ohio and had to get out of there. Him for false charges by the crooked government; me because I killed two men and they were getting closer."

The silence was deathly for a while until Doc spoke. "You killed two men? Do you want to elaborate, or is it none of our business? I'm good with either answer."

Rosey looked steadily at his feet for a bit, then raised his eyes to theirs and proceeded to tell his story, holding nothing back. He stressed his guilt and shared his anger and fear during the difficult time. Doc and Kenny looked at each other for a bit, then Kenny spoke.

"Ya know, Rosey, Christ died for all those mistakes, whether accidental or deliberate. I'm sure the others shared that with you, but I like to make sure."

"I guess I need to finish my story, fellas. The day Morgan and I decided to do this operation, he insisted on reading his Bible before deciding. He read, our wives went into another room and read, and then we got back together. It was scary. The part Morgan read was the SAME PLACE our wives read! It seemed to point to our needing to do the mission! So... the decision was made, and then Morgan prayed. For a really long time. During that prayer, I felt a presence of some thing or some one, I swear I did, and it was then I realized there was really something to the things they had been trying to tell us about God. I hear what you're saying about this forgiveness, and I hear what you're saying about heaven. I guess I'm ready to go with this stuff you're telling me." A long silence again, then, "Yeah, I AM ready. Tell me what I do next."

Doc dug into his doctor's bag and produced his small, crinkled, folded up, moth-eaten looking Bible and proceeded to teach their patient what he needed to know. After they prayed together, Rosey was very quiet, and crawled away to be alone. The others just left him go as they rejoiced and prayed silently for their new brother in Christ.

When dawn broke the next morning, Kenny went to the horses and grained them with the last of their oats. As they munched in their nose bags he worked over Rosey's saddle, fashioning a sheepskin around the horn and devising a makeshift sling to help support the right leg as it protruded over the left side of the mount along with his other leg. It would be clumsy at best, but with the right sides of the riders scraping the cliff at times there was no way Rosey could withstand the pain and suffering he would have had to endure. When he was satisfied with his work he returned to camp for breakfast.

Once they were loaded they first prayed together, something Rosey had not been aware was happening each morning. Just forty minutes after setting off Kenny led them around a point to a cliff ledge that swallowed the world on which they stood. He could hear the intake of breath by his two companions and smiled as he turned to watch their expressions.

Stretching as far as they could see was a network of ridges and valleys that were several thousand feet below their vantage point. Kenny let them drink it in for a while before interrupting their fascination.

"Those ridges are three thousand feet below us, guys. We literally ride off this cliff right here to start the trip down. I don't need to tell you how dangerous this is without a bad leg and a crude side saddle setup; but just in case you haven't grabbed onto it yet – this is just plain crazy to start down! It was crazy the first time I did it alone, and it's still crazy today.

"Take your time, if at any place you have a doubt about your horse or yourself, you holler, and holler loud. Rosey, there will be places where I will need to come back and lead your mount around some sharp corners; when you see me disappear from sight, stop and wait. Everybody ready?"

Doc growled a "No" but grabbed the lead ropes for the two pack animals he was leading.

"Just get them between you and Rosey, Doc, and they'll follow along on their own. Believe me, they don't have a choice. If one balks at a spot, call me, I want to be the one to get them around again. Okay? Here we go!"

John Rosenthal had flown most of his life, having soloed on his sixteenth birthday, he took one look over the rim where Kenny had disappeared from sight and panicked. His heart pounded furiously in his chest until he wasn't certain it would remain there as his breathing went ballistic. How anyone or anything could even step close to what appeared to be a three thousand foot drop-off he could not understand.

Fortunately for Rosey, his mount was a mountain bred and raised horse and simply stepped onto the narrow trail with no urging whatsoever. After all, the one giving him his grain was just ahead, and he wasn't about to hang back from that!

The first couple of hundred feet of the descent found Rosey with his eyes closed! He felt faint, was sweating profusely, and was shaking like the proverbial leaf. Doc, even with his

241

experience in the mountains was not much better off. The first hundred or so feet was so narrow the horses' bellies hid sight of the trail when the riders looked own. As the descent continued the shelf widened a couple of feet for the next hour and both greenhorn "descenders" became rather calm and accepting of their plight.

As the old proverb says, "All good things must come to an end," and such was the case for the three fugitives and their mounts. Kenny stopped an hour and a half into the descent at a "wide spot" as he put it. It was such that he could walk past his horse instead of crawling between its legs to get back to his companions.

"We break here for a few minutes and then we hit the worst section for half an hour or so. After that, it's almost like vacation time because the trail goes to ten feet wide. We're halfway down, guys, and it's going good"

"Ha! That's YOUR story redskin," said Doc. Kenny could tell his sense of humor had returned because he never teased Kenny about his Indian heritage unless he was relaxed and feeling mischievous. They often referred to each other as redskin and paleface when sparring back and forth verbally. Those were actually terms of endearment for the two of them.

They got Rosey down from his saddle and massaged his arms and legs to renew circulation for him. He had done amazingly well considering the horrible position of his body in the side saddle configuration. Doc dug out his needles and received the ire of Rosey when he started poking medicine into him.

"You bloodthirsty sawbones, what you think you're doing? Trying to drug me up so I'll fall off?"

Doc just smiled and continued his "poking" until he was done. "It was time for your antibiotic, my friend, the pain I cannot help any more for a few hours. I'm sorry."

"Hey Doc, ya know, it really hasn't been all that bad. I'm so blamed scared out of my socks that I don't notice the pain as much. I think my body is just happy to not be splattered on the rocks way down there to consider the pain!" He patted Doc's arm as he spoke and the two exchanged knowing looks.

"Okay guys, let's mount up and finish this thing."

They got Rosey back in the saddle and tethered fast, mounted up and then proceeded. It took just fifteen minutes for Kenny's prediction of the worst place to prove him a prophet. He came to a place on the ledge where the trail seemed to simply end at the projection of a corner of the cliff. From their vantage point at seemed there was no more trail.

Kenny dismounted and crawled between his horses front legs. He faced the cliff and slowly led the steed forward until the front half disappeared from sight. The hind quarters followed and before long Kenny reappeared around the corner. The fact he was sweating profusely was not lost on Doc and Rosey and did nothing to relieve their fear.

"Rosey, see where the cliff is overhanging the trail about six feet up? I need for you to lay back on his rump as flat as you can so you fit under that spot. Might be good to get an extra grip on the cantle as you do and close your eyes. I don't need for you to react in a way that makes him even more nervous than he's gonna be shortly. You might wanna be praying as well, just for the extra safety He can give."

Rosey scrunched himself as flat as possible, grunting as the pain hit a bit harder and definitely prayed. He prayed for the horse, for himself, for Kenny, for the cliff not to move! He was absolutely terrified. He could feel the horse's body flexing with the turning and felt really precariously perched in his present position. Then there was the feeling of the horse suddenly relaxing and he knew they were around.

Kenny's soothing voice to the horse ceased and told him to set up and get as comfy as he could, saying that Kenny was going back for Doc and the pack horses. Another fifteen minutes and the ordeal was over for that turn. Kenny took no break, but forged on to the next terrifying obstacle. It was only ten minutes away.

During the next hour they encountered three more such places in the descent and suddenly they realized they were descending into the tree level. Doc stated he had never seen trees look so green or wonderful! The old fellow was totally wiped out, and for him rather than Rosey, Kenny called a break for a couple of hours. He built a fire and made coffee, almost their last, and made some sourdough biscuits for a mid-afternoon snack.

"Can you see that break in the skyline there to the north guys? It's maybe ten miles and that's our last camp. We'll see the ranch from there, our campfire will be a signal fire, and you two can get off your horses for good."

"How can we do that, youngster? Will they send a truck out for us?"

"No, a chopper, most likely."

"WHAT?"

"Hey Doc, remember I told you this is a huge operation. You guys are about to be flabbergasted as never before with the scope of the military operation there.

"It's just a matter of time before the government discovers it via satellite. If and when that happens there's gonna be a horrible battle, 'cause these people are the most extreme radicals you'll find anywhere. Keep that in mind while you're there, some of them are a bit unstable, but they're on our side."

"When you say, 'unstable', just what do you mean and how unstable?"

"Just don't get in any political debates or discussions and you'll be okay, Rosey. Hey, you're putting quite bit of weight on that leg, fella, way to go."

Doc spoke up, "Not so, my fine, feathered friend. That means there's a lot of healing that has taken place and we might not be able to do a successful surgery to keep him from having the leg heal crooked."

"Hey Doc, crooked or straight, I'm just happy to have a leg on that side and to be here to even HAVE a leg, period!"

Doc smiled and nodded, feeling satisfaction for Rosey's attitude.

Their mid-afternoon respite over, Kenny doused the fire, cleaned up the site, tightened the cinches on the horses and motioned for his charges to mount up. He smiled as he watched Rosey hobble over to his mount and attempt to climb on without help. His zest for life was returning.

They moved out, the far off horizon in their sights.

Ten miles on a highway with a good walking horse is only a couple of hours. If the mounts had been Tennessee

Walking horses, they could average around six miles per hour. When those ten miles are mountain miles, the picture changes drastically, and it was four hours later they drew up at the summit and gazed down the incredible long slope on the other side. Both Rosey and Doc uttered exclamations of wonder at the scene.

Over twenty miles away, and at the bottom of that long stretch of undulating sage covered mountain side were the tiny buildings of a ranch of tremendous proportion. As the two of them stared, Kenny climbed down and started gathering material for their fire. There was still enough daylight for them to be discovered.

He lit the fire and as soon as it was burning high he piled on some green grass and sage to make a big smoke. Then he fired his rifle three evenly spaced shots at the ground.

"They won't hear those, Ken, it's way too far."

"Actually, Rosey, they just might. Sound travels really far in these mountains, and there have been times I've not even had to build the fire. But, for today I want to be sure they see us so you two can get off the horses."

They waited for several minutes, close to twenty in fact, and then saw a speck rise from behind a large building. Well, at least it appeared to be a large building from that incredible distance. As the speck rouse higher they realized it must be a chopper.

"Now guys, when they get here in a few minutes, make absolutely no moves that I don't tell you to make. And...don't say anything until I give you a nod. You won't believe how paranoid these guys can be!"

His instructions were acknowledged with nods and they settled in for the wait. It didn't take long for the craft to cover the twenty-odd miles and the closer it got, the more they could identify it as a military attack helicopter! It settled down several yards from the fire and shut down. When the rotors had stopped turning two men climbed from the door, M-16s in hand.

"What'd ya bring us here, Morningsong?"

"Hi captain. The gentleman here with the sour look is my friend Doc I've told you about before, and John Rosenthal, here, was captured over in Struthersburg by the spy consortium after rescuing the scientist you knew about. Rosey has a very nasty leg break from the blast over there and needs attention; Doc can't go back because he helped me get John out of there before he was tortured into revealing the coordinates of the valley settlement we talked about last time we met over home. I can't go back, either, so I think I'll check on helping at the valley settlement. That's still up in the air. All been quiet here?"

"Yeah, very quiet, but we're still adding on to the security systems just in case. We sent out a platoon thet is battle ready last week; just waiting for the next to come in for training. I don't like these periods when we're so low on troops, I gotta tell ya. We only have a couple hundred men here right now."

"I hear you. Well, can we get these two frazzled companions of mine loaded up and down to the infirmary?"

Doc looked quickly up and said, "Infirmary? They have one here? No…"

The captain smiled and nudged Doc on the shoulder with a gentle hand as he replied, "You'll be shot down big time when you see this, my friend. Big time.

"Ken, you'll bring the pack animals in yet today? You're gonna run out of daylight if you try."

"No, I'm gonna set right here 'til daybreak. You wouldn't have any coffee on that bird would you?"

The fellow chuckled and shook his head. "Sorry, Indian, no coffee. If I did it would be yours."

"Captain, I have a thermos I was just filling when you called me!" yelled the other soldier. "It's his, he's probably earned it!"

With that, he returned to the chopper, retrieved the thermos and tossed it to Ken who smiled and nodded gratefully. The men loaded up, the turbine started to whine and within minutes Kenny Morningsong watched as his two companions were lifted off and headed for more comfort than they had experienced for close to three weeks. "Good bunks for tonight," he surmised to himself. "I need to remember to warn the people here about the south entrance to the cave down home being no more."

Chapter 26

When dawn pushed its way insistently into night's command of the light the next morning it found Kenny Morningsong already five miles down the slope leading the animals as they straggled reluctantly behind. He had awakened early, stiff with the damp cold air, and decided to skip breakfast as he drained the rest of the soldier's thermos and proceeded to saddle up.

As soon as he threw the pack saddles on those steeds he grabbed the lead ropes and trudged off, choosing to walk the first several miles to loosen up. He paused from time to time to use the field glasses as he carefully studied the ranch complex below. Kenny had always felt apprehensive as he approached the ranch turned military base for some reason. During the last couple of years he had been called on to assist several people in their quest for the facility for safety. Since roads were not only scarce but also watched via satellites his approach was the best route available.

He finally mounted up and picked up the pace, satisfied with what he saw as far as smoke starting to rise from the chimneys and signs of life showing around the barns. Ranching was still a prime activity here in spite of the military presence. Being a seasoned traveler and with good mounts he covered the twenty miles in record time and set down to the noon meal with his two friends. A good horse can average four to five miles and hour at just a walk, and Kenny's mounts were capable of alternately trotting and cantering for hours at a time with only occasional walking and grazing breaks. He had covered over eighty miles in a day before and this twenty was a cakewalk for him since it was over relatively easy ground.

"Well, my fine feathered friend, how was your night?" Doc asked.

"Cold."

"That's it, just cold?"

"Yep. Rosey, they helping you here yet?"

"I slept so great in that rack! A real treat, I tell you. I get x-rays today, Kenny! Here! In this forsaken backwoods place they have x-ray machines!"

Doc joined in at that point, "I'm shocked at the modern equipment they have here, fella, I'm thinking I might just settle in here for the duration to help out. They say they need another doctor and would welcome my experience. I mean, what else am I gonna do since you got me tossed out of town back there?" The twinkle in the old gentleman's eye looked on Kenny with a father's pride.

"Hey, you old renegade, it was your idea to bail this malefactor beside us out, not mine."

"Hey! Malefactor? What you talkin' about, redskin? You're the one kidnapped ME! I was perfectly comfortable there, ya know."

Just as the byplay was getting well underway to hilarity a couple of ladies brought them trays laden with enough food for thrashers and they dug in like wolves on a cold winter day. Silence and peace then prevailed for a time.

An hour later Kenny and Doc sat with Rosey as he waited for the x-ray results. Rosey had been thinking about his dear wife back in the valley and spoke to that.

"Guys, I gotta get word to Paige. I know she still thinks I'm dead, and that's horrible to think about. Do you know of any way that could happen from here, Kenny?"

"Let me ask at headquarters, Rosey. I'll go over there now and see what I can find out."

He walked to the main house and entered through the front door without knocking. He went straight to the desk in the corner.

"We have this wounded guy with us who is from a secret establishment buried somewhere deep in the mountains. They have reason to think he was killed and would like to get word to them to the contrary. Any way you can do that here?"

"I seriously doubt if our commander will authorize any transmission from here for at least another week. We've detected some electronic surveillance of our place recently and he's very nervous about that. I'll get him to look your guy up as soon as he can and see what he says."

"Thanks ma'am, we appreciate it." He trekked back to the large metal "barn" that was actually the infirmary and delivered the word to Rosey.

"Thanks, Kenny. They looked at my breaks, want to do surgery to try and put things back right. But Doc here, he says I've healed too much already for them to be able to help and recommends I refuse the surgery.

"He says I'll always have a nasty limp, but I should still be able to fly in spite of it. That's good enough for me. If I can fly, and can see my wife and friends sooner, I'm better than good, I'm wonderful! I feel God has blessed me way beyond anything possible because I'm still alive. How soon can I get out of here?"

"Don't know, Rosey. We should find out yet today, 'cause the big guy is supposed to look you up soon."

Late afternoon arrived and a stooped, slender old rancher approached the trio as they rested on the front porch of the ranch house.

"You three must be our travelers I need to see. Hi Kenny, how was this trip?"

"It was especially tough, Grant. Rosey here had a really miserable trip since he was so busted up. Sometimes, just getting him in the saddle would nearly put him out for a while."

"I can relate to that. Mister Rosenthal, I understand your family and friends don't know you're alive?"

"I think that is correct, sir. Is there a way to notify them? I'm very concerned for my wife's well being."

"Unfortunately, thet isn't right now. We're being watched right now, and all radio transmissions are disallowed at this time. However, I think we can get you out of here at night in a small chopper. Is there a place for you to go that is not your family's location? We could drop you there sometime yet this

249

week if you can guide us. I understand you're a seasoned pilot?"

"Yes. I can give you coordinates for the valley so you can calculate how far it is from here."

"No, don't do that. We do NOT want that kind of information here. Please understand, this nation is on the edge of exploding internally, and we stand to be invaded here at any time. The less information we have, the better.

"I am very concerned for the next thousand troops on their way here for training. There's a good chance they might be followed, and if they are, we may find ourselves in one heck of a brawl!"

"What kind of training do you give here, sir?"

"We're training all the troops we can on enemy recognition techniques. If these people are fighting other Americans, nobody wants to see the wrong people shot down. You need, and they need, to realize we are perched on the edge of civil war, and we do not want to be killing indiscriminately."

"Wow. Well, in that case, there's a hunting ranch I could go to and he could get me home. Home, never thought I would refer to that hidden valley as home. Home is back in Ohio."

"I understand. I'll assign a pilot to you and get you there yet this week."

"Sir, we have no medical resources in the valley, and they are continually sending us activists and such in the planning for a secret headquarters for the militia. Is there a possibility we could have your coordinates so we can get any emergency needs here?"

"No, I don't like that idea at all. Any direct flights could definitely endanger us; and you."

Doc spoke up at that point. "Rosey, I'll go back with you. They can just do without me here in favor of taking care of you folks."

"Doctor, I really urge you to stay with us. With the numbers we pass through here, we can definitely use your help."

"And just leave this band of non-military folks high and dry? Not on your life, I can recognize a stronger need when I see one. I go with Rosenthal."

"I could just deny him the trip if I wanted to."

Kenny quickly spoke up. "Sir, you try that, and I'll upset

your applecart right here and right now. You rely on my help here for your connection to the enemy's spy center. Forget you, and forget my help. I'm done with you. If you can't treat friends like American compatriots, I'm history. Not only that, I'll saddle up the horses and haul these two out of here and we'll make our way on our own. Try and stop me, and that fight you're so worried about will start right here between you and me.

"I've never liked your policies here, but it's been necessary to tolerate them in the interest of the common good. That's over, and you can bank on that."

"I certainly hope you don't try to enforce that, Morningsong, but understand this, I just gave my word that we would get Mister Rosenthal out of here and I always keep my word. As for the good doctor, I haven't made up my mind yet."

Kenny was on his feet with the rancher's shirt balled up in his fists in a split second, slamming the man against the wall of the house.

"I told you," he said in a perfectly calm voice, "You're likely to start the war right here and right now. You try and keep either of these men, or me, here against our will, and I'll tear you apart. You have no idea what damage I can do to you and your so-called help here. Now back off."

Two ranch hands ran to the aid of their boss, stopping short when they were confronted by a 44 magnum revolver looking at them in full cock. Rosey had found his trusty side arm and retrieved it from the packs the night before.

"Kenny, please let the good rancher go for now, I'll handle this from here on out. You men, your boss is not in any danger, you have my word on that, so just stroll calmly back where you were. Sir? Would you tell your men all is well?"

"If this impertinent young man will let go of me, yes." As soon as Kenny released him he motioned for the men to leave, nodding at them to affirm his order.

"We obviously have a very serious disagreement here, gentlemen. You apparently do not consider my position here as being in total command. I assure you, nothing happens here that I do not approve. Mister Morningsong, I intend to have you locked up for a few days for this, then maybe you'll be a bit more reluctant to resort to such actions with a command person."

"You know, Grant, you and I have never really been friendly, and, as I said before, I've never really approved of some of your tactics. You try to lock me up and someone is going to get hurt really bad. If you're close when it happens, it'll be you. If not, I guarantee you'll lose some good men. Rosey, I'm going to your valley with you to se if I can help there in some way. This has been my last trip for these people.

"Grant, they told me when I first started making these trips for you that you were a bit unbalanced, and maybe even a lot of Bonaparte was in your blood; I see what they mean now. You may be doing the great work here that others have told me about, but from now on you can just sneak your own spies through the mountains. I'm done, and I'm NOT staying here another day."

With that rather long speech for Kenny, he wheeled around and headed for the supply barn. Fifteen minutes later he emerged with two pack saddles laden with supplies and headed for the barns. Rosey looked at the commander with a raised eyebrow in question as to his actions that might be forthcoming. He fingered the handle of the Smith & Wesson as he did so. The old rancher fumed as he watched that action. No one had ever challenged him since the base had been established. Now, three men were doing it.

Minutes later the Shoshone emerged from the barn leading three saddled mounts and two pack animals. He mounted and rode up to the porch, cocking a questioning eye at Doc and Rosey when he drew to a halt.

"I'm not sure he can be trusted any more, fellows, so you're welcome to come with me if you like. No hard feelings if you don't."

Doc walked from the porch and placed a foot in the stirrup, pausing there. "Rosey, if he doesn't follow through with his promise, SHOOT the devil. I would like to use a different term, but I won't lower myself just because of the likes of him."

"Don't worry, Doc, I'll be fine. And thanks for the offer of helping in the valley, that means a lot."

Both the rancher and Rosey noted that Kenny carried his

rifle across the saddle as he and Doc rode out to the north, and Grant was fuming at the audacity of the young Indian

"I hope he doesn't think I'll let him get away with this. This is treason and desertion and I won't have it!"

"Really? Do you have Kenny's signature on any kind of paper, sir? As I understand it, he simply volunteered for the service he provided."

"Doesn't matter, he's in more trouble than he ever thought possible. Now, mister Rosenthal, hand over that weapon."

That was absolutely the wrong thing to say to the fiery-tempered Rosey at a time like that. He drew the 44, cocked it, and as he looked Grant straight in the eye and asked, "Or what?"

Then he stood and motioned for the old rancher to do the same. "Come on, my friend, we're going for a walk. Get going over to the choppers. NOW!"

Fortunately they made the hanger without anyone observing them. Rosey went to the attack unit and promptly opened the door. Then, without getting in, he went next to the small four place and motioned the rancher to get in. He proceeded to start the engine right there in the hanger and wheeled the now whirling ship around to where he could see the panel of the other bird.

Six horribly loud explosions sounded out as the complex instrument panel on the military unit shattered into nothing useful as the 44's slugs smashed into it in six different locations. Then Grant was shoved out onto the floor of the hanger and the little craft rose a foot off and transitioned to the clear air out side. Rosey lifted it off and rapidly roared off to the north, following the direction of the horse-mounted pair of his friends.

Kenny and Doc heard the engine start in the clear, mountain air, then the shots, then the roar of the lift-off.

"What in blazes has Rosey done back there?" Doc exclaimed. Just then the little chopper rose into sight and roared over them. Rosey hovered for a little bit and motioned north, then motioned for them to follow. He flew about a mile until he saw a small clearing to let down in. It didn't take long for the horses to arrive at a dead run.

Kenny and Doc leaped off and quickly stripped the saddles

for the horses, grabbed personal gear from the packs and leaped in. The horses, unburdened by saddle or bridle, would be fine and free to fend for themselves.

"Are you CRAZY? We can't get away with this! That other chopper will knock us down inside of five minutes!" Doc was furious. He failed to think about the fact that he had jumped aboard!

"That thing won't fly for at least a week, Doc! I shot it in the heart six times. I doubt if they have all the necessary parts to get it airworthy very soon. When you know where to plug a bear, you can kill him for sure, right? Well, I know where to plug THAT bear and I did it."

Rosey then veered off to the west and flew up a series of valleys as he wound his way first west, then south, then back west, then north just so it would hard to tell the direction to his destination.

As it neared dusk, he set down in a clearing and they made camp there for the night. Rosey gritted his teeth as he exited the chopper and stood on the bad leg. His next statement took the others by surprise.

"Tomorrow we ditch this antiquated piece of junk and head north without it."

"What do you mean, ditch it?" Doc asked.

"Well, I did grab it without doing a preflight, and we're almost out of fuel. Not to worry, though, I swiped a handheld GPS and know where we're headed. We'll get some help there."

"And just where is that, my surprising transport pilot?"

"Well, before I hooked up with Roy Turnbull I hunted with a guide from this area and I remember the coordinates because I flew into his local airport where he picked me up. He's a radical patriot and I know he'll help us out."

"If he's so great, why did you drop him as a guide?" Kenny asked.

"He retired. Said it was time to kick back and live off the money he'd made from all his rich clients! Feisty old turkey."

"Okay, now explain to me what we do with this 'antiquated piece of junk' you referred to."

"I have an idea that should drop it out of sight forever, even if they've been able to track us somehow. You'll like it, I'm sure.

Now, I need to drop dead for a while, this leg is killing me."

Kenny and Doc took care of the camp chores while Rosey collapsed and they soon had a skimpy supper going over the fire. Morning would see them up early.

When Rosey set the chopper down in a front yard of a rustic log cabin the next morning, what seemed like thousands of hunting dogs ranted and raved around them as soon as the rotor stopped. They remained in the chopper until an ancient old fellow hobbled toward them, rifle at the ready.

"What in tarnation ya think you're doin', ya crazy idiot? Ya think this is a truck stop or somethin'?"

"Hey Silas, it's me, John Rosenthal. Remember me? I used to hunt with you until you got lazy on me!"

"Aww, fer cryin' out loud. Whut the bejeebers you think you're a doin', John? You lost or somethin'?"

"No, but I need to be. Listen, Silas, while I weave you a story too awful to be true, yet it is." With that, Rosey gave a very abridged account of how the three of them had arrived at his front door in the chopper.

"So you see, we need to ditch this thing where it will never be found, and then get north to Roy's place."

"Ha! Gotcha covered, John. Remember that loggin' road out back? And remember that high ledge where you bagged that spindly elk last time you were here? We'll get it there by air, pile it over the edge, and I'll bring you back here for a day while we make ready for the trip to Roy's.

"We gotta load the horses up, though, cain't get to the top by pickup. Best I can do is 'bout three miles away.

"Aww, heck, cain't go there, cain't turn the truck and horse trailer around there. I guess it'll be more like eight or nine miles by horse. I sure as blazes ain't a backin' no trailer up for several miles!"

"Silas, you do what you have to, we'll do the rest, and thanks a bunch, you're a life saver."

"Could be, John, could be. Now, can you find that ledge?"

"I sure can, I'll just follow the logging road to the end and it's just a couple of miles to the west of there. Listen, Doc, you stay here, Kenny and I can lever this junker over the edge."

"You know, I think I'll just ride along with Silas, except for the horseback ride part. I can stay with the truck while he retrieves the two of you but I think I'll feel better sticking to you that way."

"Suit yourself, Doc, but know we don't expect it from you."

Kenny grabbed his rifle and strode to the chopper, looking back at Rosey as he went. "You comin', or gonna talk all day?"

Rosey hobbled to the craft, started it up, and lifted off without another word. Twenty miles later he slowly let down in a small clearing at the lip of the high ledge some five hundred feet above the floor of the adjacent gorge.

"Kenny, I'll let you get out, then I think I can turn this thing so your side is over the cliff edge and set it down there. I'm not so sure we can dump it without the help of gravity!"

"Just be careful, I didn't bring you out of Egypt to lose you to the Philistines!"

Rosey laughed as the youngster exited and then turned ninety degrees right as he carefully let down. He opened the door on his side and unbuckled his belt before doing so, then moved sideways until the skid on the left side was actually over the edge.

As soon as his skid touched rock he jumped! As he landed on his bad leg he screamed in agony but it was in harmony with the desired results he had sought because the chopper crunched down with a lurch, the precession of the main rotor leaning it precariously to the side. Kenny rushed in and gave a heave that was quite unnecessary and watched the old craft plunge over the side to a mighty crash some 500 feet down. It disappeared into the trees when it did so, and, miraculously, there was no fire.

It appeared the thing was totally hidden from sight from above. As Kenny turned to help Rosey he found him rolling in agony on the ground and rushed to his side.

"Never gave a thought to not landing on this stupid leg! Just jumped. Man, this hurts like hobs."

Kenny helped him back into the trees and settled down to wait for Silas. A couple of hours later he heard the sounds of hooves coming and lifted the 30-30 to a ready position just in case. "Man, I'm really getting jumpy," he thought to himself. He glanced at Rosey to see if he had observed only to find an understanding grin looking back at him. Rosey simply nodded and continued rubbing his sore leg. Silas whistled minutes later and Kenny answered him.

It took them both to get Rosey mounted, but several hours later they were setting around the kitchen table at Silas' cabin as they planned tomorrow's trip. They would soon be at Roy Turnbull's ranch, and soon after that, the valley!

Chapter 27

All of Washington was in a quandary; the White House, the Pentagon, and congress. In addition to that, many state capitols were in like condition. The cause? Literally hundreds of thousands of troops were AWOL. They were army, marines, most national guard units in many of the sates, in addition to navy and coast guard personnel.

There was no accounting for the mass disappearance of these men and women, there were simply too many to successfully hide somewhere; at least that was the thinking in the capital. If those in Washington had only known of the subterfuge leading up to this they would have packed up and run away.

Carefully orchestrated transfers of the desired personnel had been going on for nearly six months until there were three main military establishments that were completely manned by revolutionary forces. It was perhaps the greatest mass assembling of such forces in the history of mankind, and it had gone off at the rate of thousands per week without any of the unsuspecting socialists detecting it.

This maneuvering was not the brainchild of one, or even a dozen men, but a coming together of hundreds of commanding officers a few at a time who were brilliant tacticians. The time was at hand for the retaking of America by those still interested in freedom as given by the original constitution. Blood would run in the streets, but hopefully at a minimum if the planning was right.

An air force transport was on approach to Dulles in the dead of night with three thousand two place skimmers on board.

Two others were already there with more on the way. They held revolution fighters and before the dawn invaded the capital, six thousand armed soldiers and marines would have their positions in the skimmers secured and ready for the invasion of the nation's capital. The militia intended to take over within hours of daylight with the targeted state capitals being taken simultaneously. It was perhaps the largest military operation in history and the "friendlies" intended to succeed at all cost.

As the civilians began to emerge into the streets to commute to their appointed places, a young boy grabbed his mother's hand and pointed excitedly at the sky.

"Look, Mom! It's a space invasion army! I bet they're from Mars!"

The two gazed fixedly at the dozens of small craft floating into view above the buildings of the city. The sky seemed dotted forever with them. The mother nervously guided her son back into the apartment building and secured the locks. She had never seen craft like those, but knew they probably were unfriendly. How she wished her husband was not gone on a business trip; he would protect them!

Many others gazed, talked excitedly, ran for cover, or gathered to plan escape as the dozens of craft floated almost noiselessly overhead in the direction of the capital. When they arrived at their destination and began to settle into the White House lawn and the streets around the capital, the secret service men drew weapons and readied to defend. Some of them, that is. Others pulled bright green armbands from their coats and donned them; one on each arm. They approached those without the bands and quietly disarmed them at gunpoint. The rebellion was on!

Jeryl Roberts leaned back in the president's chair with his feet on the desk in the oval office. Before him on the desk was a half-empty latte and the remaining crumbs of three donuts. He had decided this was his day to take over the office of president. It was strange that this decision came in conjunction with the militia's decision to begin the revolution, but had he known of the coming battle he would have still planned the murder of Marcus DeLoyac. The man had finally stepped off the deep end.

The day before DeLoyac had called three opposing senators and one congressman into the oval office and threatened them with their lives if they failed to vote the way he instructed them. A full platoon of soldiers stood in the hallway at the ready to form a firing squad at his command.

One of the senators called what he thought was DeLoyac's bluff and found himself being offered a blindfold out in the hall. He still refused to believe it and shook his head. He was shot.

Jeryl's consternation ran rampant as he jumped all over the president only to find two soldiers waiting for the word to shoot him as well should they be ordered to do so. He left and tracked down his own goon squad of overpaid security men and gave them their instructions. This morning they would relieve the nation of its madman president as soon as he arrived at the office.

Roberts had the strange desire to be the one to pull the trigger, but wasn't sure he could really do it. He was spared the decision. As the president opened the door to the office the two of them heard machine gun fire down the hall. DeLoyac spun to see the cause as Roberts grabbed the automatic pistol from a desk drawer and fired two rounds into the president's back. As DeLoyac fell, Jeryl quickly ran for a window and fired into it to break the glass for an escape from whatever fracas was occurring outside. The shots failed to penetrate the bulletproof glass, which was really half-inch thick lexan, and troops flooded into the room within seconds.

They had leaped over the bleeding body of the president and captured Roberts immediately after doing so. One of them knelt by the body and started first aid. DeLoyac was still alive, but barely.

In other sections of Washington people watched as strange craft floated down in droves. They settled in the lawn of the White House, into the center and perimeter of the Pentagon and the capital. Many of the skimmers descended all around the strategic positions of those three structures and armed soldiers quickly flooded the buildings with a nearly bloodless coupe.

In the pentagon especially this was the case, because men and women wearing green arm bands exited office after office, armed with automatic pistols and quickly disarming any security not wearing those green bands. Truth be told, there weren't many of those. The underground work of the militia to find patriotic Americans had been thorough and complete.

The capital was secured in less than three hours and the takeover by the "new military" was complete. Those generals, admirals, and others assigned to establish order were soon putting things in order for a true and effective marshal law; one aimed toward the good of the people. It would oversee the establishment of a newly elected government while those would-be socialist rulers found themselves behind bars.

As this assault was taking place, Roy Turnbull watched guardedly, rifle in hand, as a pickup truck roared up the dusty road to his headquarters. The driver looked familiar, but they were still too far away to tell.

When the "cowboy Cadillac" slid to a gravel tossing halt and the occupants dismounted he experienced a mighty shock. As he stared, tears formed in the eyes of the normally taciturn and unflappable guide. He walked like a man in a trance as he approached Rosey until they were just a couple of feet apart. Then he leaped on the hapless man and engulfed him in a monstrous hug and rocked back and forth in a very uncharacteristic manner, silently trembling.

Rosey reacted in the same manner as he realized the attachment this quiet man of the mountains had for him. After what seemed long time, Roy released him and held him at arms length, as though he was confirming that Rosey was real.

He choked out, "John…John…it's really you. We heard you were killed in a cave in. John, what happened? Tell me, quick, what happened?!"

Rosey choked back the tears and stood shaking his head. "First, Roy, you HAVE to let Paige know I survived! You gotta! Please, Roy?"

"We'll do that right now, come with me. Hurry!"

The others stood silently as the two hurried off to the house. Rosey actually was keeping pace with the tall, lanky guide. Well, for the first few steps, anyway. Then he grabbed Roy's arm and slowed him down, pain gripping his face.

Kenny looked down at his feet for a while, realizing he had a huge reunion. He shuffled around a bit until Doc touched his arm with the understanding look he needed. He smiled a weak grin and nodded at the old physician, the man who had raised him like a father.

Twenty minutes later, in the valley, Brent burst out of the com' shack on the run. He pulled the 410 "snake pistol" and fired three evenly spaced shots into the ground as he ran. That was the established signal for all to gather quickly at the fire ring for an emergency meeting. It was the equivalent of the shipboard Navy's general quarters. Brent was adding his own version of three shots with his voice – screaming with every step for all to hurry.

If one had been looking down on the gathering as the people hurried to the ring he would have found one common denominator; everyone carried a firearm, even the ladies. All but Paige, that is, she simply wandered in the general direction as in a mild trance. She was the last to reach the seats.

Brent shouted in his excitement even though they were gathered closely together. "Roy just radioed us and Rosey just showed up at the ranch alive!! He's alive, do you get it?! Rosey…is…ALIIIIVE!!!"

It was as though Brent had kicked a bee hive. They all flocked to him at once asking questions he couldn't answer and grasping at his sleeve to get his attention to each one's query. He finally shook them all off and rushed to envelope Paige in a hug, twirling her around in the air as he danced with her. When he put her down she simply stood gawking at him.

"Why are you trying to do this to me? Why are you doing this horribly cruel thing to me?"

Instead of answering her he shouted at Morgan. "Morg', ready the big chopper, Roy says to bring Paige there, and that they have three people, counting Rosey, to bring here. Hurry! He wants us there ASAP."

Morgan was off like a shot, Brian and Cal right beside him. They pre-flighted the chopper together while Kay led Paige by the hand to the craft.

"I'm riding along, guys. I need to help Paige in this." As they stood waiting for the turbine to be started she carefully began to groom the hair of her diminutive dear friend. Jennifer came running with a makeup kit, knowing instinctively what Kay intended. As she handed it over, Cal encircled her with his arm and grinned at his mother and Paige. Tears ran down each face present as the turbine began its excited whine and spooled up to speed, Morgan motioning wildly for those going to climb in and buckle up. They were in the air in less than twenty minutes, raising rapidly above the two thousand foot lip of the valley canyon and then tipping to the north, reaching top speed in what seemed like an instant.

At the Turnbull ranch, Silas and Doc fought the afternoon nap tendency while Kenny and Rosey related the events of the weeks just past. Doc would occasionally add his bit when he was alert enough and was in the act of doing just that when they heard the sound of a large chopper approaching. Roy turned, startled, and said, "It's way too soon for them to be here, everyone on the alert, now!"

They ran to Roy's truck and zoomed to the strip. A large military craft set down and as soon as it touched down, General Sikes and Hagan Marshall dropped to the ground. They were obviously very excited as they ran to the group in the pickup.

Hagan spoke quickly, "We have just taken Washington in a coupe! Very little firing, only a few casualties and only one serious. The rest are all minor wounds! It was the most successful coupe ever recorded!"

"You can't be serious! We knew of no plans for such an operation! How in the world?"

"Roy, we kept the plans very close to our vests and circulated only those plans to those who needed to know them. I tell you, nothing like this has ever happened in ANY military force before. And you know the key? SKIMMERS!! Those amazing little things took our people to the places where they needed to be silently, quickly, and put them right down in the president's office! Well, almost that good."

"I bet that turkey is fit to be tied."

"Well, he might be dead by now, the vice president put two 45 caliber slugs in his back. Our military leaders are establishing power and control even as we speak; at least in Washington.

We also pulled off coupes in three critical state capitals, Ohio, Florida, and Texas. California is still underway, and is the only one in that situation right now.

"We have a very long way to go to get all of the country behind us, but with the response we have already seen from both citizens and military; the amazing thing is that we do not see how the socialists gained so much power! I guess the best example is to go back to when they tried to confiscate all firearms and the people stood up and waved those same firearms in the faces of those who tried. This country has been free far too long for power hungry crooks and politicians to take completely over like that. We ARE going to re-establish this country, folks, we simply ARE!'

As he finished his impassioned speech they heard the sound of another chopper far to the south.

Roy drew a deep breath and looked at Rosey. "John, how is your heart right now? You're gonna need some major strength and control in a few minutes; Paige is almost here."

Rosey turned pale at the thought, tears flowed freely down his face, and Doc and Kenny moved to his side for support as they awaited the arrival of the "valley people."

When the chopper landed, Rosey was hobbling painfully to it without waiting for the rotors to even begin to slow their whirling song. When the door slid open he leaped aboard and fairly landed in her lap. She had already unbuckled and the two fell to the floor clasping together as if their lives depended on it. Paige could be heard sobbing while Rosey just went into a shaking silence as he wept bitterly.

The others quietly climbed from the craft and slipped out to greet those on the ground with smiles and tears at the tremendous reunion going on behind them. Doc and Kenny were introduced and then the little party strolled to the waiting vehicles to allow the reuniting of the couple to run its course. Not a soul thought of interrupting them.

Hagan then began to catch Morgan, Kay, and the "valley people" up on the situation. As Morgan listened, his heart tried to leap from his chest while Kay leaned heavily against him. Then she could keep silent no longer, "Does this mean we can go back to our homes? Does it?"

"Yes, Mrs. Montgomery, it does. And another thing about your home; as you know, I operated out of the northern Ohio, southern Michigan area at first and that was where we formed the first really effective militias, so I am back there often.

"I recently spoke to the law enforcement's spy who was implanted at the provost office and he indicated the local sheriff and one of the deputies have kept the officials away from your homes; all three of them. So, you DO have a home to go back to.

"However, we wouldn't want you to go back for at least a month, just to allow some stability to take hold there."

"I can do a month standing on my head!" she shouted. "As long as I know I am going to leave that rattlesnake ranch behind and have running water, telephones, flush toilets, and my KITCHEN again! And I will NEVER strap another handgun to these curvy hips again!"

Morgan's eyes popped open at that and then he broke into uncontrollable laughter.

"Curvy hips? You finally admit you have curvy hips?" Then her hand clamped over his mouth and she turned a beet red.

"You just hush your trap, Morgan Montgomery, unless you want to suffer for the rest of your life for your comments."

He choked off his laughter and silently shook all over. Brian gave Sue a hip and she swatted him, shaking her finger at him to insure his silence at that moment. Then Kenny spoke up, "What do you suggest Doc and I do, sir?"

"You are the one we call the 'spy deliverer', are you not? The one we depended on out of Struthersburg?"

"That's right. And Doc, here, was my accomplice for most of those deliveries. We both became known to the enemy when we broke mister Rosenthal out from under their clutches. We can't go back, I don't WANT to go back, but I know Doc has a nicely equipped office there with a lot of expensive equipment in it."

"First, thank you two for three years of great service, I can't begin to tell you how much impact your help has had on this result. Secondly, we're cleaning out that little town and returning it to the normal citizens. If you want to go back, you can in a few weeks."

Doc spoke up, :I don't really need to go back there, I want to find some backwoods place to set up housekeeping and just disappear from society like a hermit for a year or so." "Hey Doc, we have a cabin over at the main complex you can have for as long as you want it. You can't be a hermit there, for both my wife and I will bug you from time to time, but we're gonna need some company for a while before the hunters start coming again. At least, that's what I figure. Same goes for you, Morningsong." Roy looked from man to man as he spoke, and was rewarded with two nods.

"For now, though, I want to see this valley I've heard so much about. If it won't put you folks out, can I go back with you? I'll gladly tent it while I'm there."

"Sure, Kenny, we'll be glad to have you. We call it the valley of the shadow because there's such a shadow of gloom hanging over our nation, our lives, and our very being. We fled there out of desperation, and these military people have set us up with whatever comfort they could, but I am so relieved we do not have to spend a winter in there.

"I WILL come back to hunt someday, I have NEVER seen so much game in one place, and the rattlesnake hunting is unequalled!"

That little jibe earned Morgan an elbow to the ribs that was hard enough to elicit a grunt. Kay thoroughly hated the creepy creatures, and hated the 410 shotgun revolver she was forced to carry because of them almost as much as the snakes themselves.

It was then that Rosey and Paige departed the chopper and walked hand in hand to the group. Hugs were delivered all around, even to Marshal and Sikes, and they were trucked off to the main ranch house to be fed.

The next several days were spent with Morgan and Rosey working on the two Cheyenne's to make sure of their airworthiness while the rest packed what they intended to take out of the valley. As much as possible would leave on the two choppers in order for the Cheyenne's to be loaded as lightly as possible for the climb out in the rare atmosphere of the high mountains.

It was obvious more than one trip would be required to

evacuate all of the inhabitants. Brent and Sally volunteered to be the last out. Brent would remove all of his critical equipment as well as Sean McTavish's and leave the valley "naked of goodies" as he put it. Only the houses and work shack lab would remain.

The Rosenthal's were inseparable, however during that time, and Paige was found anywhere Rosey happened to be. No one complained. During the departure preparation time, the military regime was busy establishing further control over the nation, and all incumbents in the capital were sent home unemployed. The masterminds of the military had planned far enough ahead that an almost seamless transition took place to begin the establishment of a new government for the people, of the people, and by the people.

It was announced that a new general election would take place inside of a year if at all possible. Candidates were quickly lining up their campaigns for the primaries and others were entering into the picture with opposition to those with any socialist policies in their background.

The main thrust of those applying to run were farmers, plumbers, electricians, common laborers and the like. America was sick and tired of politicians and was showing that with a strong voice. Some military officers were resigning commissions in order to run; in other words, it certainly looked to be a unique and different atmosphere for the elections when they were, at last, presented as the primaries in a few months.

A date was selected for the exodus from the valley, and when that time came, they gathered and watched as first Morgan, and then Rosey, poured full throttle to the turbines of the Cheyenne's and rocketed down the makeshift strip. The nearly antiquated twins rose faithfully from the earth, climbed rapidly in a tight turn representing a chandelle in order to easily clear the two thousand foot sides of the canyon and headed off to the north. Tears were in abundance as all who watched realized another chapter in their lives was beginning. Would it be better?

Epilogue.

Full winter had been long established in northwest Ohio, and the complete stillness that settled on Liberty Center was exceeded only by the nearly daylight appearance presented by the full moon glancing off the new fallen three inches of fresh snow. The earth fairly glittered and one needed not use a flashlight to walk anywhere. The cold was ear biting and the stillness only made it seem colder.

A few miles to the west the reception hall of the American Legion was rocking with laughter at the end of Brian Montgomery's hilarious and scandalous toast to brother Cal and his bride, Jennifer.

At the nearest table mother Kay leaned to Morgan and whispered, "He'll pay for that one sooner or later if I know Cal."

Morgan nodded through his tears of laughter and looked to Rosey with a nod. Rosey sat with his bad leg propped up on a chair. That served a dual purpose; it eased the pain and also allowed easier access to the recent plaster cast on the surgically repaired leg for folks to sign it.

Paige was next to her husband with her body pressed as closely to him as could be accomplished. Brent and Sally Shaffer were the others at that table. At the table next to theirs, Roy and Helen Turnbull smiled as Doc and Kenny exchanged barbs at one another over the toast, each declaring it also applied to one of them.

When Cal and Jennifer announced their engagement just one month after the return to their home, they insisted on inviting every valley resident and arranging for transportation.

They had truly become family while in the valley, and the Turnbull's were just as much a part of that family as anyone.

John Hall and Ted Sawyer circulated among the reception guests in their uniforms, patting a shoulder here, whispering to another there, and seemed to both end up at Rosey's side together, even though they had approached from different directions.

They knelt down by him and John spoke very quietly. "Just in case you should be wondering, mister Rosenthal, we spoke with some very informed people yesterday about some cases the military had ongoing in Henry County, and it seems the main officer involved has been thrown out of the army, and all involvement in those two cases has been dropped. We thought, for whatever reason, you might be interested in knowing that. I know I was."

With that, they rose, and each renewed their cruising of the guests tables.

'I couldn't help but hear, my brother, and that is great news!" Morgan smiled and patted Rosey on the shoulder.

"I guess it is, Morgan, but ya know, God had already forgiven me, so that's all I was concerned about. I'm learning, my friend, I'm learning."

As the wedding reception was at its peak, back to the east the little village sat in the cold, still night with life seeming to have resumed in a normalcy not recently enjoyed. Lights from the houses invaded the moon's brilliance with rectangles of yellow light gleaming on the snow while Monopoly boards occupied dining room tables; a teenager sat on his bed, guitar in hand as he learned some new chords; popcorn was taken from the microwave to supplement the Hallmark movie on in a living room television, and the still tranquility of the night stood watch over the outside gleaming world of near daylight.

In the wee hours of the early morning the tranquil scene was broken by the rasping noise of the garage door at 405 East Maple Street as it made its clumsy way up and allowed entrance to the garage for the Montgomery's auto.

The perfect, unbroken surface of the glittering snow was wounded and scarred by the feet of Morgan and Kay as they walked to the side door of the house. Lights flashed on inside, but only temporarily, and soon it was dark again as the two snuggled down into the heated mattress cover on the bed.

Kay Montgomery was a very typical wife with that sixth sense of just the moment her husband was about to succumb to sleep and she exercised her wifely right to talk at that precise moment.

"I thought Jennifer's dress was just magnificent, didn't you? And Sue and the other bridesmaids were perfect. Do you think John Hall and Ted had a reason to wear their uniforms to the reception, Morgan? And aren't we glad we don't have to spend a winter in that horrible valley? This heated bed feels sooo wonderful. How soon do you think the new election will be, Hon'? Honey? Morgan?"

"*ZZZZZZZZZZZZZZZZZZZZZZZZZZZZZZZZZZ*"

Will Riley Hinton was born and raised in the foothills of the Appalachians in southeast Ohio. He grew up on a farm with a grandfather who had made his living with horses and as a result, Will literally grew up on them. Having a mother who encouraged his active imagination along the lines of role playing and storytelling at a young age contributed greatly to his creative writing.

He was consumed by a love of horses, books, and airplanes. He served a hitch in the Navy and afterwards spent time as a part time flight instructor and crop duster. Will is married and has two grown children with five grandsons and two great grandchildren. Not surprisingly, his reading preferences are westerns and folklore.

Also by Will Hinton

Read every episode in the ongoing
Rocky Mountain Odyssey adventure series:

Book 1: Lonely are the Hunted
Book 2: Rocky Mountain Odyssey
Book 3: Shadow of Vengeance

Order your copy now from:

www.whitefeatherpress.com

www.amazon.com

For a signed copy, order from:

www.authorwillhinton.com

Valley of the Shadow